Lisa Scottoline is the bestselling author of several novels. She has been given the Fun Fearless Female Award by *Cosmopolitan* magazine and has also won the Edgar Award, for excellence in writing suspense fiction. She serves on the boards of the National Italian American Foundation and the Mystery Writers of America. A former trial lawyer, Lisa also teaches justice and fiction at the University of Pennsylvania Law School, her alma mater. Her books are published in more than twenty languages, and she remains a lifelong resident of the Philadelphia area.

D

LADY KILLER

Mary DiNunzio is a big-time business getter at Rosato and Associates. Unexpectedly, her old school rival, Trish Gambone, walks into her office one morning. Trish was the head Mean Girl, but now she's terrified of her live-in boyfriend, an abusive, gun-toting drug dealer for the South Philly mob. Trish is unaware that Mary also had a crush on him. Then Trish vanishes and a dead body turns up in an alley, and suddenly she's plunged into a nightmare: her job, her family and even her life is threatened. She goes on a crusade to unmask the killer, and on the way finds new love in a very unexpected place. But a shocking denouement forces Mary to confront the profound effects of lifelong love, and hate.

Books by Lisa Scottoline
Published by The House of Ulverscroft:

ROUGH JUSTICE
MISTAKEN IDENTITY
MOMENT OF TRUTH
THE VENDETTA DEFENCE
COURTING TROUBLE
DEAD RINGER
KILLER SMILE
DEVIL'S CORNER
DIRTY BLONDE
DADDY'S GIRL

LISA SCOTTOLINE

LADY KILLER

Complete and Unabridged

CHARNWOOD
Leicester

First published in Great Britain in 2008 by
Macmillan, an imprint of
Pan Macmillan Ltd.
London

First Charnwood Edition
published 2009
by arrangement with
Pan Macmillan Ltd.
London

British Library CIP Data

Cottoline, Lisa.
   Lady killer
   1. Rosato & Associates (Imaginary organization)- -
Fiction. 2. DiNunzio, Mary (Fictitious character)- -
Fiction. 3. Rosato, Bennie (Fictitious character)- -
Fiction. 4. Women lawyers- -Pennyslavania- -
Philadelphia- -Fiction. 5 Suspense fictiobn.
   6. Large type books.
   I. Title
   813.5′4–dc22

   ISBN 978–1–84782–807–1

Published by
F. A. Thorpe (Publishing)
Anstey, Leicestershire

Set by Words & Graphics Ltd.
Anstey, Leicestershire
Printed and bound in Great Britain by
T. J. International Ltd., Padstow, Cornwall

This book is printed on acid-free paper

TO MY BFF, FRANCA PALUMBO

Hates any man the thing he would not kill?

William Shakespeare, *The Merchant of Venice*,
Act 4, Scene 1, 66–7

1

Mary DiNunzio sat across from the old men, deciding which one to shoot first. Her father, Matty DiNunzio, was the natural choice because he was the most stubborn, but his three friends were tied for second. They sat next to him at the conference table, a trinity of Tonys — Pigeon Tony Lucia, Tony-From-Down-The-Block LoMonaco, and Tony Two Feet Pensiera, who was called Feet, making him the only man in South Philly whose nickname had a nickname.

'Pop, wait, think about this,' Mary said, hiding her exasperation. 'You don't want to sue anybody, not really.' She met her father's milky brown eyes, magnified by his bifocals, as he sat behind an open box of aromatic pignoli-nut cookies. Her mother wouldn't have let him visit her, even at work, without bringing saturated fats. Besides the cookies, waiting for her in the office refrigerator was a Pyrex dish of emergency lasagna.

'Yes, we do, honey. The club took a vote. We wanna sue. It's about honor.'

'Honor?' Mary tried not to raise her voice. She loved him, but she was wondering when he'd lost his mind. A tile setter his working life, her father had always been a practical man, at least until this meeting. 'You want to sue over your honor?'

'No, over Dean's honor.'

'You mean Dean Martin?'

'Yeah. He was a great singer and a great man.'

'Plus a great golfer,' said Tony-From-Down-The-Block.

'*Great* golfer,' repeated Feet. 'And Bernice disrespected him. In public.'

'But Dean wasn't there.' Mary stopped just short of saying, *He's dead*. Or, *Are you insane, too?*

Tony-From-Down-The-Block nodded. 'Dean Martin wasn't his real name, you know. It was Dino Crocetti.'

Mary knew. Dean Martin, born in Steubenville, Ohio. Adored his mother, Angela. Everybody Loves Somebody Sometime. She hadn't grown up her father's daughter for nothing. In his retirement, her father had started the Dean Martin Fan Club of South Philly, and she was looking at its four copresidents. Don't ask why there were four copresidents. The fifth had to step down from prostate problems.

Mary asked, 'How does it avenge his honor if you sue?'

'Mare,' Feet interrupted, indignant. 'Bernice insulted him. She called him a drunk!'

Mary winced on Dean's behalf. Her father shook his head. Tony-From-Down-The-Block reached for another pignoli-nut cookie. Feet's slack cheeks flushed with emotion, trumping his Lipitor.

'Mare, she hollered at him like a fishwife, in front of everybody. The *mouth* on that woman. So Big Joey hollered back and before you know it, he's holding his chest and falling down onna

2

floor. She gave him a heart attack.' Feet pushed up the bridge of his Mr. Potatohead glasses. 'That can't be legal.'

'I saw on *Boston Legal*, it's motional distress.' Tony-From-Down-The-Block brushed cookie crumbs from a red Phillies T-shirt, which matched his unfortunate new haircolor. He was single again, a fact that his red hair blared like a siren. Also that he might not own a mirror.

'That's how they always are, that club,' her father said. 'They never shut up. Sinatra this, Sinatra that. They think Frank was the best, but Dean had the TV show. They forget that.'

'Dean was the King of Cool, 'at's all,' added Tony-From-Down-The-Block, and Mary's father turned to him.

'Don't get me wrong, Sinatra was good, my Vita loves him. But he hogged the spotlight. A show-off.'

'A showboat,' Tony-From-Down-The-Block agreed, and Mary listened to the two men have the same conversation they'd had a thousand times. Pigeon Tony sat silently on the end, dunking a cookie into his coffee. At only five foot two, he was more wren than pigeon, with his bald head inexplicably tanned, his brown-black eyes small and round, and his tiny nose curved like a beak. He was quiet because his English wasn't that good, and for that, Mary felt grateful. Two Tonys were enough for one lawyer.

'But, Pop,' Mary interrupted, trying to get them back on track. 'Big Joey's fine now, and Bernice didn't cause his heart attack. He weighed three hundred pounds.' *Hence, the Big*

3

part. 'In an intentional infliction case, you have to prove that the act caused the harm. And the statement she made wasn't outrageous enough.'

'How can you say that, honey?' her father asked, stricken. 'It's outrageous, to us.' His forehead wrinkled all the way to his straw cabbie's hat. He was wearing an almost transparent sleeveless shirt, dark pants with a wide black belt, and black socks with pleather sandals. In other words, he was dressed up.

'Mare,' Tony-From-Down-The-Block interjected, 'the drinking wasn't for real on Dean's TV show. They put apple juice in the glass, not booze. It's show business.'

Feet's face was still flushed. 'Yeah. They just spread that rumor to make Dean look bad. They're always trying to ruin his reputation. Can we sue about that, too? If Dean was alive, he could sue, so why can't we? He can't help it he's dead.'

Mary sighed. 'Slow down, gentlemen. It costs money to sue. Even if I don't charge you, there are filing fees, service fees, all kinds of fees. You have to have money.'

Feet said, 'We have money.'

'Not this kind of money.'

'We got seventy-eight grand in the kitty.'

'*What?*' Mary couldn't believe her ears. 'Seventy-eight thousand! Where'd you get that?'

'Dean's got a lot of fans,' Feet answered, and her father added:

'Dead fans. Angelo, you know, the barber down Ritner Street. Remember, his wife Teresa passed two years ago, and they had no kids. Also

4

Mario, who had the auto-body shop on Moore, and Phil The Toot, got that nice settlement from the car accident. He passed, too, poor guy.' Her father paused, a moment of silence. 'They left their money to the club. We had three hundred and twelve dollars before that, but now we're rich. We can sue anybody we want.'

'Anybody says anything bad about Dean, we're suing,' Feet said.

'We don't even care if we lose,' said Tony-From-Down-The-Block. 'It's the principle. We're sick of Dean gettin' kicked around. It's gotta stop somewhere.'

'Right!' Mary's father pounded the table with a fleshy fist, and Pigeon Tony looked up from his coffee. Her father and the Three Tonys looked determined, their lined faces an Italian Mount Rushmore.

'Gentlemen, how's it gonna look if you sue?' Mary fought the urge to check her watch. She had so much else to do and was getting nowhere fast. 'You club is mostly male, right?'

'Yeah, it's true.' Her father shrugged his soft shoulders. 'What are you gonna do? Dean was a man's man.'

'It's 'cause of the Golddiggers,' Feet explained, and Tony-From-Down-The-Block sighed like a lovesick teenager.

'Weren't they somethin' else?'

Mary gathered the question was rhetorical. 'As I was saying, your club is mostly men. Isn't the Sinatra club mostly women?'

Feet interjected, 'It's not a real club, like us. They call it the Sinatra Social Society. They

5

don't even have bylaws, just parties.'

'Their name don't even make sense,' Tony-From-Down-The-Block said. 'It has too many *s*'s. You oughta hear 'em. Sounds like snakes with dentures.'

'Women,' Feet said, but Mary let it pass. A flicker of regret crossed her father's features. He knew where she was going, and she went there.

'Pop, let's say you take the Sinatra club to court and even that you win. How's that gonna look? A group of men beating up on a group of women? Is that really what you want?'

Her father blinked.

Feet and Tony-From-Down-The-Block exchanged looks.

Pigeon Tony dropped his cookie into his coffee. *Plop*, went the sound, and a pignoli nut bobbed to the black surface.

Mary pressed on. 'Is that what Dean would have wanted?'

'No, he wouldn't want that,' her father said, after a minute.

'But we don't like people insulting Dean,' Feet said.

'Plus, we gotta set the record straight,' said Tony-From-Down-The-Block, and Mary got an idea.

'Tell you what. Why don't I call Bernice, and ask her to apologize. Then you get what you want and nobody gets sued. You can even put it in the newsletter.'

'You sound like your mother,' her father said with a wry smile, and Mary laughed, surprised. Her mother would have sued. Nobody loved a

6

good fight more than her mother. She'd take on all comers, armed with a wooden spoon.

'Bernice Foglia will never apologize,' Tony-From-Down-The-Block said, and Feet shook his head.

'She buried two husbands, both from heart attacks.'

'Let me try, gentlemen. Let's not get crazy.' Mary needed to resolve this fast. She had three hundred things to do. Her slim BlackBerry Pearl sat next to her on the table, its e-mail screen dark and its phone set on Silent. She hated being tethered to the device, but it was corporate oxygen nowadays. Mary touched her father's hand. 'Dad, why don't you take the money you'd use on a lawsuit and do something positive? Something good, in Dean's memory. Something that honors him.'

'I guess we could buy somethin' for the playground,' said her father, cocking his head.

'Or sponsor a softball team,' said Tony-From-Down-The-Block.

'Or have a party,' said Feet, and on the end, Pigeon Tony looked up.

'*O andare al casinò*.'

And for that, Mary didn't need a translation.

Fifteen minutes later, she had ushered them out of the conference room, hugged and kissed them all, and walked them out to the reception area. The elevator doors slid open, and the Tony trifecta shuffled inside, followed by her father, to whom she gave a final hug, breathing in his characteristic spice of mothballs and CVS aftershave.

7

'I love you, Pop,' Mary said, surprised by the catch in her throat. It was paranoid, but she always wondered if it would be the last time she would see him alive. The man was perfectly healthy, but she couldn't shake the thought. It was a child's fear, and yet here she was, over thirty, with no excuse except a congenital flair for melodrama.

'Love you, too, honey,' her father said softly. He patted her arm and stepped back into the elevator. 'I'm so proud a you — ,' he was saying when the stainless-steel doors closed, leaving Mary facing her blurry reflection, wearing an unaccountably heartsick expression and her best navy blue suit.

'Mare?' said a voice, and Mary turned, recovering. It was Marshall Trow, their receptionist, walking from the hallway in a blue cotton shirtdress and tan espadrilles. Her usual smile had vanished, and her brown eyes were concerned. 'I just put a friend of yours in your office. I didn't want to interrupt your meeting.'

'No problem.' Mary switched her BlackBerry back on, and e-mail piled onto the screen, making a mountain she could never climb, like an electronic Sisyphus. 'What friend?'

'Her name is Trish Gambone.'

Trash Gambone is here?

'You know her, right?' Marshall blinked.

'Sure, from high school. *Here?*' Mary couldn't process it fast enough. Trash, er, Trish, Gambone personified every slight she'd suffered at St. Maria Goretti High School, where Mary had been the myopic straight-A president of the

8

National Honor Society, the May Queen, and the all-around Most Likely to Achieve Sainthood. During the same four years, Trish Gambone had flunked Religion, chain-smoked her way through Spanish I twice, and reigned as the quintessential Mean Girl.

'She said she had to see you and it was confidential. She was beside herself.'

'Upset?'

'She was crying.'

'Really?' Mary felt her heartbeat speed up. A classic fight-or-flight reaction, but she didn't know which to do.

'I wouldn't have taken her into your office, but I couldn't leave her here, hysterical.'

'No, sure, you did the right thing.' Mary slipped the BlackBerry in her pocket, where it began to vibrate like crazy. It if were in her pants, she'd be having a really good time.

Marshall handed her a thick stack of phone messages. 'These are for you. I put your mail on your desk, and don't forget you have the Coradinos coming in fifteen minutes, then the DiTizios and Mrs. Yun.'

'Thanks. Get my calls, please?' Mary hurried from the well-appointed reception area, passed the gold-plated Rosato & Associates sign, and hustled down the hallway, where her best friend Judy Carrier called out from her office.

'Mary!' Judy's lemony blond head popped through her doorway. She had large, sky blue eyes, chopped chin-length hair, and a gap-toothed grin, which somehow looked good on a face as round as a dinner plate. 'How about hello? Time for how-was-your-weekend.'

Mary was about to burst with the news. 'Guess who's in my office right this minute.'

'Who?' Judy had on a hot pink T-shirt, yellow cargo pants, and kelly green Dansko clogs. Read, dressed like the colorblind.

'Trash Gambone.'

'That *bitch*!' Judy's eyes flew open. 'She's *here*?'

'In the flesh.' Mary appreciated that Judy reacted with the appropriate hate, even though she'd never met Trash. Only a true girlfriend would hate someone on your say-so. In fact, that's what girlfriends were for.

'She's a jerk,' Judy added, for emphasis.

'A skank.'

'A slut. What does she want?'

'I have no idea. Marshall said she was crying.'

'Goody!' Judy clapped. 'Maybe she's in trouble with the law?'

'We can only hope.' Mary almost cheered, then caught herself. 'Wait. I feel guilty.'

'Why? She deserves it.'

'I thought I was nicer than this, but I'm not.'

'It's human nature. Delight in the pain of your enemies. The Germans have a word for it. Schadenfreude.'

'The Catholics do, too. Sin.'

'It's not a sin to be human,' Judy said with a smile, but Mary let it go. Of course it was, but she'd given up on saving Judy's soul. Her clothes alone were sending her straight to hell.

'I can't believe Trash needs my help. What should I do?'

10

'I smell payback.'

But deep inside, all Mary smelled was nervous. Trish and the Mean Girls had bullied her during lunch, assembly, and Mass; anywhere you could make someone feel smaller, uglier, and more myopic than she felt already. Was she the only person who had post-traumatic stress syndrome — from high school?

'Did your dad bring us food?' Judy asked, hopeful.

'In the conference room.'

'Woot woot!'

Mary hurried down the hall, passing Bennie Rosato's office, which was empty. She was glad that Bennie had a jury trial this week because she didn't want the boss to see her dark side, which she didn't realize she had until this very minute. She'd always heard that what goes around, comes around, but she didn't know that it really happened.

I smell payback.

Mary reached for her office door, with its MUST WEAR SHIRTS sign. Lately, she had so many clients from South Philly that the sign had become necessary. She was pretty sure that was a first for a law firm.

And when she opened the door, her hand was shaking.

2

Mary stepped into her office, which reeked of perfume and cigarette smoke, Obsession with notes of Marlboro Lights. Trish Gambone was sitting in the club chair opposite the desk, facing away from the door. A curly tangle of raven-haired extensions trailed down the back of her flashy fox jacket, and she wore a black catsuit that ended in black boots, with stiletto heels that met the legal definition of a lethal weapon.

Trash? 'Trish?' Mary closed the door behind her.

'Hey, Mare.' Trish looked up and swiveled around in the chair, barely over her crying jag. She looked like a streetwise Sophia Loren, but her lovely features were drawn with anguish and her flawless skin mottled under a spray tan. She dabbed a soggy Kleenex to eyes as brown-black as espresso, but they were bloodshot from tears.

'Are you okay?' Mary asked, hushed.

'What do *you* think?' Trish shot back, her voice thick.

Mary cringed, as if Trish had swung a machete and hacked off her self-esteem. She flashed on them both in their white shirts with Peter Pan collars, heavy blue jumpers with the SMG patch, and white stockings worn with navy-and-white saddle shoes, like Britney Spears before rehab.

'You look so professional.' Trish checked her out quickly. 'Better than you did in school.'

12

'Thanks.' *Kind of.* Mary reminded herself that she wasn't fifteen years old and there was no such thing as an esteem-whacking machete. She knew she looked better than she had in high school; she had a nice smile now that her braces were off and she'd grown into her strong cheekbones and nose, so that her husband used to call her striking, even beautiful. She'd traded her glasses for contacts, so her round brown eyes showed better, and she'd cut her thick, dark blond hair to her shoulders. She reached only five foot two, but she had a compact, curvy figure. All in all, Mary wasn't a troll anymore.

'Sit down, will ya?' Trish blinked wetness from her eyes. 'I'm so freaked, I'm runnin' outta time.'

'So what's the matter?' Mary walked around to her desk chair, sat down, and placed her phone messages on the stack of morning mail.

'I need help. I'm in real trouble.' Trish pursed her perfectly puffy pair of lips, their lipstick long gone. She had always been the sexiest girl in their class, but she looked older than her years. Dark eyeliner emphasized her eyes, and she still had the smallest nose that qualified as Italian-American.

'Okay, fill me in,' Mary said.

'First off, I'm not askin' you for nothin' I can't pay for.' Trish swabbed at her eyes, leaning forward in the chair. Her fox jacket parted, revealing a killer body — curvy hips, a tiny waist, and breasts that had been a healthy C cup, even in sixth grade. 'I'm not asking you to do anything free 'cause we're Goretti girls.'

Don't worry. 'Okay.'

'I'm the top colorist at Pierre & Magda's. I make good money. I know lawyers are expensive and I can pay in installments, like layaway.' Trish pulled another Kleenex from a large black Gucci bag.

'We'll work it out.' Mary became vaguely aware that she wasn't looking directly at Trish, as if eye contact could be dangerous, like with Medusa. She picked up a pen and wrote on her pad, WHAT IF SHE CAN SMELL FEAR?

'I came to you because you were always a major brain.'

Mary wrote, WHICH YOU MADE FUN OF, BUT NEVER MIND.

'It's my boyfriend, I gotta get away from him. I can't take it anymore, I hate him, I just hate him.'

'That's so terrible.' Mary wrote, THAT'S SO JUICY.

'He's a bully.'

NOW YOU KNOW HOW IT FEELS.

'My mom had his number from day one, 'cause my dad used to knock her aroun', and my girlfriends hated him, too. But I didn't listen to any of 'em. You remember them — Giulia, Missy, and Yolanda.'

'Sure.' Mary suppressed an eye roll. Giulia Palazzolo, Missy Toohey, and Yolanda Varlecki. The Mean Girls, who evidently took literally the F in BFF.

'They all hate his guts. They been tellin' me to leave him, but they don't know the whole story. Lemme tell it in order or I'll get messed up. It started with him screamin' and yellin' at me, all

14

the time. He's crazy jealous, even though I'm not runnin' around, and he calls my cell like thirty times a day. If I don't pick up, he calls the shop.' Pain etched Trish's features, and she needed no encouragement to continue, the story pouring out with a force of its own. 'He's drinkin' more and more, and that makes it worse. He calls me 'pig,' 'whore,' the whole nine.'

'That's terrible.' Mary felt a pang of sympathy despite her better judgment.

'He won't let me go out except to go to work. The house has to be perfect, the dinner on a table. His clothes have to be perfect. I even iron, everything perfect.' Trish's words fell over themselves, coming out in an urgent rush with a South Philly accent. 'Last year, he started hittin' me, then he'd feel bad after. Now he hits me all the time, he never feels bad. If I do somethin' wrong, he hits me. If I do it right, he hits me.'

'He *hits* you?' Mary forgot about payback. Trish was desperate, and she was beginning to understand why.

'He's smart, too, he hits where you can't see. Punches my belly, my back. Kicks me on my ass, or my arms, even when I'm on the ground. I tol' my friends and my mom that he roughs me up a little, but that's it. I didn't tell how bad it is, or they'd go crazy. Last week, when he was drunk, he did this.' Trish reached for the collar of her catsuit, pulled the zipper down to her ample cleavage, and moved a heavy gold necklace and her black jersey to the side. Above her breast was a vicious, ugly bruise. 'You see this? He bites me during sex. He likes that. It turns him on.'

15

Mary felt disgusted. She didn't know where to start. 'You have sex — '

'He makes me. I won't show you the rest.' Trish zipped up the catsuit, her lower lip trembling. 'Last week he said he was gonna kill me, and when I saw the look in his eyes, I knew he meant it. That's when I realized, like, from a stupid Oprah show, that I'm abused. That girl on TV, that girl's *me*.' Suddenly Trish's voice broke and she stifled a deep sob, pressing the Kleenex to her nose. 'You believe that? Me, livin' afraid all the time, like a little mouse? Like *you*?'

Mary's heart went out to her, despite the insult. 'Did you take any pictures of your injuries?'

'Yes, I kep' a diary, too.'

'Good.' Mary was drafting a restraining order in her mind. She had gotten two in her time, in far less ugly cases. 'Did you go to the doctor or the hospital?'

'No way.' Trish wiped her nose. 'He told me he'd kill me if I did.'

'Your neighbors must hear it, when he yells.' Mary was thinking about potential witnesses.

'We live next to the corner store, Filantonio's, only now it's Korean and they don't speak English. You remember, back in school, it was my corner.'

'I remember.' Mary didn't hang on the corner, she memorized Latin declensions. But back to business. 'Do they hear him yelling in the store, do you think?'

'No, he yells at night when they're closed, and he has a gun. He carries it, a Glock.' Trish

16

hiccupped another sob. 'He points it in my face, he holds it to my head. Yesterday he stuck it down my throat, like he was gaggin' me.'

Mary gasped.

'Don't worry, I have a gun, too, a Beretta. I bought it a long time ago for protection, and I got one for the girls and my mom, too, for Christmas.'

In another mood, Mary would have made a joke. One size fits all.

'Only thing is, he knows how to use one and I don't. Alls I got to help me shoot straight are the Pink Sisters.' Trish laughed sadly, an abrupt break in the stormclouds. 'You remember the Pink Sisters?'

'Of course.' Mary managed a smile. The Pink Sisters were a cloistered order of nuns in the Fairmont section who would pray for you if you slipped a request in their front gate. They had gotten Mary through the bar exam, her wedding day, and her husband's funeral. She asked, 'When did you go to the convent?'

'I didn't. They have a website that takes prayer requests now. You believe that?' Trish smiled, wiping her eyes, and Mary felt a flicker of closeness to her.

'Incredible. And did you hear there's no more limbo?'

'I know, right?' Trish smiled again, and the moment passed, her beautiful face falling into fearful lines, her forehead wrinkled with anxiety. 'It's hell, Mare. I'm walkin' on eggshells all the time. Yesterday he told me he's got a big surprise for me on my birthday. That's today.'

17

Yikes. 'Happy Birthday.'

'Yeah. Real happy.' Trish's lower lip trembled, but she maintained control. 'This is why I hadda see you, I'm outta my mind. I think the surprise is he's gonna propose, and if I say no, he'll kill me. Tonight.'

Mary had heard enough. She set down her legal pad. 'Trish, you don't have to live like this another minute. On these facts, especially with your diary, we can get you a restraining order. The court requires a reasonable fear of imminent danger, and we can go over there right now and — '

'No, I can't do that.' Trish's reddish eyes flared with new fear. 'I can't go to court.'

'Why not?'

'He's connected.'

'To what?'

Trish snorted. 'Where'd you grow up? Duh.'

Whoa. Mary felt stricken. Everybody in South Philly had a love/hate relationship with the Mob, but her relationship was more hate/hate, except when it was hate/terrified.

'He deals drugs for them, heroin and coke.'

Mary took mental notes. I'M NOT HEARING THIS.

'Also he's takin' a cut on the down.'

'What's that mean?' THE MAFIA DOES NOT EXIST.

'Takin' money. Skimmin.' If they find out, he's dead. They don't play that.'

THE MEDIA CREATES A VICIOUS STEREOTYPE OF ITALIAN-AMERICANS.

'I never sleep anymore. Alls I can see is them

18

breakin' down the door, shootin' us both up. He's not made, so we got no protection. He's playing craps with my life. If he don't kill me, they will.'

IT'S ALL TONY SOPRANO'S FAULT. ALSO AL PACINO'S.

'And, trust me, he knows how to use that gun.'

YOU DIDN'T JUST SAY THAT.

'I don't know what to do.' Trish's voice thinned with fright. 'I'm *dyin'* here. What do I do? You get my problem?'

'Yes — it's how do you break up with a mobster, right?'

'Right!' Trish wailed. 'It's, like, no-win. What do I do? I'm *trapped*.'

Mary's thoughts raced ahead. 'Hold on, not yet. How about we go to the cops? I'm sure you have information they could use, and we can get you into the witness-protection program — '

'Are you *nuts*?' Trish fairly shouted. 'He'll kill me. *They'll* kill me!'

'You can't be sure of that.'

'I'm sure, believe me. What are you, stupid?'

Mary let it go. There had to be a solution. 'You sure you won't go to court? We can get the protective order and — '

'They're not worth the paper they're printed on.'

'But maybe he'd pay attention to it, knowing you'd haul him into court. He certainly doesn't want that exposure.'

'He'd kill me before I got there. Wise up! You're not helpin'!' Trish started to get upset again, her eyes welling up.

19

'Stay calm. We can figure this out. How about you get out of town? Just go.'

'Where'm I gonna go? He'll find me wherever I go.'

'No he won't.'

'Yeah, he will, and what do I do when I get where I'm goin'?' Trish threw up her hands. 'What'm I supposed to do? Leave my mom, my friends, my job? It took me years to build up my book at work. I don't wanna leave my life.'

'Your life is on the line, Trish.'

'It won't work anyway, Mare. He'll find me. He won't stop until he does.' Trish edged forward on the seat. 'Mare, don't you *get* it? Nothin' you're sayin' will work. The man is an animal, and you're talkin' *law*!'

'I'm a lawyer,' Mary said, nonplussed.

'Well, the law isn't helpin'! You're smart, think of somethin'!'

Mary wracked her brain. 'Okay, wait, listen. If you don't want a legal solution, then I'm telling you what I'd do. Go far away. Take a vacation. I'll even lend you some money.'

'*This* is what you're tellin' me, Einstein? Get outta town?' Suddenly Trish leaped to her boots. 'How's that different from the witness protection?'

'It's not like witness protection, that's forever. I'm saying just go for a while, a month or two.' Mary rose behind her desk, softening her tone. She'd never seen Trish have a moment's self-doubt, much less a meltdown. 'By the time you come back, he'll have cooled down and — '

'It won't work. He loves me. He's obsessed.

He's not gonna get over it, Mare.' Trish shook her head, then covered her face with her hands. 'I can't believe this is really happening. I can't believe this is my life. He was so sweet, so great, in high school. Why didn't I see it then?'

'Stay calm, Trish — '

'We always thought we'd get married, everybody did.' Trish uncovered her face, and her skin was flushed with emotion, her eyes frantic. 'How did I get myself into this? You remember how nice he was? How sweet?'

'I don't know him.'

'Yes, you do. He went to Neumann.'

Great. Bishop Neumann, Goretti's brother school, was graduating mobsters now. Mary wished for her legal pad. WONDER WHAT HE GOT IN RELIGION?

'What was I thinking?' Trish raked manicured fingernails through big hair. 'I thought I was so lucky. He was the hottest thing. We were so in love.' Then Trish said his name.

Oh my God. Mary's heart stopped. The room slipped out of focus.

Trish was saying, 'We dated in high school, senior year, remember?'

So did we.

'I broke up with him but then I went back. What a mistake. He was obsessed with me even then, I used to think he was so romantic. Now I know he's crazy.' Trish kept shaking her head, then stopped abruptly. 'So what are you tellin' me to do, Mare?'

Mary snapped out of it. 'If you won't leave or go to court — '

21

'I can't! He'll *kill* me! *Tonight!*' Trish hollered, full bore, all of her anguish channeled now to rage. 'And you'll sit there and do *nothin*'!'

'The only way out is — '

'I need *help! Help me!*'

'I'm trying but — '

'*Screw* you, Holy Mary!' Trish exploded. 'That's what we all used to call you, you know that? Holy Mary, Mother of God! Little Miss Perfect, that's you! Thanks for *nothin*'!' She whirled around, grabbed her purse, and stalked to the door, then flung it open and left.

'Trish, wait!' Mary went after her, but Trish was running down the hall toward the reception area.

'Please, wait!' Mary almost caught up with her, but let her run for the exit stairs when she saw a surprised receptionist and a waiting room full of uncomfortable clients, all of whom were hers. There were Dawn and Joe Coradino and daughter Bethann, a well-dressed family from Shunk Street; Jo-Ann Heilferty, whose new yard needed regrading; and Elka Tobman, who wanted a new business incorporated. They'd heard the shouting and were waiting for an explanation. Mary collected herself and managed a shaky smile. 'Dawn and Joe, the doctor will see you now.'

And when she turned to lead them back to her office, an exuberant Judy Carrier was standing in the hallway, flashing her a joyful thumbs-up.

22

3

Mary and Judy walked among the crowds packing the sidewalk at lunchtime. Men wore ties and wrinkled shirts, their ears plugged with iPods and Bluetooth receivers, and women talked and laughed in groups, toting oversized purses and undersized cell phones. Sunlight filtered through the new leaves of skinny city trees, and everybody but Mary was enjoying the freshness of the cool day, one of the nicest so far in a chilly March. She felt haunted after the morning meeting with Trish.

Judy walked along, wrinkling her upturned nose. 'You have nothing to feel bad about. You tried to help her even after all she did to you. She made your life miserable.'

'That was high school.' Mary walked with her head down, making her feel even shorter than usual next to Judy. Her best friend, at a full foot taller and from northern California, was like a walking sequoia.

'I wasn't mean in high school, and neither were you.'

'Still, she doesn't deserve what's happening to her.'

'Okay, there I agree with you.'

Mary couldn't shake her bad feeling. She'd had Trish in the back of her mind all morning, unable to concentrate on her mail, e-mail, meetings, or phone calls. She'd even forgotten to call Mrs. Foglia about Dean Martin. 'What if Trish is right? What if he kills her tonight?'

'If she won't get help, there's nothing you can do.' Judy looked grim. 'I'd say we should call the police, but that could endanger her further, and what she told you is privileged anyway.'

'I called the salon but she hadn't come in yet, and her home number is unlisted.'

'Gangsters like their privacy.'

Mary didn't laugh, and Judy touched her shoulder.

'Don't worry. It sounds like he's an abuser, not a murderer.'

'I hope you're right.' Mary couldn't believe he was either, not the way she remembered him.

'Also you said she was a drama queen in high school.'

'But I feel really scared for her. I have a bad feeling, like my mother, you know how she gets vibes? She can tell things.'

'You mean like that evil eye business?' Judy scoffed. 'You're just upset.'

'I feel guilty.'

'You wake up guilty.'

Mary managed a smile. 'Did I let Trish down?'

'No. She got herself into this mess. How could she fall for such a loser?'

Mary kept her own counsel, studying her navy pumps. She wasn't about to tell Judy that she'd dated him, too, and that he was the most popular guy in their class, a football player with a wacky sense of humor. All the girls loved him, and when he asked Mary out, she was sure he did it for free tutoring.

'What is it about bad boys?'

'He wasn't bad,' Mary blurted out, but Judy was looking at her funny.

'Did you know him?'

'Not well, and that was pre-Mob.'

'What's that? Like pre-med, with weaponry?' Judy grinned, but it faded. 'Look, you couldn't have done more than you did. If Trish won't leave town or go to court or the cops, there's nothing you can do. You're a lawyer, and the law has its limits.'

Mary looked up, almost comforted. Judy's white-blond hair caught the breeze, and it blew her bangs back, the strands fine as dandelion seeds. She loved the law, having caught the bug in law school. Mary never did; she still vacillated about whether she wanted to be a lawyer. At work, she daydreamed about other jobs and at night, she cruised www.monster.com like it was online porn.

'Now, Mare, enough about Trish. I have big news.' Judy stopped on the pavement, holding a brown bag of their leftovers, take-out Chinese. The scent of chicken lo mein wafted from the bag's open top, and foot traffic flowed around them. 'I got a call from Marshall this weekend because she couldn't figure something out on payroll. So I went over and got to see the billing for everyone in the office. You, me, Bennie, and Anne.'

'Isn't that confidential?'

'Not when Marshall needs help, it isn't. So here's the amazing thing I learned.' Judy's blue eyes glittered. '*You* are responsible for bringing

25

in more fees to the firm than Bennie.'

'What?' Mary couldn't have heard her right.

'You're billing the most hours, of all of us. You're at almost 215 a month, which is killer. Anne and I come in at about 160 each, and so does Bennie. We're all busting our asses, but you, my dear, bill more time and collect on more bills than Bennie, and that's been true for the last three quarters.'

'Quarters?'

'Business quarters, dufus. Bennie bills you out at $250 an hour, but pays you only $125. Same with me and Anne, but we do her work, not our own clients, like you.'

Mary was getting confused. It had been a long morning. The conversation felt vaguely illicit. 'So what's the point?'

'The point is, the income you bring in is *huge*. You're a profit center.'

'That can't be. None of my bills is more than five grand and they're all defective sunroofs, storm windows that leak, and garage doors that don't open. This morning, I arbitrated a dispute between Dean Martin and Frank Sinatra.'

'Whatever, they pay on time.'

'Well, that's true.' Mary knew that her base clients, the children of immigrants, were like her parents; they paid their bills before the due dates, in the naive belief that it maintained their reputation with the American aristocracy, which existed only in their own minds.

'Right now, and for almost the entire year, you've been bringing in more in fees than Bennie does.'

'Huh?' Mary was astounded. 'But Bennie is the owner.'

'Right, and *you're* keeping her firm afloat, as far as I can see.'

Mary couldn't wrap her mind around it. It was topsy-turvy.

'Your numbers look like they're growing. Bennie has big cases, mostly trials, and they only pay, like, once every two years. Those civil rights cases, and the police brutality, they don't pay until the court approves the fee application. Take it from me, those are the matters I work on, and I haven't billed anybody in three months.' Judy's eyes focused with a piercing clarity. 'You know what that means?'

'No.'

'You should ask Bennie to make you a partner.'

'*What?*' Mary looked around nervously, for no reason except that the conversation was high treason. Luckily no one was listening, and the only attention they were getting was because of Judy's crazy outfit. 'That's so wrong.'

'No, it's so right.' Judy grinned, but Mary didn't.

'I feel sick.'

'You should feel great. You attract clients. You should be a partner.'

'But we're associates.'

Judy shook her head happily. 'Anne and I should be, but not you. You're the rainmaker of South Philly. Think of it. Rosato & DiNunzio.'

Mary felt her knees give way. She looked around for support but the closest object was a grimy fire hydrant, which she lurched toward and sank onto anyway. 'Ouch.'

Judy followed with the fragrant bag, and bypassers flowed around them. 'I'll e-mail you the docs. They'll show you your billings and Bennie's.'

'Don't. I don't like knowing things I'm not supposed to know.'

'You really should talk to Bennie about making you partner.'

'That would be like Pluto asking the sun for equal billing, and Pluto's not even a planet anymore. It got demoted, like Saint Christopher, who I always liked.' Mary shifted on the fireplug. She felt queasy. It had to be the lo mein, wafting in her direction. 'And now there's no limbo. Purgatory's next. What's going on in this world?'

Judy was looking at her funny. 'Mary. Don't you want to make more money? Or, at least, keep more of the money you generate for the firm?'

'I make enough money,' Mary answered, but they both knew she wanted a house and still couldn't afford the down payment, though she was close to the amount, having saved like a city squirrel. She shook it off. 'That's not the question. I don't want more money if I have to take it from Bennie.'

'She's taking it from you, right now. You earned it. It's yours.'

'No, it's hers. I work for her.' Mary had never thought about it any other way. She recorded her hours, sent her bills out on time, and the rest took care of itself. She was a born employee. It could be worse. She could be in the Mob, which didn't exist.

'I knew you'd freak.' Judy smirked.

'I'm not freaking.'

'Are, too. You look green.'

'It's the reflection off your clogs.'

'Very funny.'

'I thank you,' Mary said, channeling Feet.

4

Mary walked to her last meeting, through the forty blocks that seemed to define her. South Philly was a small town in a big city, where everybody knew everybody else, if they weren't first cousins. Twilight was coming on, and a coppery sun, useless as a penny, dropped behind the flat asphalt roofs. Satellite dishes and loopy TV antennae made a familiar silhouette against the darkening sky, criss-crossed with sagging phone and cable wires. Old brick rowhouses lined skinny streets parked with older cars, and blackened gum and grime pitted the sidewalks.

Mare, don't you get it? Nothin' you're sayin' will work.

Soft light filtered through gauzy sheers in the front windows, which displayed plastic flowers, Virgin Marys, and little Italian and American flags, as each family declared its identity in its front window, a bumper sticker for the home. It had been this way for as long as Mary could remember. The new immigrants — Vietnamese, Korean, and Mexican families — displayed their stuff, too, proving that tackiness was universal.

The man is an animal, and you're talkin' law!

Mary's heels *clack-clack*ed on the pavement, a clatter behind her thoughts of Trish. She hadn't been able to reach her and prayed she'd be safe tonight. Suddenly a front door swung open on her right, interrupting her thoughts. The bluish gray head of elderly Elvira Rotunno popped out, followed by her flowered dress and an apron, accessorized with terry-cloth slippers. She was one of Mary's clients, and her hooded eyes lit up behind rimless trifocals. 'Mare, you here to see Rita?' Elvira hollered.

'Yes.' Mary stopped at her steps. 'You know, her name is Amrita, not Rita. She's Indian, not Italian.'

'I know that, so what?' Elvira waved her off. 'She's an Indian religion where they think God is an elephant. It's okay by me. I got a cat, and he thinks *he's* God.'

Mary let it go. 'Great talking to you, but I'm late.'

'I know. You were supposed to be here a half hour ago, but Rita won't mind. I tol' her, you're better than Matlock.' Elvira pointed up with a knotted index finger. 'See my new awning? It's beautiful! You saved me twelve hundred bucks. You didn't let 'em take advantage.'

Mary smiled. 'Thanks, Elvira.'

'Mare, why'n't you stop in, have somethin' to eat after you're done with Rita? Dom's not workin' tonight, and I got tiramisu.'

'I can't, thanks. 'Bye now.' Mary kept going. She was never getting fixed up again and especially not with Dominic Rotunno, who still lived at home and was trouble from the third grade. Maybe she should resign herself to a life of celibacy. Sister Mary DiNunzio, Esq.

He bites me during sex. He likes that. It turns him on.

She reached Amrita's house, walked up the

31

stoop, and rang a black metal doorbell. The front window contained a child's diorama inside a gray-and-orange Nike box. The scene showed Noah's ark, and a McDonald's French-fry container, cut in half, served as the bright red ship for animals of molded plastic. Green camels and pink lions from the dollar store. The front door opened, and Amrita let her in with a weary half smile. A dental tech, she was still in her scrubs, decorated with smiling molars in red sneakers.

'Sorry I'm late.' Mary stepped inside.

'No worries, I just got in myself,' Amrita said, in her Anglo-Indian lilt. She and her husband were Londoners, transferred to Philly because of his job. She brushed back a black tendril and tucked it into her long ponytail. 'How are you, Mary?'

'Fine. And you?'

'Crazy busy.' Amrita's eyes, wide set and almond shaped, flickered with fatigue, and her generous mouth turned down slightly.

'How's Dhiren?' Mary asked, and Amrita gestured behind her as she shut the door. A boy in a striped T-shirt and tan shorts flopped on a patterned couch, and his head of wavy dark hair was bent over his Game Boy. His legs, dark skinned and skinny, dangled over the couch. He was nine years old, a fourth-grader at the local public school, where he was going under.

'Dhiren, say hello to Ms. DiNunzio,' Amrita said, but the boy kept playing. 'Dhiren, I won't tolerate such bad manners. Please.'

'Hello, Miss DiNunzio,' Dhiren answered in

his cute accent, but he didn't look up. Amrita frowned, about to rebuke him when Mary put an arm around her shoulder.

'Let it go. I want to talk to you first. By the way, why didn't you warn me that Elvira's trying to fix me up?'

'I expected you could handle the situation. Run screaming, my advice.' Amrita smiled, motioning Mary through the dining room to the kitchen, the standard layout for rowhomes. They entered a cozy kitchen, smelling of fish and cooking oil, and Mary pulled up one of the wooden chairs around a small table, with two places marked by yellow plastic mats.

'Did you eat?' Amrita opened a refrigerator plastered with Dhiren's crayoned dogs and giraffes, from before it had all gone wrong.

'Yes, thanks,' Mary lied. Amrita had enough to do without serving her dinner.

'Tea, then?'

'Yes, thanks. Just plain is fine.' Mary pulled a file and a legal pad from her briefcase. 'We still haven't heard from the school district.'

'I assumed so.' Amrita filled a mug with water, scuffed to the microwave on the counter, and pressed the button after she put the mug inside. 'They just wear one down. That's their strategy.'

'It won't work with me. I thrive on rejection.' Mary was losing sleep over this case. Dhiren could barely read and write.

'I don't know why they make it so hard.' Amrita stood by the microwave, and inside the mug turned around and around, a spinning shadow behind frosted glass. 'The child cannot

33

read. This, they know.'

'I understand, but we need them to test him. They have a legal obligation to identify him and initiate the testing.'

'They should simply hand him a book. Watch him struggle, like I do.' Amrita punched the button to open the microwave door. 'My parents have been saying it for years. He's dyslexic. They know, they are physicians, both.' Her voice was edged with an anger that came off as haughty, but Mary knew better.

'The tests measure IQ, cognitive ability, and achievement.' She had been boning up on special-education law. 'If there's a significant disparity, they'll find him eligible for special ed and pay for the right school.'

Amrita frowned. 'I told you his IQ. It's 110. Very high. Obviously, he should be reading better. He should be writing better. His writing is unintelligible.'

'I know that, too.' Mary had Dhiren's papers, with words that faced backward or looked like alphabet soup. 'But they won't take our word for it, and they won't give him an IEP without the tests.'

Amrita plopped a teabag into the cup. 'I never make a proper cup anymore. This will have to do. Don't tell Barton.'

'I won't.'

'So what do we do, Mary? What is our plan?' Amrita fetched a spoon from the silverware drawer and the mug of tea, its paper tag fluttering like the tiniest white flag. She came to the table and set the spoon and mug down, the

34

tea releasing a humid cloud.

'We've requested the testing, so they have sixty days.'

'In the meantime, Dhiren suffers.' Amrita sat down heavily in the opposite chair.

'There's another way, but it's expensive. We can do an independent evaluation, but it costs. Three thousand dollars.'

'We can't afford that. Can't you get us somebody sooner, cheaper?'

'I'll look around.'

'Let's crack on, then.'

'Will do.' Mary got the gist of the Briticism and noted that Amrita made the decision without Barton. A software programmer, he traveled for work and wasn't Indian, which Mary sensed had strained the relationship with Amrita's parents. 'Now, tell me how Dhiren is.'

'Not good. I don't know what I'd do if I worked full-time. He says he's sick, most mornings. He doesn't want to go to school.'

'That's typical. They call it schoolphobic. How many days did he go last week?'

'Two only.' Amrita closed her eyes, trying to remember. 'Before that, he went three days. Of course that only makes it worse. He falls behind. He misses class discussion.'

'Did you start volunteering at school?'

'Yes, twice, as you asked. I see what happens now.' Amrita sighed. 'They started a new unit on the Revolutionary War. They write entries in a battlefield diary, as if from Valley Forge, and read them in class.'

Mary's heart wrenched. It would be a disaster for Dhiren.

'I helped him with the diary, but he had to read it himself, out loud. They mocked him. Dummy, they called him, instead of Dhiren. They mocked his accent as well. This I heard with my own ears.' Amrita's expression remained stoic. 'Imagine, with all this talk against bullying on the TV, on the news.'

Mary thought again of Trish.

'Last week, he got into a fight. One of the other boys called him dummy, and Dhiren hit him. The teachers, appalled, sent Dhiren home. I had a strop, a hissy fit, you call it, and now, it gets worse. I'll show you.' Amrita stood up. 'Dhiren, please come here.'

'I got a present for you, Dhiren.' Mary reached into her briefcase, and by the time she'd pulled out the bag, the boy had arrived at the threshold, his dark eyes shining. She handed him the wrapped package. 'I don't know how to work this, but I expect a smart guy like you does.'

'Cool!' Dhiren ripped off the paper and pulled out a shrink-wrapped box, a new game for his Game Boy.

'Say thank you, Dhiren.' Amrita frowned.

'Thank you!'

'Hope you don't have this one, it's called Dogz.' Mary pointed to the word, though its corrupted spelling wouldn't help the cause. 'You choose a puppy and you get to name it.'

'Dhiren, bend your head down for me,' Amrita said, and the boy bent over while his mother rooted around in his gorgeous hair, then exposed a bloody scab on his scalp. 'See, Mary. Look at this.' Then she let the hair go and displayed another scab behind his ear, bloodier. 'And see this, here.'

'Who did this to him?' Mary asked, disgusted. 'The kid he fought with?'

'Not him.' Amrita removed her hand, and Dhiren straightened up, his knees wiggling again. 'Son. Tell Miss DiNunzio what happened in school.'

'Did someone hit you?' Mary asked, softly.

Dhiren shook his head.

'No,' Amrita answered for him. 'The hair is gone in patches. It's pulled out at the root.'

'Yikes.' Mary could only imagine how much that hurt. 'Who pulled your hair, Dhiren? Please, tell me.'

Amrita answered, 'He goes in the boys' room and pulls it out himself.'

Mary gasped, astonished, but Amrita remained impassive.

'He does it himself. He's so upset, so frustrated, he's tearing his own hair out. It started last week. Tell her why you do this, son.'

Dhiren kept looking down, his new video game forgotten. 'I don't know. I go and do it. I can't help it.'

'You *can* help it,' Amrita snapped. 'You must not do it. Simply, you must not.'

'Dhiren,' Mary interrupted, 'can I ask you a favor? When you feel like pulling out your hair, could you please pretend your hair is like a puppy and pat it instead? Like in the game?'

Dhiren nodded. 'Can I go now?'

'Yes, you can,' Mary answered, though she knew he was asking his mother. 'Go. Play. Have fun.'

Dhiren hurried off, leaving the two women in the still kitchen.

Amrita's features slackened, and she surrendered to a sadness as familiar as an old sweater. 'Please, Mary,' she whispered, over the untouched tea. 'Won't you save my son?'

'I'll do everything I can,' Mary answered, sick at heart. She had no better answer. The law was failing everyone today. Or she was.

Outside the kitchen window, it was getting darker.

And nightfall was Trish's deadline.

5

A troubled Mary left Amrita's house and stood outside for a moment, surveying the street. A cold night had fallen but lights were on in the rowhomes, glowing a warm gold. TVs flickered behind gauze curtains, sending bluish flashes into the night. Down the street, a young woman stood smoking on her stoop, the cigarette tip burning red.

He'll kill me. Tonight.

Mary slid her BlackBerry from her purse, ignored the e-mail, and hit Redial. She listened to the phone ring and ring, but there was no answer at Trish's mother's house. Where was Trish now? Was she okay or was she lying dead somewhere? Mary hit End, slid the phone back into her purse, and scanned the city skyline, looking for answers that weren't there.

She hadn't gone two steps when a door opened and Elvira Rotunno reappeared, a stocky silhouette in the doorway, her timing too good to be coincidental. she called, 'Yo, Mare, did you eat yet?' she asked, which came out like *Jeet jet?*

'Yes,' Mary lied again. 'I gotta run.'

'Why don't you come in for some dessert? Dom wants to say hi.'

'No thanks, gotta go.' Mary looked around for a cab, or a gun to shoot herself.

'Where you goin' this time a night?'

'To my parents',' Mary heard herself answer,

though she hadn't thought of it until this minute. It was a good idea. She needed an escape, a meal, and a hug, but not in that order.

'Hold on then. Dom can give you a ride. You won't get a cab out here, you know that.'

'I can walk.'

'To your parents'? That's twenty blocks.'

Mary made a mental note to move. 'I'll get a bus.'

'Here he is.' Elvira was joined at the door by an equally wide silhouette in jeans and an Eagles sweatshirt.

'Ma,' Dominic bellowed. 'I can't drive nowhere, you keep forgettin'. I got no license since the DUI.'

Gulp.

Suddenly a silvery Prius turned the corner and slowed to a stop in front of the rowhouse. 'Oh, here's my Ant'n'y.' Elvira walked down the steps, holding on to the wrought-iron rail. 'He can take you home, Mare.' When she reached the sidewalk, she pulled Mary close and whispered in her ear, 'I'd fix you up with Ant'n'y, but he's gay.'

Perfect.

Mary turned in time to see Anthony emerge from the driver's side of the Prius. She didn't know him from high school, but she knew only the boys who needed tutoring. Anthony Rotunno looked like a nice guy; tall, slim, and ridiculously well dressed in a brown leather jacket, white shirt, and charcoal pants.

'Ant, this is Mary DiNunzio,' Elvira said, gesturing. 'You know Mary. Her parents live

40

down the block from Cousin-Pete-With-The-Nose. Can you give her a ride home?'

'Sure, Mary, climb in.' Anthony smiled, opened the passenger-side door, and gestured her inside while he crossed to the front stoop, kissed his mother on the cheek, and handed her an envelope. 'Sorry, Ma, I almost forgot.'

'Love you, Ant. Such a good son.' Elvira gave him an extra kiss on the cheek, and he hustled back to the car and climbed in.

'Thanks for the ride,' Mary said, when he slammed the door.

'Sure.' Anthony put the car in gear and they took off. The car was quiet, with all manner of glowing gauges on the dashboard and a politically correct hum coming from the engine. 'It's the least I can do, after what you did for my mother. She's in love with her new awning. I never saw somebody so excited about molded plastic.'

'Fiberglass.'

'Excuse me.'

Mary smiled. 'It's the simple things.'

Anthony laughed. 'So where we going?'

Mary told Anthony the address and relaxed into the neat little car. She could see in the dim light that he had a handsome profile, with thick, dark hair, big brown eyes, and a slim, straight nose. His cologne was on the strong side, but it only reminded Mary of her old friend Brent Polk, who was also gay. Brent had passed years ago, and she still missed him. She felt instantly comfy with Anthony because of Brent, like a gay associative principle.

41

Anthony said, 'My mother wants to hook you up with Dom. She loves you, and she smells grandchildren. Fee-fi-fo-fum.'

Mary moaned. 'Uh-oh.'

'It's a love match. You can keep him out of jail, free.'

Mary smiled. 'So what do you do for a living?'

'I'm on sabbatical from St. John's to write a book. Nonfiction. I published one modest volume on the trial of Sacco and Vanzetti.'

'Interesting.'

'Happily, the critics thought so, and both of my readers agreed. Now I'm working on another, about Carlo Tresca.'

'Who's he?'

'He was an anarchist, a contemporary of Emma Goldman, who was shot and killed in New York in 1943. His murder was never solved.' Anthony steered the car around the corner, negotiating double-parkers with a native's skill, and they picked up speed past the rowhouses, lighted front windows, and people walking mutts. 'They think it was the Mob who did it, or somebody against the unions he was trying to organize.'

'Whoa.' Mary considered it. 'So these are Italian-American subjects.'

'Exactly. I teach Italian-American studies.'

'My life is Italian-American studies.'

Anthony laughed.

'So what do you do about Carlo Tresca? Research the case?'

'Research it and educate people. Right now I'm trying to subpoena the rest of his FBI file, under the Freedom of Information Act. The forms are a real pain.'

'You don't need a subpoena, just a request.'

'Really?'

'Yes. I can help you with that,' Mary said before she realized she didn't have the time to help anybody with anything.

'Would you mind if I called you, to pick your brain?'

'Not at all.' Mary dug in her purse for her wallet, extracted a business card, and stuck it on the console as they stopped at a red light.

'Thanks.' Anthony smiled warmly, and Mary felt a pang of sadness for Brent, then for Dhiren and Trish, and for everything that had gone so very wrong.

'It's good to go home,' she blurted out, her chest suddenly tight.

'It's always good to go home,' Anthony agreed.

★ ★ ★

'How nice you come viz'!' Vita DiNunzio cried, meeting Mary in the living room, throwing her soft arms around her, and enveloping her in a hug redolent of old-fashioned Aqua Net and fresh basil.

'Honey!' her father boomed, wrapping her in his embrace, completing the one-two punch of the DiNunzio love attack.

'Hey, Pop, long time, no see,' Mary said, and they laughed, them at her joke, and she at the joyful realization that she could come home whenever she wanted, get loved up, and forget

43

about bad things, at least temporarily. She wanted to drown her sorrows in tomato sauce, having long ago realized she was an emotional eater. After all, what other reason was there to eat?

Her father kept his heavy arm around her, her mother took her other hand, and together they half-led and half-carried her like a parental sedan chair to the kitchen, The Place Where Time Stopped. The small room was bright, ringed with white wood cabinets and white Formica counters, unchanged since Mary's girlhood. A church calendar on the wall depicted an old-school Jesus against a cerulean background, his eyes so far heavenward the whites showed, and next to him were photos of Pope John, JFK, and Frank Sinatra, attached with yellowed Scotch tape. Wedged behind the switchplate was a brittle spray of palm and Mass cards, the fancy ones laminated. The collection had grown since last month, but Mary didn't want to think about that.

'So, how are you guys?' she asked, sitting down. On the table were a few old screwdrivers, one with a yellow plastic handle that she would always remember as one of her father's tools. 'You fixing things, Pop?'

'Your mother's put me to work.' Her father pulled up his chair opposite her, easing heavily into the seat and placing a hand flat on the table.

From the stove, her mother answered, 'For . . . *macchina da cucire*.'

'Your sewing machine?' Mary translated. Her mother, an Italian immigrant, had spent her

44

working life sewing lampshades in the basement of this house, having almost gone blind with the effort. Mary didn't get it. 'You sewing again, Ma?'

'*Si*. Your father, he fix alla for me. Alla work good now.' Her mother's face lit up, and her small brown eyes flared behind thick glasses whose stems disappeared into teased white hair, like an airplane into clouds.

'Your mother's got a business idea,' her father said, with a soft smile. 'Tell her, Veet.'

'*È vero, Maria*,' her mother answered, her flowered back turned as she twisted on the gas under their dented perk coffeepot, then went into the refrigerator, fetched a pot of tomato sauce, and set it on the stove near the dish rack. Her parents didn't own a coffeemaker or a dishwasher; her mother was the coffeemaker and her father the dishwasher. The DiNunzios were like the Amish, only with brighter clothes.

'What's the idea, Ma?' Mary asked, mystified.

'*Aspett', Maria, aspett'*.' Her mother turned the knob to fire up the gravy pot, then scurried from the kitchen and disappeared into the darkened dining room.

Mary turned to her father. 'She's starting a business, Pop? She doesn't have to work, does she?' She offered them money all the time, but they consistently turned her down, their finances a state secret.

'Nah, she wants to work, and the babysitting took too much outta her.' Her father shrugged happily. 'What's the harm?'

'Okay, but let me get her a new machine. She

45

can't use that old one from the cellar.'

'The Singer with the pedal? Runs like a top.'

'Pop, please.' Mary moaned. 'We have electricity now.'

'She loves that machine.'

Mary gave up. Usually, you couldn't fight progress, but progress never met Vita and Mariano DiNunzio. 'Okay, you win. Tell me, how's Angie? You hear anything?'

'She's still in Tunisia. Says she's fine.'

'When's she coming home?' Mary asked, suddenly missing her sister, a stab of longing like a phantom pain.

'She'll be back in three months, the letter said. I'll show you later, it's upstairs.' Her father leaned over, his elbows on the table. 'Hey, what did Bernice say? She gonna apologize about Dean?'

Oops. 'I forgot. I'm sorry. I'll call tomorrow.'

'It's okay, Mare. Don't worry.'

It got Mary thinking. 'Pop, you hear anything about Trish Gambone lately?'

'From high school? She was one o' the fast ones, right?'

'Yes.' Mary hadn't heard the term in years. 'She was in my office today. She's living with a guy in the Mob.'

'That, I heard from Jimmy Pete. He said the wiseguy is that kid you used to teach. Remember him?'

Boy, do I. 'Yes, it is him.'

Her father clucked. 'I thought he was a nice kid, but you never know.'

'No, you never do.' Mary didn't want to dwell

46

on it, not here. The coffeepot started to boil but her father didn't hear it, despite the hearing aid curled behind his ear like a plastic comma. She rose to get the coffee and turned off the gas under the pot before it percolated into its eleventh hour, then retrieved three mismatched cups and saucers. She set the table and got the pot, then poured her father a cup in a glistening arc, releasing the dense aroma of DiNunzio Blend, coffee distilled to brown caffeine.

'*Eccoli*,' her mother said from the door, and Mary set the coffee-pot down in astonishment. Displayed across her mother's arms was a perfect little gown of white cotton. Layers of miniature pleats fanned out from its sweet yoke, crosshatched by the finest threads, and its neckline curved like a tiny shell. Cap sleeves puffed from either side like the ears of a child's teddy bear. Smiling, her mother asked, '*Che carino, no?*'

'Ma, this is beautiful. It's amazing!' Mary stepped closer to see better. 'You made this?'

'She makes christening dresses,' her father answered, with quiet pride. 'She did that one by hand and three others. Each one takes her a week, so I figured we had to get the old machine goin' again.'

'It's lovely!' Mary marveled, and her mother beamed, displaying the dress like a human store window. 'How did this come about?'

'She was sweepin' the stoop, and Mrs. D'Orazio said she was gonna spend $150 on a christening dress for her granddaughter. Your mother tol' her she could make it cheaper and she did. Then she sold it for seventy-five.' Her father clapped his heavy hands together. 'For a dress the size of a baby doll.'

'*Si, Maria, è vero.*' Her mother nodded happily, and her father continued:

'So then the grandbaby had it on at the christening, and Mrs. D told everybody how cheap it was, and now all them want the dresses for their grandkids. Then this Puerto Rican lady from Wolf Street found out and she told all the other Puerto Ricans in their parish, and you know they love to dress their kids up.'

Mary flinched. 'Don't say that, Pop.'

'Why not? It's true.'

'It sounds racist.'

'I'm not racist, you know that.' Her father looked wounded, his forehead troubled, and Mary felt horrible. Matty DiNunzio wasn't racist in the least. He'd been a foreman and always gave his crew an equal shot at jobs and overtime, even bringing them home to dinner in an era when it raised eyebrows.

'I'm sorry, Pop. I'm just tired.' Mary sighed, and on the stove, the gravy began to bubble, warming the kitchen with the aroma of tomatoes, garlic, basil, and fresh, peppery sausage.

'I know, I can see.' Her father sipped his coffee, then his smile returned. 'Anyway, your mother's in business. She's got twelve orders already.'

'Wow.' Mary managed a smile, and her gaze strayed to the little dress, so small and white. She could almost imagine the baby in the gown, pure and pink, its arms sticking out of the puffy sleeves. Her husband Mike had wanted kids, but she had always thought that would come later. But she had been wrong about that and many other things. A wave of despair swept over her, as she stood at the intersection of life and death.

'Mare?' asked her father.

'Maria?' echoed her mother.

Mary put on a happy face. 'I'm hungry,' she said, and her parents brightened, knowing exactly what to do.

But tonight, not even spaghetti would do the trick. All through dinner, Mary thought about Trish.

★   ★   ★

Mary got home to her apartment, ignored the day's mail, and went to her bedroom, where she undressed quickly, changing into gray sweats and her old Donovan McNabb jersey. She stopped by the bathroom, unpeeled contacts from her corneas, and washed off her eye makeup, leaving two attractive skidmarks in the white towel, then finger-combed her hair into its Pebbles ponytail and slipped on her glasses.

Mike.

Grief struck without warning, an emotional mugging, and Mary stood still at the sink, steadying herself, resting her fingertips on the chilly rim. Then she fled the room, padding barefoot to her home office, and headed for her computer. She moved the mouse, and her home page, *www.phillynews.com*, burst onto the screen. The headline read, **SOCIETY HILL BABY ABDUCTED**. She scanned the story, reporting that a year-old baby girl, Sabine Donchess, had been kidnapped from the home of a wealthy family. An Amber Alert had been issued, and the police were hunting for suspects. Mary felt relieved. No news about Trish.

He's connected. He deals drugs, heroin and coke.

Mary sat back in her chair, her memory unspooling. Even though she'd only known him in high school, he'd been her first real love. He'd come to her house for a full year of Wednesdays, and the two of them sat at the kitchen table while she tutored him in Latin, so close she could have kissed him. He was a jock in a black Neumann sweat-shirt, sweaty from a shower after practice, smelling of hard soap and Doublemint gum. Always antsy in the chair, his big legs jiggled under the table. She kept her crush to herself, so far gone that she used to look forward to going to bed at night, just so she could think about him.

She breathed a sigh, knowing she had dodged a bullet with him. He had grown into a nightmare. When had that happened? How, when she could still remember the sound of his laugh, most often directed at himself? He would say, *I'm so dumb.* He'd run his hand through his hair as he puzzled over the translation. He'd grip his pencil like a little boy, throttling it between thick fingers. His handwriting was terrible, and to Mary, even that was proof that he was such a *guy.*

Her apartment was so quiet, and the silence left Mary alone with her regrets. So many things she couldn't undo. So many problems she couldn't solve. So much she knew now that she hadn't known before. She stared at the computer screen without seeing anything. She had tons of work to do, plus she had to answer the e-mail she hadn't checked for hours, and now poor Dhiren. She could be up all night and never make a dent in her caseload.

And when she closed her eyes, in her own darkness, Mary couldn't help but sense that something terrible was happening, somewhere.

6

Mary charged off the elevator before the office had even opened. She held a half-full cup of Dunkin' Donuts coffee, and her newspaper, bag, and briefcase. She was a girl on a mission, perfumed and caffeinated, dressed in a burgundy suit and a white shirt, her hair loose to her shoulders. She'd checked online and ascertained that there was no new news about Trish, which was good news. But she had another problem to solve.

She powered down the hall and made a beeline for Bennie's office, where the light was on. Voices came from inside; it would be Bennie and the other associate at the firm, Anne Murphy. Mary reached the office, and court papers, depositions, and files blanketed the desk, credenza, round table, and even the striped couch against the wall.

She stuck her head in the open door, but her nerve wavered. 'Maybe this isn't the best time,' she blurted out.

'Hi, Mary.' Anne looked up from the back table and tucked her glossy red hair behind an ear, her makeup perfect, her green eyes sparkling, and her body sleek in a russet knit dress. She was so gorgeous she deserved to be hated, which happened from time to time. Three is never a good number for women, especially if they have law degrees.

'Hey, Anne,' Mary said, bucking up at Anne's warmth.

'DiNunzio, did you say something?' Bennie stood behind her desk, her unruly golden blond head bent over a deposition, and she was putting yellow Post-its on lines of the transcript. An elite rower, she had broad shoulders and stood so tall in her granite-gray suit that she looked like a skyscraper.

'Can I talk to you for a minute?' Mary made herself ask. Behind Bennie, glistening crystal awards, gold-toned plaques, and framed citations stocked her bookshelves and covered her walls. Bennie Rosato was one of the most highly regarded trial lawyers in the city, a maverick who fought for civil rights. Which, Mary now knew, didn't pay as well as broken sunroofs.

'Come in and make it fast.' Bennie turned to Anne. 'Murphy, can you leave us alone? DiNunzio's having a hard time asking me something. She may faint. Stand by.'

'I'll call 911.' Anne laughed and headed for the door. 'By the way, thanks for the lasagna.'

'You ate it, you thief?' Mary tripped Anne when she passed, and Bennie gestured her to a seat.

'DiNunzio, come in, close the door, and state your business. You know how I get before cross-examination.'

'Cross?'

Bennie didn't smile.

'I have something to talk to you about.' Mary lowered herself into a chair, still holding her stuff. If she put her coffee cup on the desk, it

53

would undoubtedly spill on important papers, resulting in an unfavorable jury verdict and loss of gainful employment. 'We need help.'

'We do?' Bennie returned to the transcript, flipping the page, which made its distinctively crinkly sound. She kept reading as she stood, her head bent, her hands braced on her desk.

'Yes, I think we need more help here.' Mary chose her words carefully, not wanting to reveal what Judy had told her. 'I'm working really hard and I have so many active matters and it's overwhelming. I have a special-ed case and I can't give it the attention it needs.'

'Can't this wait?' Bennie flipped the page.

'No, because I think we need to hire another associate, as soon as possible. I could keep her or him busy.' Mary had thought about it last night, when she'd gotten only three hours sleep. 'I know it's an all-woman firm, and I don't care if we hire a woman or a man, obviously. I don't even know if you intended the firm to be all women or not.'

'No.' Bennie flipped another page and kept reading. 'You three were the best people, ovaries aside.'

Mary blushed. She knew she had reproductive organs, she just didn't want to discuss them at the office. 'Okay. Well, whatever the gender, I really need help.'

'No.'

Mary had thought there'd be more discussion. It threw her off balance. 'Can I ask why not?'

'We don't have the office space for another person right now, and I've been thinking about

54

moving. So we can't expand before we have the space, for one thing.'

'We could put the new person in the library, temporarily.'

'We need the library and the conference room.'

'Then they could work out of the office, or even at home.'

Bennie looked up sharply, her gaze a fiercely intelligent blue. 'DiNunzio, I appreciate that you're working hard. We all are. But this is a terrible time to discuss this. I have a jury trial this week.'

Mary swallowed hard. 'I know, but — '

'I know you're doing a terrific job, bringing in a lot of business right now.'

Right now?

'Your new clients and cases will cause a strain on you. It's inevitable. But I can't take on another associate just because you have a good quarter.'

Judy said three.

'I can't take on someone and then let that person go when the cases aren't coming in.'

But Judy said they were trending up.

'You remember when I almost lost the place? I don't have to remind you that they had an eviction notice on the wall.' Bennie frowned. The phone on her desk rang, but she ignored it. 'I can never put myself, or any of you, in that position again.'

'What about a contract lawyer?' Mary had prepared for this argument. 'Won't the business I bring in pay for that person?'

'Money's not the problem.' Bennie's unlip-sticked mouth curved into a tight smile. 'Look, every six months or so, you feel overwhelmed. It's a pattern. But I have faith in you, and you can get it all done. If you're still feeling overwhelmed six months from now, we'll talk again.'

But that will be too late. 'Okay.' Mary juggled her coffee and got up.

'That's a concession, DiNunzio. You're getting better.' Bennie half-smiled. 'By the way, I know some special-ed law. Come to me and we'll talk about it, just not when I'm on trial.'

'Okay,' Mary said, though she knew she wouldn't. They both did. When you feel dumb, the last place you go is the boss.

Suddenly, Anne appeared in the open doorway, slightly agitated. 'Hate to interrupt you, Bennie, but that was me on the phone.' She gestured to Mary. 'There are some clients here to see you.'

'At this hour?' Mary asked, going to the door.

'I'll be right back, Bennie,' Anne called over Mary's shoulder, then grabbed the door and closed it behind them. 'Trust me, you don't want her to see this.'

'What's going on?' Mary asked, puzzled, as Anne hurried them both up the hall toward reception.

'Actually, I'm not sure they're your clients. They look like your clients.'

Mary knew what she meant. Code for South Philly. Big hair and workmen's comp appeals. 'I'm not expecting anybody this morning.'

'They're really pissed off at you.'

'Why?' Mary asked, and they'd gotten almost all the way up the hall when three women came charging from the reception area toward them, a flying wedge of curly extensions, big chests, and stiletto heels.

'Mare!' they shouted, from down the hall. 'Mary DiNunzio? That you? Get your ass out here!'

At the middle of the hall, Judy, who must have just come into work, opened her office door and popped her head out, her expression astonished. 'Who's yelling? What's going on?'

'I don't know,' Mary answered, mystified until she recognized the three women. The Mean Girls — Giulia Palazzolo, Missy Toohey, and Yolanda Varlecki. Each wore tight blue jeans, huge gold earrings, and a form-fitting leather jacket in shades of black, black, and black, respectively. They all had long, matte-black hair in elaborate ringlets, distinguished only by the color of their highlights. Giulia's streaks were ruby red, Missy's bleached white, and Yolanda's electric blue, our nation's colors gone terribly wrong.

Giulia shouted, 'You're ignorant, Mare! This is all your fault!'

Missy yelled, 'You don't give a crap about anybody but yourself! I always hated your guts!'

Yolanda hollered, 'I could effin' kill you myself!'

Mary froze. Anne took her arm. Judy came out of her office. The three lawyers faced off against the three Mean Girls, but it was no contest. The lawyers had advanced degrees, but the Mean Girls had acrylic tips.

'What are you talking about?' Mary asked, but Judy stepped forward and put up a hand.

'Please stop yelling at my friend. That's so not cool.'

'Yeah, cut it out,' Anne yelped, just as Missy shoved Judy backward, knocking her off balance. Mary leaped to catch her, dropping her coffee, purse, and briefcase, but Giulia yanked her hair and Yolanda screamed cigarette breath in her face. Mary struggled to get free, somebody with too much lipliner threw a punch at Anne, handbags and clogs went flying, and in the next second, Rosato & Associates hosted its first, full-fledged catfight.

'STOP THAT!' came a shout from down the hall, and Mary looked up from Giulia's chokehold to see Bennie running toward them like a superhero, her suit jacket flying. Giulia only tightened her grip, but in the next moment Mary felt Bennie's powerful hand clamp down on her arm and yank her out of harm's way.

'STOP RIGHT NOW!' Bennie hollered.

'You're scum!' Giulia yelled, pointing a lethal fingernail at Mary, who staggered to her feet and watched Bennie bring order to chaos. The boss grabbed Judy by the T-shirt, extricating her from the melee, and shielded Anne as she scrambled to her Blahniks and scooted from the fracas.

'STOP THAT THIS INSTANT!' Bennie shouted, stepping forward and grabbing Giulia by her padded leather shoulder. 'HOW DARE YOU!'

58

'Who're *you*?' Giulia practically spat. 'A freakin' Amazon?'

'Go.' Bennie released Giulia, who tottered slightly on her stilettos. 'Get out of my office before I call the police.'

'Call them,' Giulia shot back. 'They're good for nothin'.'

'Wrong, crazy.' Bennie towered over the Mean Girls, who seemed surprisingly intimidated. 'They're good for charging people with crimes. I'll make sure they charge you with assault, battery, terroristic threats, and trespassing. Now get out of my office and don't you ever, *ever* touch one of these girls again.'

'Ha!' Giulia erupted in a laugh. 'You should know that your *girl* turned her back on our best friend — and now she's *gone*.'

'You mean Trish?' Mary felt sick.

'Yeah, she's gone.' Giulia's mascaraed eyes burned with outrage. 'And so's he. All because you couldn't be bothered.'

'How you live with yourself?' Missy yelled, and Yolanda glowered.

'I bet she's dead right now because a you.'

Mary was stricken. Judy caught her eye. Anne cowered in the rear.

Bennie turned, her cheeks flushed. 'DiNunzio, are these women speaking a language you understand, or are they merely delusional?'

'I understand,' Mary answered, miserably. *Trish. Gone.* 'Don't throw them out. I know them from high school.'

'You feel safe with them?' Bennie frowned.

59

'Fine. DiNunzio, I leave this situation to you. I have a case to try.'

'Okay, sorry, thanks.' Mary nodded, and Bennie turned to Giulia.

'You. Go to the reception area. She'll call you when she's ready. Do what I say or leave.'

'Whatever.' Giulia turned away and pivoted on her spike heel, and Missy and Yolanda followed suit, all of them stalking off, trailing a crowd of perfume and adrenaline. Bennie and the associates watched them reach the reception area.

Judy couldn't hold it in any longer. 'Those girls are wack.'

'They're *girls*?' Anne finger-combed her hair back into place.

'Sorry.' Mary picked up Judy's clog and handed it to her. 'Thanks for the help.'

Bennie shook her head. 'Is everybody okay?'

'Fine,' Judy and Anne answered.

'Thanks.' Mary scooped up her purse, while Judy retrieved her briefcase. Anne got the Dunkin' Donuts cup, mopping up the spilled coffee with the newspaper.

'DiNunzio, I'm surprised you agreed to meet with them.' Bennie frowned. 'I wouldn't reward that behavior. I'm still not sure you'll be safe.'

'I'll be fine. They're just emotional.'

'Hormonal,' Judy said.

'Certifiable.' Anne looked up from the wet rug. 'You shouldn't be around them. You could catch really bad taste.'

'They'll settle down.'

Bennie motioned to Judy. 'Stay with her,

60

Carrier. Don't leave her alone with them.'

'Okay.'

Bennie put a soft hand on Mary's shoulder and looked at her in a way that was almost maternal. 'Don't let them push you around, understand? They're not worth one ounce of you.'

The boss never talked that way, and Judy and Anne looked over in surprise. But Mary barely heard the praise, engulfed by guilt. She flashed on Trish, crying in the office, her life dependent on a gun and the Pink Sisters.

Gone.

7

The Mean Girls were no longer homicidal by the time they all sat down at the conference table, and Mary could see the individual differences in them that she'd missed when they were trying to kill her. Giulia looked Italian, with large, warm brown eyes, a biggish nose, and full lips, each feature a bold stroke on an olive-skinned canvas, like Botticelli on acid. Missy Toohey had small, light blue eyes, a little nose with the tiniest bump, and heavy foundation that obliterated a freckled complexion, as if she were erasing her Irishness. Yolanda Varlecki looked like a working-class Angelina Jolie with round brown eyes in perfect symmetry with a lovely nose and lips like hot dogs.

Mary began, 'So tell me why you say she's missing.'

'How about you tell us why you blew her off?' Giulia's eyes flashed with anger. 'She came to you for help, Mare. You're from the neighborhood. You too good for us now?'

Mary's mouth went dry. 'I didn't blow her off. I told her I'd take her to court but she didn't want to go.'

'She was worried he'd kill her. Now maybe he did. Ya happy?'

Judy raised a warning hand. 'That's enough. Whatever happened, it's not Mary's fault and you know it.'

Giulia shot back, 'Shut up, you don't know me at all.' Then she fixed her dark gaze on Mary. 'Alls I know is, my best friend's missing and I don't know what to do about it. Her mother's outta her mind from worryin'. We're all sick about it.' She glanced irritably around the conference room. 'What's the deal? Can I smoke in here?'

'No,' Judy answered, and Giulia's eyes glittered.

'I don't like you, girl.'

'Love is all around.' Judy flashed her a peace sign.

'Giulia,' Mary broke in, 'tell me what happened, as best you know. It was Trish's birthday, right? And he had some kind of surprise?'

'Yeh. We thought he was gonna propose, and she was afraid because she didn't want to say yes. The only way she'd accept is if he put a gun to her head.'

Mary felt a chill, bone deep. 'Do you know if he was taking her out to give her the surprise? Or was he bringing it home?'

'They never shopped for a ring, but I dunno. Wait. Lemme think.' Giulia calmed down as she sorted out her confusion. 'She called me at seven o'clock, all nervous that he'd be home any minute. Now that I think about it, she did mention they were going out.'

'Okay. Did she say anything else?'

'We set it up so she'd call me after the surprise, to let me know if she could go out to celebrate.'

'Would he let her do that?' Mary asked, surprised.

'No way, never. We only said it so she had an excuse to call me after she got the surprise, so I'd know she was okay.'

Mary's heart ached at the scheme set up by these women, desperate to protect themselves.

'But she never showed up and she never called. We called her cell about a million times and her house. Then we went and stopped by her house and she wasn't home. Neither was he. We chilled there awhile and — '

'Where? At her house?'

'Yeah, I have keys. I used to go over there a lot, borrowin' clothes. So anyway we went to T's house but she never showed up, and then we went home. She never even went on the computer. We IM each other at night but I didn't get nothin' from her. No e-mail, no IMs. Nothin'.'

Mary understood why the Mean Girls had behaved the way they had. This was the worst-case scenario.

'None of us slep' a wink.' Giulia turned to the others for confirmation, and they nodded unhappily. 'So we went back over her house this morning, and she still wasn't home, so we called the cops.'

'Good,' Mary said.

'Not really.' Giulia snorted. 'We told 'em what happened, and they said she mighta eloped, which we know she didn't. They said they couldn't do nothin' about it because it wasn't forty-eight hours yet. They said, what if they went on a vacation? Or a cruise?'

'You believe that?' Missy muttered, disgusted. 'They were all about that baby girl who got kidnapped, Amber Alert.'

Mary didn't enlighten her. 'Giulia, did you tell the police that he was in the Mob?'

'Totally. We thought it would get them interested, but with that dumb baby, it's like T don't even matter.' Giulia threw up her hands, nonplussed. 'They had like fifty million phones ringin'. The cop said, if she isn't a little kid or an old guy, she has to wait the forty-eight hours.'

Yolanda shook her head, gravely. 'T's dead, I can feel it. I had a dream.'

Mary's gut tightened, but she knew enough not to ask anybody from South Philly about their dreams. She wanted to finish today. 'You called the salon, and she's not there?'

'We didn't have to call. We all work there. T got us our jobs. She didn't show up today, and we didn't either. The boss said it was okay.'

Yolanda sniffed. 'On the other hand, if we don't show, the world don't end. We only do manicures, except for G, who's gettin' into waxin'. She's movin' up. Or down.'

'Shut up!' Giulia shoved her, but didn't miss a beat. 'Mare, if T didn't go to work, something's wrong. She'd never ditch a full book. Plus it's not like her. No matter how hungover she was, she always went in. I'm scared, Mare. Real scared.' Giulia's eyes glistened, and she wasn't so streetwise anymore. She was just a girl whose best friend could be dead. She wiped her eye with the side of an index finger, and Mary

65

handed her a Kleenex box from the credenza, but Giulia waved it off. 'I'm not cryin'.'

'It's to wipe your mascara, then.'

'I don't wear mascara, it's eyelash extensions. T has 'em, too.' Giulia drew an airy circle around her eyes. 'Plus, see, my eyeliner ain't runnin'. It's permanent. Me and T got it tattooed on, together.'

'Tattooed *on your eyes?*' Judy interrupted, incredulous, and Giulia nodded.

'Yeah, sure. You never have to reapply, and your eyeliner always looks good, even when you wake up.'

'My lipliner's permanent,' Missy added, and Yolanda nodded.

'So's my eyebrows.'

Judy looked, dumbstruck, from Giulia with her tattooed eyes, to Missy with her tattooed lips, and finally to Yolanda with her tattooed eyebrows. Mary was too upset to care. She put down the Kleenex box.

'Didn't it *hurt?*' Judy asked, astounded, and Giulia shrugged.

'No more than a Brazilian.'

Mary couldn't hear anymore. Catholics shouldn't get Brazilians. In fact, the words Catholic and Brazilian should never appear in the same sentence, except for: Brazilians are very good Catholics.

'Anyways, I'm not like some very negative people.' Giulia jerked a spiked thumb toward Yolanda. 'I'm not saying he killed her. I can't go there, not yet. Alls I know is she *never* woulda gone away without tellin' us. That means she's in

66

trouble, real trouble.'

Mary felt it, too. It was too coincidental to be otherwise. 'Has anyone seen him?'

'No, he's gone, too. They're both gone.'

'Does he go to work?' Judy interjected.

'Whaddaya think, blondie?' Giulia looked at her like she was crazy. 'He packs a peanut-butter-and-jelly in a paper bag?'

'There's no call for that,' Mary said. 'She's only asking if he has a regular job, on the side. A front or whatever you call it.'

'No, he doesn't.' Giulia leaned forward in the chair, her eyes meeting Mary's directly. 'You gotta help us find T.'

'I'm in,' Mary said, her chest tight.

'Great.' Giulia smiled briefly, and Missy sniffled.

'Preciate it, Mare.'

'Me, too,' Yolanda said, grim.

Judy touched Mary's elbow. 'Can I talk to you a minute?' she asked, then turned to the Mean Girls. 'Would you wait for us in the reception area, please?'

'We get the message.' Giulia rose with a smirk, pushing out her chair, and so did the others.

'Thanks,' Mary said, and both she and Judy waited while the Mean Girls left the conference room. In the next minute, low laughter came from down the hall. Judy cringed, then turned to her.

'Mary, don't let them guilt you into this. This isn't your problem, and it could be dangerous. He's in the Mob.'

'I can't not.' Mary felt a tug in her chest. She

had a full day of work, including calls for Dhiren and another for Dean Martin, but Trish was out there somewhere. She couldn't help but feel responsible. 'I have to help, this time.'

'Why? They're using you, don't you see that?' Judy gestured outside the door. 'They're laughing at us, right now. Didn't you hear?'

'It's not for them, it's for Trish.'

'What do you owe her? She was horrible to you.'

'This is life and death, Jude. You saw them. They need help. They're . . . '

'Dumb?'

'A little.'

'Rude?'

'Okay.'

'Bitchy?'

'All of the above.' Mary met Judy's eye, so blue and clear, and she could see the love there, and the loyalty. 'I have a deposition to defend at ten today. It should take an hour, tops. It's a contracts case, a roof that leaks. The client's a sweet old guy, Roberto Nunez. Will you go for me?'

'This is crazy.'

'I prepared him last week. I even gave him a list of questions, so he's good to go.'

'Mary, they tattoo their *faces*.'

'And you pierced your you-know-what.'

'Touché.' Judy smiled. 'Anyway I let it close.'

'The point remains.'

Judy rolled her eyes. 'Okay, get me the file, you loser.'

8

'Keep the change.' Mary handed the aged cabdriver a ten, and he accepted it without taking his rheumy eyes from the butts of the Mean Girls piling out of the backseat. She climbed out of the cab while they took their first drags on their cigarettes, and she surveyed the block. It was typical South Philly, a little grimy even in full sun, with identical brick rowhouses differentiated by their stoops, awnings, and bumper-sticker front windows. The Korean grocery store Trish had mentioned was to the left of the house, a dingy stuccoed affair with its windows covered by painted plywood and a faded Dietz & Watson sign that read HOAGIES CHEESE FRIES PLATTERS.

Next to the grocery, Trish's house was well maintained, of newly painted brick with shiny black bars over the glass door and a blackframed bay window. Nothing was in the windowsill. Mary eyed the cars parked in front, a dusty lineup of older American cars, except for a shiny white Miata with a vanity plate that read DYE JOB. She pointed at the Miata. 'Is that Trish's?'

'Ya think?' Giulia laughed, emitting an acrid puff of smoke, and the others joined her.

'What's he drive?' Mary asked, trying not to breathe.

'A BMW, what else?'

'Where's he park it?'

69

'Anywhere he wants to,' Giulia answered, and they all laughed again. She pointed at an empty slot behind the Miata. 'That's his spot. You wanna be the jerk who takes it?'

'What color and year is his car?'

'Black. New.'

'Does he have a vanity plate, too, like DYE JOB?'

'Yeah, WHACK JOB,' Giulia answered.

'BLOW JOB,' Missy said.

'HAND JOB,' Yolanda added, and they all started laughing again except Mary, whose exasperation got the best of her.

'You ladies want to help or not? Because when Trish shows up, I'll be happy to tell her how funny you all were.'

'Okay, whatever,' Giulia said defensively. 'I don't know his license plate. It wasn't a vanity plate. It was normal.'

'Thank you.' Mary cleared her throat. 'Okay, so obviously, wherever he and Trish went, they took his car. So she probably went with him voluntarily, because he couldn't have forced her into the car and driven it at the same time.'

Giulia stopped smiling, and so did the others. She squinted through the cigarette smoke, or maybe her tattooed eyeliner made it look that way.

'He coulda drugged her,' Missy said.

'He coulda killed her and put her in the trunk,' Yolanda said, and Giulia turned on her, red-and-black curls flying like a blurry checkerboard.

'Shut up with that, Yo. It's like you *want* T to be dead.'

'I don't want her to be dead,' Yolanda shot back. 'Ga' forbid!'

Mary sensed another catfight. 'While you guys mix it up, I'm going inside and look around. Can I have her house key?'

'Here.' Giulia clamped her Marlboro between her lips, dug in her black purse, and produced a key ring that held a red Barbie pump, a Taj Mahal ersatz-gold horseshoe, two red plastic dice, and a St. Christopher medal. Mary took the key ring without bringing up what had happened to St. Christopher, then walked up the two-step stoop, unlocked the door, and pushed it open, surprised by the sight.

In contrast to the house's mundane exterior, inside it was glistening, modern, and expensive, with warm white walls, a shaggy white area rug, and white marble flooring. It had been remodeled to make one large room out of the first floor, with the entrance hall, living and dining room divided by frosted white screens, like a high-end Winter Wonderland.

Would this have been my life?

Mary walked through the contemporary entrance area, where a fake ficus provided a splotch of color, passing a white laminated side table and a louvered closet. Light shone from a white Murano-glass chandelier, and when she walked around the divider, the focal point of the living room was an oversized, colorized photograph of the couple, he in a wide-lapel tux and she in a low-cut, melon-hued dress. Mary's gaze

71

shot to the boyfriend, who had once been her boyfriend, at least for a time. His face hadn't changed; the same eyes, the strong, wide nose, and a smile just this side of I-don't-care. He had prominent cheekbones and a strong chin, and Mary used to imagine it on an ancient gold coin, but she was always too into Latin Club.

'That picture was taken at my wedding,' Giulia said, coming up from behind, her stilettos clacking on the marble floor. 'The first one, that is. T was my maid of honor both times.'

'So how long have they been living here?'

'Five years or so.' Giulia crunched an Altoid, releasing a blast of toxic peppermint. 'They remodeled the whole thing. Gorgeous, huh?'

'Yeah, wow.' Mary looked around. A sectional couch of white leather sat against the wall, catty-corner to two matching chairs and a white laminated coffee table, spotless but for a white marble ash-tray and three silvery remote controls. Hanging on the opposite wall was a huge plasma TV.

'To me, it's too clean, but T had to keep it that way, for him.'

'Trish told me.' Mary looked back at the entrance hall. 'No sign of a fight or struggle on the way out.'

'Maybe Missy's right. Maybe he drugged her. Or slapped her one.' Giulia pursed her lips. 'I know he knocked her around. T told me once, and I think it was worse than she said.'

'I do, too.' Mary considered it. 'But if he hit her, how would he get her out, then? Carry her?

72

It's still light at seven o'clock this time of year. People would see.'

'He could kinda hold her up, like she was drunk or somethin'.'

'Maybe, but look.' Mary gestured at the entrance hall. 'The rug near the door is still flat, not even moved or wrinkled. It's the kind that slips easily. That suggests they went peacefully.'

'You're right, Mare.'

'We'll see. It's just a working theory.'

'I like it, a workin' theory.' Giulia smiled. 'That sounds good. Now what do we do? I mean, what're you lookin' for in here?'

'I'm trying to learn what I can and hope it gives us a clue about what happened to Trish. We'll test our theory as we go along.'

'Another good idea. Thank God you're here.' Giulia clapped her on the back, and Mary couldn't help but smile.

'Giulia, what kind of coat does Trish usually wear?'

'Call me G, everybody does. I'm G, Trish is T. Yolanda is Yo.'

'What's Missy?'

'A pain in the ass.'

Mary laughed. 'When Trish came to my office, she had on a fox coat.'

'That's what she wears to dress up. The one she normally wears is just like mine.' Giulia gestured at her coat. 'We bought them together.'

'Okay, so do me a favor. Go check in the closet and see if her fox coat or her leather coat's in there.'

'I'm on the case.' Giulia pivoted on her heel

73

and *clack-clack*ed over to the entrance hall.

'Thanks.' Mary walked ahead into a white dining room, which had a long, white laminated table and eight high-backed chairs. A matching breakfront displayed a Franklin Mint plate of Madonna and Child, next to photos of the couple with their arms wrapped around each other in front of Epcot Center, the Christmas tree at Rockefeller Center, and on the boardwalk in Atlantic City. There was even one of them in front of some palm trees with Joey Merlino, the mobster who kept South Philly on the crime map.

'Mare,' Giulia called out, *clack*ing back to the dining room. 'Her fox coat's not there.'

'Interesting, good. So she took her dress coat and she had time to take it and to make a choice. So she wasn't drugged. She went voluntarily. So far, our theory is holding up.' Mary picked up the photo with Joey Merlino. 'They went away with Merlino?'

'Nah, that was taken in prison.'

Mary blinked. 'But there's palm trees.'

'That's a fake background they have in the joint. Didn't you know that?'

Uh. 'No.' Mary set it down. 'I was just looking at the photos, and they seem so happy. When did it turn bad?'

Giulia squinted, thinking. 'About two years ago.'

'What happened?' Mary opened a drawer in the breakfront, but it was empty, then reached for the next.

'He's old school. He wanted her home at

74

night, dinner on the table, makin' babies. Like a homebody, a wife. But T''s not that type. She liked to have fun.' Giulia's expression darkened. 'Then he started drinkin' more and more. I hate him, I hate the way he treated her. He was a loser and he blamed her for everything, like that he wasn't movin' up fast as he wanted.'

'In the Mob, you mean?'

'Yeah, the *Mob*. Oooh.' Giulia made claw-hands with her fingernails, but Mary walked into the kitchen area.

'So why did she stay with him?'

'In the beginnin', she kep' hopin' it would get better, then she was too afraid to leave him. I woulda been, too.' Giulia crunched her Altoid. 'The only way out was if he dumped her. My husband says if you're with a wiseguy, it's like a roach motel. You're gettin' in, but you ain't gettin' out.'

Mary glanced around the kitchen, so clean it appeared unused. She walked over to a pad under the wall phone, and nothing was written there. She asked, 'When did he get involved with the Mob?'

'After high school, I think.'

'I don't remember that. His family wasn't in the Mob, were they?'

'Sure, and his brother might even be made.'

'There's something to be proud of.' Mary started searching the kitchen drawers, which contained only ladles, silverware, and the like. While she looked, she tried to remember what she knew about his family. He had an uncle who had raised him and an older sister. She didn't remember him talking about a brother, but most of their conversations were about school or the Gallic war.

'Anyways, we haven't hung here for a while. My house is our hang.'

'I didn't see Trish's purse. Did you?' Mary thought that Trish's big black bag would have stood out on the sea of white.

'I don't see it, either.' Giulia frowned, looking around.

'I keep mine in the living room.'

'So do I.'

'Hers isn't here, not that I saw. If it's not upstairs, then she took it with her, which supports our theory, too.' Mary opened the next drawer. 'She took her purse and coat.'

'Our workin' theory is workin'!' Giulia grinned, and Mary went through the contents of the drawer, but it held only potholders and napkins.

'Doesn't she have a junk drawer? I thought everybody had a junk drawer.'

'I dunno,' Giulia answered, just as Mary reached the last drawer and pulled it out. It was a mess.

'Bingo.' Mary rifled through the drawer, keeping an eye out for receipts or anything that might suggest where they could be. Or maybe even the diary Trish had mentioned, or the gun. But there was nothing inside the drawer except old Chinese take-out menus, Valu-Pak coupons, and a YMCA brochure, along with pencils, pens, matches, and more matches. 'You were telling me about how they were in the beginning, and

76

why it went wrong.'

'Okay, right. At first, T liked it he was connected, and we all thought it was cool. My husband's got a plumbing supply business, and Missy sees a maitre d' at Harrah's. Yo broke up with a guy works the docks. T was the one who got the bit catch.' Giulia leaned against the counter. 'Least that's what we thought, then.'

Mary kept looking in the junk drawer, but wasn't finding anything, which made sense because she didn't know what she was looking for.

'He was so crazy about her. He loved her since high school. T was everything to him.'

Mary felt a stab of envy, then caught herself. Was she really jealous of an abused woman? Lusting after a mobster? Had she lost her mind? She closed the drawer and reached for the phone, lifted the receiver, and heard an interrupted dial tone, which meant there were messages. Verizon was the most common Philly carrier; Mary had it at home, too. She pressed 00, reached a prompt, then turned to Giulia.

'What password does Trish use generally, do you know?' Mary asked. 'I want to check her messages.'

'Try Lucy. She uses that for everything. It's her mom's old dog.'

'Thanks.' Mary pecked the keys, then the voicemail said that there was one new message. She pressed 1, but it was a telemarketer. She hung up. 'Rats.'

'No luck?'

'Not yet.' Mary thought a minute. 'Trish told

77

me she kept a diary. That's probably in her bedroom, right?'

Giulia frowned slightly. 'No, she didn't. She said that? You sure?'

'Yes. She had a gun, too, didn't she?'

'Sure.' Giulia seemed distracted, her forehead creased slightly. 'I don't think she had a diary. She woulda tol' me.'

'Do you know where she kept the gun?'

'No.'

'I'm wondering if she took it with her.'

'I don't know. Prolly.'

Mary thought the gun and the diary would be upstairs. 'Let me ask you something else. Where would he take for her birthday? Which restaurant?'

'I don't know. He didn't like to take her out. He liked her home. It drove her nuts.'

'Okay, where does he go when he goes to work, or whatever Mob guys do?' Mary didn't know much about organized crime and wasn't going to pretend otherwise. 'Where does he sell drugs?'

'I dunno. We never talked about it. She didn't wanna know the details, and neither did I.'

Mary remembered Trish had said that. *They don't know the whole story.*

'Once she told me that the boys hang at Biannetti's, down Denver Street. But he never took T there.'

Mary made a note on an imaginary legal pad. AVOID BIANNETTI'S AND DENVER STREET. 'Did she ever mention any friends of his in the Mob, or just guys he knew? Maybe Mob guys he

78

hung with at Biannetti's? Guys who might know where they went?'

'No. Like I said, we didn't talk about it.'

Mary scanned the kitchen and dining room one last time. 'How many bedrooms in this house?'

'Two, one and a half baths, no cellar.' Giulia frowned again. 'I can't remember the last time I was even upstairs. It's like she's not allowed to have girlfriends.'

'How can you get along without your girlfriends?' Mary was thinking of Judy, and Giulia smiled.

'For reals.'

'Did Trish mention any other friends she had? Maybe a friend who might know something about where they could be?'

'No way. She had us. She was loyal to us.' Giulia frowned, and Mary let it go.

'Did you check the bedroom? I'm curious to see if her clothes are missing. Or if there are any signs she packed anything, or he did.'

'I didn't check.'

'Where does she keep her suitcase, do you know?'

'I dunno. We keep ours under the bed.'

'I'll check that, too.' Mary filed it away. 'By the way, where's their computers?'

'He didn't have one, I know that. She told me he never liked 'em. He said he had ADD.'

Mary thought back. He had been a poor student. He could have been undiagnosed, back then. 'No e-mail or anything?'

'T had it.'

'I want to look upstairs.'

'I'll go out and smoke.' Giulia turned, but Mary touched her arm.

'Wait, I have a job for you and the girls. I want you to go up and down the street and interview the neighbors.'

'Why?' Giulia frowned.

'When there's a crime, cops canvas the neighborhood to find out what people saw. They interview them to get witnesses.' Mary walked into the dining room and picked up one of the photos from the credenza. 'Take this with you. Show it to the neighbors when you talk to them.'

'Don't need it. I got a picture of them in my cell phone.' Giulia's eyes narrowed, so that with the eyeliner tattooing, they looked like two black dashes. 'So what do I ask in this interview?'

'Ask people if they saw Trish last night, or recently. Ask if anyone saw them leave and if they were alone.' Mary was thinking out loud. 'Ask them, what time was it? Did they carry suitcases? Did they leave alone in the BMW? Did someone go with them and maybe follow them? Did it look like she was forced? Did they hear any yelling last night? How about a scream?'

Giulia frowned in confusion.

'I'll write it down for you.'

'That's what I'm talking about!' Giulia reached into her purse for her cigarettes.

9

Mary entered the bedroom and flicked on the light switch, feeling oddly as if she were walking into her alternative life, the world of what-if.

He was so crazy about her. He loved her since high school.

She shook the thoughts off, disturbing as they were, and concentrated on the task at hand. A large king-size bed sat against the far wall, between two windows covered by closed shades. The bed's black quilted comforter was completely flat and four zebra-print pillows sat in neat layers, but at the foot of the bed lay a heap of clothes. Mary picked up the top one. It was a woman's sweater, black with silvery glitter scattered on one padded shoulder, reeking of smoke and perfume, and underneath it lay another sweater, red with tiny red beads in the shape of a heart. It had to be Trish's clothes, and from the looks of it, she'd been trying to find something to wear at the last minute, or maybe packing to go somewhere.

Mary set the clothes back down and looked under the bed for suitcases, but there was nothing there, not even a single dust bunny. She straightened up, looked around, and out of curiosity, went to the dresser. It was neat and clean, covered with more photos of the beaming couple. Flush against the large dresser mirror sat two open jewelry boxes, his and hers. His was smaller, of black leather, and most of the tray was empty except for a few gold chains, sets of cufflinks, a stainless-steel Rolex, and a set of black studs. Something glinted underneath the studs, and she moved the jewelry aside with an index finger.

A high school ring winked back at her, and she remembered the day he'd gotten his class ring. Their first date had been that night. He'd asked her out one Wednesday at their session, their books side by side on the kitchen table, momentarily forgotten.

You mean, like a date? she had asked him, amazed. It was all that she had hoped for.

That night, in the car, he'd showed her his ring, and she'd misunderstood, thinking for a thrilling moment he was going to offer it to her. He didn't, but the ring and the romance were knotted together in her mind, unsettling as it was, in retrospect.

She shooed the memory away and looked at Trish's jewelry box, which looked like the treasure chest in a Disney cartoon. Gold chains of all sizes glittered from a hanging bar on the open lid, golden bangles sat stacked in a lopsided heap, and gold earrings overflowed their little trays. Mary lifted up the tray. Underneath, more gold chains and bangles covered the bottom, almost hiding a set of car keys, still with the rubber keychain from the dealership. They must have been an extra set. Impulsively she took the car keys and slipped them into her jacket pocket. Then she went quickly through dresser drawers, piles of neatly laundered and folded undies, socks, polo shirts, and shorts. Neither Trish's gun nor her diary was there.

Mary straightened up and eyeballed the room. A long closet stood open, its louvered panels slid aside, and she went over and searched the pockets on the hanging jackets and pants. No diary. No gun. She grabbed a footstool, undoubtedly used by Trish, and searched the top of the closet, stocked with sheets and electric blankets. No gun. Then she bent down and searched the bottom of the closet, where shoes lay in piles. No gun, no suitcases, no nothing. Mary stood up and dusted herself off. Beside the closet was a bathroom, and she looked inside, turning on the light.

It was large and white, with two side-by-side sinks on a single, long, superclean vanity. On Trish's side, an electric toothbrush upright in a holder, and a thin bar of Neutrogena sat in a white plastic dish, and his side was almost a mirror image. A chrome blow dryer sat on the sink, and all the towels on the racks had been folded and were in size order, from bath towel to facecloth. The mirror over the sink had to be a medicine chest, and Mary opened it.

The left side was plainly male, an orderly lineup of shaving cream, deodorant, aftershave, and a clean silvery razor. Nothing remarkable, so she opened the other side. It was Trish's, and it had a push dispenser of Cetaphil moisturizer, foil tubes of Bobbie Brown masques, and jars of La Mer and Lancôme creams that lined the skinny shelves. Underneath, front and center, lay a yellow blister pack that read Tri-Sprintec. Birth-control pills.

Mary picked them up and examined them. Sunday was the last pill missing. Monday's pill hadn't been taken yet. Today was Tuesday. So, assuming that Trish took her pill at night, when the rest of the world did, that meant she hadn't taken her pill last night before bed. She must've thought she'd be right back.

Mary felt a chill. She surveyed the clutter with new eyes, then saw, next to the soap, a pair of women's wire-rimmed glasses. That meant Trish wore her contacts last night. Again, she must've expected to be right back, if not the same night, the next day. So wherever they'd gone, it had to be in the city or driving distance from it, to return the same night.

Still Mary was no closer to knowing where Trish was, and it would be nice to find a suitcase or two. She returned to the bedroom, where she noticed something she hadn't before. Two night tables flanked the bed; again, the one on the left held a *Sports Illustrated* magazine, a black electric clock, a small lamp, and an ashtray. On the other side of the bed, the top of the night table was clear, with an electric clock and an empty ring stand. Evidently, Trish's. But no ashtray.

Odd. Trish smoked, so there should be an ashtray next to the bed.

Mary went over to his night table, then pulled the drawer open. She half-expected to find an arsenal, but no. The drawer was almost empty, save for some pens, a pack of Hall's cough drops,

84

and some receipts. She went through the receipts, looking for anything unusual, but they were for clothes, shoes, and undershirts, from JoS. A. Bank, Nordstrom, and Target. She closed the drawer and walked around the bed to Trish's night table. The surface was characteristically neat, but dull-looking in the lamplight. She ran a finger over the surface and checked her fingerpad. It was dusty. And again, no ashtray.

Mary pulled open the drawer, and it contained a few *Cosmopolitan* and *People* magazines. She checked their dates. December; months ago. She followed her hunch, left the room, and went down the hall to the other room and turned on the light. It was a spare room with a desk. An overhead fixture illuminated a single bed, neatly made, flush against a light-blue wall, across from a wooden desk with an older Dell laptop. Trish's computer. Mary went over and moved the mouse. The screen came to life, the screen saver yet another photo of the couple. She clicked on AOL, which signed on automatically, and watched the e-mail load for the screen name TRex193.

Mary skimmed the list of incoming e-mail, the usual spam about penis enlargers, stock tips, and pleas for money from Ethiopian royalty. Seven e-mails piled in from Giulia, Missy, and Yolanda, and Mary clicked on one, which read: T, WHERE ARE YOU? I'M OUTTA MY MIND! She clicked on a few of the others, also from the Mean Girls. She closed the e-mail, logged on to the Internet history, and scanned the websites Trish had visited last. They were all the same:

www.protectionorder.org, www.domesticviolence.org, www.womenslaw.org.

Mary's heart sank, and she turned away. Next to the desk was another louvered closet, and she slid the door aside. Black Tumi suitcases sat piled one on top of the other. So they hadn't gone on a trip. She searched the closet for the guns, just to make sure, but found nothing. She turned around, preoccupied.

Next to the bed sat a white night table with an electric clock, a pump bottle of Jergens hand cream — and an ashtray. She walked over to the night table and opened the drawer. *People* magazine from last week. She stepped back and almost tripped on the black cord of a cell phone charger, then put two and two together:

Trish had to have been sleeping in here. It made sense, together with the fact that she was miserable. The birth-control pills were a loose end, but Mary didn't need to go there. They had separate bedrooms, or at least fights frequent enough for Trish to sleep in here. Mary closed the drawer. No gun, no diary. Trish could have the gun with her, but where was the diary? Then a thought struck her.

She still had one place left to search.

* * *

Outside, Mary chirped Trish's Miata unlocked, using the keys from the jewelry box. She opened the door and climbed inside. The car matched the house, with its gleamy white enamel paint and beige interior, and it was equally clean. She

86

shut the door and opened the tan console between the seats. Nothing but a cell phone charger, E-ZPass statements, and an open pack of Trident. She closed the console lid and popped open the glove box. The lid hung open, revealing a multicolored stack of folded maps.

Mary blinked, surprised. There had to be at least ten maps squeezed in there, which was nine more than most people from the neighborhood had, and ten more than most women, especially from the neighborhood. She herself had one map of Pennsylvania in her car, which her father had given her and she'd never used. She pulled out the maps, wondering if the gun was hidden behind them. It wasn't, but sitting in the glove box was a slim clothbound book, also black.

Mary reached for it and opened it up. The first page read, **Patricia Maria Gambone**, and it was written in ballpoint in perfect Palmer method, with detached capital letters. She opened the book near the front and read the page:

I know he'll just love it and I can't wait to see his face when he opens it! I never thought I'd be this happy in my life!

The diary! In a car? Mary considered it, and it made sense. Trish couldn't leave her diary in the house, where it could be found. Her car would be the second-best place, both secure and private. She flipped ahead, scanning the entries. Evidently, Trish didn't write in it every day, only from time to time. *God knows what we'll do for Valentine's Day. He's drinking again, and when I called him out, he blew up. He started screaming that I was a lying whore and that he was going to*

87

kill me with his bare hands. Mary turned the page and a Polaroid picture fell out, and she picked it up.

It was a horrifying photo of Trish, and it looked as if it had been taken in the bathroom. A hideous red bruise, just beginning to go purple and black, covered her upper arm. The edge of the photo caught her profile, and she had obviously been crying. Mary's mouth went dry. She replaced the photos and read ahead a few pages, picking up words here and there. *Terrified. Scared. Screaming. Punched. Hurt. Bruised. Cut. Gun.* There were more photos. Red bruises to a taut stomach, and one that made a cut near her navel. It sickened Mary, and she put them back with care. It was the perfect set of proofs for a lawsuit that would never go to trial. She felt disgusted and bitter at the law, at justice, and most of all, at herself.

She skipped to the most recent entry, praying it could provide a clue about where Trish had been taken. She turned to the last page, and her cheeks flushed hot: *I went to see Mary but she didn't do anything. Now I don't know what to do. If you're reading this now, whoever you are, I'm already dead. But at least this can prove he did it.*

'Hey, Mare, yo!' somebody shouted, and Mary slapped the diary closed with the photos inside and looked through the windshield.

'MARE!' It was Giulia, hollering from down the street, because South Philly was a neighborhood without volume controls.

Mary waved to Giulia through the windshield, shoved the diary in her purse, and slipped the maps back in the glove box. She gave the car one last look around, got out, and chirped it locked, while the Mean Girls *clack-clack*ed down the sidewalk like a tiny black locomotive, puffing smoke.

And it looked as if they'd picked up a passenger.

10

Giulia, Yolanda, and Missy stood beaming in Trish's living room, surrounding an older Asian man who had a lined face and a delighted, if slightly bewildered, expression. He wore baggy black pants and a thin plaid shirt buttoned up to his neck wattle, and his hair was thin, steel gray, and slicked back. He was very short and never took his eyes from Giulia's face. Okay, chest.

'Mare, look.' Giulia looped her arm around the tiny man and squeezed him close. 'This is Fung Lee. He's Oriental.'

'Chinese,' the man corrected good-naturedly, in thickly accented English.

'We went up and down the street like you said, and nobody saw nothin' except Fung.'

'Good work, ladies.' Mary introduced herself and shook Fung's hand, though his attention remained glued to Giulia. He nestled next to her body, fitting neatly beside her breasts, obviously enjoying his new best friends.

Giulia smiled down at the man. 'Fung goes to the corner store the same time each night to buy a lottery ticket. He always goes at six thirty, right before they announce the winner, because he thinks that's good luck.'

Fung nodded, ensconced.

'So I showed him the photo, and he recognized T because he sees her all the time, goin' in and out of the house. He lives around the corner with his daughter and her husband.'

'Got it.' Mary held up a hand. 'Let's let him say what he saw, in his own words, okay?'

'Sure, Mare.' Giulia bristled, but Mary didn't want words put in Fung's mouth.

'Fung, what did you see last night?' she asked. 'Can you tell me?'

But Fung only smiled up at Giulia, his free arm encircling her waist.

'Fung?' Mary repeated.

'Talk louder, Mare,' Giulia said, snuggling him, but Mary suspected his hearing wasn't the problem, unless a breast blocked his ear. She raised her voice before he reached orgasm.

'Fung! What did you see? Did you see something at the house last night?'

'Tell her what you told us, doll,' Giulia said, gesturing at Mary. 'It's okay. She's a lawyer. She can't help being mean.'

Fung answered, 'I see woman. Woman from picture.'

Giulia interjected, 'I showed him Trish's picture.'

Fung continued, 'Woman very pretty. She with man. Leave with man and go in car.'

'What kind of car, do you know?'

'Black.'

'Was anyone else with them?'

'No. Woman and man only.' Fung looked up at Giulia.

'Did they seem happy or unhappy?'

'Not happy. Man very angry. Door close. *Bang!*'

Mary felt her gut tense. 'Did the man yell? Shout?'

'Yes.'

'What did he say?'

'*Wo bu zhi dao*. Don't know.' Fung pointed to his ear, and Mary understood he didn't hear that well.

'What was the woman doing?'

Fung shook his head.

'Nothing?'

'Nothing.'

'Was she crying?'

'No.'

'Did she call to you, or anybody?'

'No.'

Mary got a bad feeling. 'What time was this, about?'

'Six thirty exact. I go store.'

Giulia interjected, 'I told you, he goes to the store at six thirty because the luck is better.'

Mary asked, 'Did the woman have a purse?' She held up her purse. 'Purse?'

Fung thought a minute. 'Yes.'

'Did they have a suitcase?'

Fung frowned, not understanding.

'A suitcase is like a big purse.' Mary wanted to double-check and played charades for a second. 'Like for a trip, for vacation.'

Fung frowned, not understanding.

Giulia held up her huge purse. 'Suitcase.'

Fung shook his head, with a smile for her. 'No.'

Good. 'And they drove away?'

'Yes.'

92

'Which way?'

Fung pointed north.

It told Mary nothing. She didn't know why she'd even asked. 'Did the woman see you, do you think?'

'Don't know. I go corner. She go car.'

'Did she try to signal you? Show you a sign?'

'No.'

'Were other people on the street?'

'Yes. Family. Baby.'

Mary looked at Giulia. 'I thought you said nobody saw anything.'

'Like I said, you wanna be the one who IDs him?'

Good point. Mary paused. 'Fung, is there anything else you can remember about what you saw?'

'No.'

'Okay, thank you.' Mary stuck a hand in her purse and extracted her wallet, then slipped out a business card and handed it to him. 'This has my phone number. Please feel free to call if you remember anything else.'

Fung took the card, then looked up at Giulia. 'You have?'

'Awww,' Giulia said, and kissed him on the cheek.

Fifteen minutes later, they were back in another cab, with Mary giving another aged driver the address and the Mean Girls squeezing in the backseat. She took the seat up front again, feeling like the chaperone on a field trip of underachievers. She twisted around in the seat and eyed Giulia, whose red highlights blew in the breeze from the open window. 'You did a good job, girl.'

'Hmph,' was Giulia's only reply. She'd barely said a word since Mary had rebuked her in front of Fung.

'We helped, too,' Yolanda said, beside her, and Missy nodded.

'My feet are killin' me from all that walkin'.'

'You all did great. Fung placed Trish's departure in time and confirms our working theory.' Mary managed a smile, but Giulia still held her grudge. 'By the way, I'm curious, did you guys know that they were sleeping in separate beds?'

'Get out.' Giulia came to life, her dark eyes wide.

'For real?' Yolanda asked, blinking.

'Why didn't she tell us?' Missy raised a permanent eyebrow.

'That's my question.' Mary looked to Giulia for the answer, and so did the others.

'I guess she was embarrassed?'

'Why?' Mary asked. 'She told you they were having problems. She told you she wanted out, right?'

Giulia nodded, curls blowing in her face, and she speared one with a long nail and pushed it back.

'So, why?' Mary asked again.

Yolanda slid her gaze toward Giulia. 'We woulda blabbed it.'

'We would not!' Giulia shot back. A frown folded in the shape of a pitchfork on her forehead.

'*You* woulda,' Missy said, and Mary let them fight it out, watching.

Giulia: 'I can't believe you said that, Miss! I wouldn'ta told nobody.'

Yolanda: 'Who you kidding, G? You woulda told Joey.'

Giulia: 'Well, yeah, Joey. I mean, whaddaya think, I'm married to the guy.'

Yolanda: 'Just 'cause you're married don't mean you have to tell him everything.'

Giulia: 'No? That's why you're divorced. Twice.'

Yolanda: 'Whatever, Joey woulda told Tommy and Tommy woulda told Jerry and Jerry woulda told Johnny Three Fingers who woulda told Cooch, who hangs at Biannetti's because he's a wannabe. And Cooch woulda told the boys at Biannetti's and T woulda gotten herself dead.'

The Mean Girls fell silent, suddenly chastened. Giulia said, 'She's right. That's exactly what woulda happened. That's why T didn't tell us.'

Mary still didn't get it. 'But Trish told you that he roughed her up. Why is it okay to blab that and not that they had separate beds?'

Giulia snorted. 'Hello? One makes him look like a man, and the other makes him look like a jerk.'

Mary didn't have to ask which was which. She'd already learned more than she wanted to know about Trish's world. They all fell silent again, and the cab lurched through the streets, the driver pretending he wasn't watching the girls in the rearview and the traffic increasing as the noon rush approached. On the radio, KYW news was reporting still no suspects in the disappearance of baby Sabine Donchess, who turned out to be the only daughter of the Gentech CEO. Even the governor had weighed in, already calling it the crime of the century.

'Stupid baby,' Giulia muttered, looking out the window.

Mary changed the subject. 'By the way, Trish did keep a diary.'

'No, she didn't,' Giulia said, certain.

'Then what's this?' Mary teased the diary from her purse, and the Mean Girls reached for it, talons outstretched.

'Gimme that!' Giulia said.

'What'd she say about me?' Yolanda asked.

'And me?' Missy asked.

'Sorry.' Mary slid the diary back into her purse, gloating like crazy. 'I'm surprised at you guys. I would think you'd respect Trish's privacy.'

'Oh, come on.' Giulia snorted. 'You read it, didn't you?'

'Of course, but I can. It's covered by attorney-client privilege.' *Sorta kinda.*

'Gimme an effin break.' Giulia rolled her eyes.

'That doesn't sound right,' Missy said.

'What a bunch a crap!' Yolanda said.

Mary turned back around in the seat, smiling to herself. 'Maybe you should've been nicer to me in high school.'

The driver looked over, lifting an eyebrow.

11

Half an hour later, they arrived at the police administration building, called the Roundhouse because it was a round concrete building, circa 1970s. The cab pulled to the curb, and Mary paid the driver while the Mean Girls piled out of the backseat and reached in their bags for their cigarettes.

'Okay, listen, kids,' Mary said. She stood downwind while they lit up. 'I can only take one of you inside. But whoever comes with me has to behave.'

'What do you mean by 'behave'?' Giulia cocked her head, eyes flinty behind the smoke.

'I do the talking, and you stop moping.'

'Whatever.' Giulia stepped forward, clearly an underboss to Trish's *capo di tutti capi*.

'Okay, let's go.'

'I'm not finished my cigarette.'

'Yes, you are.' Mary turned and walked toward the building through the parking lot, which buzzed with media covering the baby Donchess kidnapping. The case had been all over the cab radio on the way over, with audioclips of the parents pleading for her safe return. Reporters milled around, talking in groups, and cameramen sipped coffee, resting their videocameras on their shoulders.

'Mare, wait up!' Giulia hollered.

'G, catch up!' Mary hurried past a male TV

97

anchor with orangey makeup and a paper towel folded into his shirt collar like a bib, doing sound checks with a logo microphone. She reached the smoked-glass entrance doors, opened them, and stopped at the plastic security window, manned by an older uniformed cop with an official smile. She introduced herself and said, 'I'm here to see Detective Brinkley.'

'This about a homicide?'

'No, I'm a personal friend of Mack's,' Mary said, using Detective Brinkley's in-the-know nickname. She had worked a case with him not long ago, and they'd become friendly. He adored her mother and had even fixed her pilot light, but that was another story. The desk cop looked skeptically from Mary to Giulia, who appeared beside her.

'Who're you?' he asked.

'My paralegal,' Mary answered, but Giulia was miffed.

'I'm no paralegal. I can walk.'

Oops. 'She likes to joke around. I'll sign us in, Officer.' Mary spun the clipboard toward her, signed them both in, and grabbed Giulia's arm, hustling her to the metal detector.

'Don't yank me around.' Giulia took her arm back. 'Like I said, I can walk.'

'The deal was, say nothing. *Capisce?*' Mary got through the metal detector, entering a lobby crowded with uniformed police and other employees. She passed display cases of old police ears, but noticed that the clatter of stilettos had stopped. She looked back to see Giulia chatting up two cops, who were smiling down at her.

Mary called out, 'Giulia?'

'Comin', Mare!' Giulia called back, looking over. She blew the cops a goodbye kiss and clacked to the elevator bank, her dark eyes reanimated. 'Are they hot or what? How's my makeup?'

'Permanent.' Mary hit the elevator button. 'They friends of yours?'

'Yeah.'

'How'd you meet 'em?'

'They arrested me once.'

'Really?'

'Okay, twice,' Giulia said sheepishly, and the elevator doors opened.

Five minutes later, Mary was hugging her old friend, Reginald 'Mack' Brinkley. Brinkley was typically well dressed in a brown sport jacket and khaki pants, with a crisp white shirt and shiny loafers. He hugged her back warmly, then held her off, smiling at her like her own father — if her father were tall, thin, and black.

'How you been, Mary?' he asked, his voice deep and soft.

'Great, thanks. How about you?'

'Good. Fine.' Brinkley was handsome, with a long, slim face, a narrow nose, squinty, if benevolent, eyes, and a tight smile. He must have been in his forties and hadn't added a wrinkle since she'd seen him last, though his short hair was a tangle of silver at the temples. 'Got remarried and all.'

'That's great, congrats.' Mary felt happy for him. He'd had a tough divorce, but he kept all of that to himself. They were friendly, but not that friendly. She introduced Giulia, who had been looking distractedly around the squad room.

'It's sure ain't like *Cold Case*,' Giulia said with a frown, and Brinkley half-smiled, leaning against his desk.

'No. They clean it up for TV.'

'They'd have to.' Mary smiled. A few detectives in shirtsleeves were talking in a group, near beat-up gray file cabinets of different sizes and colors. Messy metal desks were placed in the largish room in no particular order, and the chairs didn't match the desks. The old-fashioned tile floor looked grimy, and dingy beige curtains that covered the expanse of curved window had brown stains on them and hung off the valance, letting bright sun into the room in odd places. It wasn't a total dump, but it wasn't ready for prime time.

Brinkley asked, 'Mary, you at the same place, working for Rosato?'

'Yes.'

'She still tough as nails?'

'Nails have nothing on Bennie Rosato.'

Brinkley chuckled. 'You got that right. How about Jack? You still seeing him?'

Mary hadn't thought of Jack Newlin for a while. 'Nah, didn't work out. Or the guy after him, either. Any day now, I'm entering the convent. Does God take lawyers?'

Brinkley laughed softly. 'If I got lucky, you will, too.' Then his relaxed manner faded, and he straightened up, folding his arms over a slight paunch. 'So how can I help you? This about a case?'

'Kind of. Can we talk alone?'

'Sure. This way.' Brinkley gestured to his left, and they went inside a small greenish interview room that needed repainting. It contained a few odd wooden chairs and an old pine typing table with a few Miranda waiver forms. Brinkley closed the door. 'Welcome to my summer office.'

Mary smiled, and after Brinkley and Giulia had taken their seats, she told him about her meeting with Trish, the Mob connection, the search of Trish's house, and what Fung Lee saw. She knew that Brinkley was respected at the Roundhouse and if she could convince him, he would make things happen for Trish behind the scenes. She argued her case like a lawsuit, with all the facts supporting the proposition that Trish's disappearance gave cause for real alarm.

Brinkley's expression grew grave as she spoke, and Giulia stayed obediently silent, even when Mary produced Trish's diary. The detective bent his neat head over the pages, and she pointed out the terrifying entries and photos, which Giulia craned her neck to see, shaken. He examined them in silence, then looked up when he was finished, his expression concerned.

'Okay, I hear you.' Brinkley closed the dairy. 'It doesn't sound like two lovebirds who decided to take a vacation.'

'No, it's not,' Mary said, holding her breath for his decision.

'Hang on to this.' Brinkley handed Mary back

the diary, then stood up, moving his sport jacket aside with both hands and hitching up his pants from the sides of a black belt. 'Here's the problem. To start with, you know this isn't my bailiwick. This is a case for Missing Persons, not Homicide.'

Giulia exploded, jumping up. 'When are you guys gonna wise up aroun' here? Did you see those pictures? What more do you want? She could be dead, and all you guys worry about is whose job it is *not* to do!'

'Whoa, settle down.' Brinkley put up his hands, and Mary stepped between him and the crazed Goretti girl.

'Giulia, *basta*!' She shot her dagger-eyes and turned to Brinkley. 'We know there are jurisdictional issues, but this really seems like a hybrid case, between Missing Persons and Homicide. We have proof-positive from the diary that Trish is in danger and that her boyfriend's a mobster. He's a man with the means and the wherewithal to kill.'

'I see that.'

'So if you spoke with Missing Persons, I'm sure they'd understand it's not the typical situation. Maybe they'll give Trish's case some attention. Speed things up, or put out an APB or something.'

'You know they have their hands full with the Donchess case. Amber Alerts get priority, it's state law.' Brinkley gestured toward the door. 'You saw the press outside. It's the Lindbergh baby.'

Giulia interjected, 'There's *another* baby, now?

Those effin babies can just wait their turn.'

Mary hushed her again. 'Reg, Trish can't be far, and if we find her, maybe we can prevent her murder. Doesn't an abused woman deserve an Amber Alert, too? Why are we making value judgments between victims, anyway? Besides, the press doesn't run the police department, does it?'

'Don't pull that on me, Mare.'

'But it's right, isn't it?' Mary felt desperate. Brinkley was her best and only chance. 'I would never ask you for help if the case didn't merit it. Trish was terrified in my office. He's going to kill her, if he hasn't already.'

'Come on, help us already!' Giulia held up her cell phone over Mary's shoulder. 'We have photos of her, right here!'

'The Mob angle makes this tougher for us, you know.' Brinkley puckered his lips, still deciding. 'The feds won't like us moving ahead without checking in. For all we know, they're watching him already.'

Mary hadn't thought of that, and Brinkley nodded.

'You know how it is when the feds get involved.'

'They make a federal case out of it,' Giulia blurted out, like a schoolgirl with the right answer. Brinkley wasn't mean enough to make her feel dumb. Mary was, but she didn't have the time right now.

'On the other hand,' she said, 'if we find Trish alive, she'll be inclined to turn state's evidence against him. Wouldn't the FBI like that?

103

Wouldn't that be a coup for them and the department?'

Brinkley thought a minute, looked from Mary to Giulia, and emitted a final sigh. 'Tell you what, ladies. I'll do my thing if you make me a deal.'

'What deal?' Mary asked, and Giulia came out from behind her.

'Anything.'

'No more searching houses or finding witnesses. No more playing cop, either of you. You're out of your league.' Brinkley folded his arms. 'What do you say?'

Mary felt her heart leap, with hope. 'Point of clarification. I assume some self-help is okay, like we can send out flyers about her, can't we?'

'Yeah, but keep it low-key. Don't talk to the press until I get back to you.'

'Time matters, Reg.'

'I know that, having been in law enforcement longer than you.' Brinkley half-smiled. 'Don't push your luck. Gimme an hour. I'll call you back. Do we have a deal?'

'Deal. Thank you.' Mary kept her reaction subdued. Brinkley wasn't the effusive type, and if he'd said that much, she knew he'd give it his all. When you win, get out of the courtroom.

'I LOVE YOU!' Giulia shouted, throwing herself into the arms of a very startled Reg Brinkley.

After a minute, he didn't look like he minded much.

* * *

Outside the Roundhouse, Mary stopped Giulia's hand before it reached into her handbag. 'Wait on the smoking, please. I need oxygen.'

'Okay, but only 'cause you did so good in there. I didn't know you had it in you.' Giulia smiled with temporary admiration. 'You really handled that detective, Mare.'

'I didn't handle him. He's a good guy and he'll help if he can.'

'It's really who you know, not what you know, like they say.'

Mary let it go. 'Where's Missy and Yolanda?' she asked, and they looked around the parking lot, which buzzed with activity.

'There, flirtin' with those guys.' Giulia pointed across the lot, where Missy and Yolanda were chatting up two good-looking men in suits and a wiry bicycle messenger.

'Okay, forget them. You're in charge. You heard Brinkley, he said it's okay to send out a flyer. Here's what you gotta do. You're good online, right?'

'Sure. I got a MySpace and I watch porn, like everybody else.'

Mary let that go, too. Then she didn't. 'You watch porn?'

'Yeah.'

'But you're a girl.'

'Yeah, so?' Giulia shrugged.

Right the first time. 'Anyway, let's use some self-help. Take the photo from your cell phone and e-mail it to everybody you know. Find some missing persons sites and post the photos there. Put it on your MySpace page and everywhere online that you can.'

'Good idea, Mare. We don't want to waste any time.'

'Right, and make a flyer, in hard copy.'

Giulia nodded. 'Like when you lose a dog?'

Uh. 'Yes. You know what it should say?'

'Yeah.'

'You want me to write it down?'

'Nah, I got it.'

'Do that right away.'

'I know, I know.' Giulia stamped her little black boots. 'Come on, I'm jonesin' for a cigarette.'

'I'm going back to work, to check in. Call me and tell me your progress with the flyer. We'll meet again in an hour.'

'When am I gonna see that diary?'

'Never.' Mary hustled out of the parking lot, with a final wave to Missy and Yolanda, who were laughing with the men and didn't notice her. She unsheathed her BlackBerry while she hailed a cab, hit the number for voicemail, then heard the first message.

Which was very bad news.

12

'What happened?' Mary said, as soon as she hit Judy's office. She'd tried to call her on the cab ride to the office, but she kept getting the voicemail, so she'd used the time to return other calls and e-mails. By the time she got back, her head was exploding and she could be liable for malpractice.

'I'm so sorry.' Judy hung up the phone. 'I was just about to call you.' Sunlight poured through the window behind her, backlighting her hair and setting her fuchsia dress aglow. A half-eaten tofu salad and a bottle of Fiji water fought for desktop with messy notes, a laptop, correspondence, pencils and pens, and a Magic 8 Ball.

'Not your fault. Nunez wouldn't go forward with the deposition?' Mary deflated into the chair in front of the desk.

'Not without you.' Judy looked regretful, puckering her lower lip. 'I told him you had an emergency, but he just got rattled.'

'Oh no. Poor guy.'

'I think he has a crush on you.'

Mary scoffed. 'He's like ninety years old.'

'He says he doesn't feel safe without you. He's supercute, for such an old guy.'

'You're creeping me out. So what happened?'

'We got as far as state-your-name-for-the-record, and he said he wanted to leave.' Judy

107

sighed. 'You'll just reschedule.'

'To when?' Mary knew her week would be crazy. She had her regular case load to deal with, plus Dhiren and Dean Martin.

'What happened this morning with Trish?'

Mary didn't have the time to fill her in, but did anyway.

'Good work,' Judy said, when the executive summary was over. 'You're doing all you can do for the dark side.'

'They're not so bad.'

'The harpies?'

'I'm doing it for Trish.'

'Watch yourself with these girls.' Judy pointed a finger. 'They're just going to hurt you, in the end, and I don't like anybody who hurts you.'

Mary smiled, touched. 'Oh, by the way, I talked to Bennie this morning.'

'You did?' Judy's eyes flared, and Mary filled her in on her meeting with the boss, which seemed ages ago. When she was finished, Judy's unlipsticked mouth made a determined little line. 'She won't even hire a contract lawyer? That's not fair. You need help.'

'It is what it is.' Mary got up. She had tons to do before Giulia called.

'If you were her partner, you wouldn't have to ask permission to hire help.'

'If I were her partner, I'd be your boss.'

Judy laughed.

'My thoughts exactly,' Mary said with a smile, then hurried back to her office.

There, she called Roberto Nunez, but there

108

was no answer and she left a message. She rifled through her mail, sorting it into Good and Evil piles, as was her habit. She ignored the ringing phone, logged on to the computer, and searched for special-education websites. She took notes, then scouted online to find an alternative place to get Dhiren tested. All the time, she was wondering when Brinkley would get back to her. She found a suburban child-study center with psychological and personality testing, then called them and was put through to the intake coordinator. Mary explained the situation, finishing with, 'He's so frustrated in school that he's pulling his hair out.'

'That's called trichotillomania.'

'You've heard of it?'

'Yes, it's unfortunately quite common. We have fifteen psychologists on staff, all specializing in children with learning disabilities. As you're seeing with your client, those disabilities affect them emotionally, so they hurt themselves or act out in school.'

'That's exactly what's happening.' Mary almost cheered. 'Great! So when can I get him an appointment?'

'Will this be paid by the district?'

'No. This is private.'

'Payment is due when services are rendered. The cost is $3025.'

'I understand. I told the boy's mother it's expensive. I just need to set up the appointments.'

'Would you like an appointment for testing or counseling?'

'Both.' Mary felt greedy. 'He really needs help.'

'I understand, these cases can be so heartbreaking.' From the other end of the phone came the clicking of a computer keyboard. 'I'd start counseling as soon as possible. I have an opening on June 11, at three thirty with Dr. Theadora Landgren.'

Mary thought she was kidding. It was months away. 'He has to wait that long?'

'I'm sorry, we're very busy.'

'He can't wait. He's in a very bad way.' Mary heard the intake coordinator's other phone start ringing.

'Excuse me. I have to get that. Please hold.'

Mary waited while they played uplifting music that didn't uplift. She was already defaulting to Plan B. She wouldn't make a counseling appointment; she'd find Dhiren another shrink, maybe closer, in the city. The important thing was the testing.

'Ms. DiNunzio, would you like to make that appointment for counseling?'

'No, that's okay. Let's go for the testing. I'll get him counseling elsewhere, if you don't mind.'

'I can even make some referrals for you.' Then came the sound of keyboard clacking, and the coordinator said, 'Our first appointment for testing is June 3.'

'June? Even for the tests? Can you really be so booked up? I mean, it's just a test.' Mary thought of Amrita saying, give him a book and see how he struggles.

'It's not that simple. Our tests include full

psychological batteries, personality testing, neuropsychological assessment . . . '

Mary zoned out while she explained in detail.

'So you can see it's a complicated process, and that's why we can't take you until June 3. But I have referrals for testing as well.'

'Thanks so much, and I can't wait until then.' Mary grabbed a pen. 'May I have those referrals?'

Ten calls later, Mary had made a testing appointment for April 10 and counseling for April 15. It was the best she could do, but could Dhiren wait that long? How could she tell Amrita? Her BlackBerry rang, and she checked the display, the caller a welcome one.

'How's my little girl?' her father asked warmly.

'Great, Pop.' Mary had trained her father to call on the cell, to be sure to get her, and put on her earphone so she could check her e-mail while they talked.

'Did you hear from Bernice yet? Feet keeps askin' me.'

Oops. 'I'll tell you what. I'll call her right now and get back to you.'

'Okay, baby. Love you. Your mother says don't work too hard.'

'Love you both, Pop.' Mary hung up, called information for Bernice Foglia's number, and pressed it into the BlackBerry while she answered her e-mail. It was the only good thing about her hated BlackBerry — when she used it with the earphone, she could do three things at once, instead of merely two.

111

'Yeah?' Bernice answered, her voice quavering with age.

'Mrs. Foglia, how're you? This is Mary DiNunzio. I'm calling about this situation with Dean Martin.' Mary couldn't believe the words coming out of her own mouth.

'I heard your father's gonna slap me with a lawsuit, me and my ladyfriends.'

'That's not true, Mrs. Foglia. I don't know how you heard that.'

'Feet told Johnny-From-The-Corner who told his wife Lillian and she knows Josephine who's my camarr from Moore Street, so she called me right away.'

Mary smiled, checking her e-mail and typing responses as quietly as she could.

'Mare, you better mark my words. Just 'cause you're a lawyer doesn't mean you can push me around. You used to be nice when you were little, but you changed. Success got you a swelled head. Hmph!'

'Mrs. Foglia, no one is suing you. They were upset about what you said about Dean Martin, is all.'

'Why? It was true. The man was a drunk.'

He was not. 'You know what I think, Mrs. Foglia?' Mary heard a noise and looked up from her e-mail. Judy was standing in her doorway, gesturing for her to come. Mary flashed her the one-minute sign, but Judy rushed in, grabbed her by the hand, and pulled her out of the chair, while she followed her with the BlackBerry.

'I don't care what you think,' Mrs. Foglia was

112

saying, and Mary let Judy lead her down the hallway by the hand.

'I think this is getting out of control. Everybody's up in arms.'

'They don't like what I said? They can lump it. That's what Frank would say.'

'Frank who?'

'Sinatra.'

'Mrs. Foglia, would you consider apologizing for saying what you said? Then I think I can get them to apologize.' Mary hurried along under Judy's power, toward the conference room.

'No, I won't apologize. They should apologize to me and Frank. They said he was crazy.'

'Who said that?'

'Tony-From-Down-The-Block. What a *cavone*. And that hair! It's red as Lucille Ball.'

'Let me ask you a question. If he apologizes, will you?' Mary followed Judy into the conference room, where Marshall was already inside, looking at the TV on the credenza. Mary couldn't see the screen because Marshall was blocking it.

'No,' Mrs. Foglia said. 'Honey, I got no regrets. I'm like Frank.'

Judy dropped her hand, Marshall moved aside for her to see the TV, and Mary's mouth dropped open. The news was on, and she couldn't believe what she was seeing.

'I chew it up and spit it out,' Mrs. Foglia was saying.

'*What?*' Mary said to Mrs. Foglia and the TV.

'I do it My Way!' Mrs. Foglia shouted, hanging up.

Leaving an incredulous Mary with the news.

13

Mary almost dropped the BlackBerry, the earphone still plugged into her ear. On the TV screen, a bright red banner read, LIVE BREAKING NEWS, and above it stood Giulia, Missy, and Yolanda, outside the Roundhouse. An excitable Giulia was being interviewed by an anchorwoman, who was flanked by the Mean Girls, like bookends with estrogen.

Mary groaned. 'What are they doing?'

Judy folded her arms. 'This can't be good.'

Marshall said, 'Nice makeup.'

Giulia said into the microphone, 'Please, please help us! Our best friend, Trish Gambone, is missing since last night and we need your help!'

Oh my God. The Mean Girls had just queered the deal with Brinkley.

'This is a picture of Trish, on vacation in Vegas.' Giulia held up her cell-phone photo of Trish, and the camera moved in for a closeup. 'She looks exactly like this, only without the spray-on. She's white, in her thirties, five foot two, a hundred and five pounds.'

'A hundred and twenty,' said a voice, off camera.

Yolanda.

'Like I said, a hundred and five,' Giulia said firmly, holding up her cell phone.

'What's a spray-on?' Judy asked, but Mary was

114

too stunned to answer.

Giulia continued, 'We're askin' everyone to keep a lookout for Trish, and if you see her, please call Detective Mack Reginald Brinkley right away. I know everybody's up in arms about that dumb baby, but doesn't an abused woman deserve an Amber Alert, too? Why do only babies get it?'

The TV reporter grabbed the microphone and managed a smile. 'You heard it here first. Trish Gambone, a South Philadelphia resident, is missing at this hour . . . '

Mary sank into a chair and pressed the number for information into the BlackBerry. 'Any lasagna left?' she asked miserably.

The operator said, 'Pardon me?'

'Sorry. In Philadelphia, Pennsylvania, may I have the number for the police department, the Homicide Division?'

'Please, hold,' the operator answered, and Judy left the conference room. The call connected but the line was busy. Mary hung up and looked at Marshall, who had a handbag and a light navy coat folded over her arm.

Mary asked her, 'How did you know this was on TV?'

'I always check the traffic report before I leave and I recognized the girls from the fistfight.' Marshall patted her on the back. 'Hang in. Gotta go. Gabe's at daycare.'

'Thanks.' Mary pressed Giulia's number into the BlackBerry, and after a few rings, the call connected.

'Mare, didja see me on TV?' Giulia sounded

115

breathless. 'Wasn't that great? It was like an infomercial for Trish, like Proactiv!'

'How did you get on TV?'

'You remember those guys that Missy and Yolanda were talking to? The one was a reporter, and he hooked us up. How'd I do?'

'Terrible,' Mary answered flatly. 'Where were you thinking? We weren't supposed to go public until Brinkley got back to us. Now we made him look bad and we broke our word. Besides, he's not with Missing Persons. He's Homicide. You gave out the wrong number.'

'Yo, Mare!' Giulia raised her voice. 'Why you gotta be so negative? Nothin' I do is good enough? First with Fung, now the phone number? So what? We got Trish on TV. Those babies don't know who they're dealin' with.' Giulia's voice cut off. 'Hold on, I got another call. It's T's mom. Call you back.'

'Wait, no more interviews. Not another one, you hear?' Mary said, but the line went dead.

She listened to the silence for a minute, trying to collect her thoughts. Her gaze wandered to the window, where the skyline, marked by the tented rooftop of the Independence Blue Cross building, the granite spike of Mellon Center, and the distinctive ziggurat of Liberty Place cut into the early evening sky. Below, people would be streaming from their offices, piling into trains, cars, and buses, and going home to their families. And somewhere, Trish was below, dead or alive.

Just then Judy came back into the conference room. 'Dinner is served,' she said, setting a cup of fresh coffee and a tiny square of lasagna on

116

the table. 'I nuked it for you.'

'Thanks,' Mary said, touched. Unfortunately, the lasagna was barely the size of a bite. 'Anne really did eat it? I thought she was kidding.'

'It's an appetizer. You can join Frank and me at dinner.' Judy meant her boyfriend Frank Lucia, the grandson of Pigeon Tony. They'd found love on a case together, but Mary couldn't even find lasagna.

'I can't go. I gotta work.' Mary moved to call Brinkley again, but Judy grabbed the BlackBerry away.

'Enough! It can wait.'

'Brinkley's gonna be so angry.'

'Give him time to cool down. Eat.' Judy pointed at the plate, and Mary picked up the plastic fork. After one mouthful of her mother's cooking, she knew it was the right thing to do. After the lasagna and Judy were gone, Mary went back to her office and stayed on the phone until she finally got through to Homicide.

When the call connected, she asked, 'May I speak with Detective Brinkley?'

'If you're calling about the missing person on TV, this isn't the number to call.' A male voice sounded testy, and Mary knew she was speaking with the detective whose job it was to answer phones on that tour of duty. 'You need to speak with Missing Persons, and I'll give you that number.'

'I don't need it. I'm a friend of Detective Brinkley.'

'Leave a number, and I'll tell him you called. He's out.'

Mary gave him her name and cell. 'Please tell him to call on the cell, so I don't miss him, and I'm so sorry about what happened, with my friend Giulia going on TV. I didn't have any control over that. I didn't even know about it.'

'Hold on.' The detective's tone cooled. 'That was your friend, on TV? Are you that lawyer from Rosato's office, was in here with her?'

'Yes, and — '

'What were you doing, going on the tube like that?' The detective's voice turned hostile. 'You know how many calls we got already? We won't be able to get our regular phone calls now, calls we need to get.'

'I'm so sorry. I can imagine.' Mary felt terrible, but couldn't resist asking, 'But were there any leads?'

'Of course not. Every turkey in the tristate area's calling Homicide. I just hung up on my second drunk dial.'

'I'm so sorry.'

'I'll give him the message. He'll definitely want to talk to *you*. 'Bye.'

Mary hung up, troubled. She should have warned Giulia not to say anything. She should have stayed in control of the situation. What if she had gotten Brinkley in trouble? Missing Persons wouldn't like Homicide usurping its role. Nobody took jurisdiction more seriously than the police department, except a federal court, or maybe a waitress.

Mary checked her desk clock. 5:15. She hadn't answered her mail yet and she still had a ton of calls to make. She started to look through her

118

mail, but couldn't concentrate, preoccupied with Trish and now Brinkley. How could she have let this happen? When was Giulia going to call about the flyer? Soon Bennie and Anne would be back from court. It set Mary's teeth on edge. She had work to do, no help in sight, and at some level, her clients would pay the price. Dhiren, Mr. Nunez. Trish. She didn't have the time to do anything. Right when she was feeling sorriest for herself, her phone started ringing.

Mary picked up, hoping it was Brinkley. 'Hello?'

'Hey, Mary? It's Anthony Rotunno.'

'Hey, Anthony.' Mary stifled her dismay. Her new gay friend. She didn't have time for the Freedom of Information Act right now. She shouldn't have picked up.

'I was wondering if I could ask you a question or two. I'm really stuck.'

No. 'Well — '

'I'm downtown today, only a block from your office. You wanna grab a quick bite? I could really use the help.'

'I'm kind of busy.'

'You have to eat. My mother says.'

Mary's stomach growled in response. She was too distracted to work and she wanted to be out of the office when Bennie got back. She wouldn't miss Brinkley because he'd call on her cell, and Giulia might be boycotting her.

'Whaddaya say, counselor? My treat.'

'Be right down.' Mary grabbed her purse.

She needed a friend, about now.

119

14

Mary had been on so many blind dates that it was a pleasure to be with a man who had a medical excuse for not being attracted to her. She couldn't pass or fail the date and she hadn't even bothered freshening her makeup. No matter how hard she tried, Anthony wasn't falling in love with anyone but the waiter.

'This is fun,' Mary said, and Anthony raised a glass.

'To Italian-American studies.'

'*Cent'anni.*' Mary raised her glass and they both sipped their wine, which tasted cold and great. She knew nothing about wines, but Anthony had selected it from a bewildering array on the leather-bound list. She said, 'Nice choice, sir. That wine list was harder than the bar exam.'

'You could have picked a bottle. It's not as difficult as people think.'

'Like the Freedom of Information Act.'

'Exactly. You answered all my questions on the way over.' Anthony grinned, his eyes crinkling photogenically. He had on a dark cashmere blazer with a white shirt and khaki slacks, and his smile was as warm and friendly as last night, if even handsomer in the candlelight, which lent his eyes the rich warmth of dark chocolate.

'Were you ever a model, Anthony?'

'No.' He grinned crookedly. 'Why?'

'You're so hot.'

'Thank you.' Anthony smiled, a little surprised.

Mary eyed the menu, feeling the wine affecting her, already. She hadn't eaten all day and was always a cheap drunk. Giulia, Brinkley, and even Trish floated farther back in her mind. The restaurant, a casual bistro, was dark and uncrowded, and the menu was completely in French. She stumbled over the béarnaise and mumbled, 'Why is the menu never in Latin?'

'What did you say?' Anthony leaned over his menu. 'You like Latin food?'

'No, forget it.'

'I cook very good Cuban. I learned it in South Beach from a Cuban friend.'

'I feel inferior, with no Cuban friends. I know people from Jersey, however.'

Anthony laughed. 'I even went to Havana with him. What a city. Very wild.'

'I'm sure. I saw *The Godfather*.'

'I memorized *The Godfather*. I even read the book.'

'That's hardcore.' Mary smiled. 'What's your favorite line?'

' "Leave the gun, take the cannoli." '

'Good one. Mine's 'Fredo, you broke my heart." ' Mary smiled again. She was buzzed. Anthony was fun. Gay men were always fun. She wished suddenly that all men were gay. 'So you're a good coke?'

'Excellent. I love to cook. My idea of a perfect night is a wonderful dinner.'

'Me, too. You know, it's too bad I didn't know you in high school. The only boys I knew were the ones who needed tutoring.'

'Not me. I studied hard, I was a good boy. In fact, I was an altar boy.' Anthony smiled, and Mary laughed.

'You're like the male version of me. It's really too bad we didn't know each other.' Her thoughts turned to Trish and the boy she did know in high school. Not a good boy, decidedly a bad boy.

'What?' Anthony asked. 'Your face just fell.'

'It's a long story.'

'So, tell me. The waiter's never coming back anyway.'

'He'd better.' Mary checked her watch but it was too dark to see it. 'I have to go back to work and this thing that's exploding. If you saw the TV news today, you know that Trish Gambone is missing.'

'How do I know that name?' Anthony asked, with a slight frown.

'High school.' So Mary told him the story, and his expression darkened.

'It's a terrible thing.' he said, after she had finished the story. 'I don't get some men.'

'Me, either.' Mary didn't elaborate.

'Wait a minute. Why is this your problem? You and Trish weren't friends, were you?' Anthony cocked his head. 'She was so conceited in high school, and he was a dumb jock.'

'She came to me for help.'

'So she's your client?'

'Not really.'

Anthony arched an eyebrow. 'Then if you ask me, I think you did plenty. You found the diary and you told the police. This is their job now. Let them do it. They'll go forward with their investigation, even though Giulia went on TV.'

Mary nodded. It was exactly what Judy would have said. 'Still, I hate doing nothing.'

'Don't be so hard on yourself. It's time for the police to take over. You're not responsible for everyone from the neighborhood.'

Yet it was exactly how Mary felt. 'But that's what a community does. That's what it is, to me. Take Dhiren for example, who lives next door to your mom.'

'I've seen him. Nice kid.' Anthony sipped his wine.

'He needs help, but I can't find a psychologist who can test him because everybody's too busy.' Mary knew that she had just divulged confidential information, but she was a little drunk, so it was permissible under the Tipsy Exception. 'Nobody feels the remotest responsibility for others in this world. It's all the bottom line and the schedule and it's-not-my-table, and a little boy hangs in the balance. Even the cops have their issues between Homicide and Missing Persons, and Trish falls through the cracks.'

Anthony set down his glass. 'You're not a big drinker, are you?'

'Does it show?'

'Absolutely, but it's cute.' Anthony smiled softly, and their eyes met over the cozy table, in the candlelight's glow. It would have been a romantic moment, if not for that pesky homosexual part.

123

'So, tell me about you.' Mary said. 'Do you have a partner?'

'What kind of partner? I teach.'

'You know, a partner. A lifemate. A lover.'

'No.'

'Oh.'

'No. Oh, no.' Anthony started to smile. 'You've been talking to my mother.'

'Your mother? About what?'

'Oh, no.' Anthony laughed, covering his face with his hands. 'This is so embarrassing.'

'What is?'

Anthony looked up from his hands. 'You think I'm gay.'

'Aren't you?'

'No! Oh my God, no. Not at all. I'm not gay.'

'What?' Mary asked, puzzled. 'Your mother said you were.'

'She thinks I am, but I'm not. She was always fixing me and my brother up, and I would never like any of the girls. Each one was worse than the next.' Anthony couldn't stop chuckling. 'So she decided that I'm gay because I like wine, good food, and books. The books alone will convict you in the neighborhood.'

Mary reached for the wine, dumbfounded. 'Why don't you tell her you're not gay?'

'Because she'll start fixing me up again. My brother Dom wishes he had the same scam, but nobody would believe such a slob is gay. She never asked me if I am, so I never lied to her. It's don't-ask, don't-tell, only I'm straight.'

Mary laughed, incredulous.

'Now, we have a running gag. Dom and my

124

sisters are on it, too. He gives me Cher and Celine Dion CDs for Christmas. My sister took me and my mother to the Barbra Streisand concert last year. They think it's a riot. I did, too. Until now.'

Mary blinked. 'What about when you bring home a girl? Someone you're seeing?'

'I say they're my friends, because they are, and she assumes it's platonic.'

'And when it gets serious?'

'I haven't met anyone I wanted to get serious about, yet.'

Mary tried to wrap her mind around it. 'The funny thing is, I only went to dinner with you because I thought you were gay.'

'Oh no. Are you seeing someone?'

'No, but I'm really sick of fix-ups.'

'Perfect.' Anthony raised his glass, his easy smile returning. 'To no more fix-ups.'

Mary took a big swig of wine, suddenly stiffening, and Anthony met her eye in the candlelight.

'So you didn't know this was a date?' he asked softly.

'Uh, no.'

'It is, and I hope it's not the last.'

Mary's mouth went dry.

'Is that okay with you?'

No. Yes. No way. Sure. Mary felt a warm rush inside, but it had to be the alcohol. If Anthony was straight, her makeup needed freshening. She set down her glass. 'Order for me, please,' she said, getting up and grabbing her bag just as her phone started ringing. She

125

stepped away, dug in her bag for her cell, slid it from its case while she fled to the ladies' room.

'Yes?' she said into the phone, on the fly.

'Mare?' It was her father.

'Pop, hi.' Mary pushed the swinging door into a tiny ladies' room. 'Sorry I didn't call you back. I spoke with Bernice.'

'That's not why I'm calling.' Her father sounded panicky. 'Can you come home right away?'

'What's the matter? Are you okay? Is Ma?'

'She's fine. Just get home. Hurry.'

Mary's heart tightened in her chest.

'Hurry.'

15

The sun ran for cover behind the flat asphalt roofs, and Anthony pulled the Prius in front of her parent's rowhouse. 'I'll park and be right back,' he said, and Mary thanked him. She got out of the car in front of her two older neighbor ladies, who were standing close together on the sidewalk. They turned and looked at her, oddly hard-eyed in their flowered dresses and worn cardigans.

Mary ran up her parents' steps. 'Hey, Mrs. DaTuno. Mrs. D'Onofrio.'

'Hmph.' Mrs. D'Onofrio sniffed, uncharacteristically chilly, but Mary didn't have time to deal. She shoved her key in the front door and hurried inside, where a small crowd filled the dining room.

'You're just in time,' her father said, upset.

'Dad, where's Ma?' Mary asked, and just then, the sound of a commotion came from the kitchen.

'Oh, sweet Jesus!' Her father took her arm and hustled her back through the crowd, as fast as he could on bad knees and slip-ons. They all frowned at Mary as she passed, but she didn't understand why.

Her father was saying, 'Thank God we got the heads-up from Cousin Joey. That's when I called you.'

'It's okay, Pop, I'll handle it,' Mary said, but

when they reached the kitchen, she wasn't so sure.

An angry Mrs. Gambone stood on one side of the kitchen table, an older version of Trish, too much makeup, deep crows'-feet, and tiny wrinkles fanning out from her lips. Stiff black curls trailed down the back of her long black jacket, which she wore with black stirrup pants and black half-boots. Mary's mother stood near the oven, distinctly Old World with her puffy hair, smock apron, and flowered housedress, and she held a clear plastic bag in her hand. Christening dresses blanketed the kitchen table, as if she'd been interrupted while she was wrapping them.

'Mrs. Gambone?' Mary asked, and Trish's mother turned on Mary, her dark eyes flashing.

'You!' Mrs. Gambone said in a chain-smoker's rasp. 'What do you have to say for yourself? You let that monster take my daughter.'

'No, that's not true.' Mary felt stung, and her mother stepped forward, shaking her fist holding the plastic bag and defending her daughter in rapid Italian.

'Don't you dare talk to our daughter that way,' her father said, a running translation. 'This is our home.'

'Don't talk to me that way!' Mrs. Gambone yelled back, straining her voice and setting her neck veins bulging. 'You're scum, Mare, pure *scum*!'

'Mary's a big shot now!' a man shouted from the dining room, and the crowd murmured in angry assent. All that was missing were the

128

burning torches, and Mary felt like Frankenstein with a law degree. If she wasn't Responsible For The Neighborhood, somebody forgot to tell the Neighborhood.

'Let me explain,' Mary began, but Mrs. Gambone cut her off with a hand chop.

'My daughter came to you for help. You coulda helped her but you didn't! Now she's *gone!*'

'I wanted to help her,' Mary almost cried out, as the words hit home.

'She knew he was gonna kill her and now he did. She's *gone!*' Mrs. Gambone's lower lip trembled. 'I told her to go to you. She didn't know what to do. She was too scared to leave him. But you didn't lift a finger! You didn't *care* what happened to her!'

'Mrs. Gambone, I did care. I wanted her to go to court and I went to the Roundhouse today — '

'Yeah, right, and you yelled at Giulia because she went on TV! She's tryin' to save my baby's life. Why didn't you help my Trish? If you had done something, she'd be home now. All safe.'

No, no. Mary felt stricken. It was true. Once she set aside her lawyerly rationalizations, the fact remained that she was the one Trish had gone to for help.

'She called me, last night, but I musta missed the call. She left a message, she said he was gonna kill her, she said where she was, but it was all static.'

'What?' Mary couldn't process it fast enough. 'Please, slow down and tell me what happened.'

'What do you care?' Mrs. Gambone shot back.

'I told the police, they know. She called me for help. She said he was with her, he was going to kill her. Then he grabbed the phone. She didn't have time to talk, she said he was comin' right back in the room.'

'What time did she call you?'

'It was around ten o'clock she called, but I didn't get her message till today. I must not a heard the phone, sometimes it's weird, it don't get messages right away.' Mrs. Gambone's voice broke, anguished. 'I came here because I wanted your family to know what you did to my daughter. She's all I had, all I had, and he *took* her! She's *gone!*' Mrs. Gambone's eyes welled up. 'My beautiful, beautiful baby. My only baby, my little girl.'

Mary felt her heart break. Her father, her mother, and the crowd fell silent, stunned by the depth of Mrs. Gambone's agony, raw and unvarnished, echoing in the quiet house.

'Can you know . . . what that feels like? To be a mother, and your baby . . . your baby's gone?' Mrs. Gambone finally broke down, and her ladyfriends supported her as she sagged, still trying to speak. Suddenly, she banged her fist on the kitchen table in sheer frustration, and the force of her hand jostled a cup of coffee sitting next to the christening dresses. Before anybody could stop it, the cup tipped over and coffee spilled on the pristine white dresses.

'No!' Mary yelped.

'*Dio!*' Her mother plucked the tiny dresses from the table, but it was too late. The espresso soaked instantly into the soft cotton, even as she hurried them to the sink. Mary sprang to her side, twisting on the cold water.

'I didn't mean it . . . I'm sorry,' Mrs. Gambone said, her tears subsiding.

'We'll pray for you and your daughter,' her father said softly. He handed her some napkins from a plastic holder, and the ladyfriend accepted them for Mrs. Gambone, who turned miserably away and left the kitchen under support, followed by the crowd. They found their way out the front door, closing it behind them, and only then did Mary notice that her mother was chewing her lower lip in an effort not to cry.

'I'm sorry, Ma. So sorry.' Mary couldn't do anything but stand by her mother's side at the sink and hug her.

'S'all right, Maria, s'all right.' Her mother ran cold water over the soggy white clump until her knobby knuckles turned red, but the coffee stains had already set. All four dresses were ruined.

'Aww, Veet.' Her father came over and rubbed her mother's back. 'Maybe we put a lil' bleach and it'll come out?'

'No, no, no,' her mother said, shaking her head, washing the dresses and trying not to cry. 'No, the dress, they no matter. I no like what they say about my Maria. *That* hurts my heart.'

'What's going on?' came a new voice, and Anthony appeared in the kitchen, his dark eyes wide as he took in the scene.

'Ma, it's okay, it's all okay.' Mary gathered her mother in her arms, meeting Anthony's eye.

Surprisingly, his pained expression mirrored her own.

Half an hour later, the four of them were sitting at the kitchen table, trying to get back to normal. The christening dresses soaked in the cellar in a pot of cold water and Clorox, and the kitchen table was set with spaghetti, hot sausage, and meatballs. Steam from the plate, carrying the comforting aromas of fresh basil and peppery sausage, warmed Mary's face. She was trying not to be bothered by the fact that Anthony was sitting in Mike's old chair, or that her parents seemed overly happy it was filled again.

Her father twirled his spaghetti against his plate. 'So you and Mare were out to dinner, huh?'

'Yes,' Anthony answered, suppressing a smile. 'This is one of the more unusual first dates I've ever had.'

Mary smiled, uncomfortably. He was a sweet guy, but she didn't know if she was ready for him to sit in Mike's chair. Or maybe she was upset at everything that happened. The image of Mrs. Gambone, weeping, would stay with her always. She'd already called Brinkley and left two more messages for him, hoping that he wasn't boycotting her. It made her feel guilty to be enjoying a meal. What had she been thinking, going out to dinner while Trish was still missing? The neighborhood was judging her, no more harshly than she judged herself.

'Mary doesn't see anybody,' her father said, and Mary looked up.

'Pop. Please.'

'It's all right. I don't either.' Anthony stabbed a meatball with a fork. His sport jacket hung over the back of the chair, and he tucked a napkin in his collar, as if he'd eaten here before. He turned to her mother, who'd finally sat down to her meal. 'These meatballs are great, Mrs. D.'

'*Grazie molto*,' her mother said, brightening.

'*Prego*.' Anthony caught Mary's eye, and she faked a smile. He didn't know her mother well enough to be calling her Mrs. D. Judy didn't call her mother Mrs. D until she'd known her for a year, or after twenty-seven spaghetti dinners.

'*Parli Italiano, Antonio?*' her mother asked, cocking her head.

Mary couldn't shake her disapproval. Her parents were practically offering Anthony the house keys.

'*Si, si*,' he answered. '*Ho insegnato all' Università di Bologna per tre anni*.'

'Excuse me,' Mary interrupted, rising with her BlackBerry. 'I want to call the Roundhouse again.'

'Sure, Mare,' her father said, and she could feel his puzzled gaze on her back as she left.

She entered the darkened dining room, pressed Redial for the Homicide Division, and listened to the inevitable busy signal while the conversation resumed in the kitchen. She was in no hurry to go back into the light and the warmth and the family around the table, with all the chairs filled. For the time being, she sat alone in the dark.

Beep beep beep, went the busy signal.

133

★ ★ ★

It wasn't until ten o'clock that Mary and Anthony got back to Center City and the silvery Prius cruised to a stop on her skinny back street. Her end of the street was dark, and everybody was inside, the windows aglow. Unlike South Philly, nobody here hung out on stoops talking or trading gossip, and everyone had quit smoking. Center City was just off the business district, revitalized by the city's young professionals. It was a neighborhood, too, but one formed by gym memberships and gourmet muffins, both less constant than church parishes and blood ties. Mary had been trying to feel at home here for years.

Anthony pulled up the emergency brake and looked over with a tight smile. 'Was it something I said?'

'Why? What do you mean?' Mary felt her face flush.

'You've been so quiet and well-behaved.'

'This, from an altar boy,' Mary shot back, more harshly than she'd intended. 'I'm sorry,' she said quickly. 'It's just that this was such an awful night.'

'In some ways. But in other ways, it was great. I got to know you.'

Mary smiled, but somewhere inside she felt like crying.

'No, really, going to your house, it felt like home. It was wonderful. It was . . . real.'

Mary heard a soft, masculine note in his voice that she liked, even though she wasn't ready to like it yet.

'Your parents were terrific, the food was delicious, and we're in agreement on my sexuality.'

Mary reached for the door handle and saw Anthony's eye catch the movement. If he was even thinking about kissing her good night, which it was way too early for anyway, she'd head it off with her patented going-for-the-door-handle move.

'I'd love to see you again. Okay with you?'

No. 'Yes.'

'Are you free this weekend?'

Yes. 'No. Maybe next, I'm not sure. Gimme a call.'

'Okay, well — '

'See you later and thanks for everything. 'Bye.' Mary grabbed her bag and got out of the car, closing the door. Through the glass she could see the corners of Anthony's mouth turn down, and superimposed on his troubled expression was her own reflection, frowning back at her. She couldn't begin to deal with him. She couldn't make it better for him. She couldn't even make it better for herself.

She turned away and escaped to her building, let herself in and grabbed her mail without looking at it, then climbed the stairs to her apartment. She was unlocking her door when she heard her phone ringing inside.

She burst through and flicked on the living room light.

16

Mary dropped her purse and grabbed the receiver. 'Hello?'

'It's Reg Brinkley.'

'Reg, thanks for calling.' Mary couldn't miss the chill in her old friend's voice. 'I'm so sorry about what happened. I didn't know they'd go on TV, I swear.'

'I figured. I got your messages but didn't want to call you from work or on your cell. This conversation is confidential, correct?'

Gulp. 'Yes, of course. I'm sorry. Nothing like that will ever happen again, I promise.'

'I gotta make this fast, we're busy tonight. Please don't call me at work anymore. You're radioactive.'

'I won't,' Mary said, taken aback. She sank onto the living room couch.

'Take my cell number. If you need to contact me, call me there.'

'Okay, thanks.' Mary grabbed a pen from the table and scribbled his cell number on her hand when he rattled if off. 'I hope I didn't get you in too much trouble.'

Brinkley chuckled, which made Mary feel worse. She'd let a friend down, not to mention endangered his job, and all because he'd tried to help her. It didn't feel good. She was screwing up left and right this week.

'Reg, yell at me or something.'

'Don't worry about it. Officially, I have to bow out of the picture. As far as your friend Trish Gambone goes, let Missing Persons do its thing. They didn't appreciate me sticking my nose where it didn't belong, but they're on it, even if they are busy with the Donchess case.'

'I heard Trish called her mom.'

'I know. How'd you know?'

'Her mom told me.' Mary gave the details. 'Do the cops have any idea where she could be? Can they locate where the call came from?'

'I'm not discussing it further. Missing Persons knows about it and they're on it.'

'So that's the only lead?'

'Enough, Mare.'

Mary took it as a yes.

'Also, please tell your nutty friend Giulia to stop calling me.'

Mary moaned. 'She's calling you?'

'All the time.'

Great 'By the way, I have Trish's diary. Does Missing Persons want it?'

'Yes. Anything in it?'

'Like what?' Mary asked.

'References to a getaway place they like. Their habits as a couple. People have patterns.'

Mary made a mental note. 'I haven't even had a chance to read it yet. Today was wall to wall.'

'Messenger it to them tomorrow.'

'I could take it over myself, first thing in the morning.'

'No,' Brinkley answered quickly. 'I don't want you anywhere near the Roundhouse.'

Mary tried not to take it personally.

137

'Sorry I can't help you anymore. Hope they find your friend. Give my best to Mama.'

'I will,' Mary said, and Brinkley hung up before she could say she was sorry again.

Half an hour later, she was leaning against the soft down pillows in her bed, wearing her Eagles sweatshirt, her hair on top of her head in its Pebbles ponytail, and wearing her glasses, getting ready to read Trish's diary. She would look for the references that Brinkley mentioned, and it could tell her more about their relationship. Not that it would be fun reading.

My daughter came to you for help.

Mary felt a deep pang, then pressed the image of Mrs. Gambone to the back of her mind. She grabbed a pen and propped her legal pad up on her knees. The best way she could help Trish was to do exactly what she was doing. She took a sip of decaf Lipton and began to read on page one.

My birthday!!! Yay, T!! We went out for a great dinner and he gave me diamond studs, 2.3 carats if you add them together!!! G's are only 1 carat each and also they're flat, so it's a cheat. They look bigger but aren't really heavier and the cut isn't as good. BTW, I'm starting a journal. But tonight, I drank too much to write much. TTYL.

Mary made a note, then thought a minute. So that was why she didn't find any other diaries in the house. She read on, and pretty quickly the November and December entries fell into a

138

pattern. Trish seemed to write at night, on a weekly basis, after they'd gone out to dinner and a movie, a club, or a party. The entries were glowing and loving. Entries about the Mean Girls concerned weight gained and lost, and the time Yolanda got a butterfly tattooed on her lower back, which led to a flock of butterfly tattoos.

It hurt like a mother!

Mary smiled, sadly. Trish could be so cute, even conscientious, recording details about work, her increasingly large number of clients, formulas for mixing lowlights, and gripes about one Shawna, who appeared to be the salon's Mean Girl. Trish wrote about her mother, worrying that Mrs. Gambone *never went out* and *needed a man*. She worried even more about Giulia, who seemed *so moody* lately, and Yolanda was *so jealous of me.*

Mary sipped some tea, and by February, the entries were changing. After the dinners, there were fights. *He drank too much, again.* Or, *He yelled at me for no reason.* There were fewer exclamation points, fewer dates they went on together, fewer notes about the Mean Girls.

Many of the entries read that *He came back late from Biannetti's, drunk.* Mary recorded and counted them, finding 28 such entries until March. And about that same time, Trish wrote that *he's skimming, I just know it. He always has so much cash on him, and always when he comes back from work.*

By June, Trish was becoming frightened. The fights became worse, the drinking more frequent, and the skimming worried her more and more. On June 4 and June 10, she worried that *they'll find out*. On June 23, she wrote that *Cadillac thinks he's stealing* because at a wedding, *Cadillac said that my watch must have cost an arm and a leg*, and said, *I didn't know your boyfriend was earning that much*. Mary made a note of the name Cadillac, but couldn't find a last name.

She read on, noticing that the verbal abuse intensified in the June entries, and she stopped flinching at the *whore, slut*, and *lying bitch*. Trish wrote that *he's slipping up on the job* and *not doing as good as he used to*. On July 4th, she felt snubbed by the other Mob girlfriends at a barbecue because he's *not doing as good as he should be even as good as his brother, who's a dumbass on top of it*.

Mary read on. The story reached a climax of sorts, when Trish confronted him about his stealing, but he denied it to her, and she wrote, *he told me I'm nuts to think he'd be dumb enough to steal from the boys, and if Cadillac thinks it, he's an idiot, too*. Cadillac keeps *having his suspicions*, which led to Trish being accused of having an affair with Cadillac, which she would never do *because he's a pig*. Again, no last name supplied.

More suspicions that led to the incident where *he shoved me in the closet and held the door closed so I couldn't get out! I was so scared he was gonna trap me or something!* Mary read the following entries, in which a newly mistrustful Trish didn't believe the apologies: *And when he socked me in my stomach like four times and I couldn't get my breath*. In the next pages, the violence escalated.

He beat the shit out of me after Biannetti's again and the very next night, *he won't stop with the biting.* More assaults after Biannetti's, more reconciliations, more I'll-never-do-it-again, and at least ten Polaroids, each one uglier than the next.

Then Mary turned the page and it got worse: *he made me suck his gun and he kept laughing and wouldn't let me stop or he said he'd shoot me and blow my brains out my neck.* Her stomach turned over. He had become a sadist, a sociopath. She shook her head in disgust and bewilderment, then kept reading. Entries in the days following were filled with *I'm so scared* and *what do I do* and *what if he sees me writing in the diary.* There were no references to any weekend getaway, as Brinkley had said, or any clue as to where they would be now. It was the chronology of a nightmare, and Mary re-read the final entry: *I went to see Mary but she didn't do anything. Now I don't know what to do. If you're reading this now, whoever you are, I'm already dead. But at least this can prove he did it.*

She closed the diary, her heart leaden, and looked aimlessly around her bedroom, hoping to see something that would lift her out of Trish's world and restore her to her own. It was a feeling she had after reading any book, a reentry issue when she was finished, as if she'd been out of earth's orbit, but this diary was more powerful than any story. It was real, and Mary herself had let the heroine down, resigning her to a fate that admitted no happy ending.

She was scared he was gonna kill her and now

141

maybe he did. Ya happy?

Mary felt her eyes moisten and blinked it away. A white ginger lamp filled the cozy bedroom with a warm glow, and a blue-and-yellow flowered chair sat in the corner. Two landscapes hung on the wall, and a pine dresser sat nearby with a large mirror, which still had Mike's photos stuck in the side. They weren't photos of Mike; rather, they were photos he'd taken, loved, and put there, of his parents, his fraternity brothers, and the class he taught, third-graders, missing teeth here and there. He had loved teaching, and every time Mary saw those photos, she remembered him. She didn't need to see his face in a photo; she had his face in her heart. She wanted to see what he saw, through his eyes. That's what the photos showed. His soul.

She felt suddenly lucky that she'd been married to Mike. She wouldn't have married anybody but him, least of all Trish's mobster. She wouldn't have changed a single thing about her life, except losing Mike. And that, she couldn't do anything about. So she set the legal pad and the diary aside, then took off her glasses and set them on the night table, faceup so they didn't scratch. She reached over and turned out the light, and darkness covered her like a down comforter.

She scooted down in bed, thinking in the silence of her room. Her solitude seemed more obvious to her now than ever, after the noise and violence of the relationship she'd been reading about, though she finally understood some

142

things. Trish had stayed in the relationship because she was afraid to leave it, that much was obvious. But what Mary learned was that Trish had gotten into it because she didn't want to end up in a bedroom alone, with her hair in a Pebbles ponytail and a mug of decaf tea cooling by the bed.

Trish didn't want to be her.

Nobody did.

Nobody wanted to be the girl avoiding a goodnight kiss from a perfectly nice and handsome man whose only fault was that he liked her. Finally, there in the dark, Mary understood something about Trish, and about herself, too.

And if Trish were still alive, Mary vowed to find her.

17

Mary's office window was a harsh pewter square, and the dawn sky cloaked her desk in a cold, gray light. She was at work by six thirty, moving the computer mouse and logging on to *www.philly news.com* for the latest. The headline read **DONCHESS BABY STILL MISSING.** She skimmed the top stories, all about the child's kidnapping, but there was no new news about Trish. Mary hadn't slept well last night and she'd come into the office to get work out of the way before she made her next move, which she couldn't do until nine o'clock. She was dressed for it, in a brown tweed suit, overpriced pumps, and with her hair back in its loose twist. Sleuthingwear.

She flipped through her phone messages from the past two days, a dangerously high stack. The top one was from somebody named Alfred Diaz, Esq., then she read Marshall's neat notation on the message: *Diaz is Roberto Nunez's new lawyer, he wants you to send file.*

'I'm fired?' Mary asked aloud, in dismay. She'd worked the Nunez case for six months, but she couldn't blame Roberto. He'd wanted his lawyer with him at his deposition and he had a right to that. She thumbed unhappily to the next message, from Tom DeCecco, canceling their appointment tomorrow on a workmen's comp case, and another was a cancellation from Delia

Antoine, of a meeting at her house on Friday, about lead paint removal.

Hmm. Mary would've rescheduled those meetings anyway, to deal with Trish, and she usually prayed for cancellations. But two? Uneasy, she sipped her take-out coffee, which tasted hot and good. Was something going on with her clients? Was it related to Trish? She flashed on the scene last night in her parents' dining room.

Mary's a big shot now.

Her BlackBerry started ringing, and she startled, wondering who could be calling so early. She checked the display, alarmed, and picked up. 'Amrita, what's the matter?'

'Sorry to bother you at this ungodly hour, but I don't know what to do. Dhiren won't come out of the bathroom. He's missed the bus. He says he won't ever go back. He's in there, crying.'

'Poor kid. Don't make him go.'

'He's so upset. He was taking a shower and one of the scabs on his head started bleeding. He's afraid they'll mock him.' Amrita sounded beside herself. 'Did you make any progress with getting him tested? I can't take this much longer, nor can Dhiren.'

'They can't see him or test him until April, but I want to improve on that.'

'He needs help now.'

'I understand.' Mary's face burned. 'I'll get on it.'

'Thank you. I must go. Talk to you later.'

'Bye,' Mary said, but Amrita had already hung up. She got back on the computer and logged on

145

to the white pages to find a qualified child psychologist in Philly. She'd skip all the red tape. She couldn't listen to Dhiren cry like that and she didn't want to let another client down. In fifteen minutes, she had a list of psychologists to call, and a grinning Judy Carrier materialized in her threshold.

'Cock-a-doodle-doo!' Judy said, fresh-faced in a yellow rain slicker. She carried a paper bag. 'I thought you'd be in. I'm bearing breakfast.'

'Wow. Why are you in so early?'

'Same reason as you. Work, work, work.' Judy flicked on the light, entered the office, set down the paper bag, and shed the slicker, revealing a funky dress with orange-and-white swirls.

'My God, you're a Creamsicle.'

'Thank you.' Judy flopped into a seat with a grin. Her blond hair was swept back from her wide face with a stretchy purple headband, emphasizing her broad cheekbones and fore-head. Mary couldn't see what color clogs she had on. She didn't want to know.

'Do they even have orange clogs?' she asked, anyway.

'Unfortunately, no.'

'They'd be perfect for deer season.'

'Or for feeling sunny and bright, on a gloomy hump day.' Judy dug into the bag and pulled out a corn muffin with a top like a mushroom cloud. 'Look, your favorite.'

'Thanks, sweetie,' Mary said, though the muffin showered crumbs on her desk, threatening to make grease spots on her letters, which she moved hastily aside.

146

'So fill me in. What's up with Trish?' Judy reached in the bag and produced two tiny golden packets. 'I got butter, too.'

'Oooh, butter,' Mary said, succumbing to the inevitable. She hit a button to print the list of psychologists' names, then cleared a legal pad for a placemat and reached over for the muffin. 'For starters, she called her mother the night she disappeared.'

'Really?' Judy asked, and Mary told her about the scene at her parents' house, and later, about Anthony. By the time she'd finished, Judy had sprouted little worry lines on her forehead. 'Hopefully, the cops will find her.'

'Right.' Mary didn't tell her about the plans for the day, because she'd be sure to object.

'But you had a date? Hallelujah!'

'I guess.'

'So what's the matter?'

'I'm not ready, I decided.'

Judy almost spit out her coffee. 'You're so ready you're dying on the vine.'

'Thanks.' Mary smiled.

'Mare, why don't you like him?'

'At my parents', he sat in Mike's chair.'

'He needed a place to put his ass. Your parents have four chairs at that table. When I eat there, I sit in Mike's chair. There's no other choice.'

'He's going too fast, is all.'

Judy's eyes glittered evilly. 'Why? Did he go for the tongue?'

'No. We didn't kiss.'

'Then how is he going too fast?'

'I don't know.' Mary tried to shrug it off, but

147

couldn't. She reached for her coffee and noticed her e-mail in-box had gotten a new e-mail the sender in boldface: **Giulia Palazzolo.** The re line read, **Have you seen Trish Gambone?** Mary said, 'Uh-oh, incoming Mean Mail.'

'What?' Judy brushed crumbs off her fingertips and came around the desk, while Mary opened the e-mail and they read it together. It was a flyer that showed the photo of Trish from Giulia's cell phone, and underneath was a description of Trish, with Giulia's phone number and Reg Brinkley's, too.

'Oh, no.' Mary moaned. 'Brinkley will go nuts. Giulia's been calling him, but I didn't get a chance to yell at her yet.'

'Not a bad idea, to send a flyer. But they're going about it the wrong way.'

'What do you mean?' Mary looked up, and Judy's clear blue eyes moved rapidly back and forth as she read the screen, its light throwing white shadows on her chin and cheeks.

'The flyer, it's all about Trish, and that's not good. They don't need to find her, they need to find him.'

Mary felt like kicking herself. 'You're right. I'm the one who told them to send a flyer. How could I have missed that?'

'They'll never find her this way. This is all wrong.' Judy gestured at the screen. 'They need a photo of him. They need to find out where he went last, where he hangs, where he was last seen, where he could have taken her. Once you find him, you find her.'

'You're a genius.' Mary reached for her phone,

searched the received calls, pressed Call, and set it on speakerphone. It was almost seven o'clock, so Giulia should be getting up soon.

'Hello?' she answered sleepily.

'Hi, Giulia, it's Mary. Sorry to wake you.'

'Wha?'

'Giulia, I'm here with Judy and we have you on speaker. First, do me a favor and please don't call Brinkley anymore. We almost got him fired. Second, I got your flyer and instead of making it about Trish, we were thinking you should do a new one and — '

'Oh, yo, Mare. Yo, Judy. Thank God you bitches woke me up to tell me what I'm doing wrong.' Giulia's voice went from sleepy to angry faster than a Maserati. 'What a relief that you called. You know, I been sleeping on my back but maybe I should turn over? Whaddaya think?'

'Giulia, it's just that — '

'What's your freakin' problem, Mare? I heard you dissed Trish's mom last night. How ignorant can you get?'

'No, I didn't.' Mary controlled her temper, remembering what Mrs. Gambone had said about her rebuking Giulia. 'I'm not trying to be critical of you. I'm — '

'We're the ones runnin' around — me, Yo, and Missy. I was up until three in the mornin'. We went to all the places where they know Trish, askin' everybody if they seen her, postin' the flyer on telephone poles around work and the bars she used to like. Everywhere she goes or used ta go.'

'That's the problem. You need to go where — '

'What's *you* doin' for Trish, Mare? Makin' with Ant'n'y Rotunno, who, p.s., in case you didn't know, is friggin' gay?'

Judy's eyes widened. *He's gay?* she mouthed, but Mary waved her off.

'Giulia, I understand that you're working hard, but you should think about going after — '

The line went dead. Giulia had hung up. Mary rubbed her forehead. 'That went well.'

Judy cocked her head. 'He's gay?'

'No.'

'Then why did she say that?'

'It's a long story,' Mary answered, sipping her coffee, preoccupied.

'You look worried.'

'I am.'

'You think she's dead already?' Judy's expression went grim, and Mary didn't want her muffin anymore.

'I pray not.' Their eyes met over the desk, and Mary lied, 'I guess I have to let it be.'

'You do, you can't help anymore. You don't know anything about the boyfriend.'

'No, not really.' Mary kept her mouth shut. She knew a lot about the boyfriend, but this wasn't the time for a confession. There was no confessional, for one thing.

'It's for the best. I don't want to worry about you getting mixed up with the Mob.'

'Me neither.' Mary faked a shudder, which wasn't difficult. She had a second chance to help Trish and she wasn't about to blow it. She got up, gathered their muffin trash, and said, 'I gotta go.'

'Where?' Judy asked, rising.

Mary tried to think of a lie, grateful she hadn't told Judy about the cancellations. 'A breakfast meeting with a new client.'

'Will you be back for lunch?'

'I doubt it.' Mary tossed her trash into the wastebasket, slid the list of shrinks from the printer tray, and grabbed the manila envelope that held Trish's diary, to be hand-delivered to Missing Persons.

'Okay, have fun.' Judy handed her her trenchcoat from the hook, and she took it with a smile.

'Thanks,' Mary said, avoiding the trusting eye of her best friend.

18

Mary hurried down the street under the gray sky, her trenchcoat billowing behind her, her handbag bumping against her side, and her pumps *clack*ing self-importantly on the filthy pavement. There was no one else on the street this early, especially in this seamier side of South Philly. Trash blew in the gutter, and the rowhouses were badly maintained, the awnings cracked here and there. Plywood boards covered most of the first-floor windows, and she hurried past a noisy auto-body shop where she drew an anachronistic wolf-whistle.

She picked up the pace. His house used to be number 3644. She wasn't sure if his father still lived here, but nobody moved in South Philly, or if they did, the neighbors would know where they'd gone. It wasn't the kind of information you got from Google. Mary approached the house, the typical two-story with shutters that needed painting, and she noted with a city-girl's eye that the brick hadn't been repainted in years. She walked up the steps, knocked, and waited. There was no answer, so she knocked again, trying not to be nervous.

In the next minute the door opened, and an older man she barely recognized stood stooped in the threshold. He had to be around seventy, but seemed much older. He was bald, and his skin was gray as the stormy sky. Lines etched his face behind greasy black eyeglasses, which sat so heavily on his ears they bent them forward. 'Yeah?' he asked, his voice quavering.

'Mr. Po, I don't know if you remember me. We met a long time ago, when you used to — '

'Pick up my son from your house, from studying. In high school.' The old man smiled shakily, his lips dry, and he pointed at her with a tapered index finger. 'I remember you.'

'How nice.'

'Never forget a face. Names, yes. Don't know your name.'

Mary introduced herself and raised a pastry box she'd brought.

'Would you mind if I come in a minute, to talk with you?'

'No, come in. I like a little company.'

'Great, thanks.' Mary stepped in as he opened the door and backed up, admitting her to a living room that had no lights on. It was modestly furnished, with an old-fashioned dark green sofa against the far wall under a rectangular beveled mirror that hung in every rowhouse in Italian-American history. If Mr. Po was in the Mob, maybe crime really didn't pay.

'Come on inna kitchen.' Mr. Po gestured, and Mary followed him into a dark square of kitchen that was the same dimensions as her parents', though it smelled of stale cigar smoke. A patterned curtain covered the only window, in the back door, and cabinets refaced with dark fake-walnut ringed the room, matching a brown Formica counter. On the right side of the room sat the sink, stove, and an old brown refrigerator covered with fading photos.

Mary sat down and opened the box of pastry while she stole a glance at the photos, some from as far back as high school. She recognized instantly those light blue eyes and that lopsided grin. He was dressed in a black football uniform, and there were pictures of another boy, bigger and brawnier, and a studious girl with glasses and long, dark hair. Mary didn't know the boy, but she recognized the girl. Rosaria, his sister, older by a year.

Mr. Po shuffled to the sink in brown moccasins. 'You like some coffee? It's instant. See, I got Folgers.' He held up the red-labeled jar like Exhibit A.

'Thanks. I bought some *sfogliatelle*.'

'Good girl.'

'Where's Rosaria these days?'

'Were you in her class?'

'No, but we were in choir together. We're both altos, so we stuck together. She was nice. How is she?'

'Got a kid.' Mr. Po shook his head, abruptly cranky, which warned Mary off the subject. She looked away, and her gaze found one of the smaller photos on the fridge: a picture of a little brown-haired boy in a green-and-gold baseball uniform. The green cap had a B on it, and the front of the shirt read Brick Titans. Mary made a mental note. 'Mr. Po, I came to you because I want to find Trish.'

'Know why you came. The police got here already, yesterday, ahead a you. You're wonderin' where Trish and my son went. Tell you what I

154

told the cops. I don't know where they are. How you take your coffee?'

Mary blinked, surprised. She broke the string on the pastry box, moving aside a *Daily News*, which lay open on the table near a black magnifying glass. A curvaceous jug of Coffee-mate, a plastic-crystal sugar bowl, and a colorful stack of Happy Birthday napkins sat in the middle of the table.

'Cream and sugar onna table.' Mr. Po spooned some Folgers into a mug he got from the cabinet, and the brown crystals made a tinkling sound. 'He always like you, my son did. Talked about you a lot.'

Mary felt a disturbing thrill. It threw her off. It wasn't why she'd come. She had to find Trish. Time was slipping away.

'Used to say you were smart. A nice girl, a good girl. Different from the others.'

Mary smiled, in spite of herself.

'Puppy love, I guess.' Mr. Po turned, lifting a sparse gray eye-brow. 'You're the one that got away, eh?'

'Nah,' Mary said, though she wasn't about to tell him what had happened.

'Too bad. He wasn't my real son, you know. I'm his uncle. My brother was his father. A drunk.'

Mary hadn't known the whole story. 'But you raised him, right?'

'Me and my wife did. Now she passed, too. We raised him with our son. Him and his sister, we treated 'em like they were ours.'

'That was very kind of you,' Mary said,

155

meaning it, but Mr. Po only shrugged knobby shoulders.

'Blood is blood.'

'When did you see him last?' Mary asked, getting to the point.

'Six months ago, maybe more. He don't come home much anymore. The things they're sayin' about him, it's lies. He didn't kidnap Trish, or whatever they're sayin'.'

'So where do you think they are?'

'They're young. They go where young people go.'

Right. 'I know they had problems, and he was abusive to her.'

'That's not true. That ain't the boy I raised. I think he changed.'

'So do I.' Mary felt surprised at the words coming out of her mouth, and Mr. Po eyed her from the stove, seeing her as if for the first time.

'Funny how life is, eh?'

'Yes. When did he start to change, Mr. Po? What changed him, do you think?'

'The wrong crowd.'

The wrong crowd being the Mob? Mary wasn't going there, at least not yet. She needed information. 'Did he ever talk to you about Trish?'

'No.' Mr. Po turned off the pot, picked up the handle, and poured the hot water, crackling in protest, into the mug. 'High school sweethearts. He started seein' her after you, right?'

Ouch. 'Right. When did you hear they were missing?'

'Yesterday on the TV.' Mr. Po reached in the

156

silverware drawer, took out a spoon, and mixed up the coffee.

'Aren't you worried about him? It's going on two days.'

'My boy can handle himself.'

Mary hadn't even considered that somebody could have abducted them both. She knew from Fung that they'd left the house alone, but that didn't preclude anything. What if they had both been abducted? Maybe a Mob thing? Maybe this guy Cadillac? Mary filed it away.

'I taught him how to take care of himself. In the basement, I taught him how to throw a punch. I made sure he knew that. That's a father's job.'

'You don't think he'd hurt her?'

'No. No way. He wouldn't hurt her. He wouldn't hurt nobody. He's lover, not a fighter. His brother, maybe, he's a fighter. But him, no. He'd never raise his hand to a woman.' Mr. Po came over and plunked down the mug of coffee, which smelled like cardboard.

'It was hard for me to believe, too, knowing him the way I do.' Mary made it up as she went along, trying to get Mr. Po to open up. She waited while he sat in the wooden chair catty-corner to her, his eyes downcast behind his glasses, which were sliding down his veined nose.

'Gonna drink your coffee?' he asked after a minute, looking up.

'Sure, thanks.' Mary shook in some Coffee-mate and spooned in sugar, then took a sip of the horrible brew, biding her time. 'I'm wondering where he could be.'

157

Mr. Po eyed the *sfogliatelle*, then pulled the pastries to him by hooking an index finger inside the cardboard box, his fingernail oddly long.

'They didn't tell anybody they were going anywhere, and her girlfriends are all worried. Giulia Palazzolo, Missy, Yolanda. You remember that crowd?'

Mr. Po snorted softly. '*Spaccone.*'

Mary translated. Show-offs.

'Not good girls. Not like you.'

Mary felt a weight on her leg and looked down. Mr. Po's gnarled right hand was resting on her skirt, while he was biting into a pastry as if nothing were happening. It was so unreal that it took her a second to process. She stood up abruptly.

'Who're you, honey?' asked a loud voice behind them, and Mary turned. A brawny man in a T-shirt and blue polyester sweatpants stood in the doorway, his expression a scowl, his posture a challenge. He thrust his strong jaw forward, threw back his massive shoulders, and displayed unashamedly his substantial paunch. His head was shaved, exposing a script neck tattoo, and he had rough features, like Mussolini in sweats.

'Used to go out with your brother in high school,' Mr. Po answered, slowly eating his pastry.

'I was wondering where he was,' Mary answered, standing between the two of them, suddenly afraid. No one knew she was here. She hadn't told anyone. She had lied to Judy. She went for the door, but the brother stood his

158

ground, blocking her.

'Where you goin'?' His breath told her he was the cigar smoker. A diamond stud glinted from a fleshy earlobe.

'I was just leaving.'

'Then why were you *comin*'?' He grinned at the double entendre, then his grin vanished. 'You one o' these bitches callin' baby bro a *murderer*? You one o' them?'

'No, I was just looking for him.'

'It's *his* business where he is, not yours.' The brother raised his voice. 'He's lyin' on a beach somewhere with his girl. He don't need anybody goin' on the TV news, tellin' this, that, and the other that he killed her.'

Mr. Po said, 'Lay off her, Ritchie. She's a lawyer. Trish went to see her, but she threw 'er out. She knows your brother wouldn't hurt his girlfriend. They go back.'

Mary's mouth went dry. She'd been foolish to think Mr. Po wouldn't have heard something, accurate or not. But it could play to her advantage.

'Right, Mare?' Mr. Po asked, looking up. 'My son's your old flame.'

Gulp. 'Right.'

'You're still in love with 'im, aren't you?' Mr. Po chuckled, dropping pastry flakes onto the table.

Mary didn't know what to say. She had to get out of here.

'You were into baby bro?' Ritchie's grin returned, menacing. He took a step closer, but Mary edged backward, like a nightmare cha-cha.

159

'Yes.'

'How come *I* never met you?'

'I don't know. Did you go to Neumann?'

'Neumann?' Ritchie laughed. 'No, honey, let's just say, I was *away*.'

'Stop scarin' her,' Mr. Po said from the table, his tone sterner, and Ritchie stepped aside with a ham-handed flourish.

'Excuse me. Please, go.'

'Thanks. 'Bye now.' Mary walked to the door as calmly as possible, but heavy footsteps pounded behind her. She startled as Ritchie appeared beside her and opened the door, flinging it wide.

'Boo,' he said, with a wink.

★   ★   ★

It wasn't until Mary was safely in the backseat of a cab that she breathed easily enough to get out her BlackBerry and plug the word *Brick* into Google. The results came up after a nanosecond: Brick the movie, Acme Brick, Brickwork Design, the Brick Testament, whatever that was, Brick Industry, and finally, the Official Township of Brick site. She connected to the link, and a glorious green-and-blue website filled the little screen. Brick Township was in south Jersey and was known locally as Brick. The site boasted, Brick Township Celebrates 'Safest City in America' Honors!

She scrolled down farther, and there was no other town on the first five pages. It had to be Brick, New Jersey, that Rosaria had moved to.

Mary logged onto *www.whitepages.com* and plugged in Rosaria with her last name, praying that she'd kept her maiden name. In the next second, a single address and phone number popped onto the screen, in glowing blue letters. She called it.

'Hello?' a woman answered, and Mary recognized the distinctive alto.

'Sorry, wrong number,' she said, and hung up. She leaned forward and asked the cabbie to take a right, toward her garage.

She'd need her own wheels.

19

It was a two-hour trip on the New Jersey Turnpike because of the congestion, and Mary returned as many phone calls and e-mails as she could without crashing. She called twelve more shrinks for Dhiren and on the thirteenth, got lucky. There was a last-minute cancellation and the psychologist would see Dhiren tomorrow. She almost cheered, then called Amrita's cell phone. No answer, but Mary left a message, her spirits soaring.

In time, the traffic let up and she hit I-95 East, toward the coastline. The clouds dissipated and the sun burst through, which she couldn't help but take as a good sign. She opened the car window and inhaled a lungful of fresh air, bearing a hint of the Atlantic, a smell she remembered from happy summers down the Jersey shore. The DiNunzios used to go to Bellevue Avenue, in an Atlantic City that didn't exist anymore.

She took a right, then a left, following the directions in *www.yahoo.com*, and finally passed a grassy stretch along the Metedeconk River. Seagulls squawked overhead, and the huge houses were uniformly lovely and well maintained, with costly cars parked in driveways. She could see why Rosaria would move here, away from the graffiti, even if a cannoli was harder to come by.

Mary was trying to find the house when she spotted a slim woman in a pink tracksuit walking a little dog that danced at the end of the leash. The woman's hair was gathered into a reddish brown ponytail that Mary recognized immediately. Rosaria had lost her studious, meek air and had come into her own, an attractive woman with the same blue eyes as her brother's, a similarly long nose, and full lips. Mary grabbed her bag, got out of the car, and crossed the street, intercepting her in the middle of the block.

'Hey, lady, weren't you in choir?' she asked with a smile, holding out her arms for a hug, and Rosaria laughed and returned the embrace.

'Mary? What're *you* doing here?'

'It's a long story.' Mary released her, and the little dog hopped on its hind legs, pawing her shins like a miniature black lion. Its fur stuck out like a fright wig and it had the ears of a kitten. 'What kind of beast is this?'

'A toy Pomeranian.' Rosaria bent over and baby-talked to the dog, 'Aren't you adorable? Aren't you?' She straightened up. 'She's my baby replacement, now that my son's in high school.'

'So cute.' Mary scratched the dense black fur of the dog's domed head, which only made her jump higher, springing around like she had pogo sticks for legs. 'Mind if I walk with you, for a minute?'

'Sure, okay.' Rosaria smiled uncertainly and got back in stride. 'How did you find me?'

Mary fell in step beside her. 'I was at your

163

father's, saw a photo, and put two and two together.'

'My *father's*?' Rosaria's expression changed instantly, her smile fading. Sunlight fell on her face, trying to fill the creases that had just popped onto her forehead. 'I hate that he calls himself that. He's my uncle, not my father.'

'Sorry.'

'It must've been an old photo.'

'Your son, in a baseball uniform.'

'Ha. Like I said. I don't send him photos anymore.'

Mary didn't know what to say, so she decided to be honest. 'You guys had trouble?'

'You could say that. Haven't spoken to the man in ages. This is about as far from South Philly as you can get, in my book.'

'Plus it has driveways.'

'There is that.' Rosaria smiled. 'So what are you doing here, out of the blue? You came to see me, after all these years?'

'I'm trying to find your brother.'

Rosaria looked grim again. 'I haven't spoken to him in about four years. I have no idea where he is.'

Mary wondered what had happened. 'You knew he was living with Trish, didn't you?'

'Yes.'

'I don't know if you heard, but he and Trish are missing.'

'Ask me if I care,' Rosaria shot back.

'The police haven't contacted you?'

'No.'

Mary let it go. 'He abducted her. She was able

164

to get a call to her mother that she needed help. He may have killed her.'

Rosaria kept walking, her dark expression contrasting with the perfect suburban setting and the happy little dog, who pranced along with her baby muzzle in the air.

'I'm trying to find them, which means I have to find him. Hopefully before he does something stupid.'

'Too late,' Rosaria said flatly, and Mary felt that chill again.

'I can't give up on Trish. She's in trouble.'

'Trish *Gambone?*' Rosaria laughed, without mirth. 'This may be poetic justice.'

'You don't mean that.' Mary hid her surprise. Rosaria had always been such a sweet, benevolent girl. 'I don't want anything to happen to Trish, I don't even want anything to happen to your brother. I want to prevent something terrible.'

'You a cop now, Mare?' Rosaria picked up the pace, her soft jowls jiggling with the faster step.

'No. They're investigating, but there's things I can do, too. Find you, for example.'

'Look.' Rosaria stopped and faced her matter-of-factly. 'I don't know where my brother is or what he did to Trish. I washed my hands of him.'

'What turned you so bitter? What happened?'

'That family was a dark, dark place to me.' Rosaria started walking again, faster this time. 'That's all I want to say on the subject.'

'Okay, I understand,' Mary said quickly. She was thinking of Mr. Po's hand on her leg.

'They're sick. My so-called father and his son, that pig.'

'Ritchie?'

'You met my cousin? What a waste of life.'

Mary couldn't disagree. And she couldn't keep up the pace, either. They had made their way all the way back to the park, and she spotted a bench. 'Can we just sit down for a second and talk about this? I need help. Trish needs help. Also my feet hurt.'

Rosaria sighed heavily.

'Please, for me? For old times' sake? For Jesus, Mary, and Joseph?'

'Oh, all right.' Rosaria smiled, becoming herself again. She tugged the little dog away from a fascinating stick, and they walked to the bench and sat down, where Mary kicked off her pumps.

'I'm so professional.'

Rosaria smiled. 'I heard you became a lawyer.'

'So news travels, all the way to paradise.'

'Is Brick paradise?'

'Looks like it to me.' Mary surveyed the huge houses across the river, which must have cost over a million dollars. They were three stories tall, with plenty of shiny windows and façades of gray stone. Other people would have called them McMansions, but Mary was no snob. She'd take a McMansion. Then she could be a McHome-owner. 'I would love to have a house.'

'Why don't you?' Rosaria asked, with the bluntness Mary remembered from high school.

'The down payment's tough, but I almost have it.' Still, Mary knew that wasn't what was

166

holding her back. 'You married?'

'Divorced.'

'Sorry.'

'Don't be. Best decision I ever made. I'm getting smarter and I got great alimony. And the dog.' Rosaria smiled.

'Then I'm happy for you.' Mary chose her next words carefully. 'Look, you don't need to tell me your personal history. I know we weren't that friendly. But if you could just tell me where you think your brother could be, or where he could have taken Trish, it could save a life.'

'No idea,' Rosaria shrugged, but close up her nonchalance looked more contrived.

Mary felt on edge. She wasn't getting anywhere, and coming here had taken so much time.

'I don't know who he is anymore. He drinks. He's mobbed up. He sells drugs. I cut him out of my life. I couldn't stand to see the path he was going down and I didn't want my son exposed to that. The curtain went down between us when he told me he opened his first 'store'' — Rosaria made quote marks in the air — 'as he called it, at Ninth and Kennick. That became his corner, though he always said that one day when he made enough money, he'd get out.'

Mary made a mental note. She knew that corner.

'We used to be so close.' Rosaria smiled at the memory, almost talking aloud, her voice soft as a tear. 'He used to tell me everything. I was his big sister, and it was just the two of us, really. He needed a best friend, and I was that, for him, all through grade school and high school.'

'He used to tell me about you.' Mary thought back, remembering.

'He used to tell me about *you*,' Rosaria said, pain flickering through her eyes. 'He really loved you, you know.'

Mary's throat caught.

'I think you were his first love.'

It was impossible to believe, given what had happened.

'You look surprised,' Rosaria said, and Mary's mouth went dry.

'Try shocked.'

'Why?'

He didn't tell you everything. 'He didn't tell me he loved me, or show me, in any way.'

'I'm not surprised. In that house we weren't exactly taught how to express affection.'

Mary felt herself go into a sort of emotional stall.

'After you broke up with him, he just shut down. Closed up. We talked about it, but I don't think he ever got over you.'

Mary felt a wave of sadness. *How did it all go so wrong?*

'I mean, it's not like it's your fault, what he did or the choices he made later. He chose to hang with Ritchie and his hoods, who were in and out of juvy. He chose Trish, too, but they were never happy, at least they never seemed happy.' Rosaria sighed. 'Then the drinking got worse. I think his life didn't turn out the way he thought it would.'

Mary let her gaze run over the lush green

grass and the shifting splotches of light that filtered through the leaves of the tall trees. An older man drove on a riding mower, its green-and-yellow John Deere gleaming like new. She wished it had all been different, or at least part of it.

'But that's in the past. It doesn't matter now.'

How wrong you are.

'The fact is, my uncle's toxic, that's what my therapist says, and so is my cousin.'

Mary came out of her reverie, her heart heavy. She had to get back to the city. She didn't have time for the guilt, for the second-guessing, for the woulda coulda shoulda.

'You okay?'

'I think so.' Mary straightened up and slipped her heels back on. 'So he sold drugs around Ninth and Kennick. Anything else you can tell me?'

'No. That's all. I have no idea where he could be now, or what he's thinking, taking Trish. You know, I used to try to talk to him, but he said he knew what he was doing.' Rosaria paused. 'Oh, wait a minute.'

'What?'

'He might have a place, somewhere.'

'What do you mean?'

'I used to tell him I was afraid for him, getting in with the boys, but one time, he said not to worry.' Rosaria frowned in thought. 'That he had a place to go, to get lost, when he finally got out.'

'Like a second house?' Mary asked, puzzled.

'I don't know.'

Mary thought of the diary. There had been no

169

mention of a second house.

'He said it, just once, and I wasn't sure he was telling the truth. I told him, you can't quit, they don't let you quit. And he said, you can quit if they can't find you.'

Mary's heartbeat quickened. 'That could be where he took Trish.'

Rosaria nodded. 'It could.'

'So where could it be?'

'I don't know.'

Mary thought a minute. 'It would have to be out of the city. Away.'

'That's possible.'

Mary felt on edge. 'You have no idea where he could have been talking about? This is important.'

'Sorry. I'd like to help, but I can't.'

'How could he buy another house? Could he afford it?' Then Mary realized. Maybe that's why he'd been skimming profits from the drug sales. She knew herself how hard it was to make a down payment. Still, where was the house? 'Did he have any hobbies, so he'd buy a house with that in mind?'

'Hobbies?' Rosaria looked at Mary like she was crazy.

'Did he fish? Hunt?'

'Are you kidding?' Rosaria laughed, but Mary didn't. She wracked her brain.

'Did he like the ocean? Would he buy in Jersey?'

'It's expensive.'

'Was there any place he talked about? A place he considered a refuge?'

170

Rosaria snorted. 'Who has a place like that?'

'I do.' Mary thought about it. 'Church.'

Rosaria stopped laughing, then looked away. 'Not that I know of.'

'Any place you went as children, that he would go back to?'

'No, not that I remember.'

'How about in summers?'

'No.' Rosaria moved back her hair with her hand.

'Where did you go on vacation? Like, we went to Atlantic City.'

'We weren't a family-vacation kind of family.'

Mary tried a new tack. 'Do you know the names of any of the guys he knew, in the Mob?'

'Only my cousin.'

Mary thought about the name in the diary. 'Does Cadillac ring a bell?'

'No. I didn't know a Cadillac. I didn't wanna know.'

'How about your father? Is he connected, too?'

'My uncle, no, but my cousin is. He is the one that got my brother involved.'

'Anybody else?' Mary was trying everything. She wouldn't get another chance. 'So he had nobody he trusted enough to tell about the house?'

'No, not that I knew.'

'Everybody trusts somebody.'

'Me. He trusted me.' Rosaria looked at her, eyes flinty. 'Honestly, I don't know anyone else he trusted. I never heard him talk about any friends. I guess he kept the house a big secret. He'd have to.'

Whoa. It struck a chord. Maybe the house was

the secret he was going to tell Trish about, on the night of her birthday. The fact that she didn't mention it in the diary suggested she hadn't known about it.

'That's all I know, sorry.'

'Thanks. If anything else occurs to you, will you call me?' Mary extracted a business card from her wallet and handed it to her.

'Sure, thanks.' Rosaria slipped it into her pocket, and the little dog jumped around, excited to be back on the move.

'Thanks for the help. It was great seeing you again.'

'You, too.' Rosaria stood up. 'Take care.'

'You, too.' Mary rose, gave her a brief hug, and turned to go.

'Mare? One last thing.'

'Yes?' Mary turned, and Rosaria's expression was pained.

'I don't want to know about it, if he kills her.'

'I hear that.' Mary turned away and hurried back to the car.

★ ★ ★

Back in the car, Mary checked the clock 2:25. She had to do something with the information about Ninth & Kennick. She considered calling Giulia, but she couldn't trust her not to blab the information and that wouldn't do any good, anyway. When traffic slowed, she reached for her phone and plugged in Brinkley's cell number, reading the pen marks still faint on her hand. The call connected with his voicemail, and she left a complete message, telling him about Ninth & Kennick. Still she felt vaguely unsatisfied.

She called information, asked for the Missing Persons department, and the call connected. 'Hello, I'm calling about the abduction of Trish Gambone. I may have information as to their whereabouts. With whom should I speak?'

'Hold, please,' a man answered, and the call went *click*, then came back on. 'Sorry, is this a tip about the Amber Alert? We're fielding calls in that case.'

'No, this is a woman, an adult. She was on the TV news last night.'

'Oh, is this the case that they had in Homicide?'

'Yes.'

'We have it logged in here. Who did you say you are?'

Mary told him, spelling her name and giving her cell number, against the background noise of ringing phones.

'Give me your information. I have to get these other calls. The Amber Alerts are just a monster.'

Mary sighed. The car moved an inch. She told him everything she knew and hung up, feeling assured of nothing. The BlackBerry rang again before she could even set it down, and she checked the display before she answered. It was Amrita, returning her call.

Yay! Mary could give her the good news about Dhiren's upcoming appointment. She pressed the green button. 'Amrita?' she said, excited until she found out what had happened to Dhiren.

Then, the good news didn't matter anymore.

20

Mary fought traffic for two hours to reach Children's Hospital of Philadelphia. She parked on the street and hurried down the hospital corridor, its tile floors gleaming. A male nurse walked past in blue scrubs, a plastic daisy attached to the stethoscope that lay doubled around his neck. At the end of the corridor, she could see two older women standing outside the door to the room, and when she got closer, she recognized Elvira Rotunno, Anthony's mother, in her old-school housedress and black plastic slip-ons, with another older woman.

'How is he?' Mary asked, walking up, and they both turned.

'Good as he can be.' Elvira managed a shaky smile. 'It's nice you came, Mare. Rita's calm now, but she was a mess.'

'I can imagine.' Mary turned and introduced herself to the other woman, whose hooded eyes and lined expression were disapproving behind her oversized plastic eyeglasses.

'Sue Ciorletti,' the woman said, barely getting the words out before her mouth snapped back to its previous tightness, like a rubber band returning to shape. She seemed too cranky to wear a pink sweatsuit that read COOL GRANDMA.

Elvira continued, 'Sue and me were talkin' to Rita when the school called, and Sue gave her a

174

ride here 'cause we didn't want her drivin' so upset. Amrita's in there with the doctors now.' Elvira gestured at the closed door behind them, with a gnarled hand. 'She's been in there for a long time. Fifteen minutes, maybe twenty, right, Sue?'

Mrs. Ciorletti didn't answer, maintaining her silence, and Mary assumed it was another neighbor who hated her.

'You okay, Mrs. Ciorletti?'

Elvira answered, 'Sue don't like hospitals because you could get an infection. Even if you're just vistin'. She heard a report on the TV news.'

'I see,' Mary said. 'Mrs. Ciorletti, you don't have to stay if you don't want to. I have a car and I'll take Elvira home.'

'I'll stay,' Mrs. Ciorletti answered. The door opened as if on cue, and the women watched as two young male doctors came out, led by an attractive woman doctor with an authoritative air, Dr. Sharon Satterfield, according to the red script embroidered on her white jacket. Three young male interns followed her, with weary faces and professional smiles.

Amrita came out behind them, her eyebrows a crestfallen slope, her large eyes somber, and her mouth a line. She shook the woman doctor's hand. 'Thanks, Dr. Satterfield. I appreciate all you're doing for Dhiren.'

'We'll get back to you when we have the results.' The doctor left, trailing interns.

Amrita sighed, then collected herself. 'Mary, how kind of you to come.'

Mary gave her a big hug. 'Sorry it took so long. How is he?'

'He's fine, and they think he'll be fully recovered in a month.'

'A month?' Mary groaned, but Amrita shook her head.

'No, that's good. When they first called me, I was terrified.' She didn't elaborate, and her dark eyes betrayed little emotion. But Elvira misted up with enough emotion for both of them, in addition to much of the eastern seaboard.

'We all thought Dhiren was gonna die,' Elvira blurted out, and Mary slid an arm around her.

'It's okay now.'

Mrs. Ciorletti's lips stretched tight, under control. 'Be strong, El. We're here for Rita, remember?'

'Yeah, I know, I'm sorry.' Elvira bit her lip not to cry.

Mary asked, 'Amrita, can I see him?'

'Sure, come in. He's asleep, still under sedation.' Amrita went back inside the hospital room, then stood aside to let Mary enter. She tried not to gasp at the sight.

The little boy looked so small, and his skin was dark against the sheets and thin white blankets. His head was bandaged, his black hair rumpled, and his left cheek was purplish and swollen. His left arm was propped up and away from his body in a cast, and the large lump under the sheets suggested that there was a cast on the leg as well.

'Thank God, he's alive.' Amrita went over to Dhiren's bed and touched the playground-dirty

176

fingers that curved out of the sleeve of his cast. She stroked his hand, though he didn't move. He was completely asleep, his head to the side. His bed sat on the left side of the room, on the same side as a sink, a small white counter, and a cork bulletin board with a crayoned drawing left behind. The other bed was empty, and the divider curtain, covered with happy giraffes and laughing cartoon tigers, drawn halfway back. A TV was mounted high in the corner, its screen black, and a largish monitor protruded from metal brackets on the wall, above an array of high-tech gauges and greenish tubes that led to Dhiren.

'So he's gonna be okay,' Mary said, confirming it for herself. 'When will be wake up?'

'The doctor said it would take a couple of hours for him to come around completely.' Amrita checked an institutional clock on the wall. 'Barton should be here any minute.'

'Amrita, how did it happen, exactly?'

'At recess, they told me. You know how the morning went. I sent him anyway. The boys were restless in class. But I left, right before recess.' Amrita shook her head. 'Right before it happened. I feel so terrible.'

'It's not your fault.'

'No?' Amrita looked up sharply, her lips tight. 'If I had been there, it wouldn't have happened.'

'You can't be there all the time. No parent can. And two can play that game. If I had gotten him some help sooner, I could have prevented this.'

'Not at all. You did what you could. The school

177

did not. The school let him down.'

Mary didn't agree. It was her job to make the school do right by Dhiren, and she hadn't fought hard enough. She had only lucked out in getting him the appointment, and even that was too little, too late. But right now, it was about Dhiren. 'You were telling me how it happened.'

'His teacher told me it started in the schoolyard. They were mocking him, and he ran away, so they gave chase. Usually he goes to the teacher, that's what I tell him to do, but this time he ran into the street.' Amrita paused, but remained in control. 'He wasn't looking, and then the car came around the corner and hit him.'

Mary shuddered. 'How awful.'

'The impact was on his left side.' Amrita gestured at her own body. 'Luckily, his head wasn't injured too badly, just some cuts and a concussion. That was their main concern, as it was mine. His leg and arm are broken, and a few ribs. But those bones can mend.'

'He must have been in so much pain.'

'Yes,' Amrita winced. 'The car was driven by a mother of a boy in the school, one of the older children, a sixth-grader. She even came to the hospital, very upset. She blames herself, but Dhiren darted in front of her. She was going under the limit because she was dropping off her child, after a dentist's appointment. If she hadn't been, Dhiren's injuries would've been far worse.'

Mary marveled at Amrita's grace. Her own mother would have beaten the driver senseless with a wooden spoon.

'But I am so furious, Mary. I played by their rules. For weeks they told me I was crazy, that he was fine. Then they told me he is simply naughty, that boys will be boys.' Amrita frowned deeply. 'Then I hired you, and we continued to play by the rules. All of this good behavior has gotten my son in the hospital.'

'I know,' Mary said, saddened.

'It's a miracle he's still alive. It's sheer luck she wasn't going faster or that it wasn't a bus that hit him.' Amrita's tone hardened to steel. 'I cannot send him back to that school. He will not go back to that school.'

Suddenly the door opened, and a tall, scruffy blond man in a white shirt and maroon windbreaker burst into the room. He looked at the bed, and his blown eyes widened with alarm and anger.

'Barton, you're here!' Amrita said, moving toward him, her arms outstretched, but her husband hugged her only briefly, his gaze fixed over her head, on Dhiren.

'My God!' he said. 'What have they done to him?'

'He's going to be fine, Barton.' Amrita released him and gave him a calm rundown of their son's injuries, but Mary could see he was barely listening. He crossed to the bed.

'This is outrageous. He could have been killed.' Barton snapped his head up, his eyes flashing. 'They permitted him to be bullied for years. They did nothing.'

'I know, Barton,' Amrita said, her voice soothing. She gestured at Mary and introduced

179

her. 'This is our lawyer. She's been helping to get him tested. She even got him an appointment for tomorrow.'

'Fat lot of good it will do him now.'

'Barton, please. Mary is on our side.'

'Then she'll understand my frustration with the bloody school district that doesn't give a damn about a child who needs extra help.' Barton turned on Mary, his lips taut with emotion. 'If you're our lawyer, I want you to sue them. This is negligence. They permitted this to happen. They're on notice, yet they permit it. He could be *dead*.'

'I know, I understand,' Mary said, but she could see she wasn't reaching him. The anxiety he had about Dhiren's condition was being channeled into anger.

'And the driver, she should be sued, too. I want them both joined in the suit. Is that possible?'

Amrita interjected, 'Barton, we know the driver. It's Suk Yun, one of the other mothers. She's very sorry.'

'Oh, she's *sorry*? She's *sorry* for putting our boy in the hospital? She's sorry she almost killed him. She should have been watching.'

'She was, dear. She's a lovely woman. She was driving very slowly — '

'Amrita!' Barton threw up his hands. 'Why are you making excuses for this woman? She could have killed our son. You expect so little of people, that's why you get so little. What are you thinking? What?'

Mary sensed she shouldn't be here, in this

180

private time, and moved to the door. 'I'll let you two talk. Call me on the cell, if you need me.'

Amrita said stiffly, 'Thank you for coming, Mary.'

'Yes, thanks,' Barton called after her, and Mary let herself out without looking back. She closed the door behind her and when she heard the shouting resume, she stepped away. Elvira was sitting in the patterned chair against the wall, a forlorn figure, her gray head bent.

'I met Barton.' Mary went over and sat down beside her, suddenly exhausted, and Elvira made a funny face, her glasses popping off the bridge of her nose.

'I don't like him,' she said. 'He's a jerk.'

'He's just upset.'

'Nah, he's always like that. Bossy. He leaves Rita alone all the time and when he comes home, all he does is gripe.'

'Where's Mrs. Ciorletti?'

'She left a while ago. I wanted to stay and make sure Rita was okay.'

'You take good care of her, Elvira.'

'She's my neighbor.'

Mary smiled, touched. 'I think she's fine now. Can I take you home?'

'Nah, you don't hafta.' Elvira waved her off. 'I called my Ant'n'y, from the nurses' phone.' She gestured at the desk down the hall. 'He'll be here.' .

Uh-oh. 'I could have taken you.'

'I didn't know if you were gonna stay or not, and he likes to help me.' Elvira patted Mary's leg. 'When you get to be a mother, I wish for you a son as good as my Ant'n'y, even though he plays for the other team.'

Mary suppressed her smile. 'He doesn't seem gay to me.'

'A mother knows these things, and you know what? I love my son. Like we were sayin' the other day, there's Hindus and there's gays in this world. It's all mixed up nowadays, and you know what? The sun still comes up.' Elvira leaned forward and looked down the hall. 'Shhh, here he comes.'

Mary helped Elvira up and caught Anthony's eye as he bustled down the hall, concerned. She had to admit that he was a great-looking man, and a nurse at the station peeked over the top of the high counter as he strode by, his tan jacket open. He had on long, slim jeans and shiny loafers, and Mary couldn't help but smile at him.

'Look at these two beautiful women,' Anthony said, giving his mother a quick kiss on the cheek, and then Mary, too, which he pulled off before she could react one way or the other.

'Sorry I didn't call you back,' she said. 'I was so busy today.'

'That's okay.' Anthony grinned, and if he was hurt, it didn't show. Then his face changed. 'How's Dhiren?'

'Okay,' Mary said, as Elvira grabbed Anthony by the coat sleeve and pulled him close to her.

'That jerk's in there, with Rita,' she stage-whispered.

'Shall we go, ladies?' Anthony looped his arm through his mother's, turned her around, and got her going down the hall. Mary fell into place

182

beside them, and Anthony looked over. 'Mary, if you didn't know yet, my mother is a woman with very definite likes and dislikes. There's no middle ground. Gray is the new black and white.'

'That's not true.' Elvira smiled.

'Oh yeah?' Anthony asked, 'What do you think of Celine Dion?'

'She's a great singer.'

'What about Barbra Streisand?'

'She's a commie.'

Mary laughed, relaxing, and the three of them walked down the hall, making surprisingly easy small talk until they got outside the hospital. It was early evening, an indigo wash darkening the sky from top to bottom, with a full moon rising. Yellow lights glowed inside the hotel across the way, and the round, orange-tiled roof of the University Museum caught the streetlamps, a bit of old Florence in West Philly.

'Where'd you park, Mary?' Anthony asked, but she was already frowning at the spot where her car had been, on 34th Street. An empty space sat where she had parked, unwelcome as a missing front tooth. 'There. But it's gone.'

'Under the No Parking sign?' Anthony pointed, and Elvira clucked.

'I wouldn't do that, Mare. They'll tow ya, around here.'

'I didn't realize it.' Mary groaned. She'd been in such a rush when she'd arrived at the hospital. No wonder she'd gotten such a great parking space.

'I know where the impound lot is.' Anthony touched her shoulder. 'Let me take you. Wait

183

here with my mother, and I'll go get the car. Be right back.'

'Thanks.' Mary threw an arm around Elvira as he left, then thought of Brinkley and Missing Persons. Her cell phone had been turned off in the hospital. But somebody should have called back. 'Excuse me, Elvira. You mind if I take a second to check my calls?'

'Nah, go head. Ant does the same thing, alla time.' She waved a hand, and Mary went into her purse for her phone. The screen said she'd missed a call. She pressed the button to return the call, and it was Brinkley who answered.

'Mary?' he said, when he heard her voice. 'We found a body.'

21

Mary sat, numb, in the backseat of the Prius, having taken the news like a physical blow. She couldn't breathe a word of what Brinkley had told her to Anthony or his mother, because it wasn't public knowledge. Luckily, the car radio was off, and the only sound was the familiar cadence of the back and forth between the two, who talked in the front seat, oblivious to what had taken place only ten blocks away.

Mary struggled to keep her composure, only half listening.

'How about Judy Garland?' Anthony was saying.

'Now *she* was a star, a real star. But Sue hates her, too.'

'Mrs. Ciorletti hates Judy?' Anthony scoffed. 'Why am I not surprised?'

'Sue's grumpy, but that's just her way.'

'It's called depression, Ma.'

'Nah. She just don't like things, or people. Like Mary here. Sue don't like her at all.'

'Ma!' Anthony said, embarrassed.

Mary's ears pricked up. 'Why not?' she asked, not that she really cared. Before Brinkley's call, she'd cared.

'There's a lotta talk about you, Mare, and it's not very nice.'

'Ma, please,' Anthony said, looking over.

'Don't be so fresh and don't make that

185

shut-up face. Mary knows I love her.' Elvira twisted around to the backseat, her coarse gray hair making a frizzy halo, backlit from a streetlight. 'People are sayin' that you forgot where you're from, you know what I mean? It started all of a sudden, with Trish Gambone, because her mother told everybody that you wouldn't help her and then it's on the TV. They're blamin' you for what happened to her.'

Mary felt sick. She could only imagine what they'd say when they knew what had happened tonight.

'Then the other day, you stood Roberto up.'

'Roberto Nunez? You know him?'

'I don't, but my camarr Linda does. She knows his son who used to buy life insurance offa her brother-in-law from St. Monica's.'

Mary didn't bother to follow it. Her head was starting to pound.

'I heard that you didn't go to his case, or his trial, or whatever it was. You were too busy. You told him it wasn't worth your time. You sent your secretary instead.'

Mary closed her eyes. It was like playing telephone.

'It's like you're gettin' a bad rep, and it's gonna get worse, with Dhiren.'

'*Dhiren?* What about Dhiren?' Mary asked, bewildered.

Anthony shook his head as the car cruised along, entering South Philly. 'I told you this was a bad idea,' he said, hitting the gas.

Elvira harrumphed. 'Don't get me wrong, Mare. I stick up for you. But you didn't get

186

Dhiren outta that school, and now he's up in the hospital. People will say you don't care about the old neighborhood no more. That's what Sue thinks. You're Center City now.'

'It's only ten blocks north, Elvira, and she's wrong. They all are.'

'I know, that's what I tell em. You and Celine Dion, I always fight for.'

'Okay, Ma, say good night.' Anthony stopped the car in front of the Rotunno house and after Mary had kissed Elvira goodbye, he got out to walk her up the steps. When he got back in the car, he asked Mary to come up front, and she took the passenger seat, stiffly. Anthony looked over, his smile warm in the darkness. 'Please forgive her.'

'It's okay.'

'Now I see what you meant at dinner the other night, about the neighborhood. Maybe I was too glib.' Anthony cocked his head. 'You wanna get a coffee? Or go straight to the impound lot? Up to you.'

'Unfortunately, neither.' Mary tried to stay in control. She hardly knew him and she didn't want to lose it now. 'Can you take me somewhere else?'

'Sure, why?'

Mary gave him the address. 'There's been a murder.'

* * *

This section of the city was normally deserted after dark, but tonight it was alive with activity.

The full moon was a bullethole in a black sky, and people filled the street. Anthony double-parked down the block, but almost before he braked, Mary was in motion, opening the car door, grabbing her bag, and climbing out onto the sidewalk. 'Thanks,' she called out. 'I'll get my own ride home.'

'I'm coming with you.' Anthony unclipped his safety harness and got out of the car.

Mary hurried heedless into the crowd. People stood smoking and talking on the sidewalks, swigging beer from a can or watching the scene at the end of the street, their arms folded over their paunches. She threaded her way through them, toward where police cruisers had been parked and wooden barricades had been erected. She got to the uniformed cops behind the sawhorses and picked one, his face shadowed by the black patent bill of his cap, then went up to him.

'I'm a lawyer and I got a call from Mack Brinkley, and he told me to come down here right away.' Mary ducked under the barricade, and Anthony followed, until the cop grabbed him by the elbow.

'Wait a sec, sir.'

'Let him go, he's with me.' Mary dug for her wallet and flashed her bar admission card, and the cop waved Anthony ahead, and he kept going.

'Thanks,' Anthony said, on her heels, and they passed groups of uniformed cops talking in tight circles, silhouetted in the headlights from the cruisers. Up ahead, she spotted the calcium white of klieg-lights and headed straight for them.

Ahead had to be where they'd found the body.

Mary screened out the noise and the curious stares and reached the TV lights, like electrified trees on their aluminum stands, with black cables that stretched like roots to boxy generators. The press was kept at bay behind the barricades, but they had cameras and lights, too, and she picked up the pace as she went toward the light, past the brick rowhouses, decrepit in this part of South Philly. On the right, next to a house with a sagging front porch, a tall, boxy white truck was parked, its side reading CRIME SCENE UNIT in reflective blue letters. The truck sat near the mouth of an alley, and Mary remembered Brinkley saying that the body had been dumped in the back of an alley.

'Almost there,' Mary heard herself say, her heart racing.

'Right behind you,' Anthony said, thinking she was talking to him, but she wasn't. There was noise and talking around them but she didn't hear it. She heard only her own heartbeat and the echo of Brinkley's voice:

I have bad news. We got a body.

Mary felt her mouth go dry when she spied Brinkley, slim and well dressed, talking with a crowd of men in suits and loosened ties, undoubtedly from the DA's office. He stood with his partner, Stan Kovich, big, brawny, and gray-blond, whom she remembered as open and friendly as Brinkley was reserved and self-contained. She made a beeline for them, giving a discreet wave to catch their attention, in case they didn't want to acknowledge her in front of the suits.

Kovich bent his head over some notes, and Brinkley spotted her first, then broke from the group to meet her. A gleaming black van stood on her right, its white MEDICAL EXAMINER'S OFFICE letters shiny in the lights, more reflective paint. The two back doors of the van hung open. It meant the gurney was out, pressed into service for the body.

Mary had gotten here as fast as she could and she guessed they would be finishing up about now. The reporters swelled toward the barricades, sensing it, too. They held cameras high over their heads, trying to get the 'bag shot.' Mary had been to some crime scenes, but not like this. Not where she knew the body.

'Mare, how you doin',' Brinkley said quietly, reaching her. 'Sorry we didn't get there sooner. We could've prevented this.'

'You tried. We all did.' Mary forced herself to say it, but she knew she should have tried harder.

'You sure you can handle it? I thought you should know.'

'Sure.' Mary glanced over, distracted. More lamps had been set up inside the alley, flooding it with light. Men in ties and coroner's assistants in dark blue jumpsuits crammed the alley, and others working at its mouth made shifting shadows, blocking Mary's view of what lay beyond.

'Who's this?' Brinkley meant Anthony, coming up next to her. 'He with you?'

'Yes,' Mary answered quickly, and while Anthony introduced himself, she kept her gaze on the alley. She caught a glimpse of a crumbling brick side wall, and when somebody in front of her moved aside, she could see that the wall was behind an overflowing trashcan. Strobes fired from a still camera, taking photographs, and there was the sound of men talking and counting off. She sensed the coroner was closing up for good, his assistants slipping the body on top of the black vinyl bag, then doing their practiced pitch-and-roll to bag the corpse with efficiency and a modicum of dignity.

Mary did and didn't want to go into the alley. She had to see, yet she didn't want to see, and in the next instant, before she realized it, she had pushed her way to its mouth as if she belonged there. Brinkley called to her from some faraway place, then Anthony, too, but she ignored them both to see. When the way cleared, she looked down at the sight.

He looked exactly the same, except that his skin was now as gray as marble, and he lay in the black body bag, which was half zippered up. His blue eyes were open, staring sightlessly at the black sky. His head lay slightly to the side, and his bangs lay fanned across his forehead, just like they always did, soft and brown. She flashed on him raking his hair back with his fingers at the kitchen table. It was so hard to believe that those hands had pummeled a woman, but Mary had seen the pictures herself. Now the coroner's assistants were tucking those same hands, each bagged in transparent plastic to preserve evidence, inside the black body bag and zipping it closed.

'He took a bullet to the back of the head,' Brinkley told her in low tones. 'We think it's a Mob hit, and so do the feds. I told them about the skimming.'

How did it all go so wrong? How did he turn up dead? And where was Trish?

'Mare?' Brinkley put a hand on her shoulder just as the assistants zipped up the body bag.

A shadow blocked Mary's view, but it didn't matter. The image had been seared into her brain. She would always see him lying there. In the next second, she became aware that Brinkley was looking at her funny.

'Mare? You losin' it here?'

'No, of course not,' she answered, but it didn't ring true, even to her. 'I'm just confused. When you told me you had a body, I couldn't believe it was him who got killed. It's Trish I was worried about.'

'So where'd you get the tip on the location?'

'The sister, in Jersey.'

'Fill me in later, will you.'

'Sure. Did I redeem you?'

'More or less. Thanks.' Brinkley half-smiled.

'Good.' Mary felt some satisfaction, if only for that reason. The body had been discovered by a uniformed cop, sent there by her tip about Ninth & Kennick. It was why Brinkley had called her when they found the body, and he had sounded grateful. Mary felt herself recovering from the shock, trying to understand. 'So where's Trish? I mean, now that he's dead?'

'I'm not gonna speculate.'

'But what do you think? He turns up dead, so is she still alive? That's possible, right?'

'Mare, I can't speculate. It's all what-if.'

'Reg, it's me. Just tell me what you think.'

'Okay, fine.' Brinkley lowered his voice. 'You have to prepare yourself for all the possibilities.'

Mary felt her knees weaken and prayed she could keep it together, especially in front of all these people.

Brinkley was asking, 'You sent that diary to Missing Persons, like I asked?'

'Sure.' Mary forced herself to think clearly. 'I had it hand delivered to them today.'

'Good, I'll get it. Anything else I should know?'

'A mob guy named Cadillac, who suspected he was skimming.'

'Cadillac?' Brinkley pulled a thin steno notebook from his back pocket and a ballpoint from his inside pocket.

'Yes. Does that name mean anything to you?'

'No.' Brinkley made a note. 'That's in the diary, too?'

'Yes. Trish was worried about him.' Mary tucked her emotions away. She had to help. If Trish was still alive, maybe it could help find her. 'His sister told me he had a house somewhere. She doesn't know where, they're estranged. He wanted a place he could get lost to.'

'What's her name again?'

Mary answered him, then asked, 'When was he killed?'

'We think late last night. That's unofficial, you

193

know that. We found Trish's cell phone on him, and it has the call she made to her mother, at seven thirteen. There's no other calls after that.'

'He had her cell?' Mary tried to wrap her mind around it. It couldn't be good. The thought made her sick. 'Did you find his car? It's a black BMW. New.'

'We don't have the car.'

'It's gotta be parked here somewhere. They left in it. The neighbor saw them. Unless it's back at home.'

'We'll check on it.' Brinkley made a note.

From the alley came the clinking sound of the gurney being erected, metal hitting metal, bearing the body.

Brinkley was saying, 'I did the notification and I also called the mother, Mrs. Gambone. She was pretty upset. Your friend was with her, the one on TV.'

'Giulia.'

Brinkley put a hand on Mary's shoulder. 'The M.E. agreed to do the autopsy as soon as possible. The body could have evidence of where she is, and one way or the other, we'll find her. Don't worry.'

Suddenly there came shouting from beyond the barricades and they looked over. A fight was breaking out in the mob, the crowd pushing and pulling. Policemen hurried from all directions toward the spot, and Mary craned her neck to see. The crowd surged toward the barricades, and the TV lights swung around and spotlighted the chaos.

'Stay here!' Brinkley took off, hustling toward the fracas.

But when Mary saw what the problem was, she knew it could take more than the Philadelphia Police Department.

22

Ritchie Po exploded through the crowd toward the barricades. Men flanked him, running interference, though cops tried to stop them, pulling them back. People shouted, and there was a panicky scream as cops brandished pepper spray. Ritchie thrashed this way and that, throwing punches. Brinkley reached the barricades and signaled to other cops to help. A metal stalk of lights toppled over, scattering onlookers and crashing to the street. People started yelling, and in the melee, reporters got shoved aside and the rowdy crowd took up for Po, hollering at the police.

'What a mess!' Anthony said, almost drowned out by the din.

'Stand aside, people!' came a shout from behind, and Mary realized that she and Anthony were sandwiched between the alley and the shouting crowd. They sidestepped out of the way, and crime techs, startled at the sudden violence, scooted from the alley. The coroner's assistants bent over and rolled the metal gurney with the black vinyl bag, rushing it bumping on the street.

Ritchie and his friends charged the barricades, and in front of him, the press struggled to catch the bag shot as the coroner's assistants collapsed the wheels of the gurney and hoisted it into the van.

'I wanna see my brother!' he was screaming. 'Get outta my way! Lemme see my brother!'

'Hurry!' The coroner's assistants shoved the gurney into the van and darted to safety as the crowd rolled toward them, Ritchie in the lead.

Suddenly, reporters and cameramen were pushed forward from behind, the barricade toppled over, and a crowd of uniformed cops, Brinkley, Kovich, and Ritchie Po trampled the barricades and barreled ahead. 'Stop right there!' Brinkley yelled, reaching out as Ritchie, carrying cops with him, rushed the van.

Mary watched, stunned. The cops grabbed Ritchie and the men around him, finally tackling them to the street. The crowd booed and shouted, and above the din, she could hear Brinkley and the cops. Ritchie stopped scream-ing, and the shoving and pushing finally subsided, ending almost as quickly as it had begun.

Mary stood speechless, trying to process what she had seen. She felt a squeeze around her shoulder and looked over, realizing that some-how she and Anthony had ended up at the edge of the crowd, out of harm's way.

'Jeez, this is incredible.' Anthony looked down at Mary with a bewildered smile. 'Is your life always like this?'

She couldn't share the joke. Someone in the restless crowd had caught her eye. There, at the edge of the white light, stood Mr. Po, in a tan windbreaker and baggy pants. He rested a gnarled hand on a remaining sawhorse, and he was looking toward the black van. Wisps of his flyaway gray hair blew in the night air, and the ragged edge of light fell on the sunken planes of his face, reducing his eyes to black slits.

Mary was struck by a single thought: *He's not half as upset as he should be.*

* ★ ★ ★

Later, Mary and Anthony followed Brinkley and Kovich down to the Roundhouse, where they were taking Ritchie Po and his father for questioning. She was dying to watch Ritchie's interview, But unlike TV and movies, there were no two-way mirrors in Homicide. Instead, Mary, Anthony, and two FBI types, Special Agents Jimmy Kiesling and Marc Robert Steinberg, found themselves thrown together in another interview room, sitting in their mismatched chairs with cooling cups of terrible coffee. The agents were undoubtedly wondering why two civilians were getting so much respect, and Mary could feel how much they wanted to be in on the Po interview. The feds didn't like to sit at the kiddie table.

'Michael Chiklis,' one of the agents said abruptly, looking from his newspaper. He was Steinberg, the quieter and older of the two, with a cute gray mustache, chubby cheeks, and ruddy skin. He'd pushed his wire-rimmed glasses on top of his head, which made his coarse salt-and-pepper hair stand up like a boar-bristle brush.

'What?' Kiesling asked, looking over with an amused frown.

'Remember I was saying that Po looks like somebody? The guy's name just came to me. Michael Chiklis. The bald guy in *The Shield*.'

'I don't watch *The Shield*.'

'It's almost as good as *Barney Miller*.'

'So you say, Dad.' Kiesling almost smiled. He was in his forties, with a pointy chin and his skin stretched tight over gaunt cheekbones. His eyes were small and brown, and his dark hair thinning. He'd mentioned that he ran marathons, but to Mary, he looked like he could use a nice cannoli.

She asked, 'So, do you two deal with organized crime?'

'We're on the Task Force.' Kiesling cocked his head. 'What do you know about the case?'

'Kind of a lot.'

'Anything that could help us? Why don't we compare notes?'

'Good idea.' Mary realized they should know what she'd told Brinkley. She wasn't about to play jurisdictional games, not after tonight's murder. 'Here's what I know that you might not: Trish Gambone thought that her boyfriend was skimming profits on his drug sales.'

'How do you know?' Kiesling asked.

'She told me, and it's in her diary.' Mary filled him in on all the details, and his expression changed. 'There's a mobster named Cadillac, who also suspected he was skimming.'

Kiesling shifted forward on his seat, and Mary caught a glint of recognition in his eyes. Steinberg eyed her over the top of his newspaper.

'Do you guys know who Cadillac is?' she asked.

'I can't really discuss that,' Kiesling answered.

'I'll keep it confidential. Who's Cadillac?'

'Sorry, I can't.'

'Listen, I'm a lawyer, representing Trish. I have a right to information that could lead to her whereabouts.'

'I wish I could tell you but I can't.'

'You said we could compare notes. I told *you* what I knew.' Mary knew it sounded lame. 'My client's out there somewhere, and I'd like to know where she is.' She couldn't bring herself to say, *or if she's dead or alive.*

'They'll find her, don't worry.' Anthony put a hand on Mary's arm, but it didn't comfort her, or shut her up.

'Are you thinking that the killer could be someone else in the Mob? Like a competitor who wanted his corner, to sell drugs.'

'Anything is possible.' Kiesling clamped his mouth shut, and Mary simmered like her mother's gravy.

'It would depend on who he sold drugs for, wouldn't it? Do you know who he sold drugs for in the Mob?'

'We can't discuss that with you.'

'I know he hung at Biannetti's. He was there all the time.'

'What makes you say that?' Kiesling cocked his neat head.

'I read it in Trish's diary. Do you know about Biannetti's?'

'I'm not going to discuss that.'

'Fine, I get it. It's a one-way street.' Mary's emotions bubbled over, which never happened with her mother's gravy. 'But here's what I *don't* get — if everybody knows the Mob hangs at Biannetti's, why don't you guys just go there and take them in for questioning? Why not take those thugs in one by one, and ask them if they know where Trish is?'

'It's not as simple as that, as you should know. You're a lawyer, correct?'

'As a lawyer, I don't understand it.' Mary couldn't help but raise her voice. 'I think you should go there and get to the bottom of this. A woman's life is on the line.'

Anthony interjected, 'Mary, I have a question, for you, as a lawyer. Ritchie Po and his father are being questioned about Trish's whereabouts. They don't have to cooperate, do they?'

'No, and they probably won't,' Mary answered, knowing that he was either trying to distract her or preempt her assault charge. 'Their lawyer's probably in there already, and he would've told them to shut up, even if they knew where she was.'

Steinberg lowered the newspaper. 'Don't kid yourself, they know where the girl is.'

'You think?' Mary asked, turning to him.

'Of course.'

'What makes you say that?'

'Don't be naive.'

Gulp. 'I admit it, I'm naive. Are you saying that's not how the Mob works?'

'No.'

'That's not how it works, or you're not saying that?'

Steinberg pursed his lips somewhere under his mustache. 'Look, in my opinion, they know where she is and they also know who left that body tonight. The brother, Ritchie, is a lousy actor.'

'I disagree,' Mary said, speaking from the heart. 'I think it was real. Ritchie was genuinely surprised that his brother was killed, but his father wasn't.'

Kiesling and Steinberg looked at her like she was too dumb to live.

Mary added, 'I saw Ritchie, and I heard him, and I know them, at least a little.'

'How do you know them?'

'From high school, and I'm from the neighborhood. To an extent, I'm of them. I know their people.'

'Their *people*?'

Anthony nodded, understanding.

'Forget it.' Mary couldn't explain the concept to the FBI agents, who her mother would have called '*Medigan*. Growing up, it took years until Mary realized that her mother was saying American, with an Italian accent. 'Let me ask you this, do you think there's a chance that Trish is alive?'

'We don't speculate about cases.'

'I'm asking in general, then. You're experts. Have you ever heard of situations in which someone is found alive, after their abductor is found dead?'

Kiesling answered, 'Usually, with adults,

kidnapping and false imprisonment happen for two reasons — ransom or sex. Obviously, ransom would be the motive in the Donchess kidnapping.' His tone lapsed into lecture mode, his expression official. 'With an adult, especially a female, we typically see a sex-slave situation.'

Mary scoffed. 'But that's not this case. Trish was his girlfriend.'

Kiesling lifted an eyebrow. 'I didn't think we were talking about this case. You asked in general.'

Oh.

'A friend of mine worked a case in Wisconsin where a neighbor kidnapped a teenage girl and held her in a basement.'

'Did they find her?'

'They did, and they prosecuted, too.'

Mary smiled, hopeful.

'She lived right next door.'

'Really? How long did it take to find her?'

'Two weeks.'

'Two weeks, and she was right next door?' Mary asked, aghast, but Kiesling was unfazed.

'More often, in the sex cases, they aren't found that quick. Take that case in Belgium, where the girl was held for ten years. She finally escaped.'

Steinberg looked up from the sports page. 'Natascha Kampusch. In Belgium, I believe it was. A man held a group of schoolgirls for over ten years. Marc Dutroux. If memory serves, two of the girls starved to death in the basement when Dutroux went to jail for car theft. Nobody knew they were there.'

Mary felt heartsick. That could happen here, and that was if Trish were still alive. Guilt, exhaustion, and grief washed over her, threatening to take her under. She needed a bathroom break and stood up. 'Excuse me, I'll be right back.'

Anthony met her eye with a sympathetic smile, but Mary felt too crappy to respond in kind. She crossed the small room and left, closing the door behind her.

She couldn't have timed it worse.

23

'What the *hell?*' somebody shouted, and Mary froze. It was Ritchie, standing with his father in the open doorway of the other interview room, his cheek bruised and black T-shirt torn from the melee. 'What're *you* doin' in there?' he bellowed.

'That's enough, Ritchie.' Brinkley strode from the interview room and put a strong hand on Ritchie's arm. Stan Kovich shot out, too, and another suit, while detectives hustled from the squad room to them, anticipating trouble. Only Mr. Po blinked calmly.

'Not here, big guy.' A stocky lawyer in an Italian suit hurried to Ritchie's side. 'We're outta here.'

'Not until she tells me what she's doin' here!' Ritchie stepped forward, but his lawyer and Brinkley restrained him.

Mary edged backward, trying to process what was happening. Ritchie wouldn't have known she was here. She and Anthony had arrived after they'd been taken in for questioning. Agents Kiesling and Steinberg came out of the interview room with Anthony.

'Mary, let's go,' he said, touching her arm.

'What's going on?' Kiesling asked, alarmed, and Steinberg stood protectively at Mary's side.

'You with *them* now, Mare?' Ritchie glowered. 'You were my brother's girlfriend. Now you're with the *feds?*'

Oh no. Mary felt exposed. Brinkley's head snapped around, his eyes narrowing, and she could read his expression. Betrayal. She didn't know what to say. She hadn't told him about her history, and he was blindsided. Kovich's lips formed an uncharacteristically tight line, his disappointment plain.

'Stay cool, big guy,' Ritchie's lawyer said. 'We're outta here.'

'Not yet.' Ritchie's eyes bored into her. 'Not until I understand what's goin' on.'

Brinkley gestured to Anthony. 'Get her out of here.'

Anthony grabbed Mary's arm. 'Let's go,' he said, and they hurried her from the squad room, to the sound of Ritchie shouting after her. She let herself be swept to the elevator, through the lobby, past the display cases and finally out the front door, where the press mobbed them with cameras, flashes, and questions.

'Ms. DiNunzio, what's your role in this?' 'Mary, do police say this is the start of a Mob war? Is the Merlino crime family involved?' Reporters surged forward out of the dark, shoving microphones in Mary's face, but she and Anthony hurried ahead, their heads down. 'Any comment on the disappearance of Patricia Gambone? Do the police have any leads?' 'Mary, Mary, look over here!' Videocameras whirred, and flashes fired from still cameras, bright and fleeting as lightning. 'Ms. DiNunzio, is there a suspect in the murder — '

Mary and Anthony broke into a light run to his car, and they jumped in. He started the

206

ignition instantly, gunned the engine, and zoomed out of the parking lot. They made the sharp left onto the Expressway entrance, and Anthony looked over.

'Let me take you home,' he said. 'We can get your car another time.'

'Okay, thanks.' Mary looked away, wondering what Anthony was thinking. She hadn't told him she knew the body in the black bag. He accelerated onto the Expressway, and Mary gripped the hand strap. Something to hold on to, when everything was falling apart.

She squeezed her eyes shut, trying to get the look on Brinkley's face out of her mind. He'd think she was a liar, playing games with him and the Homicide Division. Why hadn't she told him? The first time she'd seen him, she'd been with Giulia and she hadn't wanted Giulia to know. But why hadn't she mentioned it later?

The car streaked uptown in light traffic, barreling through the black night. The body bag flashed through her mind. The marble-gray of the flesh on his cheek. The blue of his eyes, frozen as ice. Could Trish be alive? The kidnapping cases that Kiesling and Steinberg had told her about were a gruesome sideshow. Dutroux. Girls dying while he was in jail.

'You okay?' Anthony asked gently, but she couldn't begin to answer. 'You hungry or anything?'

'No, I'm okay,' she answered finally. She spent the rest of the car ride facing out the window, watching the passing cars, red taillights, and drivers on cell phones, hiding her face from Anthony, and from herself. They reached her street in no time, and it was quiet and still, with most of the neighbors gone to sleep, the houses dark. A parking space was open near her front door, and Anthony pulled into it and turned to her.

'Thanks so much,' Mary said, making her door-handle move.

'I'd like to come in, if you wouldn't mind.' Anthony's voice sounded soft. 'I don't think you should be alone just yet.'

'I'm fine, thanks.' Mary retrieved her house keys and got out of the car, but so did Anthony, closing his door.

'At least let me walk you in.'

Mary went to the doorstop, dug her keys from the bottom of her purse, and looked up as Anthony appeared in front of her on the sidewalk. He had shoved his hands into the pockets of his sport jacket, and his dark eyes were concerned.

'Listen,' he said. 'Why don't you let me come in? I won't attack you or come on to you. I know you're not interested.'

Ouch. 'It's not that. It's that . . . I don't think I'd be great company tonight.'

'I don't mind. Let me come in for a bit. You could use a friend. A nice, safe, gay friend.'

Mary couldn't find a smile. She felt empty and numb. She couldn't believe what she'd seen tonight, and what it meant for Trish.

'Come on,' Anthony said softly, slipping the keys from her hand. 'Let's go inside.'

Mary entered her apartment, and Anthony followed, throwing the deadbolt and putting her keys on the side table. She'd grabbed the mail downstairs and set it on the coffee table, then shed her purse and jacket on a chair in the dark living room. On autopilot, she headed for the kitchen across the hardwood floor. She switched on the light and found herself going straight for the fridge.

'Can I get you anything?' she asked, surveying its contents. Two old tomatoes, a slim container of skim milk, and a plastic tub of mozzarella balls, which she knew would stink. She hadn't been food-shopping since her last confession.

'Come here.' Anthony took Mary's arm and gentled her into a kitchen chair. 'Please, sit. The doctor is in.'

'You're doing the honors?'

'Yes. You stay there and check your BlackBerry three hundred more times.'

'I'm not that bad.'

'Oh yes you are. You're more addicted than I am. We should enter rehab.'

'Hey, I left it in my purse.'

'Uh-oh, it won't like that.' Anthony slid out of his jacket, placed it around the chair opposite her, and rolled up the sleeves of a white shirt with a European fit, showing lean forearms. His waist was trim in a nice black belt, and his dark pants kept a perfect crease. He went to the fridge and opened the door. 'Sure you're not hungry?'

'Not at all.'

'Got wine?'

'In the cabinet.'

'Which one?' Anthony shut the door, turning, and when Mary pointed, he went to the cabinet and opened the door. 'Let's see, a can of white clam sauce, *ceci* beans, and four boxes of Barilla spaghetti, each half full. Here we go. A single bottle of merlot. You sot.'

'It was a gift.' Mary's head was still pounding.

'Corkscrew?' Anthony asked, and Mary pointed until he had located a corkscrew, two wineglasses, two napkins, and a wedge of hard locatelli that he shaved into fragile, thin slices and set on a salad plate with green olives. He smiled, holding the wineglasses crossed in one hand. 'Let's go in the living room. It'll be more comfortable. Come along.' He tucked the wine bottle under his arm, grabbed the corkscrew and the cheese plate, then led the way into the darkened living room, where he set the stuff on the coffee table.

Mary trundled behind, as if it weren't her own house. 'I'll turn on a light.'

'No. Let it be. It's better.'

'Leave it off?'

'Sure. It's not that dark. I can see.' Moonlight streamed through the front window, falling on Anthony's back, bringing out the whiteness of his shirt and making a ghostly circle of the rims of the wineglasses. He bent over and poured some wine, which made a sloshy sound when it hit the glass.

'Okay.' Mary sank onto the couch and kicked off her pumps.

'Drink up. Doctor's orders.'

'Thanks.' Mary took her first sip, which was delicious. She couldn't help feeling awful that she was home, drinking merlot, while Trish was missing, maybe dead.

'This is good wine.' Anthony sat in the soft chair catty-corner to her, the moon shining on the dark filaments of his hair. Shadows obscured his eyes, but not his smile, which was a little sad. After a minute, he said, 'I can't imagine how you're feeling.'

Mary took another sip of wine, the thin crystal warming under her fingers. 'That makes two of us.'

Anthony didn't laugh, which was good because she wasn't kidding. He leaned over and slid the cheese plate close to her. '*Mangia, bella.*'

Mary felt herself respond to his voice, soft and deep, or maybe the Italian, the language of her childhood. She broke off a piece of locatelli and nibbled it before it crumbled between her fingers. It tasted tart and perfect with the wine.

'You're exhausted.'

'You might be right.'

'I won't stay long.'

Mary looked out the window, and from her third-floor vantage point, she could see the lights of the other rowhouses, and beyond that, the Philly skyline, twinkling in the distance. She wondered if Trish was somewhere in the city, then thought of Mrs. Gambone. 'People are crying in the city tonight.'

'Yes. It's all very ugly and sad.'

'You're right. Well said.' Mary felt at such a

loss. She rubbed her face. She sipped her wine, then changed it to a gulp. 'I can't believe this all happened. That Trish is gone. That he's dead.' *He's dead.* 'It's awful.'

'I won't mind if I never see another crime scene. I think they'll find Trish, though.'

'Why? How do you know?'

'They learn so much from the body, like Detective Brinkley said. They'll find clues as to where she is.'

They're doing the autopsy right now. He's on a metal table.

'Brinkley seems pretty damn competent to me.'

'He is. Still it feels so selfish to be sitting here. I should be doing something.'

'You've done enough. You're the one who gave them the tip tonight. You helped them find the body sooner rather than later. As you said, that matters, in terms of finding Trish while she's still alive.'

'If she's still alive.' Mary heard herself say it out loud, for the first time, the wine loosening her tongue.

'She is. You have to have faith, and you did an amazing thing tonight, tipping them off.'

Mary couldn't hear it. 'That's not why I said it, for you to tell me how great I am. I know when I mess up and I messed this up to a fare-thee-well.'

'You can't feel responsible for what happens to Trish.'

'Let's not make this about me, okay?' Mary drank more wine, hoping to speed its effect.

'There's a woman missing, and she's who it's about. Not me.'

'Okay. Fair enough.'

Mary tried to get back in emotional control, glad of the darkness.

'Fine.' Anthony cocked his head, with a smile. 'Is this a fight?'

'No.'

'Good. In any event, I would worry if you got any more involved in this case. You made an enemy in Ritchie Po tonight, and he's a scary dude.'

Mary shuddered. 'You afraid of the Mob?'

'Damn straight I am.'

'Me, too.' They laughed together, and Mary could feel the alcohol bringing a welcome fuzziness to her thoughts. She couldn't remember the last time she'd eaten. She could still taste the locatelli, salty and grainy on her tongue.

'I told you I'm researching Carlo Tresca's murder, didn't I? He was shot dead in the middle of Little Italy, and the case was never solved. It's the Mob, only the names and the places have changed.' Anthony chuckled ruefully, then it died. 'The cops know what to do, and if Brinkley wants to reach you, he'll call.'

Mary shook her head, and her brain sloshed from side to side. 'I should have told him. I didn't get the chance.'

'Told him what?'

My secret. But Mary wasn't drunk enough to give that answer. She felt so tired suddenly, burdened with all of it. With what she had done, with what she hadn't done. With lives lost

213

tonight, and before. 'I'm a widow, you know.'
'I know. I'm sorry.'
'My husband died.'
Anthony nodded, and Mary heard how stupid she sounded.
'Sorry, I sound dumb,' she said.
'No, you're just beat.'
Mary took another sip. 'I knew him, I guess you heard Ritchie say that.'
'You knew who?'
'The deceased.'
'Your husband?'
'No.' Mary's thoughts caromed off the walls of her skull. 'The man in the body bag. I dated him in high school.'
'I heard Ritchie. I didn't know if it was true.'
It was.
'I didn't know.'
'No one did. It didn't last very long. He thought I dumped him, apparently.' Mary was remembering what Rosaria had said, on the bench in Brick. 'It was a misunderstanding.'
'That's too bad.'
'I'll say.'
'Were you in love?'
'Yes.' Mary didn't hesitate. It wasn't love, like with Mike, but it qualified. It was first love.
'Was he?'
'In love? I didn't think so, until recently.'
'Sorry then, about your loss.'
Mary blinked. It was her loss, wasn't it?
Anthony said, 'That explains a lot.'
'What?'
'You've survived two men you loved, already.

214

That's odd, for our age. It's a lot.'

Mary absorbed the observation. It hadn't occurred to her before. But he wasn't exactly right. 'Actually, it's three, with my friend Brent.'

'That's three too many.'

It's four, all told.

'No wonder it's hit you so hard.'

Mary felt like she wanted to tell him. That she had to tell somebody. She wanted to make a confession, without a confessional. At least it was dark and maybe it was time. She'd held it in for so long. Nobody knew, not even Judy and certainly not her family. She set down her wineglass. She asked, 'What happens to a Goretti girl who gets an abortion?'

After a minute, Anthony answered, 'You tell me.'

'She keeps it a secret. A big secret.'

'Really?'

'I was May Queen, you know, at the special Mass. Wore the white dress, the flower crown. The whole faculty voted for me. I was the one who most embodied her virtues.'

'Whose?'

'Goretti's. You know the fable.'

'Of course.'

Then Mary didn't have to tell him. Maria Goretti was a young Italian girl who died defending her honor, when a man had tried to rape her. She had died to remain a virgin. The irony was too much. Mary swallowed hard, noticing that Anthony didn't look away from her or seem to judge her. At least she could tell, in the moonlight. Maybe he wasn't that religious

215

anymore, or he would judge her later, on the way home.

'Things happen, Mary.'

'Evidently. I felt like a fraud. I feel like I cheated them, all those teachers, all those nuns, everybody who loved me. Who had confidence in me.'

'You didn't.'

'I did. I didn't die protecting my virginity.'

'So, you're not a saint,' Anthony said softly, and it comforted Mary a little. But she fell silent and after a moment, he asked, 'So was he the father? Trish's boyfriend, Bobby Mancuso?'

'Yes,' Mary answered, without hesitation. It felt right to say it out loud, to acknowledge Bobby in public. She couldn't have confessed the pregnancy to her family, who would have been devastated. Or to Judy, who would have been hurt that she hadn't been told long ago. Mary sensed that this was her public declaration, and that she was doing it for the baby. Her baby. *Their* baby, who never made it to the christening, and never got to wear a little white gown. 'I see.'

Mary cleared her throat. 'I got pregnant in the backseat of a car, my first time ever. How's that for luck?'

Anthony groaned.

'Bobby said he had blue balls, whatever that was, and he sort of guilted me into it, but I admit, I was in love. I wasn't ready to go all the way, but I did love him. Even after.'

Anthony fell silent.

'We saw each other a few more times, but we

216

never had sex again, and I couldn't even look him in the eye. When I missed my period, I knew. I had the abortion and I didn't tell anyone, not even him. Especially not him. I was too embarrassed to see him ever again. I quit tutoring him. I thought he was ignoring me, but I was ignoring him. I avoided him. And it, just, ended.'

'I can understand you not telling him.'

'Can you?' Mary felt her throat thicken. 'I regret it now. I've regretted it for a long time.'

'Why?'

'I used to regret it because I thought he had a right to know, but that's an intellectual concept. Abstract. Legal. Now I regret it because things might have been different, if he had known. If I had told him.'

'How different?'

'Everything.'

'You would have been the one who lived with him, and not Trish?'

Mary considered it, and for the first time, knew the answer. 'No, not per se.'

Anthony smiled. 'Now that's a lawyer's answer.'

'It's the what-if that gets me. What if it had been me? Would he have turned out differently, good instead of bad?'

'I see.'

'I mean, aren't there some decisions in your life that are so critical, so central to everything that follows, that they change everything? The whole course of your life, and not only that, the course of the lives of the people around you?' Mary wondered aloud, giving voice to thoughts

217

that had been running through her mind since that first day in the office, with Trish. 'If I had told him or we had stayed together, would he have followed the straight and narrow? Would he have gone to college? Would he be alive tonight? And Trish? Would she be safe?'

'I understand.'

'What if I had lived with him? Would I have died with him, too?'

'Good question,' Anthony answered, and they both fell silent.

Mary set down her glass, leaned back in the soft couch, and closed her eyes. Her body sank into the couch, and she felt her strength ebb from her muscles and her every emotion leach through her skin. She was worried about Trish, but she couldn't do anything to help her right now. She had to let it go. She had to let everything go, all of her regrets. She thought of Dhiren, oddly, and felt him beyond her, too. All of it, just out of reach. In time, she must have drifted off to sleep, and later, when she woke up, Anthony was gone and the moon had deserted the sky.

Leaving Mary in total darkness.

24

It was barely dawn but Mary was awake, showered, and dressed to match her mood, in a black dress with black pumps. Her makeup was light because she didn't take the time to do it right; her hair fell unprofessionally loose to her shoulders because she didn't bother to blow it dry. Her eyes had turned red from falling asleep in her contacts, and her face was puffy from the wine. In short, she'd remain single another day.

She got off the elevator at Rosato & Associates and went straight to Judy's office, because they'd agreed to meet early for a private confab. Mary needed help and wasn't ashamed to say so. That was another thing girlfriends were for, especially genius girlfriends.

'Mary, Jeez!' Judy rose the moment Mary opened the door and came around her desk to give her a hug. The window behind her showed a cloudy sky above the office buildings, and only a few windows were lit at this hour. 'You poor thing. You must be so upset.'

'I've been better,' Mary said, feeling vaguely guilty, an improvement over insanely guilty. No matter, she didn't have time to tell Judy about Bobby and the past. She had to find Trish. 'Thanks for coming in this early.'

'No problem, except I didn't want to wake Frank up, so I had to get dressed in the dark.

Look at these clothes.' Judy threw up her arms. 'I'm disgusting.'

'What do you mean? You look great.' Mary wouldn't have recognized Judy but for the yellow Danskos; she looked fantastic even without makeup, in brown tailored pants that hugged her slim hips and a beige knit V-neck. The chic neutrals complemented the golden sunniness of her hair, and Mary was dumbfounded by her dismay.

'I look horrible.' Judy almost wailed. 'I'm shades of brown.'

'Of course you are, your clothes are. That's how normal people dress.'

'But it's so matchy-matchy.'

'No, it's color-coordinated. Everything's from the same color family.'

'That's my point. It's like eating a meal composed entirely of meat. Everything's from the same food group.'

'What?' Mary didn't follow.

'You wouldn't eat steak, a side of chicken breast, and pork chops for dessert, would you?'

'No.'

'So why is it okay with clothes?'

'Because clothes are different from meat?' Mary asked uncertainly, thinking that Judy was either really dumb or really smart. She was going with really smart, since she had come to her for advice. She sat down in a chair opposite the desk. 'Okay, whatever, we have to talk about Trish.'

'Whatever.' Judy leaned forward. 'Sorry I didn't call you last night. Frank and I were at a movie, and when I saw the news online, I figured you'd already gone to bed.'

'That's okay.'

'So what's happening? You barely said on the phone, and this is some story.' Judy gestured at the newspaper on her desk. 'They're talking about a Mob war. It's all over The Inquirer.'

'I know. But the bottom line is, Trish is gone, maybe dead, or maybe he locked her in a basement somewhere.'

'What a nightmare, even for Trash.'

Mary winced. 'We like her now. Get with the program.'

'Done. Next?'

'His sister says he has a house somewhere, because he wasn't always going to stay in the Mob. So all we have to do is find the house.'

'We?' Judy grinned, brightening. 'Yay! We need a new adventure. Lately I'm feeling so brown.'

'No, sorry, I didn't mean us. I meant me. You stay and cover my desk. Please, please, please, I beg of you.' Mary slapped her hands together, praying hard as a Communion photo. 'I can't do what I have to do if my desk isn't covered.'

'But your desk is even more boring than my desk.'

'I need you. I'm getting dropped by half my clients as we speak.'

'I heard.' Judy puckered her lower lip. 'Marshall told me you got another cancellation yesterday afternoon.'

'Great. I liked it better when I was the Neighborhood Girl Who Made Good.' Mary tried not to think about it. 'So please, will you cover me for just one more day? I'll owe you, big-time.'

'Okay, but you do owe me.' Judy sighed. 'I want food.'

'Fine. What's your favorite food?'

'I don't have a favorite food. Food is my favorite.'

'Okay, I'll take you out for food. Meantime, I made a list of my matters today.' Mary got the paper from her purse and gave it to Judy, but she set it down.

'Hold on, I have a more important question.' She picked up one of the newspapers from her desk, and it showed a picture of Mary, her head down as she left the Roundhouse. Anthony was looking at her, his hand on her arm. 'Who's this hottie?'

'The guy I told you about. The not-gay one.'

'How'd he get invited and not me?'

'Pure bad luck.'

'Hmph.' Judy eyed the photo. 'Check out the way he's looking at you. He's got the look of love, girl.'

'Don't be silly,' Mary said, but felt herself flush. Anthony had washed their wineglasses and cheese plate, which raised new questions about his sexuality.

'Are you two dating?'

'We could have been, but I blew it, which isn't what we need to talk about right now.'

Suddenly there was a noise outside in the hallway, then footsteps, then humming, and Mary and Judy locked wide eyes. They both knew what it meant. The boss.

'What's she doing in so early?' Judy whispered.

'Damnit!' Mary whispered back. 'Now I'll never get out.'

'Think she'll cuff us?'

'Not funny.'

'Calm down. She's on trial. She won't have time to talk. She'll stick her head in to say hi.'

'So what do I do?'

'Say hi.'

In the next minute, Bennie materialized at the threshold in her trenchcoat, her hair drying in a wide tortoiseshell barrette. She held a Starbucks venti, which was when Mary realized that Bennie *was* a Starbucks venti.

'Hi!' Mary and Judy said, in unfortunate unison.

'Well, gee, hi, ladies.' Bennies eyes widened slightly, and she smiled. 'How did you two beat me in?'

'We're younger,' Judy said, and Bennie laughed.

'You look different, Carrier. What's different about you today?'

'I'm very brown. Shades of brown, from the same brown family. Basically, I'm wearing meat.'

Bennie laughed again, then eyed Mary. 'DiNunzio, I'm seeing you everywhere and getting calls from all quarters. You at the Roundhouse. You on TV and on the front page. What's going on?'

'I've been a little busy, I guess.' Mary told herself to act natural, or failing that, less nervous than natural.

'Is this a criminal matter?'

'Yes. And, no.'

'Two matters, huh?'

Uh, no.

'Whom do you represent?'

Mary stalled. She couldn't lie. It was wrong, and also she sucked at it. She decided to shade the truth, which would consign her only to purgatory, at least until that went out of business, too. 'Trish Gambone. She came to me for a restraining order against her boyfriend. She's the woman who was kidnapped.'

'That's terrible.' Bennie frowned, alarmed. 'So the restraining order didn't do any good?'

'Uh, well, I didn't get one.'

'You lost?' Bennie frowned, more deeply.

'No, as it happened, we didn't go to court. This is from the other day. Those girls who came in and started the fight, remember?'

Bennie snorted. 'I should have known. So why were you at the Roundhouse?'

'I had to give information about Trish to Reg Brinkley, if you remember him. He sends his regards. He's that detective from the Newlin case, who helped us out.' Mary hoped that if she kept talking, she would use up the two seconds Bennie usually allotted for small talk. 'He was the tall one, he's black, and he loves jazz. In fact, he was telling me to say hi to you when I — '

'I remember Reg,' Bennie interrupted. 'I read that the boyfriend, Mancuso, was found dead last night. He was connected?'

'Yes.'

'They're talking about retaliation from within the Mob. None of this bodes well for your client.

224

Our friend Reg has a tiger by the tail, trying to find her.'

'Luckily, he's the man for the job.'

'Yes, he is. It's not your problem, correct?' Bennie eyed her meaningfully as she sipped her coffee, and Mary shuddered. Being cross-examined by the boss was bad enough, but on espresso, it could be lethal. Judy looked like she was holding her breath, and Mary shook her head.

'Of course it's not my problem,' she answered.

'I'm betting that you're far too busy to be running around, if what you said the other day was any indication.'

Mary flushed. 'I am. Far too busy.'

'Good.' Bennie seemed satisfied. 'Anyway, I'd like you both to clear your calendars today, to give me a hand at trial. Last night, Anne got food poisoning at dinner with the client, and I'm putting on a slew of witnesses.'

Gulp. 'Poor Anne.' Mary had to stall until she could think of a reason not to help. Or maybe the office would catch fire. 'Where did you eat?'

'Muggy's, on Walnut Street.'

'What did Anne eat?'

Bennie blinked. 'Something that made her sick.'

'No, I meant, what was it she ate that made her sick?'

'Does it matter?'

'It would, if I were taking a client to Muggy's.'

'Are you?' Bennie asked.

'Hell, no. Not anymore.' HELP!

Judy cleared her throat. 'I can give you a hand,

Bennie. I've got the whole day. You won't need Mary if you have me.'

'No, I need you both.' Bennie turned to Judy. 'Carrier, you'll sit second-chair, in court. There's about three hundred documents in this case, so I need the assist.' She turned back to Mary. 'DiNunzio, I need you to prep witnesses for me. I'm starting our case in chief today. Can you free up?'

Mary froze.

'I know you're busy, but it's an emergency. All hands on deck.'

'I can't do it,' Mary blurted out.

'Why not?'

'I have a meeting out of the office,' Mary answered, shakily, and in the background, even Judy started frowning.

'What kind of meeting?' Bennie asked.

'A meeting about a case.' Mary felt panic rising. She wished she had a Starbucks venti. She felt pretty sure she could lie better if she were sucking down a Starbucks. She would use her Starbucks for good, and not evil.

'What case?' Bennie asked, impatient. 'And why do I have to take your deposition to find out?'

'You don't,' Mary answered, though it wasn't funny anymore. She didn't have to lie. She wasn't going to lie. She had a good reason to be doing what she was doing, and that was that. She straightened up. 'I can't help you today. I'm sorry. I have something important to do, and I have to get going.'

'But there's work to be done here.'

'I have work, too, and I can't drop it. It's about Trish. She's still missing, and I'm going to help find her.'

In the background, Judy's eyes flared, and Bennie's eyes narrowed.

'So it's not a case. Weren't you the one telling me you were so inundated with work? Now you can take a day off?'

'I know, I am inundated. But I can't turn my back on this girl.'

'Your clients are firing you. Is this why?'

Mary felt stricken, wondering how she'd found out.

'I know what goes on here, DiNunzio. It's my firm.'

'They're firing me because they think I turned my back on Trish.'

'And you're doing this for them?'

'No.' Mary shook her head. 'I'm doing it for me.'

'Either way, it's unprofessional and dangerous. Mancuso was in the Mob.'

'I'll be careful.' Mary reached for her bag. 'I'm sorry, but I have to go.'

'Don't go. Your place is here.'

'I have to.'

'Are you walking out on me?' Bennie looked as angry as Mary had ever seen her.

'I have to go, Bennie.'

'But I forbid it.'

'I'm sorry.' Mary locked eyes with Bennie, in an interoffice version of the age-old struggle between parent and child. 'I have no choice.'

'You always have a choice.' Bennie stiffened. 'If

you go now, then don't come back.'

No. Mary felt stricken.

Judy yelped, 'Bennie, really? She's just doing what she thinks is — '

'Enough.' Bennie raised a hand, never taking her eyes from Mary. 'DiNunzio, you're either an associate here or you're not. If you are, you'll stay. If you're not, you'll go. For good.'

Mary didn't know what to say. She felt her chest tighten but she couldn't speak. She didn't want to cry. She had worked for Bennie for as long as she could remember, but she couldn't turn her back on Trish, not again. She looked from Bennie to Judy and back again, then decided. She slipped her bag on her shoulder, turned, and left the office without another word.

'Mary!' Judy called after her.

But she didn't look back. She hurried down the hall, her eyes filling with tears.

25

Mary grabbed the stiff hand strap as the Yellow cab lurched down Market Street and around City Hall in stop-and-go traffic. She had to pick up her car from the impoundment lot; she'd need it for her next move. The morning rush hour was coming on, and the sky was clouding up, as if heaven and earth were on nasty parallel tracks. Mary tried not to take it as a bad sign. Or maybe you saw bad signs everywhere after you'd walked out on your life.

'Reg?' she said into the cell phone, having finally reached Brinkley. 'First, I want to explain about last night, about me and Bobby Mancuso.'

'No need.'

'I dated him in high school, and that's it. I would've mentioned it to you but didn't get the chance, and it's kind of personal. It really didn't — '

'No matter, thanks for the tip,' Brinkley said coldly, so Mary moved to her next point.

'Anything new on Trish?'

'No.'

Mary could've guessed as much. She'd been checking online like a fiend. 'I assume Ritchie and his father didn't tell you anything last night.'

'Can't go into that. By the way, I hear you talked to the feds.'

'I thought it would help the cause. I hope that was okay.'

'Sure,' Brinkley said, but Mary wasn't convinced.

'Did you learn anything from Mancuso's autopsy?'

'I can't discuss that with you.'

'I swear, Reg, the more I know, the more I can help.'

'Don't help. Sorry. Listen, I gotta go.'

'But what about Trish?'

'Mary, we'll follow up.' Brinkley's tone softened a little. 'We'll do our job. Go back to work. Make like a lawyer.'

Gulp. Mary pushed those thoughts away. 'Just tell me, what did the trace evidence show? I would assume there'd be dirt on his shoes, threads on his clothes, stuff that would show where he'd been and where the house could be — '

'That's for us, Mary.'

'The feds know who Cadillac is, but they wouldn't tell me.'

'Please, God in heaven, don't go anywhere near the Mob.' Suddenly Brinkley sounded like himself again, her pal of old. 'If anything happens to you, your mother will never forgive me.'

'Okay, but I thought of something else.' Mary had a new idea this morning. 'A good place to look around would be his old friends. Trish's diary doesn't mention any old friends, but everybody has old friends. He needed a friend, that's what his sister told me. If he were going to confide in someone about his house, obviously it wouldn't be someone in the Mob. It could — '

230

'Mare, I gotta go. Stay out of it. We'll find Trish, one way or another. See ya.' Brinkley hung up, and the cab stalled past the federal courthouse, heading east toward the Delaware River.

Mary pressed the button to end the call, feeling suddenly at a loss. She inched farther from Bennie, Judy, and her job, and watched traffic fill Market Street. She was unsure where she was going, even where she'd been. A white SEPTA bus rocked side to side in front of the cab, then took a right turn, unblocking the orangey sun that rose at the end of Market, bathing the street momentarily in a golden light. She squinted at the momentary brightness, then held on tight as it flickered away, thinking to herself.

And planning her next move.

Half an hour later, Mary had parked outside the main entrance of her old high school, St. Maria Goretti. The school occupied a three-story yellow-brick building in the heart of South Philly, at Tenth and Moore Streets. It had since been renamed Neumann-Goretti High School, having merged with its brother school, but it was housed in the same building, remarkably unchanged paneled windows with steel sills and a bank of stainless-steel-framed glass doors. A tall concrete statue of St. Goretti watched over Tenth Street, and Mary hurried past her up the steps, an unexpected lump in her throat as she pulled open the door and stepped inside.

The school was smaller than she remembered, but it smelled the same, an overheated mix of

231

city street, floor wax, and drugstore hair product. It was characteristically quiet because classes were in session; an empty, glistening corridor with tan floor tiles extended ahead of her and to her left. The cinderblock walls had been repainted beige, and the lockers that lined the hall were a matching color. Inside was the same as when she'd been here, except that the walls had been white, and when she turned the corner she stopped short at the sight of the old school uniform, displayed in a glass case, as if she herself were an artifact.

Mary felt a pang, standing there in the fluorescent lights, eyeing the heavy blue jumper with the SMG emblem displayed next to a set of four ribbons, each a different color. The ribbon used to be fastened to the uniform at the underarm, to hold her locker key in her jumper pocket, and they all used to twirl it endlessly, a Goretti trademark. For a minute, she couldn't leave, standing in front of herself, her emotions rushing back at her, all the joy and shame of her senior year.

Then she straightened up and willed the feelings away. She had to get to work.

Not long after, Mary was sitting in the cozy Development Office, at a spare desk near a turquoise tin of imported almond biscotti, neat piles of the school's promotional materials, and a coffeemaker. Carolyn Edgar, the development officer, was an attractive middle-aged woman with a warm smile, a chic brush of grayish-blond hair, rimless glasses, and a camel-hair sweater she wore with herringbone slacks. Mrs. Edgar was new to the school, and her position hadn't existed when Mary had gone here, before God needed marketing.

'Here we go, dear.' Mrs. Edgar set the two Bishop Neumann yearbooks in front of her, one padded green, with the Crystal and Crossroads crossing over each other like an X, embossed with the old Neumann logo. On top, Mrs. Edgar set a red yearbook that read Goretti Graffiti. 'I thought you might like to see yours, too.'

'Good idea.' Mary smiled, though it wasn't on her agenda. She picked it up and opened to a page of black-and-white photos, big-haired girls in itchy jumpers, recognizing the faces right away. Joyce DelCiotto, Madeline Alessi, and Eileen Duffy, all wearing their NHS pins proudly as a cartoon sheriff wears a badge. 'I remember the dress code. Earrings no bigger than a quarter.'

'We still have that rule.'

'Good. I suffered, so should they.' Mary skipped ahead to her own picture in the seniors section. 'Oh, no.'

'Everybody says that.' Mrs. Edgar smiled, taking a seat behind her orderly desk and hitting a few keys on the computer.

Mary cringed at the way she used to look. Her eyes were tiny behind thick glasses, her curled hair stiff with hairspray, and her teeth a tangle of braces. It wasn't until then that she remembered Trish used to call her Tinsel Teeth.

'Why is it you needed those Neumann yearbooks again?' Mrs. Edgar asked, looking through her bifocals at the computer monitor. A

233

large wooden crucifix hung on the cinderblock wall, and behind her were bookshelves and an air conditioner wrapped with a Hefty bag and duct tape.

Mary tried to think of a good reason. 'I'm doing a reunion party, and I just want to jot down a few old addresses.'

'Oh, you don't need the yearbook for that. I'll just print you out a copy from the database. It'll only take a minute or two.'

Uh-oh. 'Great. Well, maybe, I'll just look at the books anyway, for fun.'

'Go right ahead. Now, you want both Goretti and Neumann addresses for your year, correct?'

'Yes, thanks.' Mary set the Goretti yearbook aside and reached for the Neumann yearbook. She opened the book and thumbed through it quickly, the front section a black-and-white flip book of grinning boys, nuns, and coaches. She slowed when she got to the next section. Sports. Bobby had played football, and she turned the pages until she saw him, front and center, in the team photo.

'Here we go,' Mrs. Edgar said, half to herself. 'I'll just print this and you're good to go.'

'Thank you.' Mary looked at Bobby's football photo, ignoring the catch in her throat. It was so hard to believe he was really gone, or that he'd grow up to be a monster. In the picture, he stood tall in a black-and-gold football uniform, grinning self-consciously and holding the football, displaying the old-fashioned Wilson script. The team grinned in a say-pizza way, and Mary scanned the young faces, none of which was familiar. Who would have been his friends, back then?

Mrs. Edgar was saying, 'I see your name and address in the database. Do I have them correct?' She read off the name and address.

'Yes, right.' Mary eyed the photos, her memories coming back. She never went to football games at Neumann and didn't travel in the jock crowd. She didn't recognize any of them except for Bobby. She read the names under the front row of the photo: **J. Ronan, M. Gordon, R. Mancuso, G. Chavone, B. Turbitt.** None of the first names was listed, and none of the last names jogged her memory. She wracked her brain. Chavone maybe, but she didn't remember that he was Bobby's friend.

Mrs. Edgar was saying, 'We've been sending you the materials for Spirit Day, the walkathon, and the new journalism scholarship. Did you get them?'

'Yes, thanks.' Mary flipped through the yearbook, looking for Bobby among the candids of boys in plastic goggles in chem lab or hanging in the hall. He wasn't in any of the activities photos, either. She skipped to the back of the book, to the seniors' individual photos, and turned pages until she found the **M's. Robert Mancuso**.

'I see that we have an office address for you, and it's a law firm. Are you a lawyer, dear?'

'Yes.' Mary looked at Bobby's senior photo. His eyes were clear and his smile broad, and her gaze dropped to the caption he'd written: **Wildwood forever! Shout out to the Bad To**

235

The Bone Gang — Jimmy 4G, PopTop, and Scuzzy! We're history!

'I ran into Sister Helena in the office while I was fetching those yearbooks, and she remembered you fondly. She had to go, but sends her love to you and your parents. She said you'd been in all the papers, apparently involved with another Goretti grad, who's gone missing. Are you she? The famous lawyer?'

'Not exactly.' Mary hid her excitement, not over the alumnae lists, but over the caption of Bobby's senior photo. Jimmy 4G, Pop-Top, and Scuzzy had to be Bobby's three best friends. Now that the caption had jarred her memory, she recalled him talking about a Jimmy. She flipped backward to the G surnames and scanned them, but there was no last name that started with a G that also had Jimmy or James as a first name.

Mrs. Edgar continued, 'I'm not surprised that you're a big success, of course. So many of our Goretti girls have gone on to be professionals. Doctors, lawyers. Kathy Gandolfo, you know, the TV newscaster, she went here.'

'Really.' Mary considered the Jimmy 4G problem. So it was a nickname, not a last name. She flipped back and scanned the pictures of the Jimmys until she found one with the last name she recognized. Waites. Jimmy Waites had to be Bobby's friend. She had no idea what the G stood for, but it didn't matter. She made a mental note.

'By the way, Mary, I notice that you haven't made a contribution to the school in quite some time. We have so many items on our wish list. We need computers, and desks for one room are $5000. Audiovisual equipment is $1000, and we still need $6000 to paint the cafeteria.'

'Really, hmm.' Mary tuned her out, searching for the other two of Bobby's friends, cross-checking their senior photos to see if they mentioned him. She skimmed the first names and found one. Paul Meloni. He mentioned the Bad to the Bone gang, too. Bingo!

'Of course, if those amounts aren't within your means, we'd be happy for any amount you can spare. It all adds up, and I know you understand that much of your professional success is due to the education and values you learned here.'

'I sure do,' Mary said, but she was turning the pages, looking for Scuzzy.

'So, do you think you're in a position to make a contribution? I hate to be so direct, but it's rare that I get a captive in my office. You're like the little fly in my web.' Mrs. Edgar laughed. 'May I put you down for a hundred dollars?'

Mary lucked out on the next page. John Scaramuzzo. He had to be Scuzzy. She set down the yearbooks, having identified all three members of the Bad to the Bone gang. She felt like cheering. 'Yes!'

'Wonderful!' Mrs. Edgar turned to the printer, slid out some sheets, and handed her the address lists, across the desk. 'Don't forget these.'

'Thanks so much.' Mary could barely hide her excitement, and Mrs. Edgar beamed.

'You're welcome. Now, did you bring your checkbook, dear?'

Huh? Mary blinked.

Fifteen minutes later, she burst through the front doors of the school with the addresses, a hundred bucks lighter.

Hurrying from her past into her present.

26

Mary found it almost impossible to believe that the short, overweight accountant in a Bluetooth and an Italian suit was Jimmy 4G Waites. He had a salesman's grin, but had aged more than his thirty-odd years; two deep wrinkles divided his eyebrows, and soft jowls draped his mouth like a pug's. His hair was almost gone, with a brown-gray fringe encircling a thick, flattish head.

'I understand, but you're not hearing me.' Waites spoke to the air, his brown eyes darting around the large, bright office, alighting on nothing in particular. 'You wouldn't be doing this if he wasn't a friend. He's asking you to invest five mil? Tell him you're comfortable with one. You can afford to lose one.'

Mary waited in a leather sling chair opposite a glistening glass desk. The accounting firm had three floors in swanky Mellon Center, and Waites's office was beautifully appointed with Danish modern furniture. A huge square of window overlooked the mirrored skyline, the reflections of the skyscrapers dull in the overcast sky. Mary had introduced herself to Waites's secretary as an old high school friend, and Waites had gestured her in just as he picked up the phone, waving his fleshy hand with enthusiasm, thinking she was someone he was supposed to recognize.

Waites was saying, 'Then if it doesn't work out, which we know it probably won't, you two stay friends. I always say, you can have bad deals with good people, but you can't have good deals with bad people. Got it? Good. See ya.' He pressed his Bluetooth to hang up. 'Sorry about that.'

'That's okay.' Mary introduced herself. 'I went to Goretti, graduated the same year you did, from Neumann.'

'You look familiar.'

'I had braces, glasses, and an inferiority complex.'

Waites laughed. 'That makes two of us.'

'But I'm here about Bobby Mancuso.'

Waites's smile faded. 'I read that he was killed last night. I couldn't believe it.'

'I know. You two used to be friends, right?'

'Hold on, not recently.' Waites's gaze darted nervously to the hall outside his office, then he lowered his voice. 'I haven't talked to Bobby since the summer after graduation. That was a long time ago. I heard he got in with the Mob, but I didn't know anything about that. Live by the sword, die by the sword.' Waites focused on her, frowning behind costly rimless glasses. 'Wait a minute. Who did you say you were, anyway?'

'I was a friend of his, I don't know if he mentioned me. I tutored him and we went out a few times.'

'I don't remember your name, but my family only moved here in the second half of senior year.' Waites rubbed his face. 'I saw in the paper they think he kidnapped Trish Gambone. I didn't even know he was still seeing her. Is that what this is about?'

'Yes.' Mary cut to the chase. 'I'm trying to find Trish. She's still missing. I thought if you had stayed in touch, you might know — '

'Like I said, we didn't stay in touch. Not at all.' Waites sounded like he was speaking for the record, though none existed. 'I don't know what he did with her, if that's where you're going.'

Mary switched tacks. 'Okay, that aside, I'm trying to locate a house he bought, where he could have taken her.'

'I didn't know he bought a house.' Waites looked outside again. 'Look, we didn't stay in touch, as I said, and I don't want to get involved.'

'Did he ever talk about a place he went, a place he liked especially?'

'No.'

'Did he have any hobbies, that you knew of?'

'Does boozing count?' Waites snapped, and Mary faked a smile.

'Did he drink, even then?'

'Oh yeah. Too much, and he was a mean drunk. Yelled. Screamed. Not good. Punched a hole through a wall more than once.'

'Scary.' Mary shuddered.

'Yes.'

'Was there anyplace you went together, back then? In the year-book, he mentioned Wildwood.' She took the photocopied page from her purse and handed it to him. 'Does that help?'

'Bad to the Bone, eh?' Waites eyed the photo, reminiscing for a minute. 'It's sad.'

'It sure is.' Mary was liking him better. 'It all turned out so well for you, and obviously not for him. I wonder how that happens.'

'I'll tell you how.' Waites looked up, his thin lips a grim line. 'I had a great dad. Bobby didn't. That guy was a jerk.'

'What makes you say that?'

'He just was.' Waites tossed the page back to Mary. 'He put Bobby down all the time. Favored the real brother, who was a thug, always in and out of trouble. Bobby's house was hell. He did everything he could to get out of it. It's the reason he played ball, I think. He never talked about it, but you could tell. Except for the sister. He was tight with his sister.'

'Rosaria.'

'Right.' Waites nodded. 'Bobby was a great guy, a quiet guy, but he kept a lot inside. You knew that, if you knew him. We did go to Wildwood, once. Rented a house there one summer, bussed tables. Kids gettin' crazy down the shore, you know.'

'Where was the house?'

'God knows.' Waites scoffed. 'I doubt it's even there anymore.'

'Did you ever go anywhere else, back then or later?'

'No.'

'Did he say he liked Wildwood or anything like that?' Mary was thinking of Rosaria, in Brick. 'Did he mention liking the Jersey shore?'

'No way.'

'Why not?'

'He couldn't swim. Almost drowned that

summer, one day when the undertow was bad.'

Mary hadn't known. She eliminated the possibility of a shore house. 'Did he have any hobbies you knew of? Fishing? Hunting?'

'Not that I know. I wasn't that close to him. Scuzzy was the closest. They were tight.'

'Scaramuzzo?' Mary's heart leaped with hope.

'Yes. They stayed in good touch, too, at least until Scuzzy died.'

'When was that?' Mary groaned inwardly.

'Two years ago. Blood cancer. He wasn't even thirty.'

'How about PopTop? Paul Meloni? Was he close with Bobby?'

'I don't know. I didn't stay in touch. I liked the guy but I'm busy.' Waites gestured at the credenza, covered with school pictures, like kiddie mug shots. 'I got six kids.'

'A good Catholic.'

'No, married three times.' Waites chuckled again, then stopped. 'Last I knew, PopTop was in drug rehab. Neumann graduated the best, but I hung with all the losers. I'm a late bloomer, let me tell you.'

'Does he still work for the school district?' Mary checked the addresses she'd copied from the library.

'No. He got fired. I know where you can find him, though.' Waites tore a Post-it from a yellow cube, scribbled an address on it, and handed it to her, stuck to his fingerpad. 'Here you go. Now, if I could get back to work.'

'Sure, thanks for your time. If you think of anything else that might help me, will you let me

243

know?' Mary stood up and handed him her business card, though now it had an expiration date. 'Call on the cell.'

'No sweat. Thanks for coming by.' Waites stood up, nodded a little goodbye, and Mary went to the door, then turned, curious.

'By the way, what'd Jimmy 4G stand for?'

'I didn't have a lot of dates, back then. It means 'Jimmy waits for girls.' Get it?' Waites smiled. 'Bobby gave me that nickname. He was king of the nicknames.'

'What was his?'

Waites paused. 'Come to think of it, he didn't have one. He gave out the nicknames, so I guess he never got one.'

'Thanks,' Mary said, and for some reason, it made her sad.

★ ★ ★

Olde City was the colonial section of the city, a grid of skinny cobblestone streets bordered by the Delaware River. The oldest street in America, Elfreth's Alley, was here, and many of the vintage brick buildings had been refurbished to house hip restaurants and artsy shops. But gentrification hadn't reached everywhere, and on one of the grimier back streets sat a skinny glass storefront, mashed like a ham sandwich between two brick houses. It was a tattoo parlor, and a chipped black-iron grate covered the front door, which bore a printed sign that read, UNDER EIGHTEEN PARENTS MUST SIGN

WAIVER! Mary yanked open the door and went inside.

Every square inch of the walls of the small room was plastered with samples of colorful tattoos: American flags, orange koi fish, flowers, hearts, banners of every color, and Chinese and Egyptian letters. Dragons with curling tails and flaring nostrils hung next to Jesus himself, and the praying hands looked incongruous, if not sacrilegious, next to hollow-eyed skulls and daggers that dripped blood. The shop wasn't busy, and a man with a shaved head and a faded CitySports T-shirt was tattooing a black banner on a younger man's forearm, which read IN MEMORY O. The machine made a loud buzzing sound, attached to a cord wrapped with electrician's tape.

'Can I help you?' asked a man behind the counter, and Mary walked over, trying not to freak at the inked tarantulas that crawled up his bare arms to encircle his neck. He obviously worked out, because his shoulder caps bulged under a jungle of green-and-black leaves, hiding a striped Bengal tiger about to pounce.

'My name's Mary DiNunzio and I'm looking for Paul Meloni.'

'That's me.' He extended a multicolored hand across the counter and they shook. His brown hair was cut so close that his head looked like a rifle bullet, and he had round, dark-brown eyes and a long, bony nose. He wore a blue tank top and jeans, and a row of small hoop earrings hung from one ear. 'How can I help you?'

'I came to talk to you about Bobby Mancuso.

245

I knew him in high school.'

'Oh, man.' Paul's features went suddenly soft under his illustrated exterior. 'What a shame, huh? I couldn't sleep last night after I saw it on the TV.'

'I'm sorry.'

'It's a cryin' shame, is what it is. Bobby, man.' Paul exhaled, looking away.

'I'm trying to find Trish Gambone.'

'I read about that, I know.' Paul's ripped shoulders fell. 'I couldn't believe it. I knew they were having problems, he told me that, but it sounds like he just lost it.'

'You two stayed in touch, huh?'

'Yeah, more or less. We saw each other maybe every couple months or so.'

Mary considered it. An odd alliance, a drug dealer and a former addict. 'Do you know where Trish could be? Where he could have taken her?'

'No idea.'

Mary tried not to get discouraged. She felt so close to something. 'Did you know he was planning anything like that?'

'No, not at all.' Paul looked puzzled. 'Far as I knew, they were fine.'

'Did he tell you he was going to ask her to marry him?'

'No, not really. We used to talk about me, with my sobriety and all, and I was on him about his drinking. Either that, or we talked sports.'

'Did he tell you that he used to yell at her, threaten her?'

'No, but it doesn't surprise me. When Bobby drank, he lost it, even in high school. We used to

246

drink together, him and me, but I been clean and sober for five years now.' Paul cocked his shorn head. 'How did you know him, again?'

'I used to tutor him in Latin.' Mary couldn't give up. 'I really need your help. I know he bought a house. Do you have any idea where that house might be?'

'Nah. Didn't even know he had a house. I thought they lived together.'

'They did, but I think he had another house he kept a secret. Did he tell you about that?'

'No. He mighta told Scuzzy, but he passed.'

'But he confided in you.'

'Yeah.'

Mary switched tacks. 'Did you know he was in the Mob?'

Paul checked behind him, but no tattoos appeared to be listening. 'Look, it got him dead, and I don't wanna speak ill. He was my friend. He stuck by me through some hard times, and when I got the job here, he'd drop by.'

Mary was starting to panic. If she learned nothing here, she was out of leads. 'Paul, I'm trying to find that house. Trish could still be alive.'

'I don't know anything.' Paul edged back from the counter, and the other tattoo artist looked over.

'Do you know if he was close to anybody in the Mob?'

'I don't know.'

'Did he ever bring anybody from the Mob here?'

'No.'

247

'Did he ever mention anybody, any names?'

'We didn't talk about that.' Paul chuckled. 'Do I look stupid?'

'Did he ever mention anybody named Cadillac?'

'No.'

'Did he ever get picked up or dropped off by someone driving a Cadillac?'

'No, he drove the new BMW. He loved that car.' Paul hesitated, then frowned, thinking. 'I heard him on the cell, a few times. He used to get calls, you know, and he'd go outside to take them. He's not gonna take a call like that in front of me.'

'So do you remember any of the names?'

'Yeah. One.' Paul leaned closer, over the counter. 'I'll tell you, but you didn't hear it from me, right?'

'Right.'

Paul looked uncertain.

'Please, I swear.'

'Okay.' Paul sighed. 'He used to get calls from a guy named Eyes. I remember that name more than the others.'

Mary felt her pulse quicken. 'Eyes. A nickname, obviously.'

'Yeah. That was Bobby, with the nicknames.' Paul looked over when the door opened behind them, and a gaggle of young women entered, chattering and laughing. He acknowledged them with a wave. 'Be right with you, ladies.'

'You know anything else about Eyes?'

'No, just what I told you.'

Mary handed him a business card she had

ready in her coat pocket. 'If you remember anything, or think of anything that might help, will you call me?'

'Sure.' Paul slipped the card in his Jeans and smiled at the girls. 'What'll it be, ladies?'

'Butterflies!' they answered.

And Mary took off.

27

The press mobbed the parking lot in front of the Roundhouse, and Mary parked in the public lot next door, to ease her escape later. She had tried to reach Brinkley to tell him about Eyes, but his cell phone wasn't taking any more messages, so she'd come to the Roundhouse to tell him. She knew he'd said he didn't want her here, but she had to let him know what she'D found out. And she'd promised she wouldn't follow up on any Mob leads, so she wanted credit for being a good girl.

Also she was a big chicken.

She parked and got out of the car, and though the sky had gone gray, slipped on sunglasses to avoid being recognized by the press. The Donchess kidnapping was still in the news, the baby fighting the Mob for space above the fold. She kept her head down and hurried to the entrance of the Roundhouse, barreling past microphones and cameras. She entered a lobby bustling with uniformed cops, staff, and lawyers, and suddenly she heard somebody call her name. She turned, and a delighted Giulia was steaming toward her with Mean Girls in her wake, trailing their red, white, and blue extensions like an American flag on a speedboat.

'Yo, girlfriend!' Giulia wrapped Mary in a warm embrace. 'I called your cell, did you get the message? Can you believe they killed Bobby?

And they still can't find T? Her mom's freaked!'

'I bet.' Mary extricated herself, feeling oddly happy to see her. 'What are you doing here? You're not bothering Brinkley, are you?'

'Nah, we're tryin' to see the dude from Missing Persons. I left him a buncha messages but he won't return them, so we're waitin' for him to come down.'

Missy added, 'He's gotta leave, sooner or later.'

Yolanda cracked her gum. 'There's only one way out. We checked.'

'Why're you here?' Giulia was blocking the elevator, so Mary moved her out of the way and the two other Mean Girls followed like shavings to a cartoon magnet.

'I'm going up to talk to Brinkley.'

'Good.' Giulia grinned. 'I knew you'd be on it. I knew you wouldn't desert us. We been outta our minds. We wanna help but we don't know how.'

'I do,' Mary said, getting an idea. 'Bobby was friendly with a mobster named Eyes. Does that nickname mean anything to you?'

'Eyes?' Giulia repeated, frowning in thought. 'No, not off the top a my head.'

'Me either.' Yolanda popped her gum. 'I know One Eye Petrone, but that ain't the same thing.'

Missy nodded. 'I know Bobby The Nose and Chicken Neck Timmy. That's it for body parts.'

Mary felt discouraged, and Giulia must have read her expression because she touched her arm. 'Don't stress, Mare,' she said. 'We don't know all the wiseguys, only the ones we slep'

251

with. How about we ask around the neighborhood who Eyes is?'

'I don't know,' Mary answered. 'It could be dangerous. Forget it. I'll tell Brinkley. The cops can follow up.'

'Are you for real?' Giulia scoffed. 'Nobody in the neighborhood's gonna talk to the cops about *that*. Let us do it.'

'Us, they'll talk to,' Missy nodded.

'Okay,' Mary said, reluctantly, 'but you have to promise me one thing, crazy. Don't go asking the actual guys in the Mob. Only ask normal people, neighborhood people. I don't want you dead unless I kill you myself.'

'No problem.' Giulia jigged with happiness, drawing admiring glances from more than a few cops. 'Now will you write down the questions for me, like before?'

'Sure.' Mary dug in her purse for her Filofax. 'Let me get some paper.'

'Use this.' Yolanda offered her the *Daily News*, and the paper fell open to the obituaries, which were dominated by a large photo of an elderly woman with a sweet smile.

'Hey, look, that's what's her name!' Giulia tapped the woman's photo with a lacquered fingernail. 'She musta died. It's a sin.'

Mary found her Filofax and glanced at the obit, of one Elisa Felton. 'Did you know her, Giulia?'

'No, but Trish did. She was one of her clients. She's Miss Tuesday Thursday.'

'What?' Mary only half-listened, opening the Filofax and pulling out a blank page.

252

'T was an assistant when she met Miss Tuesday Thursday and when she got old, T went to her condo at the Dorchester every Tuesday and Thursday at lunch and blew her out.'

'Like room service for your hair.' Missy explained, and Yolanda nodded.

'Miss Tuesday Thursday tipped Trish a hundred bucks each time. You believe that? A hundred bucks! Must be nice.'

Mary wrote sample questions on the tiny sheet of paper, each a variation of Do you know a guy named Eyes?

But Giulia was studying the obit. 'Hey, this is whack. It says that Miss Tuesday Thursday was in the hospital for a long time. She even went into a coma last week.'

'Wrong.' Missy frowned. 'Show me.'

'Where?' Yolanda asked, and the women clustered around the newspaper while Mary finished writing her questions. When she tore off the sheet, they were looking at her in confusion.

'I don't get it.' Giulia help up the obit. 'It says here Miss Tuesday Thursday was in the hospital for two months. But T blew her out last Thursday. She told me. T got a two-hundred-buck tip from her, last time. She even showed it to me when she got back to the salon.'

'I saw the money, too. I was there.' Missy chimed in. 'But how could Miss Tuesday Thursday get blown out if she was in a coma?'

'T lied to us,' Yolanda said flatly, and Giulia shoved her angrily.

'Don't be runnin' T down, Yo. You don't know she lied. I'm sure she had a good reason.'

253

'She *lied*, G!' Yolanda snapped. 'Don't go takin' up for her. She's been lyin' about it for the past two months, she had to be. So where's she been at lunch, every Tuesday and Thursday?'

Missy lifted an eyebrow. 'And where'd she get that tip money from?'

Giulia thrust the article at Mary, upset. 'Read this for me. We must be readin' it wrong.'

'Okay, trade me.' Mary gave her the questions for the newspaper and skimmed the obit. Mrs. Felton lived in the Dorchester, on Rittenhouse Square, and was heiress to the Welder fortune. Hospitalized for two months. Fell into a coma last week. Mary looked up, intrigued. 'Sorry, but Trish couldn't have done this woman's hair last week, or anytime in the past two months.'

'So where did T go on Tuesday and Thursday?' Giulia frowned, mystified. 'Where's she been goin'? Why didn't she tell me? I'm her BFF.'

'No, I am.' Missy looked over with a scowl.

'No, *I* am.' Yolanda folded her arms. 'Or I *was*, but I'm not anymore. I knew it all along.'

'Knew what?' they all asked, including Mary.

'I knew she was cheatin' on Bobby.'

'Yo!' Giulia yelled, and every head in the lobby turned toward them.

'Shhh!' Mary said, but her thoughts raced ahead. Every Tuesday and Thursday, Trish was going out at noon? Returning with cash in hand? And Bobby a nightmare at home? Yolanda was right. Trish had to be seeing somebody.

'G, get real.' Yolanda sniffed. 'T got hit on all the time by those rich guys at the salon. Remember Mikey the divorce dude? He had a

254

mad crush on her. And the stockbroker, Damon? Sooner or later, she musta hooked up.' Yolanda wagged a finger. 'Maybe that's why Bobby freaked on her, on her birthday. He musta found out.'

'For real?' Missy asked, and Giulia stalled, momentarily.

Mary had to admit, it made sense. She remembered reading about his accusations of infidelity in the diary. They had seemed unfounded, but if Trish really were cheating, she wouldn't take the risk of recording it, even in a hidden diary. Had Bobby killed Trish for cheating on him? Had that been his dark surprise for her birthday? In the next moment, the crowd behind them seemed to part, and a group of men hustled toward the exit. Mary looked up to see Brinkley heading out, flanked by two other men in suits.

Giulia pointed. 'Look, Mare, that's Reg Mack, with the dude from Missing Persons!'

But Mary was already in motion. 'Reg, hi!' she called out, and Brinkley caught her eye, though his face fell the moment he spotted the Mean Girls. She sped up and fell into step beside him. 'Reg, I need to talk with you and couldn't reach you on the phone.'

'Make it quick, Mary.' Brinkley took her arm.

'Missing Persons Dude!' Giulia called out, as the Mean Girls surrounded the other man. 'You got any word on T? We're worried sick since Bobby got shot. We gotta find her.'

'Settle down.' Brinkley raised his large hands. 'Settle down right now.' He turned to Giulia with a scowl. '*You*. Don't call me or Missing Persons anymore. We're all working very hard to find Trish Gambone, but the more you keep bothering us, the less we can do our job.'

'Don't tell me what I can and can't do,' Giulia shot back. 'It's a free country, and my best friend's still missin'.'

'Shhh!' Mary nudged Giulia. Every head in the lobby had turned to watch. She recognized two lawyers she knew from when she was gainfully employed, earlier this morning.

'What did you find out, Mary?' Brinkley asked, his voice low.

'Bobby was close with a guy in the Mob whose name was Eyes. He might know where Trish is, or maybe where that house is.'

'Thanks, but I thought you were getting back to work. No more playing cops.'

'I'm not. That's why I'm telling you about Eyes.'

'Good girl. Keep it that way.' Brinkley made a beeline for the exit. 'Take care. We gotta go.'

'You get back here!' Giulia shouted, but Mary blocked her with raised arms, like an overeducated school safety. After Brinkley and the suits had gone, Mary lowered her arms and turned to Giulia.

'Girl, you need to calm down.'

'It's not my fault my nerves are shot.' Giulia rubbed her forehead, raking it with her acrylic tips. 'I'm so afraid she's dead.'

'Aw, don't think that way.' Mary threw an arm around her and hoped she sounded convincing.

256

'Come on, we got work to do. Trish is counting on us.'

'You really think she was cheatin'?'

'It doesn't matter now. We gotta find Eyes.'

'Okay.' Giulia smiled shakily. 'You're so smart. You always know what to do.'

'Thanks.' Mary gave her a squeeze, feeling like a fraud.

In truth, she had only one move left.

28

The gray sky spit drizzle, and Mary put the Mean Girls in a cab and followed them in her car part of the way, then turned off. She didn't want to do this, but she couldn't leave it to anyone else and Eyes was her only lead. She thought it would be safe enough, especially in daylight. She drove down a few blocks, past neat rowhouses, then found a parking space. She glanced through the rain-spotted windshield at the lighted sign down Denver Street. *Biannetti's* read black letters on a white plastic sign, next to a martini glass set sideways, a Rat Pack rewind. A modest corner tavern, a converted row-house, squatted at the end of the street, an alleged Mob hangout not twenty blocks from City Hall. She cut the ignition, braced herself, grabbed the newspaper and her bag, and left the car.

The air smelled damp and humid, and she walked to the restaurant with her head down against the wet mist, telling herself that Biannetti's was a public place like any other and people from the neighborhood ate there all the time. She walked along and checked out the cars on the street, wondering if any FBI agents were surveilling the place, after the murder last night. There were not telltale white utility vans in sight, only an array of older American cars. The street seemed unusually parked up, with a full line of double-parking, which Mary couldn't explain until she reached Biannetti's door, pulled on it, and went inside. The place was dim, but the noise level came up before the light, the loudness of a packed restaurant abuzz with animated chatter and laughter.

At first Mary startled, thinking she'd walked into a party, but then her eyes adjusted to the scene. It wasn't even noon, but all the tables were full, stocked with men and young women yapping away, gulping coffee, and smoking despite the city-wide ban. Almost every table had today's newspapers spread out on top of red-and-white-plastic table-cloths, and people mingled, reading the articles over each other's shoulders. It was tailgating, at a mob murder.

She slipped on her sunglasses, just in case someone had seen her picture in the paper. On the right was a short bar, where a crowd stood riveted by a TV that blared the local news. On the screen, a bright red banner read MOB WAR, complete with gang-related crawl. The crowd talked through the broadcast, waving Pilsner glasses, mugs of coffee, and unfiltered cigarettes to make their points. At the bar, older men hunched over their shots, their backbones curved like bows under pressure. Mary couldn't see their faces, but their bifocals disqualified them as Eyes. They weren't mobsters; they were retirees, with a calcium deficiency.

She scanned the patrons, and none of them looked like criminals, either. They had lined faces that came from second mortgages, car payments, and Powerball losses, and they wore polyester sweatshirts, baggy pants, and pleather slip-ons. If anything, it looked like a roomful of people's parents, none of them young enough to be a friend of Bobby's, or even to drive at night. They gobbled pork sandwiches, an aroma Mary associated with Holy Communion lunches, Confirmation dinners, and wedding receptions. To the DiNunzios, any sacrament was a good excuse for a nice roasted pork.

No hostess came to seat her, so Mary chose the only open table and pulled out a chair that faced the door, so she could spot entering felons. She put her purse on the other chair and her newspaper on the wipe-clean plastic tablecloth, then opened her newspaper like everybody else. She turned a page for show, but stole a glance at the patrons on the far side of the room. Same thing. A table of painters in spattered white pants loudly discussed the murder with two Coke delivery guys in red shirts. The only exception was a table of four elderly women, looking at Mary with disapproving frowns. She wondered if she was paranoid or if they had heard gossip about her.

She looked away. None of these people was Eyes, it was obvious. What would she do now? How would she find him? Her gaze fell on the newspaper, and her own image stared back. It was the photo of her with Anthony, and she lingered on his expression to see if he really did have the look of love, suppressing the tiny quiver she felt inside. She remembered his voice, soft and tentative. She thought of the way the shadows fell on his face and back. She had told him everything last night, confided in him in a way she hadn't anyone before, and he hadn't judged her. On the other hand, he hadn't called today. She pulled her BlackBerry from her purse and checked her call log, all of which were clients. She noted three e-mails from Judy and shot her back a quick I'm-fine, so she wouldn't worry. Then she set the BlackBerry on the table in case Anthony called.

This is what happens when single girls stalk the Mob.

Mary got back on track, turning the pages and pretending to read a sidebar editorial, by one of the snarkier columnists whose byline she recognized. The headline alone scared her. THE PHILLY MOB: DEAD OR ALIVE? Her mouth went dry. Even though Biannetti's seemed safe, she didn't like tempting fate by reading about the Mob in a Mobbed-up restaurant.

'Coffee, honey?' a waitress asked, and Mary jumped.

'Sure, thanks.'

'You hungover?'

'What?' Mary didn't understand.

'The sunglasses.' The waitress set down a red plastic menu, and on the front was a stereotypical Italian chief with a Mario Brothers mustache, holding a plate of steaming spaghetti and meatballs.

'Right, yes. Ouch.'

'The coffee will help.' The waitress plunked down a thick white mug and poured coffee into it from a Bunn glass pot. She had a pretty, if careworn, face, and was in her fifties, with brown hair in short, dark layers. She had on a casual

261

blue blouse with mom jeans and seemed approachable enough, so Mary gestured casually to the newspaper.

'Pretty weird, huh? Think it's a Mob war?'

'Sure do.' The waitress nodded. 'It's been a while. You know what they say in *The Godfather*. It's time.'

'But that's a movie.'

'Oh yeah? Look around.' The waitress winked. 'Try telling the fans that.'

'Is that really why everybody's here?'

'After last night? You bet.'

'You'd think they'd avoid the place, if there's going to be trouble.'

'No way. They wanna be where the action is.'

Mary shuddered. 'But it might not be safe.'

'The Mob ain't like those rappers, shootin' the joint up. They only whack their own. Today, Biannetti's is the safest place on earth.'

'So Mob guys really do hang here?'

'Why do you wanna know?' The waitress smiled slyly.

'I'm just interested. None of these men look like gangsters to me, unless AARP's fronting.'

'This is the lunch crowd.'

'So at night is when the Mob guys come?'

'Midnight or later.' The waitress shifted her weight to the other hip. 'You like the bad boys?'

No. 'Yes. Does it show?'

'Please. You're not the first girl to come in here, lookin' to hook up.'

Yikes! 'I'm not?'

'No way. Girls come in all the time, and they all look just like you. They got the Coach handbags, the cell phones, the nice suits. They're like groupies. No offense.'

'None taken.'

'Ever since *The Sopranos*, business is crazy. The owner's talking about opening for breakfast. I see it all the time. You professional types like to take a walk on the wild side.'

'Color me guilty,' Mary said, and they both laughed.

'My husband says, you got women's rights and all, and you ladies give orders all day to your secretaries and assistants, and sometimes, you just wanna get ordered around in bed. Me, I'm married thirty-five years. I'm dead below the waist.'

Mary laughed, then turned to the front page of the newspaper and pointed at the photo of Bobby. 'You know,' she said, 'I used to hook up with this guy. Bobby Mancuso.'

'The one that got killed?' the waitress asked, in admiration.

'The very same.'

'He was made, wasn't he?'

'No, just connected,' Mary answered, eager to try out her new lingo.

'Still, he's so good-lookin'.' The waitress leaned over like a coconspirator. 'Was it *great*?'

'Beyond great.' Mary suppressed a twinge.

'Too bad they whacked him.'

'It happens.' Mary paused. 'You know, he always talked about this guy named Eyes, a friend of his. He said Eyes was a great guy.'

'Eyes?'

'Yeah. I'd like to meet him, but I can't find him.'

'Ha!' The waitress grinned crookedly. 'You're not wastin' any time, are you, girl?'

'The King is dead, long live the King.'

They both laughed, and at a nearby table, an older man raised his coffee mug, requesting a refill, but the waitress ignored him. 'So you're interested in Eyes, huh?'

'Do you know him?'

'It doesn't sound familiar.' The waitress frowned, thinking. 'What's his real name?'

'I forget. Bobby always called him Eyes.'

'What's he look like?'

'I don't know.'

'I never heard of a guy named Eyes.'

Damn. 'Maybe he came in with Bobby.'

'The dead guy? I never saw him either, but the boys come in at night, after midnight. I'm not on then.'

'Who is?'

'Barb. Barb Maniaci.'

'Maybe you could put in a good word for me, with her.' Mary reached for her wallet, extracted as many twenties as she could grab, and stuck them in the red menu, which she folded closed and handed to the waitress, who accepted it with a discreet wink.

'I'll let Barb know you wanna meet Mr. Eyes.'

'Great. Can you make it happen tonight?'

'Tonight is tough. They're all layin' low today. Nobody knows when all hell's gonna break loose.'

'I can't wait.'

The waitress arched an over-plucked eyebrow. 'You gotta, if you don't know his real name. We been sendin' sandwiches and baked ziti out all morning to, like, twenty different houses. For them, we deliver.'

'Good move.' Mary considered it. Of course, everybody would be over at the Pos' house paying their respects. Maybe even Cadillac.

The waitress pulled out her white pad. 'Now, hot stuff, what'll ya have for lunch?'

'I'm not eating,' Mary answered abruptly. She had to get going.

Even if it meant passing up a pork sandwich.

29

The drizzle had let up, and Mary was back in the car. She drove down the street, and the neighborhood seemed electrified by the murder, with people hanging out on their stoops, talking to each other. She turned on the windshield wipers and cruised ahead, then took a right, slowing down as she turned onto the street where Ritchie Po and his father lived.

She suppressed a tingle of fear and cruised past the house, watching the people going in and out of the Po house. Some were older neighborhood types bearing pastry boxes, but most weren't. Brawny guys in dark tracksuits climbed the front stoop, and black jackets got out of cars that double-parked out front. Mary checked them to see if they had funny eyes, but no.

Then she got down to business, scanning the parked and double-parked cars and all of the cars that dropped people off at the house. She spotted one Cadillac, then another, and started counting. She even circled the block twice, checking the cars on each trip, ending up at twelve Cadillacs. She felt her hope slip away. Maybe it wasn't such a great plan, since a Caddy was the official car of the South Philly Mob.

Mary took another turn around the block, and when she stopped at the corner, a memory came drifting back, floating out of her subconscious.

This wasn't the first time she had driven around this block, semistalking Bobby's house. She used to drive by in high school, after they'd broken up. She'd hoped to see him coming out of his house or going in; she was trying to decide whether to tell him about the baby, even after the fact. She felt a weight on her chest, like the one she'd felt when Mike died, and for a second she didn't know who she was mourning, as if both loves had gotten tangled together, her first love wrapped around her last love like a sucker vine, choking the life from her.

HONK! went a car horn, and Mary yelped. A red VW Golf with a teenage boy driving screeched through the intersection. She'd run the stop sign.

'Sorry!' she called out, lowering her window, but the teenager flipped her the bird, then zoomed off, which was when she looked out of her open window.

Rolli's, read the neon sign, flickering. It was another neighborhood restaurant, on the corner. She remembered that Bobby used to mention the place. He used to bus tables there, after school, in the off-season, and once, driving past, she'd seen him coming out. She flashed on the memory, like a snapshot: a tall young man, his bangs catching the wind, wearing a football jacket. He lets the screen door bang closed behind him. He slides a toothpick into the side of his mouth.

Mary pushed it away and eyed the place. Rolli's was only two blocks from Bobby's house, and now that she knew how miserable his home life had been, she understood why he'd hung out there. She considered it. If he used to go to Rolli's a lot, maybe he still did. What was it Brinkley had said? People like patterns. Maybe Bobby had taken Eyes in there. Maybe Mary didn't have to wait until tonight. It could be time that Trish didn't have.

Mary pulled over and was braking when her phone range. She checked the screen. 'Anthony?'

'Mary?'

'Hey.' She heard the warmth in her own voice. She had to admit she couldn't sound cool. She didn't feel cool. She felt melty, emotional, and caffeinated, and she was crashing at the intersection of three men.

'How are you?' Anthony asked. 'I was thinking about you, after last night.'

'Me, too,' Mary heard herself say.

'Kind of a heavy night. Did you sleep?'

'Not really.'

'Where are you?'

'In the neighborhood.'

'What are you doing here?'

'Uh . . . a case.'

'Really?' Anthony sounded dubious 'You're not looking for Trish, are you? You heard Detective Brinkley.'

'Uh, no. I'm working.'

'After your meeting, why don't you take a break? Come over for lunch. You haven't had my Bolognese sauce, which I learned to make in Bologna.'

'I can't. Work, work, work.'

'When then?'

'I'm not sure,' Mary answered. She felt distracted by Rolli's. Thinking about all the things she should have done, but didn't.

'You there?'

'Huh?' Mary caught herself. She had to go. She didn't have time for this. If she could just put him on hold. How can you tell a man to wait while you track down a dead mobster? It's not a good way to start a relationship.

'You know, I can't figure you out. Half the time you're blowing me off, and half the time you're not.'

Gulp. 'Anthony, I'm not blowing you off but I have to go. I'll call you back in half an hour.'

'Forget it — '

'No, really, I will, I swear it.'

'Okay, great,' Anthony said abruptly, then hung up.

Mary slipped the phone into her purse, parked the car, and went into Rolli's, which turned out to be the opposite of Biannetti's in every way. It was tiny, but bright and clean, with only one of twelve tables occupied. Cheery flowered table-cloths covered the little square tables, and the air smelled like stale Parmesan and Lysol. An old TV mounted in the corner played ESPN with closed captioning, but there was no bar. Mary looked around for a hostess, but seeing none, sat down and waited. She looked over at the occupied table, where two older women sat behind plates of ravioli. After five minutes, she called out to them, 'Excuse me, is there a waitress around?'

'Wha?' one of the women asked, her gnarled

269

hand fluttering to her ear, feeling if her hearing aid was turned on. Mary knew the gesture. Her father had a hearing aid he turned off whenever the Phillies started losing. She craned her neck to the back of the room, where fluorescent light spilled from an open doorway into what had to be the kitchen. She got up and went over.

'Hello?' Mary called out at the threshold, but there was no answer, so she stepped inside. It was empty. Stainless-steel counters ran the full length of the room, and an array of steel ladles, spoons, and spatulas hung from hooks on the back wall. A huge pot of gravy sat on the stove, but it wasn't bubbling, and the kitchen smelled oddly of sawdust. 'Hello?'

'Be right there!' a voice called back, and a short, middle-aged man with black hair and dark skin emerged from the back pantry, holding a commercial-size can of Cento tomatoes. 'I'm Jorge, can I help you?' he asked, his accent Hispanic.

'I didn't see a waitress.'

'Sorry, she's late. please, go sit, and I'll be right out.'

'Actually, I'm looking for a man named Eyes. I don't know his real name, but I think he was a friend of Bobby Mancuso, who worked here a long time ago. I'm hoping that he still might come in here and that he brought Eyes with him.'

'Bobby?' Jorge asked, his expression somber. He set down the big tomato can, *clank* against the steel counter, then wiped his hands on his full-length apron. 'We're all so sad about Bobby. So sad.'

'You know him?' Mary asked, surprised.

'Yeah, sure. Bobby, he come in here, all the time. It's terrible he died. Such a young man.'

'He was.' It struck Mary that nobody at Biannetti's had looked like they were in mourning, even the day after his murder. 'How often did he come in?'

'Like I say, all the time, for dinner. He liked the cannelloni. Three times a week, maybe more.'

'Was this recently?' Mary felt her heartbeat quicken.

'Sure, all the time.'

Mary didn't understand it. Trish's diary had said that Bobby went to Biannetti's all the time, but there hadn't been any references to Rolli's. Between here and Biannetti's, he must have been in a crab frenzy.

'You a cop, Miss?'

Mary introduced herself. 'No, I'm an old friend of Bobby's, from way back.'

Jorge's dark eyes narrowed.

'For real. I dated him in high school. Did he ever come in with a man named Eyes?'

'No.' Jorge shook his head. 'He come in alone.'

'Always alone?'

'Yes.'

Damn. 'Not even with Trish, his girlfriend?'

'No.'

Mary made a mental note. She was fresh out of leads, unless she wanted to follow a fleet of Cadillacs. 'So you don't know who Eyes is?'

'No, sorry,' Jorge answered, then gestured at the doorway behind Mary. 'But she might. This is Latreece, our waitress. She used to wait on Bobby all the time.'

Mary turned around, and standing in the doorway was a petite black woman wearing an oversized Baby Phat coat with tight jeans and a midnight green Eagles cap, pulled low.

'Sorry I'm late. It was just too hard to get here today.' Latreece slid the cap from her head, and Mary almost gasped. She was a young woman with a beautiful face, and her skin set off her most striking feature — a stunning pair of jade-green eyes, faintly Asian in shape.

'Eyes?' Mary blurted out, in disbelief.

30

Mary and Latreece sat down in white plastic chairs in a hallway to a tiny pantry of unpainted drywall, lined with boxes of canned goods and rolls of plastic-wrapped paper towels. A panel of fluorescent lighting cast harsh shadows on Latreece's face, but it couldn't make her ugly, even grieving as she was. Her eyes, puffy and slightly bloodshot, still shone that exotic green and her fine, high cheek-bones tapered to a delicate chin and soft mouth. She wore her hair natural and short, with simple gold hoops. In a different life, Latreece would have been a model, and Mary wanted to know everything about her.

'So you're Eyes?' she asked, amazed.

'Yes. Bobby called me that the first time I waited on him.' Latreece smiled, her face lighting up. 'I loved it. Made me feel like a spy. Most men, all they see is my boobs.'

Mary believed it. Latreece had on a stretchy black T-shirt, revealing an amazing body. 'Not a problem I have.'

'You're lucky.'

Right. 'So when did you meet him?'

'About four years ago. I waited on him and we got to talking.' Latreece's tone was feminine and girlish, which made sense, because she looked about twenty-five. 'He worked here a long time ago. He loved this place, even though, well, you see it.' Latreece gestured down the hall. 'It's had better days. He said it was like some old TV show. *Cheers.* He always said Rolli's was a place where everybody knows your name.'

Mary thought of Rosaria. It had been about four years ago that she had become estranged from Bobby.

'We got to know each other, and we started, you know, seeing each other. I knew about Trish, but that didn't matter, not really. He loved me and he took good care of me and my daughter. She's seven.' Latreece's lower lip trembled. 'Damn, I thought I was all cried out.'

'I'm sorry.'

'I know what it sounds like. What I sound like.' Latreece recovered, eyeing her pointedly with those fiery green gems. 'Just so you understand, it wasn't just sex. We loved each other. He had a good side, a wonderful side, and I loved him.'

'I understand.' *More than you know.*

'I didn't want to marry him. Stop. I'm lying.' Latreece paused. 'Well, in the beginning I did, but then I saw it wasn't gonna happen, and the way it was, it worked for us.' She got lost in thought, momentarily. 'Early on, I kept thinking, maybe he'll leave her. But I always knew he wouldn't. My brain knew better than my heart, you know?'

'Yes.'

'He was crazy about Trish. He loved her.'

Mary flashed on the horrific Polaroids, in the diary. 'But he abused her, Latreece.'

'I know, I guessed it. I'm young but I wasn't born yesterday. I left home when I got pregnant and I've been supporting myself since then. I

274

danced for a long time.'

'Danced?'

Latreece laughed softly. 'In a club.'

'Oh.' Mary smiled. 'That kind of dancing. I don't get out much.'

'Anyway, I knew he had a temper, especially when he drank.'

'He drank a lot.'

'I know. It was part of the reason I didn't wanna marry him.' Latreece shook her head sadly. 'But I can't believe what happened . . . it's horrible.'

'Do you think he killed her? She was terrified he would.'

'God knows.' Latreece looked crestfallen, her eyebrows sloping down. 'I don't think he would. Not if he thought about it, not if he had the chance to think. Not if he was sober.' She emitted a deep sigh. 'He wasn't mean, inside.'

'Did he say anything about asking to marry her soon? Or would he not talk to you about that?'

'Sure, he talked about it. We'd be in bed, talking about it.' Latreece shrugged. 'Sounds weird but it's true. We talked about her a lot, mostly that he thought she was cheating on him.'

Whoa. 'Really?'

'He used to worry she was, all the time. He got obsessed. He called her all the time, to try and catch her.'

Mary didn't get it. 'But he was cheating.'

Latreece smiled crookedly. 'So? Okay if he did it, not if she did.'

'Did he suspect any man in particular?'

275

'Anybody, everybody. Men who came into the salon, mostly.'

'Did he name anyone, that you remember?'

'No.'

Mary wasn't sure why she'd asked, anyway. 'Did you see him last week at all?'

'Sure, twice.'

'At the restaurant?'

'He came in late, ate, and then took me home. That's what we always did.'

Mary thought of Trish's diary, and the fights they'd had after he'd come home from Biannetti's. Rolli's hadn't been mentioned once. The conclusion was obvious. 'He didn't tell Trish he came here, did he?'

'No way.'

'I think he told her he went to Biannetti's, but really, he came here, where he could see you.'

'Probably.'

Mary filed it away. 'Did he mention that he was going to ask Trish to marry him, on her birthday?'

'No.' Latreece thought a minute. 'But he was in a bad mood. He was drinking a little heavier than usual though. I thought he had a lot on his mind.'

'Did you ask him why?'

'I thought it was work.'

'So you knew he was in the Mob.'

'Of course.' Latreece smiled without mirth. 'I knew what he did for a living, but I knew him as a man, too, and I don't judge.'

'Even with the drug sales?'

'Please. Bobby isn't the first person I know

276

who sells, and he won't be the last.' Latreece shook her head. 'He was jus' lost, like a little boy. He was gonna get out and he almost did.'

'Did he mention any friends he had, in the Mob?'

'He didn't have any friends in the Mob.'

'Did he ever mention a guy named Cadillac? Or a woman?' Mary had learned her lesson.

'No.'

'Ever bring them in here?'

'No way.'

'Okay.' Mary had to get to the point. 'I spoke with his sister and he told her he had a house, one that he could get lost to, when he left the Mob. Did he tell you about that?'

'No.'

'Are you sure?'

'Positive.' Latreece nodded. 'I didn't know anything about that.'

Mary tried not to get discouraged. 'If he were to buy a house, do you have any idea where it could be?'

'No.'

'Please. Think.'

'Why?'

'I'm wondering if he took Trish there.'

Latreece only shook her head, again. 'I don't remember him ever talking about anyplace other than the neighborhood. He went to school here. He'd never been anywhere else.'

Like me. 'Let's think about this. His sister told me he wanted to get out of the Mob someday, get away from them.'

'He used to say that but I never took it

277

serious.' Latreece snorted. 'Good luck.'

'Did he ever mention a vacation spot he liked?'

'No.'

Mary wracked her brain. 'I keep thinking that if I were going to buy a house, I'd buy it near something I liked to do. For example, if I fished, I'd buy near water.'

'He didn't fish,' Latreece said.

'Or swim.'

'He didn't swim? How could he not swim?'

'City boy. I can't either.' Mary asked, 'Did he have any hobbies you knew of?'

Latreece only chuckled.

Mary wracked her brain. 'Did he ever mention to you any trips he took out of town? Like when he came back?'

'No.'

'But he'd have to go out of town to find a place, to buy it, and to check on it once in a while.' Mary was thinking out loud. 'If it needed work, he'd have to work on it, or close it up for the winter, or do whatever people do.'

'Winterize.'

'Whatever.' Mary had no idea.

'Gotta turn off the water, wrap up the hot water heater, put some dehumidifiers in, so mold won't grow on the walls.'

'How do you know that?'

'Everybody knows that.'

'I don't.' Mary smiled.

'That's because *you're* a city girl.'

'Aren't you?'

'Hell, no. Why'd you think that? Because I'm black?'

278

Yes. 'No.'

'I'm a country girl from up north, near the Poconos. I grew up in Bonnyhart, north of the Delaware Water Gap. You know the area?'

'I've heard of it but I've never been there.'

'Oh, it's a beautiful place, near the Jersey border. Don't get me started. Trees, forests, all natural. You can walk in the woods forever. I love it up there.' Latreece's grin transformed her face. 'The air is so fresh, and the people so nice. My daughter loves it, too. I go up all the time to see my daddy, who still lives there. We were the only black family in town, but we had been there so long, we were accepted. Everybody was friendly, too. Everybody was a neighbor, not like here.'

Mary let go of the irony. 'You grew up there?'

'Sure did. We lived in a cabin in the woods. Daddy hunted, and I took care of the chickens and a pig we had. Oinker. We had deer meatballs, deer jerky, deer everything. We practically lived off the land.'

'I thought the Poconos were more developed than that. I mean, you see all the honeymoon packages.'

'Not in Bonnyhart, even now. There was nobody there. You could walk for days and not see another person.' Latreece's voice grew lighter. 'It's the most *beautiful* place in the world and it's right here, in Pennsylvania.'

Mary's thoughts raced ahead. 'Did you ever tell Bobby about this town?'

'Sure.' Latreece laughed. 'You couldn't shut me up about it. My daughter, neither. He used to tease me all the time. He said, 'If I had a dime

279

for every time you talked about Bonnyhart, I'd be set for life.'' Suddenly her eyes widened, and Mary had the same thought.

'Maybe that's where he bought?' She felt a tingle of excitement. 'Can you give me directions to Bonnyhart?'

31

Mary listened to the phone ring three times, then Anthony's voicemail came on, so she said, 'Sorry I didn't call you back. If you're there, would you pick up?' She listened to the silence, then swung the car onto Broad Street. 'I'm not blowing you off, but I got held up at my meeting, and I'm sorry. Please call when you can.'

She pressed End, then put her emotions aside. She couldn't worry about her love life now; she had a decent lead to follow. She could be up there in three hours. She started the ignition, hit the gas, and headed for Broad Street, toward the Expressway. She set the phone on the passenger seat, in case Anthony called back.

But she had a feeling that that wasn't happening anytime soon.

★ ★ ★

Three hours, one talk of gas, and two Mobil-station hot dogs later, Anthony hadn't called back, but Mary finally pulled into Bonnyhart, a town marked by a closed gas station. Dense stormclouds had swallowed the sun, darkening the sky prematurely, and rain had begun to fall hard. The windshield wipers pounded, but Mary was having trouble seeing the paved highway that cut through the woods.

There wasn't a house or a person in sight, and she'd passed the last car fifteen minutes ago, even though this would be rush hour anywhere else in the world. She pulled over to the side of the road, gravel and rocks popping and rumbling under her tires.

She put the car in park and checked her watch. Almost five o'clock. Too late to find any hall of records to look up the recorded deeds, but no matter; Bobby wouldn't have bought the house under his real name, anyway. She took a sip of cold coffee, thinking how to go about this. Then she remembered she'd seen a realtor's sign at the last town. It could be a good place to start, and she didn't have much time before dark. She hit the gas, then turned the car around and doubled back.

It was raining harder by the time she reached the clapboard house, which had been converted to contain two small businesses, the realtor and a taxidermist. Lights were on inside, and Mary parked in the almost-empty lot, next to a hand-lettered sign: **Deer! Bear! Elk! Antelope! Your quality turkey-taxidermy mount will give you a sense of pride!**

Mary wasn't in South Philly anymore. She cut the ignition, grabbed her bag, and held it over her head as she dashed out into the rain, running past the taxidermy store to the realtor's office. She went to the small front porch, then shook herself off, scanning photos of houses posted in the window. They were in the $100,000 to $200,000 range, two and three bedrooms, and underneath were the usual hackneyed captions:

282

ALL THE BELLS AND WHISTLES; HANDY-MAN SPECIAL; COZY RANCH; LAKE-VIEW MASTERPIECE; and DIAMOND IN THE ROUGH. It was the last photo that caught her eye, a brown ranch with the caption TOTAL PRIVACY.

Perfect. Mary went inside, and a little bell went off above the door, letting someone know that she had come in. The small office contained three metal desks, each with an aged computer, and the front desk was littered with multicolored Beanie Babies. A middle-aged woman with frizzy red hair bustled from a door in the back, reapplying coral lipstick as she walked.

'Oh, my, I didn't know anybody was here,' the woman said, with a fresh, if practiced, smile.

'Sorry if I startled you.'

'Are you lost? You look lost.' The woman twirled her lipstick closed, tossed it into a bulging makeup kit, then threw it in her purse. 'Out-of-towners always get lost.'

Mary smiled. 'How can you can tell I'm an out-of-towner?'

'No four-wheel drive and no flannel.' The realtor laughed, then she extended a hand with lacquered nails. 'Julia O'Connell. Sorry about my bad manners.'

Mary introduced herself. 'I know a guy who bought a second house up here, and he loves it. He wanted total privacy, he's from Philly. He told me the address but I lost it, and now I can't reach him on the cell. I'd love to see the house and was wondering if you sold it to him.'

'I only started last month and I haven't sold

283

anything. I'm on my second career and my third husband.' Julia laughed uncertainly. 'Maybe one of the other gals worked with him. What's his name?'

'Bobby Mancuso.' Mary held her breath, in the hope that the news of his murder hadn't reached the boonies yet. Or betting that Bobby wouldn't have given his real name when he bought his hideout. It wasn't like he'd be applying for a mortgage, with proof of employment.

'Doesn't sound familiar,' Julia answered, after a moment.

'He's kind of eccentric, so he might have bought under a different name. Maybe you heard one of the other realtors talking about it. I think he might've paid in cash.'

'Cash!' Julia's eyes lit up. 'I didn't hear anything about a cash deal, but like I say, I'm not here that long. I'm sure the owner, Mary Alice Raudenbush, would know, but she's gone for the day and I'd hate to bother her at home. Maybe we should wait until your friend calls back.'

Mary thought a minute. 'Are there other realtors that sell in Bonnyhart?'

'Locally, a few. Of course, anybody can sell anywhere these days. The MLS is online and such, and some of those Philly and New York realtors, they take their clients themselves, and we cooperate with 'em, you know.'

'He wouldn't have done that.' Mary started working on a new working theory. 'The reason I'm asking is I'd like to find a house like his.'

'Really?' Julia's expression brightened. 'You

and your husband?'

'No, just me.' Mary warmed to the role. She really did want to buy a house and now she could, in an alternate reality. 'I'm on my own, and I wanted something private.'

'You've come to the right place. We sell all around Carbon and Luzerne counties, very private Pocono properties. Let's make an appointment, shall we?'

'I wanted to look tonight.'

'Now? It's raining like crazy.' Julia groaned as she checked her watch, moving it faceup on a slim wrist. 'I was just closing up, too.'

'If I knew the houses that have sold in Bonnyhart, let's say in the past two years, I could go look at them myself, maybe get an idea of what I want. I don't have a lot of time. I'm in the neighborhood only tonight.'

'I could give you the comps for Bonnyhart, but I'm not supposed to do that. I'm supposed to drive around with you.'

'What's a comp?'

'The comparable sales for Bonnyhart. You'd use them to decide what to ask for your house, or to evaluate the asking price of a target property.' Julia sounded like she was reciting from the realtor's exam. 'Comps show the square footage, number of bedrooms and baths, lot size, like that.'

'Great. I'd like the comps.'

'I'm really not allowed to do that. If you come back tomorrow, we can go together.'

'I don't have time for that and I'd prefer to go alone.' Mary played the part of a tough businesswoman, a partner at Rosato & DiNunzio. Or even DiNunzio & Rosato. 'If you give me the comps, I'll look at the houses and get back to you.'

'That's not the way they do it.' Julia's lined eyelids fluttered.

'That's the way I do it. If you want your first sale.'

'Okay, hold on.' Julia leaned over the desk and hit a key on the computer, and Mary learned that hardball wasn't all that hard. All you had to do was ask for what you want and shut up. Two hours later, she was driving through the rain, armed with Julia's map of the Bonnyhart area and two pages of comps, with twenty-one houses total. Her windshield wipers worked overtime, and her high beams struggled to cut the driving rain. She wound her way along dirt roads, splashing through muddy puddles and around downed tree limbs that snapped under her car tires.

The first seven houses were occupied, all of them clapboard or brick three-bedrooms set back in the woods, priced around $100,000 to $150,000. None of them had black BMW's in the driveway, but Mary had waited at the curb in front of each one, the downpour and darkness allowing her to snoop from the car and see what was going on inside the houses. Everybody kept their curtains and blinds open, maybe because they lived in the middle of nowhere, and the first two houses got eliminated because they were filled with kids.

Inside the eighth house, an old couple

watched TV, side-by-side on a plaid sofa, the lights from the screen flickering on their glasses, sudden as lightning. At the ninth house, nobody was home and the lights were off, so Mary had stolen up to the front window, covering her head from the rain with her purse, and looked inside with a flashlight. Four cats gazed at her from the back cushions of the couch, their eyes reflective in the dark, and she crossed that house off the list.

Mary got back in the car and hit the gas, heading for the next house. She told herself to stay the course. The plan made sense. It was logical that Bobby had taken Trish up here. The house could have been the surprise. If the diary was any indication, Trish didn't know about the house. So what would've happened? Did he take her with him? Did he kill her up here and go back downtown? Did he lock her up in the house and then go? Could she still be alive, locked inside the house, like those schoolgirls in the Dutroux case? Or was she buried in its backyard?

Mary was slowing to a stop around a bend when she saw a large deer and two spotted fawns crossing the road, the littlest one springing from a standstill onto the hillside next to the road. She took two more right turns, then a left, following the map in the interior light, and reached the mailbox for 78 Tehanna Lane. She pulled over in front of the house, cut the headlights, and eyed the place through the trees.

There was no car in the driveway, but a light was on inside, a yellow square sliced by the trees in the front yard, their leaves dripping rainwater.

287

The house was as nondescript as the others, and she flicked on the flashlight and scanned the comps in the car. Two bedrooms, one and a half baths, 1,320 square feet, half an acre, well water only, sold for $98,000 a year ago.

Mary shut off the flashlight and sat in the car a moment, watching to see if anyone was inside. The house was clapboard, but it must have been painted a darkish color, because it was barely visible at night. It looked like it had a front porch, because she could see an overhang sheltering a picture window and the gutter dripping water, twigs, and leaves. There were the twin shadows of two chairs sitting on the porch.

She checked the mailbox again. It was black, unlike the more decorative ones painted with fishing rods or deer heads. It had no plastic box underneath for the local paper, and there was no name on the mailbox, also unusual. Many of the other boxes had the owners' last names in old-fashioned white stenciling or cute hand-painted script, and the houses had been given vacation names, like Hernando's Hideaway. But if this one was a hideaway, it was well hidden.

Mary looked at the house, aware that her heart had started to beat a little harder. Raindrops pounded on the hood of her car and sluiced down the windshield in a sheet. Her shoes were still wet from last time, and her clothes felt clammy. She stalled a minute longer, in no hurry to run out in the rain or, oddly, to leave the safety of the car. She became aware that she hadn't eaten in hours and checked her watch, its dial glowing a ghostly greenish circle. Almost ten

288

o'clock. She was too nervous to feel the least bit hungry and edged up in the seat, keeping an eye on the house for movement.

No movement, no nothing. No other cars were on the road, and she shook off a spooky sensation, then grabbed her purse helmet and bolted out of the car. She ran around the front and scooted up the slick driveway. Cold rain hit her cheeks and splashed onto her ankles as she darted for the front porch. She clambered onto the floorboards, next to two chairs of a cheap white wire, and she kept her gaze on the picture window. There didn't seem to be anybody inside the living room, and she walked to the front door on sopping feet, ready to knock if she got caught snooping.

The picture window revealed a small living room, furnished sparely with a brown sofa and two chairs. There were no magazines or newspapers on the coffee table, as in the other houses; in fact, there was no clutter anywhere at all. It hardly looked lived in. She walked closer to the front door, her heart beginning to hammer. She was raising her hand to knock when she noticed that inside, where the brown rug ended, a green ceramic lamp lay smashed on the hardwood floor, its shards laying about, sharp ends up.

Mary felt her senses spring to alertness. What could have knocked the lamp down? There didn't seem to be any pets around. Why would anyone leave the broken pieces lying there? Why not pick them up? She stood at the door, wondering. Barely breathing. Listening hard.

There was no sound but the rushing of the rain around her.

She knocked, then waited, telling herself to calm down. No dogs began barking inside, and no cats blinked back at her. She knocked again out of sheer nervousness. No answer. She pressed her eye to a slit in the curtain on the door, which gave her a sliver of the small dining room beyond the living room. The light was on there, too, but there was no movement, just a long wooden table, and on it, a brown shopping bag, standing upright. Something about the bag caught Mary's attention. She squinted until she could see better, and her heart leapt to her throat. On the bag, a heavyset chef with a Super Mario mustache held a steaming plate of spaghetti and meatballs. The Biannetti's logo.

'Trish!' Mary heard herself scream, against the wind and rain. She twisted the doorknob, but it was locked. She pounded on the door. 'Trish! Are you there?' The downpour drowned her cry. She felt as if someone had flipped a switch, throwing on all of her circuits, all at once. It had to be Bobby's house. Trish could be inside, Trapped. Dying. Alive. Maybe it wasn't too late.

'Trish!' Mary screamed. The sound reverberated in her ears. Her thoughts ran scared. She could go back to her car and call the cops, but when would they come? Were there cops up here, anyway? Trish could be inside the house. It was an emergency. Mary wasn't standing on ceremony or law. She shoved the door with her shoulder, then ran back a few steps on the porch and hit it again with all her might. It budged, but

290

didn't open. Her shoulder hurt like hell.

She looked wildly around. The wire chair on the porch. It was heavy enough to do the job. She reached over, grabbed the chair, raised it over her head, and in one motion, brought it crashing through the window in the door. The glass shattered with a tinkling sound, spraying to the ground.

'Trish!' Mary yelled. No one came running from the house or anywhere else. It made her more nervous than before. Her mouth went dry.

She flung the chair aside, poked her hand through the broken window, and felt around inside for the knob, calling Trish's name. She felt herself give in to panic. She twisted the lock frantically one way, then the other. She tried the knob again. It unlocked, and she extracted her hand and swung the front door wide open, then hurried inside.

32

'Trish?' Mary called out, closing the front door behind her. She scanned the living room. It was as she had seen from the window. Nothing out of order except the broken lamp on the floor. She stepped over the shards from the lamp and the window, then moved quickly through the dining room. She could be contaminating a crime scene, but it was an emergency if Trish was alive. And if she wasn't, her killer was beyond conviction.

Mary called out again, the tremor in her voice echoing throughout the house. She reached the Biannetti's bag and peeked inside. A stack of tinfoil trays with white cardboard lids sat inside. She felt the bag. It was stone cold. She eyeballed the room. A new dining room table with four chairs. Nothing on the walls, and it smelled like fresh paint. She glanced at the walls, eggshell white, and imagined a likely scenario: Bobby had brought Trish here, to show her the house and even got take-out diner to celebrate. Then he'd dropped the question, and all hell had broken loose.

Mary turned and looked behind her at the shards on the floor, wondering. Had he hit Trish with the lamp? Dragged her out to the car? Taken her somewhere? Killed her? Could she still be alive in here?

'Trish!' Mary went from the dining room to

the kitchen, then looked around. All cleaned and untouched. A six-pack of Bud sat on the counter, unopened, next to a bottle of Chianti and three of Smirnoff vodka, one half full. Next to them sat a white cake box with dancing musical notes around the side, from Melrose Diner. She peeked inside the box's clear plastic window, knowing what she'd see. *Happy Birthday, Sweetheart*, read the pink icing.

'Trish!' Mary hurried from the room and up the stairs, her heart pounding. If Bobby had killed her, would he have done it in the bedroom? Would there be a body there? She flashed on Trish's mother, heartbroken in Mary's parents' house, and then the Mean Girls, hysterical in her office. She stowed those thoughts in the back of her mind and reached the top of the stairs, then entered the first room on the second floor, holding her breath as she flicked on the light switch.

No body. Nobody. Merely a queen-sized bed, with a white coverlet and flanking night tables, just like in the house in South Philly. Not slept in. Nothing on the walls. A small single closet with an open door. Empty. No clothes or shoes inside, or anything awful, either. Mary glanced around. There was no bathroom off the bedroom, so she went back out in the hallway, sick with fear. Where could Trish be?

Mary came upon a doorway next to the bedroom, braced herself, and flung the door open as she flicked on the light, then looked inside. Nothing. A new, bright white bathroom, also apparently unused. She turned around,

293

puzzled. There was only one room left, off the hall, at the darkened end. She swallowed hard and crossed the hall, then reached inside the door for the light switch.

'Trish?' she said, hearing the fear in her own voice. She couldn't find the switch with her fingers and got so nervous that she raked the wall with her hand until the room came to life, illuminated. Nothing. Another bedroom. Nothing in it except a double bed and a single night table. She blinked, confused.

'Trish!' she called out, then jogged back down the hall, went downstairs, and looked around for a cellar door, then found one in the kitchen. She hadn't seen it before. She told her heart to stop jumping around, and her brain began to function. If Bobby were going to kill Trish, he wouldn't leave her body in his basement, incriminating him, would he? Maybe she was locked down there, alive?

Mary descended the skinny staircase. It had no rail, and as she went down she could see that nothing was amiss in the basement. The concrete floor was clean, with a new washer and dryer against one wall, of gray cinderblock. A hot-water heater sat on the right, next to the usual collection of incomprehensible heating things. She reached the bottom and looked around. No Trish.

She went back upstairs, unaccountably spooked that somehow she'd be locked in the basement for the rest of her life, then breathed a relieved sigh when she reached the kitchen again. She took the time to search the drawers, which had been filled with new kitchen gear. She found a set of striped dishtowels, still with their price tags from Target. Clearly Bobby had been setting up house. She turned to the last drawer and pulled it open. It was full of bills and papers, and she recognized the logos for Verizon, and PECO. She picked up the first few and looked at the name: **Marty Slewinsky**.

Mary knew that name, heard it like an echo from her past. It was a name that Bobby always called himself when he felt dumb. His stupid alter ago. He'd be struggling with his declensions, and when she quizzed him and he got the answer wrong, he said it was Marty Slewinsky. She didn't know if anybody but her knew the nickname. Bobby wouldn't be telling his fellow mobsters about his insecurities, and by the time he'd grown up, he'd be masking those feelings with vodka. She reached for a thick packet of papers and opened the trifold. The yellow one on the top was a purchase agreement for a Ford 150, 4WD, also in Marty Slewinsky's name. She remembered what the realtor had said, no four-wheel drive and no flannel.

Bobby would need that truck in this terrain. So this *was* his house. His bills. His new identity, just waiting for him whenever he left the Mob. But where was the truck? Had he driven it back to the city? And what was his grand plan, anyway? Trish would leave her mom, friends, and job for a cabin in the middle of the woods? And if he had proposed that to her, what had happened?

Then Mary remembered about the cheating,

295

and Trish's nooners with Miss Tuesday Thursday. Had Trish told him she'd been cheating? Had he found out? What would he do to her if he did? She shoved the bills back inside the drawer and went over to the lamp, broken on the floor. She examined the shards without touching them, bending over, which was when she saw it, on the jagged edge of one of the broken pieces. Red-brown droplets spattered against the light green. She looked closer. The flecks were dried blood.

'Trish,' she heard herself whisper.

* * *

Mary ran back to the car in the rain, hardly feeling the chilly drops. The sight of the blood had set something loose inside her. Her worst fears. She ached to find Trish. It wasn't a lot of blood. It hadn't been a mortal wound. Maybe she was still alive.

Mary hit the gas. She had to tell Brinkley about the house and the blood. He would know what to do. She fumbled for her cell phone as she drove, then pressed in his cell number, heading for the main road, which she remembered was off to the left. The call connected, and she waited while it rang and rang.

'Please pick up, Reg,' she said, but the call went to voicemail. She cursed to herself, then waited for his message to end. 'I found Bobby's house in the Poconos, but no Trish. Call as soon as you can.'

She pressed End, taking one turn in the

woods, then another. Should she call 911, for the local police? Did that make any sense? Maybe. She pressed 911 as she drove.

'What is . . . emergency?' the dispatcher asked when the call connected, but Mary could barely hear her for static and the rain.

'I was just at 78 Tehanna Lane in Bonnyhart and I believe a woman may have been injured, if not killed in that house. She's been missing for two days and her name is Trish Gambone.'

'Did you . . . see . . . woman?' the dispatcher asked, breaking up.

'No, but I saw her blood.'

'Who . . . you, miss?'

Mary filled her in, but couldn't hear what she was saying. 'Hello? Hello?'

'Miss . . . you must . . . cell phone. You've reached the Bruman Police . . . New York.'

'What?'

'We must be the nearest . . . relay station . . . not a bona fide emergency . . . Pennsylvania State Police . . . they can follow up.' The dispatcher gave Mary the state police number, and she repeated it while she drove, then pressed it in and waited for it to connect.

'Pennsylvania State Police,' the new dispatcher answered, and the connection was improved, but still not good. Mary had just begun when the dispatcher cut her off. 'Excuse me, but we're stretched pretty thin tonight with this weather, and it doesn't sound like we need to send a car over there tonight.'

'But you do. She could be in the vicinity, still alive. She could be hidden somewhere or even

297

buried alive.' Mary had been spinning nightmare scenarios in the back of her mind since she'd seen that blood. 'I almost got out and started looking myself.'

'I'm sorry, but it sounds as if the Philadelphia police are handling the matter, and we wouldn't interfere with them.'

'But the house is up here, I think he brought her here, and I can't reach anybody in Philly.'

'Miss, please give me your name and number and we'll call you as soon as we can.'

'When will that be?' Mary sensed she was pressing a lost cause but she couldn't help herself.

'Tomorrow, business hours. That's the best I can do for you, miss.'

'Okay, thanks.' Mary gave her the information, then hung up, and when she set the cell on the passenger seat, she looked up and realized she didn't know where she was. She slowed to a stop at an intersection of two gravel roads, disoriented in the woods and the rain, then pulled over and flicked on the interior light to read the realtor's map. She traced the route from Bonnyhart with a finger, then looked around for a road sign. Rain pounded the windshield, and she could barely see outside. There were no street signs. She couldn't use the map if she didn't know where she was.

She set the map aside, switched off the light, and drove farther, sensing that the main road had been in this direction. She tried to plug the street name into the BlackBerry but didn't have enough info to retrieve the map. Last, she tried to call Judy to tell her what was going on and ask her to help, but there was no answer and the phone kept cutting out. Fifteen minutes later, Mary still hadn't hit any paved road. She must have been wrong. She started to panic a little. Where was she? How had she gotten so turned around? She thought the turnpike was off this way, but she'd been mistaken. She checked the dashboard clock. Almost midnight.

Brinkley still hadn't called her back. She took a right, then another right when she saw some lights through the trees, then kept on the roads that headed toward the lights, vowing to buy herself a navigation system when she got back to the city. In another half hour, she saw the lights getting closer. They were the lights of a snowmobile and used-tractor dealership, but up ahead twinkled new lights.

'Yay!' Mary shifted upward in the seat and hit the gas, feeling reassured as she took a right onto a paved road, which counted as progress. Ahead was an auto-body shop and a hunting-supplies store, both closed, but at least she was out of the woods. The sky glimmered gray up ahead, and she guessed it was the reflected lights of a town or maybe from the turnpike. She breathed easier and accelerated, and when she took a left turn, found herself behind another vehicle, an old red Jeep.

'Mirabile dictu,' Mary said, a little Latin for the road, and honked to get his attention. She wasn't too proud to ask for directions, but the Jeep driver must have misunderstood her, because he sped up. She honked again, more lightly this time, and the driver stuck his hand out the window and flashed her the bird.

Mary kept heading toward the light, growing brighter in the sky. On the left, down the road, was a blinking sign for a cheesy motel that read EZ-Stop, which she took as a good sign that she was going the right way. Another car pulled out from a side road in front of the Jeep, and she began to relax as they slowed to a stop to permit the car to turn onto another dirt road.

Mary glanced idly at the motel, left over from the sixties but trying to be modern. Its sign read AIR COND, C BLE TV, in front of the space-age building, and its rooms overlooked the parking lot. The all-glass office was barely lit, though the lot was almost full, probably with travelers too wise to drive on such an awful night. Mary squinted through the rain, and her eye caught one of the cars parked near the front. Its distinctive European grille stuck out in a lot crowded with older American SUVs and trucks. It was a new black BMW.

Mary wiped the steam off her window and double-checked. The shiny grille winked at her from the parking lot. She had been right, but she didn't know if it mattered. There were lots of black BMW in the world, and if not in this part of the world, then easily off the turnpike.

But when the jeep took off, Mary turned left into the motel lot.

33

Mary entered the lot and pulled into a parking space beside the BMW, then cut the ignition, eyeing the car. It glistened darkly, its inky hood slick with rain, and it had been parked by reversing into the space with its grille facing front. She looked at the other cars. All of them had been parked the normal way, with their back bumpers facing front. She herself never reversed into a space because she was the world's worst reverser. Why would somebody park that way? To hide the BMW's license plate.

She peered through the porthole she'd made in her window. She couldn't see inside the BMW because of the darkness and rain. She checked the lot behind her, which was quiet, and there were only a few lights on in the rooms. The place was silent and still, with mostly everyone asleep. She grabbed her trusty flashlight, switched it on, and shined it on the front seat of the BMW, then the backseat. the circle of light wandered over plush black leather upholstery and gleaming chrome appointments on the console, and ended in a crowded ashtray, slid partway open.

Hmm. Other than the cigarettes, there was nothing to link the car to Bobby, and lots of people smoked. She got out her purse hat, her nice Coach bag practically ruined, checked behind her car again to see if anybody was watching, then climbed out with her flashlight.

301

She let her car door close softly, slipped between the two cars, and sneaked to the back of the BMW, where she checked the license plate: FG-938. It was a Pennsylvania plate, which made sense, and the number meant nothing to her, since the Mean Girls hadn't known Bobby's plate number. The car could have come from anywhere. Pennsylvania was a big state. She directed the light to the back of the car and the shimmer of the chrome plaque surrounding the license plate. De Simone BMW. Marlton, NJ.

Mary considered it, shivering in the cold rain. Marlton was right outside Philadelphia, over the bridge to Jersey. People from South Philly shopped in Marlton and its environs all the time. They usually bought their cars in the South Philly Auto Mall, but the Auto Mall didn't have a BMW dealership. So it wasn't impossible that the BMW was Bobby's. But then how did it get here, to this lot?

Mary slipped out from behind the BMW, scurried across the lot to the motel office, and yanked open the glass front door, leaving a hardware-store Open sign swinging on a plastic suction cup. But it didn't look open. The front counter, a dingy white with a rounded edge, was cluttered with tourist brochures that flopped over in little wire racks, and there was no one behind the desk. She cleared her throat and leaned over, which was when she looked into an office behind the counter and saw a middle-aged woman sleeping in a beach chair.

'Hello?' Mary called out, and the woman stirred, fluttering her eyes.

'Oh, sorry.'

'That's okay,' Mary said quickly, running on adrenaline. 'Sorry to wake you. I just have a question or two.'

'Question?' The woman rose and stretched, soft as a teddy bear in a Bon Jovi sweatshirt and wide-legged jeans. She wore no earrings or makeup, but her long brown ponytail gave her a fresh, cute look and swung a little as she stretched and ambled over to the counter. 'You don't want a room?'

'No. I'm wondering about that black BMW in the lot.' Mary pointed, but the clerk didn't bother looking. 'I assume that it belongs to a guest?'

'Guess so.' The clerk shrugged sleepily. 'I only work the night shift. I checked in a lot of people tonight, and I expect more'll be coming if the storm keeps up. There's flooding, I hear.'

'Is there a way we could look up whose car it is?'

'No.' The clerk shook her head, and her ponytail swung back and forth like the Open sign. 'We don't have 'em write down the plates or anything. Most people come here, stay the night, and get back on the turnpike early next morning. Or they stay an hour or so, if you get my drift.'

'Do you think I could get a look at your register, if you have anything like that?'

'Nah, we don't, and I couldn't let you look at it, anyway.'

Mary figured as much, and the clerk was looking at her funny, now that she was fully awake. Her small brown eyes glinted with suspicion.

'Why do you care whose car it is?' she asked.

'My old boyfriend has a BMW like that, from the same place, and I'm wondering if he's here.' *It almost wasn't a lie.*

'Gotcha, but I can't help you there.' The clerk grinned wearily.

'Then there's only one choice. Can I get a room in view of the parking lot?'

'It's the only view we got, hon,' the clerk said, and they both laughed.

So Mary bought herself a $68 motel room, which included olive green patterned chairs, a matching bedcover and ratty rug, and complimentary dust mites. She turned on the forced-air heater, which smelled like burning hair, and kept an eye on the BMW while she kicked off her wet shoes and made herself a cup of coffee in the one-cup coffeemaker. After it was ready, she turned off the lights and took up permanent residence in a chair in front of the window, peeking through the curtain in the dark.

Rain pounded against the glass and sluiced down in crazy rivulets, and Mary assessed her view with satisfaction. She was on the first floor, directly across and not fifty feet from the BMW, so she'd see the moment anybody crossed to it, if she could stay awake long enough. She hoped to God this wasn't the dumbest thing she'd ever done, but even she was beginning to think it was crazy to keep driving in the storm. She kept her phone at hand in case Brinkley called and fought the impulse to leave him another message. She gulped the dreadful coffee and kept an eye on the BMW, babysitting an inanimate object.

Two cups later, she was beginning to feel dangerously sleepy, but was too paranoid to turn on the TV. She kept slumber at bay by watching a car pull in to the lot. It pulled in slowly, and Mary played a guessing game with herself, trying to predict whether it would reverse into the space. But the car didn't park. It idled in the middle of the lot, and she watched, her chin in her hand, her eyelids heavy. In the next instant a man got out of the car, opened up a blue-and-white golf umbrella, and ran around to the passenger side of the car. He let a woman out, which Mary thought was nice. So chivalry wasn't dead.

Then she did a double take. Mary couldn't see the face of the man or the woman because they were hidden under the umbrella, but she'd know that fox jacket, tight pants, and stiletto boots anywhere.

'Trish?' Mary sat bolt upright, stunned. The man and the woman crossed onto the pavement right in front of her window. The gold umbrella read Dean Witter. She ducked, and if she hadn't, they would have looked right into her face. Then they took a right, passing her window.

'Yikes!' Mary plopped down the coffee cup, jumped out of her chair, and went to the front door. She undid her chain lock at warp speed, flung open the door, and peeked out. The man and Trish were walking close together to a door a few down the row, then they were pausing in front of the door. Their bodies came close together under the umbrella, as if they were kissing.

So Trish was alive, and this must be the guy she was cheating with! But what were they doing up here? Mary felt about a thousand feelings at once, notably, joy that Trish was still alive, followed quickly by rage that Trish had worried her to death.

She squinted through a crack in her door as Trish disappeared inside the room, and the mystery man under the Dean Witter umbrella ran back to the car, opened the driver's-side door, and climbed in, then closed the umbrella. Mary squinted but couldn't make out any detail of his face or even build. She tried to see the model of the car, but it was too dark and rainy. It was a black sedan, four doors, a new-model something, and she wasn't about to let it get out of sight.

The car drove around the parked cars in the middle heading for the exit, and Mary darted into the rain. She reached the exit a split second after the sedan pulled out, just in time to see his license plate.

'RK-029,' Mary said aloud, so she wouldn't forget it, but that wasn't what struck her. Above the plate was an emblem she knew well. The car was a Cadillac.

She flashed on Trish's diary. **Cadillac thinks he's stealing. Cadillac said that my watch must have cost an arm and a leg. Cadillac keeps having his suspicions**. Her questions rushed at her, one after the other. Was Cadillac the mystery man under the umbrella? Why was

Trish running around up here with another man, not one day after Bobby's murder? What the hell was going on, anyway?

Mary turned on her heel and made a soaking-wet beeline for Trish's door.

34

Mary knocked gently, guessing Trish would think it was the mystery man coming back. The door swung wide open, and Trish's expression morphed from delicious anticipation to abject shock. She had on a tight black sweater with sequins around its deep V-neck, and her makeup looked fresh as a tattoo. She'd expected a lover but got a lawyer, and it hardly seemed fair.

'Mare?' Trish asked, her mouth a perfect circle.

'What's going on?' Mary pushed past her into the motel room, which reeked of burning cigarettes, rather than burning hair.

'I can't believe you're here. How did you find me?' Trish closed the door behind them, and Mary turned on her, not bothering to keep anger or hurt from her tone.

'Never mind that, Trish. You think I'm playing a game here? I've been worried sick about you. I thought Bobby killed you. So did the girls and your mom.'

'Mare, calm down. I know what I'm doing.'

'*What?* What's going on? Do you know Bobby's dead? Murdered?'

'Yeah, I do.' Trish edged backward. 'I found out.'

'How? How did you find out? Did your boyfriend tell you?' Mary could see the question strike a chord, because Trish stiffened, defiant.

'It's not your business.'

'Who's your boyfriend?' Mary almost spat. 'Was that Cadillac from the diary? Or the stockbroker from the salon?'

'My diary? You read my diary?' Trish's eyes flew open in outrage.

'Sue me,' Mary shot back. 'Now what are you doing here? Why didn't you call and tell everybody you're alive?'

'What are you, stupid? I couldn't. I was afraid for them, if they knew. Somebody whacked Bobby. They could be after me, next. Do you know what that's like for me?'

'For *you*?' Mary shouted. 'What about everybody else? Your selfishness is breathtaking! The cops are looking for you. My friend Reg is looking for you. Giulia and the girls have been out there looking for you, for days, and your mom's a holy mess. What the hell are you doing here? What happened on your birthday, at the house?'

'Who do you think you are, yelling at me? I'm not a little girl.' Trish's tone echoed the old Mean Girl years, which only made Mary madder.

'Tell me what happened or I'll call the police right this minute.'

'Fine.' Trish reached for a cigarette from a pack on the night table. 'If you shut up and let me talk.'

'I'll wait.'

'Good.'

Trish lit her cigarette and Mary took a seat in the chair opposite the bed, neither woman

309

speaking for a moment, as if they were two prizefighters, returned to their corners. Trish sat on the olive green bed, sucked on the cigarette one last time, then stubbed it out in the ashtray in the light from a cheap brown lamp.

'The night of my birthday,' she began, 'Bobby came home and said he had a surprise and we had to drive to it, so we came up here and he showed me this crappy little house in the woods.' Trish snorted. 'He said he owned it and he was gonna get outta the Mob, and we were gonna move up here, have a slew a kids. He said I was gonna marry him. He didn't even ask me, he told me, like I was some dog, and he had this ugly ring and I freaked and threw it at him.'

Trish's tone rang true, though Mary couldn't help but doubt her. Finding her with Mystery Man was too weird, and she couldn't wrap her mind around it yet.

'So when I did that, he freaked. Crazy mad, madder than I ever saw him before. He'd been drinkin' the whole way up, so I knew I was in trouble.' Trish wet her lips, her cadence slower. 'He tried to hit me but I ran around the dinin' room, and he hollered at me was I cheatin' on him and I told him I was because I wanted him to let me go, that I couldn't marry him ever, and I wanted out.' Trish's voice caught with fear, and Mary studied her face to see if the emotion was real, but couldn't tell. She didn't trust Trish any longer, and worse, she didn't trust her own instincts.

'Okay, so then what?'

'Then I realized that nobody knows where I

am, I'm in the effin' mountains and he could get away with killin' me, so when he grabbed me, I picked up the lamp and hit him on the head.'

The lamp. The blood. It was Bobby's, not hers.

'He dropped like he got shot, unconscious. I'm no dummy. I took his car keys and drove away.'

'In the BMW?'

'Right. He had another car there, a black pickup truck. I didn't even know he had a second car.' Trish shook her head, disgusted. 'I didn't know he had any of this goin' on. I don't even know how he found out about this hellhole.'

I do. 'Okay, go on.'

'So I called my boyfriend and we found this place to hide out in.'

'Is your boyfriend Cadillac?'

'No. Cadillac's a wiseguy that hates Bobby.'

'How did you know Bobby was dead?'

'He told me.'

'Who?'

'My boyfriend.'

'Who is he?'

'Just a guy. A married guy. I met him at the shop, a businessman who doesn't need any of this crap.'

'The stockbroker?'

'Yes.'

Mary thought a minute. 'So he's Miss Tuesday Thursday?'

Trish's eyes narrowed. 'How do you know about that?'

'Why didn't you write about him in your diary?'

'I was too scared to, in case Bobby ever found it in the car.' Trish eyed her directly. 'Mare, I kept up that diary to make a record of what he was doin', in case they found me dead. Gimme a break.'

'Why didn't you tell Giulia and them about the boyfriend?'

'Are you for real?' Trish chuckled. 'The mouths on them? Why don't I just put it on MySpace?'

'I thought you guys were so close.'

'They're close to me, but I'm not close to them.' Trish's tone was matter-of-fact, and so frank that Mary knew it was true. Nobody ever got close to the Queen Bee, which made her the loneliest girl of all.

'Okay.' Mary let it go. 'Get back to the story. You called your boyfriend.'

'Right, and he drove up, and he told me to sit tight until we can figure out what to do.'

'Great advice.' Then Mary remembered. 'Wait. When did you call your mom?'

'When we first came up to the house. Bobby went outta the room, and I saw what was gonna happen and I started to get scared. So I called my mom, but the connection was bad and I left a message. Then he came in and took the cell phone from me, and I could tell by that look in his eyes, that animal look, that he was gonna lose it. I was gonna be dead on my birthday.' Trish's mouth twitched with something like pain, but Mary couldn't stop doubting her story.

312

'Trish, be honest with me.'

'I *am* being honest with you.'

'What happened to Bobby that night, after you ran out of the house.'

'I don't know.'

'What do you think? Spin it out for me. You know him.'

Trish sighed. 'I think he went back home in the pickup, to the city, lookin' for me, to kill me. And then he musta got a call to do some business, and somebody set him up and whacked him. Maybe Cadillac or maybe another guy did him. They're cutthroat, like any other business. They all want what the other one has.'

Mary mulled it over, but something nagged at her. 'I don't get why you didn't call anybody. The girls, your mom, somebody.'

'Like I said, I knew Bobby would ask them where I was. He mighta killed them if they knew. That's why I didn't go back to the city right away. If he's lookin' for me, they're all lookin' for me. Any one of them coulda taken me out. I couldn't even go home.'

Mary wasn't buying it. 'But you called your boyfriend. You told him. Why?'

'Dummy, because nobody knows about him, not even the girls, so I couldn't get him killed. He lives in the burbs, he's legit. He was the only one I could call.'

'You could've called me.'

'You're not my friend.'

'Thanks.' Mary burst into laughter.

'Sorry.'

Then she had a darker thought. 'I didn't find

313

your gun. Where is it?'

'I got it with me.' Trish gestured at her purse on the bed, a black leather clutch. 'I took it with me when we went out. I told you, I was afraid of what was gonna happen.'

'Then why didn't you use it when he attacked you?'

'I couldn't get to it fast enough.'

Mary thought about it, and it made sense. Trish was a hairdresser, not a ninja.

'The next thing I hear, Bobby's dead.' Trish heaved a sigh. 'We both knew the cops would think I did it.'

Mary felt her blood run cold. She'd been thinking the same thing, but hadn't admitted it to herself until now. 'Well, did you?'

'No, of course not. You believe me, right?'

Mary didn't know what to think. She couldn't process it fast enough.

'Thanks, back at you.'

'Honestly, I don't know.'

'Whatever.' Trish waved her off like a fly. 'Anyway, my boyfriend came up and we went out to this burger joint because I was starvin' and this dump doesn't even have a coffee shop, and he calmed me down. Then you showed up.' Trish cocked her head. 'How'd you find me, anyway?'

'Tell you on the way back,' Mary answered, rising.

'To where?'

'Either home or the Roundhouse, if I can get a hold of Brinkley.'

'The cops? You think that's a good idea?' Trish

looked up, worried. 'My boyfriend said — '

'Forget what he said. I'm your lawyer, and you have no choice. We go and tell the truth.'

'But what if they charge me? What if they think I did it?' Trish didn't move from the bed.

'They won't. You were checked in here the night he was killed, and we can prove that.'

'No I wasn't. I only found this place the next day, the morning after.'

Huh? Mary frowned. 'Where were you when Bobby was killed, Tuesday night?'

'Hell if I know. I drove around and around, and I got lost. It was all trees and more trees. I never been in the mountains before. I didn't know where I was at.'

That, Mary understood, but she also knew that I-don't-know-where-I-was-at sucked as an alibi.

'There's no stores, no bars, no nothin' up here.' Trish's eyes widened, incredulous. 'You believe people live like this? It's nuts!'

'Okay, so what did you do?'

'I was too freaked to keep drivin', and Bobby had my cell. I didn't know what to do. I couldn't find an effin pay phone. So I went off the road into the woods and parked there all night, outta sight.'

'You slept in the car?'

'Yeah, and the next morning I drove around till I found a phone and called my boyfriend and he came up. I didn't check in here till Wednesday.'

'Okay, so you'll tell them that. It is what it is.'

315

Mary shrugged. 'We gotta go. People are looking for you.'

'But I have no alibi, and I do have a motive to kill him. It's like you said, how do you break up with a mobster? Only one way. You kill him.'

'You're just being paranoid.' But Mary remembered, and it was making her nervous.

'You know, I used to lie awake at night and pray he'd get killed, that one of the boys would off him, or even he'd end up in a car crash.' Trish snorted. 'Now that it finally happened, I can't believe it. I can't believe that he's dead and I didn't kill him.'

'Nice talk, T.' Mary couldn't manage a smile. She felt her anger rising again. 'If this is supposed to convince me, try again.'

'I'm not trying to convince you. It's the truth.'

'Look, get up, we're going to the cops. As a legal matter, it takes more than motive to charge somebody with murder, even if you have no alibi.'

'Like what?'

'Like evidence. For one thing, the ballistics won't match. They'll be able to tell that the bullets that killed him didn't come from your gun. They know by the grooves.'

'But the cops could say I used a different gun.'

'Where would you get another gun?'

'You kiddin' me, with my connections? I could get you one, if you wanted it.'

Um, right. 'You weren't in the city. You were up here.'

'So what? I had enough time to drive back to the city, find Bobby on his corner, kill him, and come back up here. I know where he worked. I coulda told you he'd be there.'

Mary felt confused and suddenly tired. 'Then why would you come back here?'

'To set up my alibi. To make it look like I didn't do it.' Trish arched an eyebrow. 'See what I mean?'

'No.' Mary couldn't deal. 'This is crazy. You're watching too much TV.'

'Face it, I look guilty.'

'Yes, but it's only a circumstantial case. They don't just charge people with murder, willy-nilly. You're his victim, not his killer. Brinkley has the diary. He knows Bobby's history, and the guy was connected, for God's sake.' Mary waved her up and turned to walk to the door. 'Either way, we're coming clean. We'll go sort this out and call your mother, too, on the way home. I can't take the guilt.'

'I'm not going,' Trish said from behind her, and a new tone in her voice made Mary turn around.

The sight shocked her. Trish was standing there, her black purse tucked under her arm, a determined expression in her eyes, and in her two-fisted grip, something Mary had never expected to see.

A small black gun.

35

Whoa. Mary put her hands up, reflexively, her eyes on the gun in Trish's hand. 'Now you're making me think you did it.'

'I didn't, but I can't take the chance in going to the cops.'

'If you didn't kill him, then you won't kill me.'

'I'm not gonna kill you. I'm just gonna shoot you a little.'

Yikes! 'Is that supposed to be funny?'

'Move over and let me go.' Trish aimed the gun higher, stiff armed, but Mary didn't budge from in front of the door. She prayed Trish wouldn't shoot her, but she wasn't about to let the girl walk out, not after all it took to track her down.

'Move.' Trish took a step closer.

'No,' Mary heard herself say, anger welling from deep inside. 'Once a Mean Girl, always a Mean Girl. Judy said you'd hurt me, but I didn't listen.'

'Move over and let me get outta here.'

'What's the plan, Trish? Lose everything? Keep running? Never go home? If you wanted that, you could've done that in the first place, when you came to my office.'

'Move. Now.'

'Never. I got fired to help you. I lost clients to help you. I drove to wherever the hell we are for you. I'm not going back without you.' Mary

318

lowered her hand slowly and held it out, before she could even judge the wisdom of her own actions. 'Give me the gun.'

'Move.' Trish took another step closer, and so did Mary, hand still outstretched.

'Give it to me. I'll take care of you. I promise.'

'You're asking me to take a chance with my life.'

'No, I'm asking you to trust somebody. Trust me.'

Trish hesitated. 'You said the law fails people like me.'

'It does. I won't.'

Trish eyed her directly, and Mary met her gaze over the gun.

'I found you here, didn't I? Please, give it to me.'

Suddenly Trish heaved a deep sigh and flopped the gun sideways in Mary's hand.

'Thanks.' Mary raised the gun and immediately pointed it back at Trish. 'Turnabout is fair play.'

'Are you nuts?' Trish recoiled in alarm. 'What're you doin', freak?'

'Teaching you something.'

'What?'

'Call your mother.'

Trish snorted. 'You're kiddin', right?'

'No. Call your mother.'

'At gunpoint?'

'If that's what it takes. Call her.' Mary smiled behind the gun, flinty as Clint Eastwood. 'Go ahead. Make her day.'

'I was gonna call her,' Trish said defensively.

'So go ahead then. Me and my new gun will wait.'

'You are so ignorant!' Trish rolled her eyes like a teenager, stalked to the phone beside the bed, and picked up the receiver, pressing in the number.

'You need to be a better daughter and a better friend.'

'You need to shut up.' Trish turned away and spoke into the receiver. 'Ma? Yes, Ma, it's me, I'm fine, I'm alive . . . don't have a heart attack . . . Ma, don't freak . . . I'm here with Mary. DiNunzio. She found me . . . and it's all right now . . . she's bringing me home . . . we should be home by morning.'

Mary lowered the gun, and when Trish started to cry into the phone, she pretended not to hear. Her arms trembled as the adrenaline ebbed from her body, leaving her with the residue of doubt. Had Trish killed Bobby? It was scary how fast the girl had come up with the scenario. Nor did it help that Trish had pulled a gun on her. It was the kind of thing that made you doubt somebody.

'Okay, love you, too.' Trish hung up the phone, turning, but Mary raised the gun again.

'Now call Giulia.'

'Mare, get over yourself. That gun's makin' you mental. You're trippin'.'

'Do it.'

'Arg!' Trish turned back to the phone and picked up the receiver, and Mary felt a certain degree of satisfaction. She'd make Trish a better person, at gunpoint.

Half an hour later, Mary was driving on the turnpike, with a silent Trish sulking in the passenger seat, her head turned to the window. Traffic was light because of the rainstorm, and she had to keep braking so as not to outrun her headlights in the downpour. The windshield wipers beat frantically, and she kept a bead on the red taillights in front of her, avoided trucks spraying water from their big tires, and switched the heat off so she wouldn't fall asleep.

While she'd waited for Trish to get her act together, she'd called Missing Persons and told them Trish wasn't missing anymore, and also left another message on Brinkley's cell, telling him she had Trish with her. He hadn't called her back yet, which was odd. They'd left the motel in her car, abandoning the BMW because she didn't trust Trish to follow her to the city, not after that little attempted-murder thingy.

Mary flicked on the radio news to keep herself awake, and after weather and sports stories, the announcer came on. 'This just in, there's been another murder in the city's rapidly escalating Mob war, which began Tuesday with the shooting death of Robert Mancuso.'

'My God. Listen up.' Mary gripped the steering wheel in surprise, and Trish shifted in the seat and cranked up the volume.

'Authorities report that the alleged mobster member Al Barbi, age thirty-four, of South Philadelphia, was shot to death as he entered his home at 2910 Redstone Street. Authorities have no leads at the present time, and a press conference will be held on Friday morning at ten o'clock to address the recent surge in violence.'

Mary put two and two together. 'That explains why Brinkley hasn't called back. He's got his hands full.'

'You're tellin' me. That's Cadillac.'

Mary almost veered off the highway. 'You serious? You mean that guy who got killed, Al Barbi, is Cadillac? From the diary?'

'Yeah.' Trish nodded matter-of-factly.

'So what's that mean?'

'What do you think it means?' Trish snapped off the radio. 'You can figure it out.'

Mary wished for a gun. 'Help me out, can you? I'm driving in a monsoon, I haven't slept for three days, and I don't know much about the Mob because I'm not a felon.'

'Whatev.' Trish looked over, her eyes glittering in the dark car. 'Cadillac knew Bobby was skimmin' and he always had the knives out for him. Plus Cadillac was totally jealous of his business, I know that. So Cadillac musta been the one who whacked him.'

Mary shuddered.

'And somebody musta got pissed at Cadillac for it. Maybe he didn't get the go-ahead. so he ended up dead for doin' Bobby.'

'The go-ahead? To kill somebody?'

'Yeah, what're you, stupid?'

Mary felt like a mother driving her kid to school. Reform school.

'Or maybe somebody didn't want Cadillac movin' up.' Trish paused. 'Not that I know.'

'You know more than you say.'

'Yeah, but if I told you, I'd have to kill you.'

Mary didn't laugh, but Trish did.

'Lighten up, yo. Way I see it, they all got what they deserved.' Trish folded her knees up and rested her spike heels on the dashboard.

'Don't do that.'

'What?'

'Put your feet there.'

'Why?'

'Because I'm the mommy, that's why.'

Trish slid out of her fur jacket, folded it in two, and put it beneath her head like a fox pillow. 'Do these seats go back?'

'On the right, there's a handle.'

Trish eased the seat back down, turned away, and curled up like a very curvy ball. 'Turn on the heat?'

'No. It makes me sleepy.'

'I know. I need it to sleep.'

'Do without.'

'I'm hungry. Can we stop?'

'Not yet.'

Trish looked over. 'What're you in such a bad mood for, Mare? Things are lookin' up. We just got some great news.'

'A man's murder is great news?'

'For me, it is.'

Mary laughed, but narcissists never get the joke.

'This proves it wasn't me who did Bobby. It shows it had to be Cadillac or somebody in the Mob.'

Mary steered through the rain. 'Not necessarily. Maybe it shows that somebody in the Mob

323

thinks that Cadillac killed Bobby. Not that he actually did it.'

'Same difference.'

'Not exactly.'

'Either way, I'm in the clear.'

Mary considered it, uncomfortably. Barbi's murder didn't prove anything, but it made Trish look less like a suspect. Still, something was wrong, off-kilter. Mary should have been happier, having found the innocent Trish, but now she was worried that Trish wasn't so innocent. Trish should have been sadder, because the man she once loved had been murdered.

'Trish, aren't you sad about any of this? First Bobby's dead, now Cadillac?'

'Bobby, a little,' she answered, though her tone sounded less than bereft. 'I never liked Cadillac anyway. He shoulda minded his own business. If he killed Bobby, he got what he deserved.'

'But what if he didn't do it?'

'I bet he did. He wasn't a nice guy, Mare. You gotta wise up. These Mob guys, they're not all nice like Tony Soprano.'

Huh?

Trish shifted in the seat, her back still turned. They traveled down the road in silence, then she said, 'I wonder when Bobby's funeral is.'

Mary felt her chest tighten. She'd been too busy to think that far ahead. 'It depends on when the coroner releases the body. He was killed on Tuesday night, so my guess is Saturday.'

'You're goin', right?'

'I hadn't even thought about it,' Mary

324

answered, but she did want to go. Odd as it was, she couldn't not.

'You're my lawyer, and if I go, you should go.'

'Okay, fine. I'll pick you up.'

'Nah, I'll meet you there, with my mom and the girls. They didn't like him, but they gotta pay their respects to his nutjob family.'

'You might not want to put it that way.'

Trish chuckled, her back turned like a sitcom husband, and Mary drove ahead, into the darkness, her own high beams suddenly no help. The red taillights she'd been using as a guide had vanished into the thunderstorm, and she drove ahead into the gray, rainy gloom. In time, she felt as if she and Trish were the only people afloat on a stormy sea, and she had to steer their little ship to harbor by herself. Weariness overcame her, and anxiety. She couldn't imagine that tomorrow morning would ever come.

'Maybe this'll work out, after all,' Trish said, satisfied.

But Mary looked over, uneasy.

36

Dawn brightened the Philadelphia cityscape, turning it shades of gray, and a steady rain fell as Mary steered through the one-way streets, far easier to navigate than the wooded curves of the mountains. She was exhausted but had stayed awake for the drive by stopping for horrible coffee and more gas-station hot dogs, ensuring that she'd be completely nauseated by the time she pulled up in front of the Roundhouse.

'Wake up, sleepyhead.' Mary had been trying to wake Trish up since they reached the city limits, but she'd only slumbered away in the passenger seat, curled up like a black cat. Black ringlets strayed across her lovely features, but more important, her makeup looked perfect. Mary gave her a hard nudge.

'Wha?' Trish's eyes fluttered open, and she frowned irritably, stretching her arms.

'Time to wake up.' Mary pulled up the emergency brake and eyed the parking lot, which was mercifully clear of the media at this early hour, maybe because they knew the press conference was later this morning. 'We're here to see Brinkley.'

'We're not going home first?' Trish shifted up in the seat, squinting against the harsh gray light. Heavy rain pounded on the roof, matching Mary's mood.

'No. He wanted to get your statement before

the press comes calling.' Mary felt her fatigue lift, replaced by pre-game jitters. Her phone conversation with Brinkley had been brief, and she'd been surprised he'd wanted to see them so early, especially given how busy he sounded. 'I think he might pump you for information, so I want you to follow my lead.'

Trish's eyes flashed with alarm. 'I'm no snitch, and I don't want to get dead.'

'I know that.'

'I'm not making any deals. No immunity, nothin'.'

'I told him that. You won't meet with the FBI at all. This is Homicide only.' Mary checked her watch. 'Best-case scenario, we're out of there by nine.'

'So this is it, huh?' Trish flipped the mirror visor down and fluffed her hair with her fingernails.

'Yes. All you have to do is tell him what you told me, about what happened at the house. Don't answer when I tell you not to.'

Trish rubbed her teeth with an index finger.

'Don't volunteer anything.'

Trish dug in her purse, found a bottle of foundation, unscrewed the shiny black top, and smeared a thin layer expertly over her skin.

'Trish. You hear me?'

'I know all that. I watch *CSI*, too.'

Mary let it go. Suffice it to say, she wouldn't miss the girl when this was over. 'Anything you say could make this interview last longer than it needs to. For your own safety, I want us out of there before the day gets started. If we do this

327

right, nobody will even know you came in.'

Trish traded the foundation for a rosy red lipstick, which she twirled open and slid over her lips.

'Don't be nervous.'

'I'm not.'

'Good.'

'Fine.' Trish shoved the lipstick back into the bag, and from the mess of Kleenex, cigarettes, and rewetting solution extracted her black Beretta, which she dangled at the end of her finger like a Christmas ornament. 'What do I do with this?'

'Jeez!' Mary pressed it out of plain view, even though no one was around.

'Chill, Mare,' Trish said, but Mary couldn't. She didn't know if she could even chill again and she didn't know what to do with the gun. If Trish killed Bobby, it was a murder weapon. But then again, maybe she didn't do it, or if she did, she wouldn't have used that gun, like she said.

'Leave the gun,' Mary answered finally, which sounded oddly familiar. Then she remembered, from her dinner with Anthony. *My favorite is, 'Leave the gun, take the cannoli.'* She hadn't thought of him at all, with so much going on. She was supposed to call him back three years ago, but she had bigger worries, like the fact that she was having reasonable doubts about her own client.

'Okay, ready to go?' Trish opened up the glove box, popped in the gun, then shut it and looked over expectantly.

'Let's rock,' Mary said, putting on her game face.

★ ★ ★

They settled into the interview room, with Brinkley looking weary from the night tour, his skin unusually shiny and a stubble shading his cheeks and chin. Still, he wore his dark suit with his tie knotted tight, rallying as he sat down across from Trish and pulled a thin pad from his back pocket. Kovich sat quietly in a chair slightly behind him, a reverse of their usual positions.

Brinkley flipped his pad open and slid a pen from the silky inside of his jacket. 'Okay, so Mare, we wanted to talk to Trish to hear what happened to her, especially in view of the fact that Mancuso's body was found Tuesday night.'

'Seems like dog years,' Mary said, and Brinkley half-smiled.

'I hear that.'

'Before we start, do you have any leads on Mancuso?'

'No.'

'What about the autopsy or ballistics tests? What type of gun killed him, anyway? I haven't read a paper in days.'

'You won't see it in the papers, not on my case.'

'So what was the gun?'

'We probably shouldn't discuss those details,' Brinkley answered, an official response that took Mary by surprise.

'We have an obvious interest in the case, and

329

'I'll keep it confidential, if that's your worry.'

'I know you well enough to know you will. We need to keep our friendship out of it, like I told you before. Let's move on, and we'll get you two ladies out of here.'

'Fair enough.' Mary let it go. 'Just tell me, has the coroner released the body yet? I'm curious about when the funeral will be.'

'It's released, and I think they're burying him tomorrow.'

'Thanks,' Mary said, looking over at Trish, who remained stony in her wooden seat, her legs pressed tightly together and her hands linked in her lap. She showed no reaction to the news of the funeral. Earlier, she had refused Brinkley's offer of fresh coffee and declined to participate in the small talk about the storm. Mary didn't know if Trish was afraid or contemptuous of the detectives, or a little of both.

'So, Trish,' Brinkley said with only the briefest of smiles, 'I'm happy to see that you're well, after your ordeal.'

Trish nodded, her glossy lips pursed.

'You've been missing since Tuesday night, around six, is that right?'

Trish nodded.

'Why don't you begin by telling us what happened that night?'

Mary cleared her throat. 'Reg, I wanted to reiterate that Trish is here at your request, that she's been through a terrible and exhausting time, and that we'd like to conclude this interview as soon as possible. Also, we won't be going into areas related to Mancuso's murder or

330

his involvement in the Mob, which Trish knows nothing about. She was his victim for many years, subject to domestic violence at his hands, and was very poorly served by the Philadelphia Police Department and Missing Persons.'

'Duly noted,' Brinkley said, and turned his attention to Trish. 'My apologies for the way your case was treated. Missing Persons was dealing with the Donchess kidnapping, as you know, and still is.'

Trish nodded again, her mouth still tight, and Mary saw her in a new light. Out of her element, with her sensational looks doing nothing for her, Trish was a Queen Bee dethroned.

'Now, please tell me about Tuesday night, in your own words.'

'What do you want to know?' Trish shot back, but Brinkley looked undaunted.

'I understand from Mary that it was your birthday, and you were going out to dinner with Mancuso, with whom you lived, correct?'

'Yes.'

'So tell me what happened the night of your birthday.'

'We went out.'

Mary kept her own counsel. If Trish wanted to be tight-lipped in the beginning, she'd let it go for a short time, but she'd stop her if it kept up. It could make her look guilty, at least it did to Mary.

'Where did you go?' Brinkley asked, his tone characteristically quiet.

'To a house.'

'Where was the house?'

'I don't know.'

Mary interjected. 'Near Bonnyhart, in the Poconos.'

Brinkley made a note.

Mary looked at Trish, who pointedly didn't catch her eye. The rest of the interview continued in that vein, with Brinkley pulling teeth to get each answer, like the most patient of dentists. Trish never relaxed, nor did she refuse to answer, cooperating just enough to get the story out. It took longer that way, probably by half an hour, but Brinkley was handling Trish with kid gloves. If he suspected her of Bobby's murder, he was too professional to show his hand. The interview seemed to be winding down when he reached into an accordion file, extracted a transparent evidence bag, and held it up. Inside was an opal ring with a gold band.

Brinkley asked, 'Can you identify this?'

Trish peered at the bag, but didn't touch it. 'Sure.'

'What is it?'

'It's a ring.'

'Is it yours?'

'Yes.'

Huh? Mary held out a hand. 'May I see that?'

'Yes.' Brinkley handed her the evidence bag, and Mary double-checked it.

'Where'd you get this, Reg?' Mary asked.

'Uh . . . in the alley, by Mancuso's body.'

Whoa. Mary handed the bag back, realizing she might have inadvertently messed up his interview. If he suspected Trish at all, he would've asked her any questions before he told her where it was found. Mary had done some fancy defense lawyering, if only by accident.

Brinkley asked Trish, 'Were you wearing the ring the night Bobby was murdered?'

'Yes.'

'Do you know how it got in the alley?'

Mary made her face a mask. The ring could've gotten in the alley if Trish had dropped it there, when she went to kill Bobby.

'He took it from me,' Trish answered.

'When?'

'That night, at the house in the woods. Right before he showed me the engagement ring, he took my ring off my finger and put it in his pocket.'

'Got it.' Brinkley made a note, as did Kovich.

But Mary couldn't visualize that scene. It didn't sound like Bobby at all, elegantly slipping a ring from Trish's finger. It sounded like some fairy-tale engagement story. He would've been drunk by that point, too. But if that didn't happen, how did the ring get in the alley? Mary avoided looking at Trish as Brinkley pulled out from the accordion a second evidence bag, which held a silvery LG cell phone decorated with pink rhinestones, thick as sugar frosting.

'This yours, too, Trish?' Brinkley asked.

'Yeah.'

'We found this on the body, too.' Brinkley rattled off a phone number. 'That's the number of the last call. Do you know that number?'

'Yeah.'

'Whose is it?'

'My mother.'

'That would be the call you told us about?'

'Yeah.'

'We're in the homestretch, ladies.' Brinkley flipped to a clean page of his notebook. 'Now, Trish, you lived with Mancuso for how long?'

'Seven years.'

'And during that time, he sold drugs for the Mob, didn't he?'

Mary interjected, 'We're not going there, Reg.'

'You opened the door. You told me he was in the Mob the first time we spoke.'

'That was when she was missing, and I had to go begging to get somebody to look for her.'

'You gave us her diary, too.' Brinkley went into an accordion file he got from the floor, and Trish's head snapped around, glaring at her.

'You gave them my diary, Mare?'

'Please,' Mary said, and at this point, she didn't know who was making her madder, Brinkley or her own client.

'Here, Mary, she discusses Cadillac at length.' Brinkley pointed to a photocopy of the diary, underlining an entry with an index finger. 'We believe that it's a nickname for Al Barbi, who was just killed, and she may have information about him that may help our investigation of his murder.'

Mary shook her head. 'That's the end of the Mob questions. She told you everything she knows about that night, and I can't let you pump her to get information.'

'Mare, I'll level with you.' Brinkley leaned forward, his elbows resting on his legs, lean in pressed slacks. 'We have information that both

334

Mancuso and Barbi were members of the Guarino crime family. They're the up-and-comers, the young Turks waiting to take over now that Stanfa's defunct and Merlino's in jail. Both were low-level soldiers.'

'Why do I care?' Mary heard herself say. Trish remained mute, watching the action.

'If she knows anything about the Guarino organization, it's going to prevent a lot of murders in this town. We have information that Barbi's murder is just the beginning.'

'I understand that, but she doesn't know anything, and it can't circulate that she does or she ends up dead.'

Brinkley frowned. 'I don't leak. You know that. None of my investigations leak. That's why you didn't read about the gun.'

'I'm not saying you'd leak it, Reg. For all we know, the Mob could be watching the Roundhouse right now. I'm Trish's lawyer and all I care about is her interest. Not yours and not the city's.'

'If she talks to me, she doesn't have to talk to the feds. You know, they can subpoena her.'

'And she can shut up.' Mary felt anger rising in her chest. She figured that this had been why Brinkley had been so nice to Trish and why he'd wanted to see her so early. 'This doesn't seem fair to me, Reg. She was ignored by the police, and I'm not gonna let her be used by them.'

'She wasn't ignored, and it was only a day. We don't move that fast, especially with an Amber Alert.'

'It was still a day she couldn't afford. She

335

wouldn't be alive today if she hadn't run away from him. She had to protect herself.'

'Trish,' Brinkley turned and appealed to her. 'We've been in touch with the feds and we can get you into the witness-protection program, if you help us. You don't have to worry. We can find Barbi's killer and prevent an all-out war. You'll be saving lives.'

'No comment,' Trish said, as if Brinkley were a pesky reporter.

'I'm sorry.' Mary rose, hoisting Trish to her feet. 'I assume we're free to go.'

'Of course you are.'

'Thanks.' Mary had her answer. They weren't charging Trish with anything, and she wasn't even a suspect in Bobby's murder. Mary felt somewhat reassured that Trish hadn't done it, because she respected Brinkley and Kovich's judgment, and they were privy to facts she'd never know. Their bets were clearly on the Mob for Bobby's killer. Mary opened the door. 'See you guys later. Hope there's no hard feelings.'

'I wish you'd reconsider,' Brinkley said softly.

'Sorry, Reg. Stan.' Mary took Trish by the arm and got her out of there, without a look back.

If only she could leave her own doubts behind as easily.

37

Mary pulled out of the parking lot, heading south, and rain sprayed into the car as Trish held her cigarette outside the passenger-side window. The Expressway was congested, heading into the morning rush hour, and Trish seemed to relax only after the Roundhouse had receded into the distance.

'Think the FBI will call me?' she asked, taking a deep drag.

'Yes.' Mary didn't see the point in lying to her. 'They know you have information and they want to pick your brain.'

'So what do I do?'

'Good question.' Mary hit the gas, frustrated. Bennie would know what to do, but God knew where that stood. 'Truth is, I never handled the FBI before. I'm not really sure of the procedure. I should probably get you a lawyer with experience in this kind of thing.'

'Not you?'

'Not me, but I can help you find somebody.'

'No.' Trish blew out a cone of smoke that blew back inside the car. 'You did good in there. You stood up for me. So all you gotta do is stand up for me when the FBI calls. How hard can it be?'

'Thanks, but — '

'You tryin' to ditch me?' Trish asked flatly, and Mary realized the truth. She didn't know for sure that Trish hadn't killed Bobby and she could never really trust her again.

'You did pull a gun on me.'

'Don't take it personal.'

Mary looked over in disbelief, and when she did, Trish burst into laughter.

★ ★ ★

They pulled up in front of Trish's mother's house in the steady rain, and almost simultaneously, the front door of the rowhouse flew open. Mrs. Gambone appeared in her threshold, throwing open her arms.

'My mom's a trip.' Trish smiled crookedly.

'She loves you.' Mary's heart lifted to see Mrs. Gambone, happy again, and she was hurrying down the steps, heedless of the rain, followed by an excited Giulia, Missy, Yolanda, and a horde of well-wishers, more jubilant than if the Prize Patrol had pulled up curbside.

Trish looked surprised. 'You believe this? It's like a party.'

'It's your fan club, girl. Enjoy it. And tell them you're sorry for worrying them.'

'Stop the lecture.'

'I can't. You have so much to learn.' Mary reached over and popped open the glove box. 'By the way, don't forget your toy.'

'Whoops.' Trish laughed, slid out the gun, and slipped it into her purse. 'Wanna come in?'

'No thanks, I gotta go. I'll call you later.'

'Where you goin'? You said you got fired.'

'Oh, yeah. There's that.' Mary faked a laugh. 'Home, then. I'm beat.'

'I'll call you if the FBI calls me.'

'See you at the funeral.'

'Oh yeah, right.' Trish gave her a brief hug just as her mother reached the car and opened the door wide.

'Thank God! My baby!' Mrs. Gambone rejoiced. She reached for her daughter and lifted her bodily from the passenger seat, and Trish returned the embrace.

'Sorry I worried you,' Trish said, with a pointed glance back at Mary, but Mrs. Gambone was too happy to hear.

'You're home!' Mrs. Gambone hugged Trish again, then let her go and waved to Mary, her eyes bright with joyful tears.

'Mare, thanks,' she called, through the open car door.

'You're very welcome.' Mary felt the warm rush of redemption, and outside on the sidewalk, love was all around. Giulia squealed and group-hugged Trish and Mrs. Gambone, and Yolanda and Missy started jumping up and down on the rain-swept sidewalk. Front doors up and down the street were being thrown open, and neighbors emerged from their houses, under umbrellas, and cars even pulled up, honking for fun.

Mrs. Gambone and Trish went back up the stoop, followed by Yolanda, Missy, and the rest of the crowd, except for an excited Giulia. She turned around and hustled back to Mary in the car, stutter-stepping in her tiny black boots, covering her hair with her hand.

'Yo, Mare,' Giulia shouted, and Mary happily

opened the car door and got out in the rain. She had started to like Giulia, who threw herself into Mary's arms. 'You found her, Mare! You did it! I love you!'

'Love you, too, Giulia.' Mary hugged her back, not surprised to find they were both professional, if not expert, huggers. Giulia's hair smelled of its trademark mousse-and-Marlboros, but for the first time, Mary almost liked the scent. It smelled kind of grown up. Maybe she should start smoking.

'You're the best. I knew you could do it.'

'You did your part, too, girl.' Mary extricated herself from Giulia's embrace.

'Not like you. I'll never forget that, ever. You never gave up. You're a good friend, Mare. Aren't you comin' in an' eat?'

'Can't, thanks. I gotta go.' Mary gave her a final squeeze and got back into the car.

'You sure?' Giulia leaned over the open door. 'We're partyin'! We been up all night waitin' for you to get back!'

'Nah, I should go.' Mary spotted Yolanda, waving to Giulia from the front door. 'Go in, I'll call you guys later.'

'Awright, see ya, honey.' Giulia hustled back to the house, and Mary turned on the ignition just as a white minivan pulled up in front of her, double-parking her in. She got out of her car to ask the driver to pull up, and when the minivan doors slid open, a stream of kids poured out, yelling and racing to the Gambones'.

'Watch for cars, you guys!' their mother called after them, emerging from the van.

'Excuse me, can you pull up?' Mary asked.

'My God, are you Mary? I saw you in the paper! Thanks for finding my cousin!' The woman gave her a hug, and Mary hugged her back, on estrogen overload.

'Thanks.' Mary went back to her car, in time to see a driver who had just double-parked down the street. He stood by his car, opening an umbrella that caught her eye — a familiar flash of blue and white.

Mary waited for him to open it all the way, then did a double take. It was the blue-and-white golf umbrella that read Dean Witter. He chirped his car locked, and she checked the car. A black Cadillac. She watched, astounded, as he walked briskly toward the Gambone house. Was it Trish's stockbroker boyfriend? Here? Only one way to find out. Mary made her way through the cars and intercepted him on the sidewalk.

'Sir, excuse me,' she said.

'Yeah?' The man smiled from under the umbrella, and if, by some chance, he recognized her from the motel parking lot, it didn't show in his brown eyes and handsome, if coarse, features. His black hair looked a little puffy and moussed, and Mary sensed he was using the umbrella because he didn't want to get it wet.

She introduced herself, then felt at a sudden loss for what to say next. *I'm the one who chased your car at the motel?*

'Oh, you're the lawyer.' The man brightened, grinning with bleached teeth. He extended a large hand in a warm, earthy way, and Mary shook it, his grip scratchy and strong as he

341

pumped away. 'My wife told me all about you.'

'Does your wife know me?'

'Everybody knows you, now. You're the one who helped find Trish, right?'

'Yes, thanks. And you are?'

'Oh, sorry. I don't have the best manners. My name's Joe. Joe Statio.'

'Oh, well hi, Joe. How do you know Trish? Are you a cousin or something?' *Which would be creepy.*

'No. I'm just a husband.'

'Well, husbands count.' *So I hear.* 'Whose husband are you?'

'Trish's girlfriend, Giulia. Giulia Palazzolo.'

Mary froze. Trish was sleeping with Giulia's husband? Trish had lied to her at the motel? Joe Statio was Miss Tuesday Thursday?

'You know G from Goretti, right?'

Mary found her voice. 'Sure, she's great.'

'Sure is.'

'So what do you do for a living, Joe?'

'Got a plumbing supply on Oregon Avenue.'

'That's good.' Mary grinned uncomfortably, which wasn't difficult. So Trish had lied about that, too. What else had she lied about? Killing Bobby? 'I thought you were some kind of stockbroker, because of the Dean Witter.'

'Who's he?'

'Your golf umbrella. It says Dean Witter.'

'Oh yeah?' Joe looked up, as if he'd forgotten he held a multicolored tent above his head. 'It ain't mine. Guy left it at the shop, and I kep' it.' He glanced toward the Gambone house. 'I better get inside. I'm late.'

'Right, see you.'

'Later.' Joe gave her a toothy smile, then hurried up the sidewalk toward the house.

Mary waited until he went inside, then pretended she'd dropped something and walked casually around the back of his car. She double-checked the license plate, hoping against hope. But it was the car from the motel. RK-029.

She looked up at the house, wondering, in the rain.

38

Mary arrived home, shed her purse and coat on the chair, and flopped on the living room couch. Her apartment was quiet, and even her block outside had the stillness that comes from endlessly bad weather. Nobody home was going out in this rain, and everybody else was at work. She felt out of sync, neither here nor there, and reflexively retrieved her BlackBerry. She e-mailed Judy a quick note telling her she'd found Trish and not to worry about her, then she read her long-neglected e-mail, trying not to think about Trish, Bobby, Giulia, or Joe Statio.

No, I'm just a husband.

Mary deflated as she scanned her e-mail, each piece an electronic demand, a mile-high mess of get-back-to-me and I-didn't-get-a-reply and you-have-to-let-me-know. Randomly she picked one to answer, but couldn't find her old groove. She didn't care about any of them. She didn't even know if these clients were still hers. She tossed the damn BlackBerry aside. Could she take her Clients with her? Should she leave them with Bennie? Would she ever work with Judy and Anne again? Could she get another job? What would she do now?

T was my maid of honor, both times.

Mary checked her watch. 10:05. Brinkley had said his press conference would be held at ten.

344

She found the remote in the cushions, aimed it at the TV, and stared glassy eyed at a Slim-Fast commercial, until the news came on. On the screen, the police commissioner, in a dark suit and tie, stood behind a lectern that bore the bright blue-and-yellow emblem of the Philadelphia police. Brinkley, Kovich, and an array of suits stood behind him, flanked by the American flag and the bright blue flag of the Commonwealth of Pennsylvania.

'Good morning, ladies and gentlemen,' he began, in an official voice. 'We would like to make a brief statement regarding the recent outbreak of violence among certain elements of organized crime . . . '

Mary listened with complete attention and somehow, in the next minute, fell sound asleep.

Bzzz! She woke to the sound of her downstairs buzzer, in a darkened room, disoriented for a moment until she realized she was home, it was Friday, and she was jobless *and* dateless. The TV flickered, and the evening news was talking about the stock market, down by sixty points. *Bzzz!*

'Coming.' Mary roused, dry-mouthed, got up, and sleepily made her way to the buzzer next to the door, navigating by the light from Katie Couric's smile. She pressed the speaker button. 'Yes?'

'Lemme in,' Judy said, her voice tinny through the antiquated speaker system.

Mary hit the button. 'We don't want any.'

'I got double-cheese, triple sauce.'

'Then hurry.' Mary switched on the living

room light, and in the next minute heard the ladylike clomping of Dansko clogs on the staircase.

'Open, sesame!'

Mary opened the door to see her best friend walking down the hall in baggy painter's pants, a turquoise T-shirt, and a jeans jacket covered with embroidered patches, colorful smiley-face buttons, and silver jewelry, all of which she wore with a pink bandanna wrapped around her forehead like an effeminate ninja.

'How was court?' Mary asked with a smile.

'Good one.' Judy balanced an aromatic pizza box on her spread fingers as she came through the door. 'You been busy, huh? You're all over the newspapers.'

'Great.' Mary closed and locked the door. 'I'm Rip Van Winkle. What year is it? Do I have a date yet?'

'Listen to you, all funny.' Judy clomped ahead to the kitchen, turning on lights as she went, and Mary followed like her small and slightly errant child.

'My self-esteem is at an all-time low.'

'So what else is new?' Judy set he pizza box on the table. 'You're not happy unless you're unhappy.'

'That's not true,' Mary said, unhappily. Or happily.

'You should be overjoyed.' Judy went into the cabinet for two dinner plates, retrieved them, and plunked them down. Amber light glowed from the ceiling fixture centered over the table. 'You completed your mission. You found Trash. Sorry, Trish.'

346

'No, she's Trash again.' Mary went for two glasses, scooped some ice out of the freezer, and grabbed two cans of Diet Coke.

'Whatever you say. She's alive, you found her, and the cops are after the Mob guy who killed Bobby Mancuso.'

'I wish them luck.' Mary popped open a soda and filled the glasses. 'Because I think Trish killed Bobby.'

'What?' Judy frowned as she opened the pizza box, filling the room with the aroma of hot mozzarella and wet cardboard.

'You heard me.' Mary sat down. 'I think she did it.'

'Then she's in trouble.'

'On the contrary, she's in the process of getting away with it.'

'Really.' Judy's eyes widened like a fourth-grader's. She took her seat, then pulled a piece of pizza from the pie and dripped goopy mozzarella onto her plate.

'You should wait before you eat that.'

'Thanks, Mom.' Judy folded the slice expertly and chomped down on the pointy end, squinting as she seared the roof of her mouth.

'First degree or second?'

'Mmmm. Burny.'

'You're so silly.' Mary smiled and slid a piece of pizza out from the pie, waiting for the slice to cool properly, Gallant to Judy's Goofus. 'Who woulda thought that between us, I'd be the one who got fired?'

Judy laughed, and then so did Mary, until they had to put their slices back down and laugh

347

some more, and when they were finally finished, Judy said, 'Okay, so fill me in.'

And Mary did.

'Quite a story,' Judy said gravely, eyeing the empty glasses of melting ice. Pizza crusts sat piled in the open box, like ribs bleached by a desert sun.

'There's at least a circumstantial case against Trish.' Mary slid off her glasses and rubbed her eyes, having taken out her contacts. 'She had motive and opportunity, and she even admitted that she had time enough to kill him and get back to the Poconos. Also, she has a gun, and they found her opal ring in the alley.'

'But why would she keep the murder weapon?'

'Good question. Maybe to throw the cops off.'

'Nobody's asking but you.'

'To throw me off, then.'

'And risk it being tested?' Judy shook her head. 'You're overthinking it, Sherlock. Sometimes the obvious answer really is the right one. Mancuso was a mobster. When murder is an occupation, death is an occupational hazard.'

'But that's not all. I have no idea when she's lying to me. I believed who she said her boyfriend was, until I met him. So now I think she was lying when she told me she didn't kill Mancuso. Or at least I'm kinda sure.'

'You're confused, Mare.'

'I'll say.'

'No, you're really *confused*.' Judy pursed her lips. 'You're a defense lawyer. Trish's defense lawyer.'

Mary looked away. She knew where this was going.

'You defended her, very successfully, so far. They didn't charge her and it looks like they won't. You handled it just right, going in to Brinkley. You did your job, and, in fact, you paid for it with your own.'

'If she killed him, she's going to walk.'

'Right, which is this little thing we call the adversary system. Ever hear of it?'

Mary felt sick. 'So, happy ending. He gets buried tomorrow, and she gets away with murder.'

'You don't know that.'

'She's sleeping with her best friend's husband.'

'That illegal now?'

'She's a bad person, Jude.'

'You knew that going in. You call them the Mean Girls for a reason.'

'Giulia's not like them. Giulia's a sweetheart. She's my girl.'

'Gimme a break.' Judy sighed. 'Look, I know you care about the justice of the thing, and so do I. But you can't do anything about that, not in your position. It would be unethical.'

Mary knew justice wasn't the problem. It wasn't even that Trish was getting away with murder. It was that Trish was getting away with murdering *him*. But she still couldn't bring herself to tell Judy the whole story, about her and Bobby.

'I don't understand why you're so on his side, all of a sudden. Please recall, off the record, that he was abusive. Inhuman. A killer. You had a

349

terrified woman crying in your office. I'm not feeling for him, are you?'

The words hit home. Mary was feeling for him, but she couldn't tell Judy why.

'You're way too involved with these people. It's like you forgot your own life. You live in a different world from them now. They're your past. They're high school. They're the past.' Judy threw up her hands. 'I went to three different high schools. I can't remember the name of even one of my classmates.'

'And I can't forget them.'

'I'm the army brat who never stayed put, and you're the hometown girl who never moved away.' Judy smiled, more gently. 'But you went to college, then law school. You got a chance to reinvent yourself and stop being who you were in high school.' Her tone grew reflective. 'The Mean Girls never got that chance, so they don't understand. You're not the loser they remember. You're a lawyer now. You got a life.'

It rang true, but Mary couldn't get past it. Somewhere inside, she sensed that she'd never get past it unless she started to look the truth in the eye, and that couldn't happen unless she came clean. She'd told Anthony about Bobby. Why couldn't she tell Judy?

'You gotta get your ass back into the office and beg Bennie for your job. Go in and face the music.' Judy leaned over the table, on her elbows. 'I didn't bring you up with Bennie, but I know she feels bad about what happened, I can tell.'

Mary wasn't thinking about her job, she was

thinking about what would have been her baby, and Bobby's. Now he and the baby were gone, and she owed it to them both to find his real killer. She realized then that was why she'd cared so much.

'Bennie's trial's over, and the jury should be back on Monday. If she wins, she'll be in a much better mood. She'll listen to reason.'

'I don't know if I can do it,' Mary said, after a minute, only because Judy was looking at her so expectantly, for a response.

'I know you can. Don't worry. I'll go in with you. I'll be right there.'

Mary felt tears come to her eyes, at the offer. 'What?'

Mary couldn't speak for a minute, her eyes filling.

'You didn't know that? Of course I would do that, sweetie.' Judy put her hand across the table, and Mary swallowed hard, then took her hand.

'I have something to tell you, something very bad.'

'Like what?'

'I had an abortion,' Mary blurted out, before she lost her nerve. For a minute, Judy remained motionless. They both did, as if the words cast a spell on them both, freezing them in a girlfriend nightmare.

'You did?' Judy asked, after a moment, her voice quiet.

'I went out with Bobby in high school and I was so happy he asked me.' Mary tried to stop her lips from trembling, but it didn't work. 'And later, in the car, we were making out and he kind of pushed the issue and told me something about his blue balls or whatever and then we sort of, we sort of, we had sex, and I got pregnant. It was my first time.'

'That's so terrible,' Judy said, her voice hushed, but Mary felt her heart breaking inside.

'I'm afraid you won't be my friend anymore.' A deep sob gave way, and Mary's nose began leaking like crazy, and while she wiped it with her greasy napkin, she heard the chair across the table move, the clogs clomp across the hardwood floor, and in the next second, Judy put her arms around her, hugging her.

'I'll always be your friend, Mare.'

'Really?'

'Yes. You know what I love about you, Mare?'

'What?'

And Judy answered: 'Everything.'

39

The next morning, Mary picked out her best suit and hung it on the closet doorknob, feeling somber and wretched after a terrible night's sleep. She didn't know how she'd get through what lay ahead. She'd showered, put in her contacts, and blew out her hair for the occasion, though she tried not to think about where she was going. She took the black crêpe jacket from the hanger and put it on, and the lovely fabric slipped chilly over her skin. Anne had made her buy the fitted Prada suit, and Mary usually felt like a million bucks in it, maybe because that's what it cost.

She buttoned up the three buttons to the jacket, then took the skirt from the hanger and stepped into it barefoot, zipping it up on the side. She wondered who would be dressing Bobby this morning. She pictured the funeral directors buttoning his white shirt, arranging his hands so they were loosely linked, then threading a rosary through his fingers. It would have black beads, the boy rosary.

She slipped into her black pumps, then went to the bathroom sink, dug in her makeup kit for her foundation, opened the bottle, and patted some under her eyes and smeared it on her face. Were they putting makeup on his face, now? On his hands, too? They had done that for Mike, she knew, because when she went to touch his hands one last time, she'd come away with a stickiness like putty on her fingertips, and when she'd looked down at her fingers, her husband's skin had made its own imprint on her. She'd cried then, for him.

And last night, right before sleep, she'd even cried for Bobby.

★ ★ ★

Outside it was still drizzling, the aftermath of the storm, but that didn't account for the traffic standstill on Broad Street. The cab drew closer to the funeral home, and Mary realized that the jam was caused by the funeral itself. Parked cars filled the passing lane that ran down the center of the street, and uniformed cops in long slickers directed gawkers and other traffic around the bottleneck. A Mob funeral was Saturday's big game.

'I'll get out here, please.' Mary handed the driver a ten and stepped out of the cab. She put up her umbrella and hurried to the sidewalk, walking with her head down against the rain, her pumps splashing water. Noise and chatter emanated from the block ahead, where a crowd had formed, their umbrellas fighting for space.

She wedged her way into the crowd, holding her umbrella high and excusing herself all the way to the entrance, where a thin, synthetic red carpet covered the steps of the funeral home, as if this were a movie premiere. Stocky men in dark suits stood smoking around the entrance, their gaze shifting toward her. One thick-necked man looked her up and down, unashamedly. Mary hurried up the steps, braced herself against a rising nervousness, and went inside as if she belonged there, a lawyer among felons.

The scent greeted her first, as she knew it would, the sickening fragrance of refrigerated flowers, and vases of gladiola, lilies, and roses lined the walls on the console tables. She'd never been in this funeral home, the showiest on Broad Street, a dubious distinction. Gold-flecked walls surrounded her, and she sank deep into the blood-red carpet. She kept her eyes down, scanning the crowd when she could, but she didn't see Trish or the girls as she made her way into the viewing room, which was packed. At the front stood a closed casket of glistening walnut, and the bier was mounded with massive sprays of flowers. To the left of the casket stood Mr. Po and Ritchie, both in dark suits, their expressions solemn.

Mary bypassed the reception line and took a seat on the right side, in the middle of the throng, hidden from the front. She didn't want Mr. Po or Ritchie to see her because she didn't know how they'd react, and she felt a tiny tingle of fear. She eyed the crowd, which seemed oddly quiet, without the incongruous, if typical, outbreaks of laughter or happy hugs when friends and relatives were reunited. Women talked among themselves in low tones, and the men gave each other quick and furtive glances. Mary wondered if they were wondering who among them was the killer, but to her the answer was simple. All of them.

355

She bent her head and said a prayer. The reception line shifted forward, and when Mary looked up, she spotted Trish and Mrs. Gambone, with Giulia and her husband behind them. She felt a pang for Giulia, betrayed by her husband and her best friend, a heartbreak double play. Trish walked with her head bent and her arm linked in her mother's, apparently grief stricken in dark coats, but Mary couldn't stop her doubts.

She hid her thoughts as Trish stepped forward to the casket and knelt down on the knee pad, with her mother hovering behind her. Every head in the room turned to the front, and all eyes focused on the scene. Trish rested a hand on the coffin, then bent down and kissed it. It was so convincing a portrayal that Mary almost wondered if it was real, and when Trish rose and turned away from the coffin, she wiped a tear from her eye, Exhibit A in the Grief Department.

Ritchie came forward and gave Trish a meaty hug and Mrs. Gambone hugged Mr. Po, and at the sight, the mourners nodded and murmured with approval. Mary had been to enough Italian funerals to recognize the big peace-making scene, though it usually took place between people who hadn't spoken because of an ancient grudge, not people who kidnapped and tried to kill each other, like, last week. But then again, every opera was different.

Giulia and her husband Joe did the same thing, then Yolanda and Missy appeared and followed suit, and Mary wondered if there was such a thing as collective amnesia. In the aisle behind her, someone said 'hey' and 'what's your problem, lady,' and she turned around to see an attractive couple bypassing the receiving line and hurrying up the aisle. The man was behind, but the woman stormed ahead, her russet hair flying and her face contorted with anger. It was Rosaria, Bobby's sister, from Brick.

Mary should have expected her, but with all that had been going on had forgotten about her. The man with Rosaria, wearing an expensive silk tie, must have been her boyfriend, because he was trying to catch her arm as she charged forward. Her gaze fixed on the casket, then shifted to Mr. Po and Ritchie, who had just released Trish and Mrs. Gambone.

'You! You did this!' Rosaria called out, storming down the aisle toward the casket. Mourners gasped, heads wheeled around, and a dangerous wave rippled through the crowd, but Rosaria was oblivious, grief stricken, her eyes teary. 'You're responsible for this. You got my brother killed. *You.*'

'Whoa, Ro,' Ritchie said, putting up his palms, and a shocked Trish, the girls, and Joe edged back behind Mr. Po, who whirled around with an agility surprising in a man his age.

'Rosie, show some respect,' he said loudly.

'Respect for *you?*' Rosaria shouted back. Her boyfriend pulled her away, but she wouldn't stop. 'Why? You're criminals, common criminals, both of you. You're not good enough to know my brother, much less bury him.'

'Shut your mouth!' Ritchie yelled, and men collected behind him.

Mary found herself on her feet with the rest of the mourners, craning their necks.

'You were nothing compared to Bobby, and you know it,' Rosaria hollered. 'You were always jealous of him. He was the star, not you. He was the one everybody loved, not you. That's why you ruined him!'

'That's enough outta you.' Ritchie gritted his teeth, and a short, elderly priest appeared up front, raising his arms and stepping between the Pos and Rosaria and her boyfriend.

'Please, no, stop,' the priest said, his voice quavering with age and alarm. 'This isn't the time or the place, not the time or the place.'

'Don't tell me, Father.' Rosaria turned on him. 'You don't know these people. They're sick, the both of 'em. You wanna know what he did to me, Father? *My* supposed father? Do I have to spell it out for you?'

'Rosaria, no!' her boyfriend shouted, finally grabbing her from behind and wrapping his arms around her, holding her fast while she writhed and struggled in his arms. Ritchie, Mr. Po, the priest and the men stood still, watching while she finally stopped fighting and dissolved into tears, collapsing in her boyfriend's arms. He managed to get her back down the aisle, and she sobbed against him for support, tears running down her cheeks, letting herself be taken from the room.

Up front, Mr. Po spoke with the priest, and Ritchie huddled with his partners in crime. Mrs. Gambone, Trish, and the girls formed a fluttery circle, and the room returned slowly to normal, with the mourners talking among themselves and taking their seats. Mary sat down, her emotions in tumult, her thoughts confused. She was thinking about Ritchie and what Judy had said.

Maybe the easy answer was the right one.

Maybe a mobster had killed Bobby, and maybe the mobster was Ritchie. Mary remembered that day at the Po house, when she'd met him.

Boo.

40

Sunlight beamed into her bedroom, and Mary felt almost herself by Sunday morning, lounging in bed in her oversized Eagles T-shirt, enjoying the unaccustomed luxury of loafing. Newspapers made messy tents all over her comforter, and *Meet the Press* was on TV, all the politicians in gray suits, red ties, and flag lapel pins. She watched idly, thinking that Tim Russert was cute in an altar-boy kind of way, but that reminded her of Anthony, who still hadn't called. She was too old-fashioned to call him. She looked over and checked the answering machine beside the bed, but nothing had started blinking since five minutes ago. She wasn't ready for a relationship anyway.

But if he calls, I'm ready.

She sighed and told herself it was a relief. After all, she'd almost gotten back to her life, having spent last night catching up on her e-mail, answering her clients as if she were still an associate at Rosato. She'd called Amrita to check on Dhiren, and he was improving, and she'd even drafted a brief due next week. She hadn't decided what to do about Bennie yet, but it had felt good to be back in business, dealing with roof leaks and slip-and-falls, and there had even been a ton of e-mail from her clients, congratulating her on finding Trish alive. She wondered if the other clients would come back, now that she had found Trish. Not that it gave her comfort, not completely. The whole time she'd worked, Trish had been in the back of her mind, and Bobby.

Mary picked up the front page and skimmed the article again. OTHER SHOE DROPS WITH BARBI MURDER read a sidebar, and the article went on about the history of the Mob in South Philly, with a list of so many Italian names it sounded like a menu. Mary hated the Mob stereotype because she knew that most Italian-Americans were smart, honest, and hardworking citizens, who kept her in business by slipping on wet sidewalks, crashing their bumpers, and winning the occasional contracts case. She scanned the other news articles, all on the Mob war, and pictured the crowd at Biannetti's, excitedly comparing notes and trading gossip, murder as spectator sport.

She turned back to the front page, and the lead article reported that there were still no suspects in the Mancuso and Barbi murders. Another sidebar showed the blurry cell-phone photo of Trish and reported that the mobster's 'former live-in-love' had returned to her family's home and wasn't returning reporters' calls. There was no suggestion that Trish was suspected of his murder in any way. Brinkley wasn't mentioned in any of the articles, and neither he nor the FBI must have contacted Trish or she would have called.

Mary watched Tim Russert and tried to think good thoughts. She was a defense lawyer, and the representation was over. Judy, the world's best girlfriend, had been right. Bobby had been buried, and that chapter of her life closed. She had to pick up the pieces, and right now they were messier than all the newspaper sections. She wanted to feel better. She was so sick of being down on herself for being down on herself, for having no job and no boyfriend, and she felt lost and empty, betwixt and between.

Which told her exactly what to do.

* * *

'Ma, I'm hungry,' Mary called from the door, but the noise and commotion from the kitchen took her aback.

'Honey!' her father called back, emerging with a small crowd following him. They flowed into the dining room and expanded to fill it, like last time. But as angry as that crowd had been, this one was joyful.

'Pop?' Mary asked, bewildered. 'What's going on?'

'At church, the neighbors were so happy that you found Trish and they came over to visit.'

'Mare, you done good.' Mrs. DaTuno smiled at her and so did Mrs. D'Onofrio, dressed in their nice church housedresses. Everyone called out 'Way to go' and 'Congratulations, Mare,' unanimously restoring her status as Neighborhood Girl Who Made Good.

'I'm so proud a you, I could bust,' her father said softly. He gave Mary a bear hug, pressing her to the freshly pressed white shirt he saved for Mass, and she breathed in his mothballs scent, mixed now with meatballs.

'Thanks, Pop. Thanks, everybody.' Mary waved like a Windsor, and they all started clapping. She swallowed the lump in her throat, her emotions mixed. Would they feel the same if they knew Trish could be guilty of murder? Or would they forgive it, given Bobby's abuse? So she hammed it up and took a low bow, feeling vaguely like a fraud.

'Maria,' her mother called, raising her arms, and Mary gave her a big hug, scooping her off her tiny feet. Her mother gestured to a flock of women behind her, also in their flowered dresses. 'Maria, my ladyfriends, you know, from church.'

'Hello, ladies.' Mary turned to them and extended a hand.

'Good to meet you,' the one said, with a Puerto Rican accent. 'Your mother, she make my baby's dress.'

'Mine, too,' said another, grinning, and the woman next to her nodded, too.

'She did a wonderful job. So beautiful, we tell our friends.'

'You have the best seamstress in the business,' Mary told them, realizing suddenly that she'd inherited her business-getting ability. Vita DiNunzio was the rainmaker of South Philly, and Mary's heart gladdened when she saw her mother beaming.

'Come, see, Maria.' Her mother took her by the hand. 'We have friend for you, for dinner.'

'Who?' Mary asked, and the crowd seemed to clear a way to the kitchen, where Anthony was

363

standing with a tentative smile. His dark eyes were bright, and he wore a tan sport coat with khaki slacks and a lightweight black turtleneck. He gestured at her mother.

'Your parents saw me at church, and they insisted I come to dinner. I hope that's okay.'

Yay! 'I think it's a great idea,' Mary answered, wishing she'd worn her contacts.

Later, the house cleared out except for the four of them, and they had a great meal, during which Mary tried to get used to Mike's chair being occupied by a another man who, by all accounts, was pretty wonderful. Anthony joked with her mother in Italian and listened to her father's old construction stories, and when dinner was finished, he even offered to do the dishes, which was when the afternoon skidded to a halt.

Mary froze at the table. Her mother construed an offer to help in the kitchen as an insult, akin to a puppy offering to take the scalpel from a neurosurgeon.

'*Grazie mille*, Antonio,' her mother answered, with a grateful smile that Mary had never seen in this situation. She watched, mystified, as her mother rose slowly and touched her father on the arm, saying, 'Come, Mariano.'

'Wha'?' her father asked, looking up in confusion until he received the Let's-Leave-These-Kids-Alone message her mother was telecommunicating via her magical eyes. Mary tried not to laugh. Her mother had a varied repertoire of eye messages, and the bestsellers were: Don't-Eat-With-Your-Fingers, Leave-That-Piece-For-Your-Father, and I'll-Never-Trust-That-German-Pope.

'That was awkward,' Mary said, after her parents left the kitchen.

'No, that was cute.' Anthony rose, picked up the plates, and took them to the sink. 'Let me do dishes.'

'No.' Mary got up with her plate. 'You're the guest and you have nice clothes on.'

'Let me, I like to.' Anthony slipped one of her mother's flowered aprons from the handle on the oven, and tied it around his waist. He grinned. 'Too gay?'

'Nah.' Mary laughed again. Actually, she loved the look. What was it about men in aprons? It was so homey, and in some odd way, kind of sexy. Maybe because it meant that somebody else was doing all the work?

'So.' Anthony turned on the water. 'You didn't mind me barging in?'

'No. I wanted to apologize, too, for not calling you right back.'

'You weren't blowing me off? 'You broke my heart, Fredo.''

'Ha!' Mary turned back to the table, ostensibly for the other dishes, but she didn't want him to see her smiling. She felt a little dorky and worried that she had gravy spots on her glasses, spaghetti blowback.

'I knew you were busy, saving the neighborhood.'

'Well, just one, who I'm not sure deserved it, anyway.'

'We both knew that.'

'I guess,' Mary said, but didn't elaborate. Her doubts were confidential, and she didn't want to spoil her nice mood. Maybe that's what moving on meant, but she didn't know. She hadn't done it before. She took more plates to the sink and set them on the counter. 'I decided I was right about the neighborhood, by the way.'

'Funny, so did I.' Anthony rinsed a dish, making a landslide of tomato sauce. 'I think you were right. That's what community is. People taking care of each other.'

'Really.'

'That's what you said.'

'It is?' *Was I drunk?* 'I mean, it is.'

'So you know what I did?'

'What?' Mary stood beside Anthony, their arms almost touching, side by side at the sink. She felt as if they were playing house, and it wasn't uncomfortable, but natural. He seemed to warm to it, too. It was the sort of domestic vibe that would have sent most men running, but not this one.

Anthony said, 'I know some people in the psychology department at school. They put me in touch with the chairman of the department, Dr. Rhonda Pollero. She specializes in educational testing of younger children and she agreed to test Amrita's son as a favor to me.'

'Really?' Mary felt a rush of gratitude, and Anthony looked down at her with a smile.

'She's one of the biggest experts in the country, and she'll even come down from New York, as soon as Dhiren's well enough.'

366

'That was so nice of you.' Mary felt touched, as if Anthony *got* her in some fundamental way. In the next minute, he leaned over and kissed her softly on the lips, as if he'd been doing that all his life. His kiss left her standing on tiptoe, and when she opened her eyes, he was smiling sweetly.

'*Cara mia*,' he said softly, in Italian.

'My dear,' it meant, in English.

Mary liked the sound of it, either way.

41

Mary was cleaning up her bedroom when she got a call on the cell, but she didn't recognize the number. She picked up. 'Yes?'

'Mare, it's me.' Trish sounded panicky.

'Did the feds call?'

'Yeah, they wanna meet with me tomorrow.'

Yikes! Mary wished she knew more about dealing with the FBI, and now she couldn't call Bennie.

'I can't talk to them. I'm sure the boys are watchin' me. If they think I'm gonna snitch, I'm dead.'

'I know, relax. We can deal with this.' *I hope.*

'You're the one who convinced me to come back. You're the one who convinced me to go to the cops.'

'You did the right thing, Trish.'

'You were at the funeral home. You saw. Everybody's crazy right now. All of 'em, on edge. That's when people get dead.'

'Where are you?' Mary asked, bearing down.

'At my mom's.'

Mary checked her watch. Eight o'clock. 'I'm leaving now,' she said, tense, and went back outside, not completely surprised to find it raining.

Half an hour later, she was standing in the dark drizzle on the Gambones' front stoop, and Mrs. Gambone opened the door. She looked tense, her affect flat, and she wore a dingy pink tracksuit with Uggs knockoffs. In her hand, she held a long brown cigarette that trailed smoke.

'Mare, thanks a lot for comin'.' Mrs. Gambone admitted Mary to the living room. 'I appreciate you helpin' out.'

'No problem.'

'You can't let her go to the FBI. She won't live another day.' Mrs. Gambone smoothed her hair into an old denim scrunchy, and she had no makeup on, showing a weepy puffiness around her eyes.

'Don't worry. Where is she?'

'Upstairs in her room.' Mrs. Gambone gestured with her cigarette, making a smoke snake.

'Thanks.' Mary crossed the darkened room, more contemporary than her parents', with blue-patterned couches and chairs under a rectangular mirror. She climbed the staircase, and at the top was an opened door, with light spilling from it into the dark hallway. 'Trish?'

'In here.'

Mary entered the small bedroom, which was like stepping into the past. A girl's bed with a pink chenille coverlet stood out from the wall on the right, and plush animals sat in a saggy little line on the bed. On the bedpost hung a mortarboard, dangling its Goretti tassel. There was an undersized wooden desk, and a bulletin board on the wall, which had black felt varsity letters thumbtacked to the top and an array of old photographs, mostly pictures of Bobby. Mary looked away.

369

'What took you so long?' Trish asked, sitting up. She'd been flopped on the bed, reading a magazine. The light from an undersized lamp on the night table showed her eyes as swollen as her mom's. 'Close the door behind you.'

Mary closed the door. 'How you doin'?' She pulled a wooden chair out from under the desk.

'How do you think I'm doin'?' Trish sniffled, smoothing back her dark hair, flowing loose to her shoulders. She had on a black Eagles sweatshirt that read Division Champions and she somehow made it look sexy. 'The government's after me.'

'They're just sending a feeler, so don't overreact.'

'Easy for you to say.' Trish crossed her legs in skinny jeans. She was barefoot, and her pedicure was perfect. 'Your ass isn't on the line.'

'Okay, so who called and what did he say?'

'Name was Kiesling. He said he wanted to come and talk to me tomorrow.'

Mary remembered. The FBI agent she had met that night at the Roundhouse. 'What did you say?'

'I told him, no, I don't know anything, and he said they could subpoena me. Is that true?'

'I think so, but like I told you in the car, I don't have a lot of experience with this. Tomorrow, let me make some calls and get you another lawyer, one who specializes in this kind of thing.'

'So you're really dumpin' me?'

'Trish, I'm not the best lawyer for you. I'd be doing you a disservice — '

370

'Good loyalty,' Trish snapped, her mouth twisting into an ugly sneer.

Loyalty? Mary couldn't help but chuckle. She flashed on Giulia, then her cheating husband Joe.

'Why is that funny?'

'Nothing.'

'No, what?' Trish shot back, itching for a fight. 'You laughed.'

Mary kicked herself for reacting. The girl was under stress.

'You don't think I'm loyal?' Trish put a spiky acrylic nail to her chest. 'I'm totally loyal. I'm a loyal girl. I went to you when I needed a lawyer because I knew you from school.'

Also you thought I'd give you a discount.

'I've had the same friends for, like, thirty years. G, Yo, and Missy, we go way back. G is my best friend from, like, when we were two.'

'Okay, whatever. Don't get all worked up.'

'I don't like you sayin' I'm not loyal, when *you're* the one who's not loyal.'

'How am *I* not loyal?' Mary couldn't help but take the bait. 'I just dropped a week of my life for you.'

'You didn't tell me about you and Bobby.'

Ouch. Mary felt stung.

'Yeah, right.' Trish puckered her lip. 'You didn't know I knew, did you? Ritchie told me yesterday, after the cemetery. He said you dated Bobby. Did you?'

Mary's mouth went dry. 'Not for long, okay?'

'Yeah, right.'

'It's the truth.'

'When was this?'

'Senior year.'

'Was he goin' out with me at the time?'

'No, you two had broken up.'

'I dumped him, he didn't dump me.'

Mary thought of what Judy had said. *You got a chance to reinvent yourself. The Mean Girls never did.*

'So how come you didn't tell me?' Trish's eyes narrowed.

'What difference did it make?'

'I don't know, it musta made some difference, because you didn't tell me. If you'd tol' me, I woulda thought it didn't matter. Now I think it does.'

Hmm. 'Trish, this is old news, from high school.'

'Yeah, well, I was *livin'* with him till last week, so it ain't old news to me. Why didn't you tell me? You said we were friends. I'd never keep a secret like that from a friend.'

'Ha.' Mary's mouth dropped open.

'What?'

'You'd never keep a secret from a friend? How about Miss Tuesday Thursday? How about your boyfriend?' Mary couldn't stop herself. 'Why didn't you tell the girls about him?'

'I thought they might slip and tell Bobby.'

'Bull! They never hung with Bobby, and you know it.'

Trish's eyes flared. 'You callin' me a liar?'

'I know you're a liar. You lied to me about who your boyfriend is.'

'I did not.' Trish flushed, and the words came

372

out of Mary's mouth before she could stop
them.

'You're such a good, loyal girlfriend that
you're sleeping with Giulia's husband.'

Trish gasped, momentarily dumbfounded.
'Yeah, *right*.'

'That's not true.'

'Oh, please.' Mary waved her off, disgusted.
'Stop it, just stop it. I don't know how you live
with yourself. Giulia's so sweet, and she's your
best friend. She went crazy trying to find you.
She cried over you in my office. She was so
worried, she didn't sleep nights. You're a terrible,
disloyal friend to her.'

'I'm a great friend to her.'

'You're the worst.'

'No, the *best*. Because I saved her life.'

Mary scoffed. 'What? When? In gym class? You
lend her socks?'

'No, you jerk.' Trish shot back. 'You think
you're so smart? I have news for you. That opal
ring they found in the alley? My ring?'

'Yes, so what?'

'I lent it to Giulia two years ago, when she got
married again. For something borrowed, something blue, you know that rhyme? And she never
gave it back.'

Mary sat stunned, not knowing whether to
believe her.

'So if the cops found it in the alley, it's
because Giulia had it on.' Trish met her eye,
evenly. 'It wasn't Cadillac who shot Bobby, or
any other wiseguy. It had to be *Giulia*.'

Mary couldn't deal. It was impossible.

373

'She musta thought he killed me. Plus she always hated his guts. She knew he worked the corner at Kennick, so she musta went over and shot him dead. And she has a gun.'

Mary was shaking her head. Giulia was such a sweetheart. It couldn't be true.

'When that detective pulled the ring out, in the Baggie, I knew right then what Giulia musta done. But did I tell them? No.' Trish leaned over, lowering her voice. '*I* took the rap for Giulia. *I* took the risk they'd think I did it, so they wouldn't go after her.'

Mary felt stunned. Trish was right, if she was telling the truth.

'So now who's the loyal friend?' Trish lifted an eyebrow. 'Yeah, I'm hookin' up with Joe, but so what? It didn't mean anything. I saved her *life*, and I'm so nice, I didn't even tell her. I didn't even want the *credit*. Would *you* do that for a friend? Would *you* be that loyal?'

Suddenly there came a noise from the first floor, and Mrs. Gambone called up the stairs. 'Trish? Trish!'

'What, Ma?' Trish called back, annoyed.

'G's here to see you! Okay if she comes up?'

Mary's gut clenched. She had to figure out what to do. She had no idea what would happen. She met Trish's eye.

'Send 'er up, Ma!' Trish yelled, and neither woman said anything, listening to the *clack-clack* of little boots on the stairs.

42

'What'sa matter?' Giulia asked, her face falling the moment she entered the bedroom.

For a minute, Mary didn't know what to say. It was so hard to believe that Giulia had pulled a gun and shot somebody, much less Bobby. The girl looked like a cherub who'd gotten into her mother's makeup kit, her chubby cheeks flushed from being outside, coloring even under her thick blusher, her lips a vivid red, and glittery blue shadow on her eyelids.

'Nothin's the matter,' Trish said, evidently playing dumb. 'Everything's fine.'

'You look upset.' Giulia came inside and closed the door behind her. 'You still stressin' about the funeral?'

'Yeah, that's it.' Trish frowned with fake grief, and Mary marveled at what a good liar she was, proof that practice makes perfect.

'So what'sa matter with you, Mare?' Giulia asked, cocking her head.

'Nothing.'

Giulia shrugged her padded leather shoulders. 'S'all right, you guys don't wanna tell me, you don't have to. I know I gained weight, if that's what you were talkin' about.'

'Nah.' Trish waved her off. 'It's the feds called, and that freaks me out.'

'For reals.' Giulia bucked up and clapped her

375

hands together. 'Well, good, because I'm here to take you out drinkin', T. I figured you'd be upset and all, after the funeral and what you been through, and so I thought we'd go out. I mean, you couldn't do it before, when that animal was alive. Now that he's gone, I mean, let's have some fun.'

Did you really say that? Did you shoot that man dead, out of loyalty? Or was Trish lying one more time?

'I don't know, G,' Trish answered.

Mary couldn't take it any longer. Trish had said she hadn't told Giulia that the cops had the ring, so she could be tested easily. 'Giulia, can I ask you something?'

'Sure, what?' Giulia smiled expectantly.

'Did Trish ever lend you an opal ring?'

'Huh?' Giulia blinked, then froze, her back against the door. For a second Mary thought she might open it and try to run, but her gaze traveled slowly and almost fearfully to Trish. 'I'm really . . . sorry, T. I never shoulda done it. I didn't have the right.'

No. 'So Trish did lend it to you?'

'Yeah, she did. For my wedding. I wanted it to be the borrowed thing. But I never gave it back.' Giulia turned to Trish again, her voice quiet. 'I'm sorry, T. Really.'

'That's okay, G,' Trish said, then looked at Mary, her chin raised. 'See?'

I can't believe this. Giulia did it?

Giulia continued, 'I shouldn't a kep' it so long, I guess. I forgot I had it. I'll get it back to you, T, I swear.'

Mary felt a chill. 'You won't able to do that so easily, Giulia.'

'Sure I will. I'll just ask Yo for it. I lent it to her.' Giulia turned to Trish again. 'It wasn't my ring to lend anybody. I didn't have the right, I know. I shoulda asked you, T, but I didn't.'

'What happened?' Trish asked, with a frown, and Mary's heart leaped up.

Giulia continued, 'Yo was over my house, sometime last year, and she saw your ring in my jewelry box, and she knew it was yours, so she asked could she borrow it. I forget why.' She thought a minute. 'It was Halloween, that's right, and she wanted to be a gypsy for that party at Rock Lobster. Remember when we all went to that party?'

Trish nodded. 'Sure, and we got so wasted on the appletinis?'

'Yeah, and I said that's a good gypsy ring because opals are like crystal balls kinda, and I lent it to Yo without askin' you.'

Mary almost cried with relief. 'So Yolanda has it? Not you?'

'Yeah.' Giulia nodded, her dark curls bouncing. 'Now can we go out? Or are you too mad at me, T?'

'I'm not mad, honey,' Trish told her with a soft smile.

So Yolanda did it. But why? The same reason? Loyalty to a girlfriend? Then Mary remembered that Yolanda was always the unhappy one, and she had a gun, too.

'We can ask Yo for it, in a minute.' Giulia gestured behind her. 'She's meetin' us here, with

Missy. I came separate because Joe and me went out to dinner.'

In the next minute, there was the sound of singing in the stairway, and the door opened. Yolanda stuck her head inside, her long hair swinging and a crooked grin on her face. 'You guys decent?' she asked, guffawing, then burst unsteadily into the room, her leather coat barely covering a supershort black dress with black suede boots.

Giulia rolled her eyes. 'You started drinkin' already?'

'Okay, so I had a lil' somethin' somethin'.' Yolanda grinned. 'Don't worry, Missy's drivin'. She's outside, she hadda park.'

'Yo.' Giulia touched her arm. 'Can you hear me?'

'Gimme a break. I'm not that out of it.'

'Listen, remember that opal ring?'

'What oval ring?'

'The *opal* ring I lent you, Trish's ring. You wore it to the party, last Halloween.'

'At Rock Lobster? When I was the gypsy?'

'Yeah.'

'Told you I'm not that drunk.'

'Whatev. Trish wants her ring back.'

Yolanda blinked, confused.

'Do you have it?'

'No.'

'Did you lose it, you idiot?'

'No.'

'What happened to it?'

'I'm trying to remember.' Yolanda squinted hard. 'That was the night with the appletinis, and it was so cold out, and we came back here, right?'

Giulia nodded. 'Right, Yo. We came back here because we drank too much and we all crashed in T's room, right here. We didn't go back to T's house because we knew Bobby would throw a fit.' She turned to Trish. 'Remember, T? You, me, and Missy slep' on the floor, and we let Yo have the bed because she passed out and we couldn't move her?'

Trish kept frowning. 'Yeah, I guess. But what happened to my ring, Yo?'

'I took it off in here,' Yolanda answered, pointing at the table. 'I put it right under the lamp. I figured you'd see it in the morning. Didn't you?'

Mary felt stricken, thinking of the implications.

Trish seemed to freeze. 'You're wrong. You didn't do that.'

'Did, too,' Yolanda said.

'You're too drunk to remember.'

'I'm not that drunk, and I remember.' Yolanda pointed again at the night table. 'I put it right there. I was sure you'd see it. Anybody comin' into the room woulda seen it. Ask your mom. I'm sure she saw it.'

Giulia looked over, nodding. 'Yeah, T, your mom probably found it. I'm sure it's safe.'

Trish looked stricken, and Mary didn't know what to say. Suddenly Missy stuck her head in the doorway and called out, 'Let's get this party started!'

Trish scrambled off the bed and onto her feet. 'Everybody, go. Now. I don't wanna go out

379

partyin'. I don't feel good. I need to just chill, by myself.'

No. Mary rose, facing her. She wasn't about to leave. 'It's not that easy.'

'Don't tell me,' Trish shot back, nervous. Her gaze shifted to the girls. 'Get out, all of you.'

'What's goin' on?' Missy asked, entering the bedroom.

'Get out!' Trish shouted, and Giulia recoiled.

'What'sa matter, T?'

Yolanda shook her head, her expression muzzy. 'No way, girl. Time to party.'

'Get out, all of you!' Trish exploded, and the girls jumped, confused. Missy fled outside, followed by Yolanda.

'Jeez, T.' Giulia was bewildered. 'All this, 'cause of a ring? What'd I do?'

'Just go, G. You and Mary, get outta my house.' Trish stepped forward suddenly and pushed her.

'What the — ' Giulia stumbled back, hurt.

'Go!' Trish screamed, and Giulia's lined eyes flew wide open.

'Giulia, please go.' Mary gave her the nod, and Giulia headed out the door.

Trish turned on Mary. 'You, too. Go.'

'No, Trish.' Mary set her jaw. 'I'm not going. This ends here and now.'

'Get out.' Trish shoved Mary against the desk, pushing her off balance, and her arms pinwheeled, knocking the bulletin board off the wall with a loud *clunk*.

'Trish?' Mrs. Gambone called from downstairs. 'What's goin' on up there?'

380

'Ma, don't come up!' Trish shouted, but Mary grabbed her arm.

'She talks to me or I tell the cops. Which is it?'

'You wouldn't do that,' Trish shot back, her teeth clenched.

'Come up, Mrs. Gambone,' Mary shouted, going to the door with Trish on her heels.

43

'What's going on here?' Mrs. Gambone appeared in the doorway. She looked down at the bulletin board on the floor, then up at Trish and Mary in surprise. 'Are you fighting?'

'Ma, don't tell her anything,' Trish said, frantic. 'Don't say anything.'

Mary ignored her. 'Mrs. Gambone,' she said, 'where is Trish's opal ring? You had it and the cops found it in the alley, beside Bobby's — '

'No, Ma, it's not true,' Trish interrupted, but Mrs. Gambone only blinked in response.

Mary said, 'It is true, Mrs. Gambone. Tell me how it got there, in the alley.'

'Ma, no.' Trish wailed and threw her arms around her mother. But Mrs. Gambone stood oddly still, her lined face a mask, and in the next second, her features seemed to surrender, her eyebrows sloping down, her eyelids sagging, and her thin lips drawn at the corners of her mouth.

'I need to sit down,' she said, wearily, and when Trish released her, she walked to the bed.

'Tell me what happened.' Mary pulled up the desk chair, and Mrs. Gambone eased onto the edge of the bed like a much older woman. She folded her hands in her lap, and her shoulders slumped, her chest almost concave in the pink sweatshirt.

Trish sat beside her, her arms around her. 'Ma, you don't have to tell her anything, you know that. They can't prove anything.'

'Yes, they can.' Mary looked directly at Mrs. Gambone. 'They know about the ring. All the girls know Trish didn't have it. Sooner or later, the truth's going to come out.'

'No, Ma — ' Trish began, but her mother cut her off with a wave.

'I want to . . . I just don't know where to start.'

'Start at the beginning,' Mary answered, her heart beginning to hammer. 'That night. Trish's birthday.'

'No, that's not the beginning.' Mrs. Gambone shook her head, and Trish seemed to grow still at her side. 'The beginning was a long time ago, when Bobby turned on Trish, yellin' at her, makin' her miserable. Abusin' her. That was the beginning.'

'Okay.'

'I couldn't do anything. Trish couldn't do anything.' Mrs. Gambone stopped and looked at her daughter with love, then reached out and brushed a stray tendril from her forehead. 'Right, baby?'

Trish nodded, tears welling in her eyes.

'It's okay now. He's gone.'

Mary felt a chill, waiting, and Mrs. Gambone's gaze returned to Mary, her manner almost conversational.

'I could see how unhappy she was, but she didn't complain. Trish was never a complainer. She was always a tough girl, a strong girl, like me. Never asked nobody for nothin'. Always supported myself. Never had a man support me. I'm proud a that.'

'You should be,' Mary said, meaning it.

'Trish's father, he was the same as Bobby. Nice in the beginning, to sucker you in, then it all turns to crap. He ran aroun', he drank, he started knockin' me aroun'. I didn't take it. I wouldn't take it. I wasn't one a those wimps you seen on TV. I threw his ass outta here. I made my own money, down at the shop. I didn't need his.'

'I understand.' Mary did. That Mrs. Gambone had lived a hard life was written all over her face.

'Trish couldn't do that with Bobby. She couldn't throw him out, not with him connected. She was trapped and she knew it. So did I.' Mrs. Gambone eyed Mary hard, her crows'-feet deep. 'How do you think that feels? A mother, knowin' your baby's dyin' a little, every day? Day by day?'

Mary couldn't answer. She was in no position to judge. For a minute, she was thinking of another baby.

'So that night, on her birthday, she told me what she was afraid of, and I was afraid, too. I was on pins and needles all week, worryin' about her, crazy that that piece of garbage would hurt my daughter — maybe even kill my daughter — on the very day I'd brought her into this world. I hated him for that, I hated him deep in my heart for that.' Mrs. Gambone's features darkened. 'That night, Trish was gonna call me to tell me she was okay. I waited for her call, but the phone never rang. When I finally got her message, she was afraid, but I couldn't hear all of it. The connection was so bad. I didn't even know where she was.'

Mary remembered. Her cell phone hadn't

worked in the Poconos either.

'I knew her voice, the way she sounded, the tone, from when she was a baby. A mother knows. She was afraid, terrified, for her *life*. The message said Bobby just left the room, and he was gonna be back and she thought he was gonna kill her. Then, next thing I knew I didn't hear anything else. The phone went dead, and I screamed. I screamed, I couldn't stop. My friends, they were all here, they couldn't stop me. I thought, he just killed my baby.'

Mary swallowed, recalling that night at her parents' house, and Mrs. Gambone's raw anguish.

'I called the cops, I called the Missing Persons, I did everything I was supposed to do. That's when I went to your parents, I was beside myself.'

Trish took her mother's hands in hers.

'After I went home, I told everybody to go, that I wanted to sleep. I needed to be alone. I sent them home, I made them go and I had my house to myself. I was alone, because Trish was gone.' Mrs. Gambone looked at her daughter again with a profoundly sad smile. Her eyes were dry but Trish's weren't, and she continued her story, matter-of-factly. 'I went into her bedroom and sat here a long time. Right here. I looked at the desk, and the shelves, and the stuffed animals and the pictures on the bulletin board. I saw all the things she loved in this room.'

Mrs. Gambone paused, her gaze wandering around the room almost happily, and Mary could see her soak in every detail, the times of a child's life, lost everywhere but in the memory of her mother.

Mrs. Gambone continued, 'Then I saw the ring, on the floor next to the night table. I gave it to her for her twenty-first birthday. It was right there, like a sign. I picked it up and I held it and I could almost feel my baby, alive again. I could see it on her finger. I could see her hand. I could even see her face when I gave it to her, how happy she was, and now she was dead. She was miserable for so long, and I let it happen. I stood by and let it happen.'

'No, Ma,' Trish whispered, but Mrs. Gambone shook her head.

'Yes, I did. I didn't take care of you. I was put on this earth to take care of you and I let you down, all that time. Maybe he didn't kill you that night, but he killed you a long time ago. You're not the girl you used to be, light and happy inside, you know that. I knew it, too, and I just watched. Your own mother just watched. I put the ring on my finger, just to have some of you, whatever was left.'

A tear ran down Trish's cheek, and Mrs. Gambone sighed.

'I went in my room and got my gun, the one Trish gave me. She got it from him, from Bobby. I thought, 'Good.' I knew he worked the corner at Kennick, and I knew that sooner or later, he had to go back to that corner to make some money.' Mrs. Gambone looked at Trish. 'I didn't know he was in the Poconos. I just lucked out, he came back to the city. God was lookin' out for me. I know that sounds strange, that God would help you do somethin' like that, but he was.'

Trish wiped the tear away, but said nothing.

'So I got in my car, and I drove to Kennick, and pretty soon I saw a pickup truck near the corner. I only noticed it 'cause there wasn't a contractor sign on the side, and if you're not a contractor, why you need a big truck like that in South Philly?' Mrs. Gambone smiled, but it faded quickly. 'And what do I see next but *him* gettin' out of it. I didn't know where he got the truck, but I'd know him anywhere. And he wasn't with Trish, so I thought he musta killed her. I mean, how could I not? We were all worried about what was gonna happen when she told him no, she didn't wanna marry him, and after that phone call, I thought I jus' heard my baby's last words alive.'

Mary blinked. It was an awful mistake, a horrendous mistake, but she could see how Mrs. Gambone had made it.

'So I followed him, and when he saw me, he was surprised, and we stepped a little into the alley. I asked him, 'What did you do to my daughter, you bastard,' and he laughed and he said, 'She's gone, that dumb bitch,' and he kinda laughed again, and that was *it*.' Mrs. Gambone's eyes flickered. 'As soon as he turned his back, I pulled the gun outta my pocket and I shot him in the head, just like that. I wasn't even thinking. It was like somebody else done it. Then I got outta the alley, back into the car, and drove home. I didn't remember about the ring. Wasn't thinking about the ring. It musta slipped offa my finger. And then I heard that my baby was alive.'

Mrs. Gambone's face changed, coming to life as if from a nightmare, and she looked over, almost confused to see Trish break down. Her voice soft, she said, 'Don't cry, baby. He deserved everything he got, and I shoulda done it a long time ago. I got everything I wanted, all my prayers answered. You're alive, and he's dead.'

Mary shuddered, watching Mrs. Gambone cradle Trish tenderly against her sweatshirt. The daughter's sobbing wracked her body, coming hoarse and deep, from the depths of her, and Mary couldn't help but feel awful for them both, despite what Mrs. Gambone had done. Not that it was right, but that it was human, a mother protecting her child.

It's more than I did.

Mary flushed with shame, distinctly unworthy to condemn Mrs. Gambone, as she watched her comfort Trish. Then another thought struck her. Mrs. Gambone had let her grief and her guilt destroy her life, and so had Mary. If she didn't let it go, it would eat her alive. It was time to put the past back where it belonged. Behind her.

'What happens now, Ma?' Trish sobbed. 'What about you?'

'I don't know, baby.' Mrs. Gambone rocked Trish in her arms. 'I don't know.' Her gaze shifted to Mary. 'You're a lawyer. What do I do now?'

'You have a few options,' Mary answered, shifting gears. 'You can turn yourself in and accept responsibility for the murder, and then you can either plead guilty and make a deal or you can go to trial and make them prove their case.'

Mrs. Gambone sighed again, but Trish tilted her face up from her mother's embrace, her cheeks stained with tears and her glistening eyes hopeful.

'Why, Mare? Why should she say anything? Why does she have to turn herself in? What if she doesn't tell the cops anything? What if she just shuts up?'

Mrs. Gambone looked over, and Mary blinked, plunged suddenly into a conspiracy of silence. She hadn't even considered the possibility that Mrs. Gambone would keep it a secret.

Trish sat up suddenly, wiping her eyes, and looked at her mother. 'Keep it quiet, Ma. The cops don't know a thing about you. The girls don't even know, and this, they'd shut up about anyway.'

Mary looked from daughter to mother and back again, realizing how naive she must have been, and how unprofessional. She'd wanted Mrs. Gambone to turn herself in, but that wasn't in her interest. It might be justice, but it wasn't law. Mary found herself in the middle of an ethical dilemma as Mrs. Gambone and Trish turned to her.

'Mare, you have to tell the cops on me, don't you?' Mrs. Gambone asked. 'You have to because you're a lawyer.'

Trish sat beside her, equally puzzled. 'No, you're not allowed to tell the cops, are you, Mare? I mean, my mom's your client, and this is all confidential, right?'

'Slow down, ladies.' Mary put up both hands, wondering how she'd gotten herself into this mess. She'd thought the hard part was figuring out whodunit, but this was even harder. 'As a legal matter, I have no obligation under Pennsylvania law to tell the cops what you just told me. But as a moral matter, I feel differently.' She paused, emotion confusing her reasoning. 'Mrs. Gambone, I understand why you did what you did that night, but I believe in the law and I don't think you can take it into your own hands.'

Trish gasped. 'Bobby was gonna kill me, Mare.'

'Not then he wasn't. Not in the alley he wasn't. He was an awful person, but he was still a person.' Mary found herself thinking not of Bobby, but of Rosaria, grief stricken. 'I'm sure the facts will help your mom get a good plea bargain, maybe downgrade the charge from murder to voluntary manslaughter. She has no record and she just lost it, thinking Bobby had murdered you. It's almost like a temporary insanity defense, and the sentence for manslaughter could be as low as five years. Or if she went to trial, the facts could even persuade the jury to let her off. It happens.'

Mrs. Gambone remained silent, her lips a resigned line, but Mary could see she was mulling it over.

'It's not for me to say, Mrs. Gambone, and I don't want to judge you. I can't put this back in the bag, or pretend I don't know, which gives you a compromised lawyer. I can't be objective about your case, so I can't be the one to represent you.'

Mrs. Gambone frowned, and Trish looked at Mary, astonished, the pain of betrayal reminding Mary of that first day in her office.

'I can't believe you're doin' this, Mare.'

'I have to. There's also a conflict of interest here, Trish. Right now, I'm your lawyer, and we both know you're not completely in the clear. There's lots more evidence to come, like that lamp in the cabin, and it'll show Bobby's blood on it. What if any of it points to you?'

Trish's outrage diminished.

'The best way for me to get you off the hook is to take your mom in to confess. Is that what you want? Should I sell your mom out — for you? That's in your interest, but not hers, understand?'

Trish nodded, reluctantly.

'You see the issue, then.'

'So you're gonna leave my mom in the lurch?'

'Of course not.' Mary rose on knees that felt surprisingly weak. 'Mrs. Gambone, I'll get you the best criminal lawyer I know. Then you can decide what you want to do, with solid legal advice. Be right back.' She crossed to the door and slipped outside, taking her phone from her purse. She closed the door behind her, then sat down at the top of the stairs, and pressed in the number, ignoring a bad case of jitters. When the call connected, she said, 'Bennie?'

'DiNunzio. It's about time you called. Are you clearing out your office tomorrow?'

Ouch 'No, uh, it's not about that.'

391

'What else do we have to talk about?'

'I . . . don't know who else to call. I just heard a murder confession.'

There was a pause, then Bennie asked, 'Are you serious?'

'Can you come?'

'Tell me where you are,' Bennie answered, and the sudden softness in her tone made Mary feel like crying.

44

Mary, Bennie, and Trish didn't leave the Roundhouse until past midnight, the three women crossing the parking lot in a silent little group. That they had left one of their number behind hardly needed saying. The drizzle hadn't let up, and the night felt heavy and muggy, the dampness making a vaporous halo around the streetlights. The lot was busy, but not with the clamoring media, only with routine hustle and bustle, the everyday business of murder and mayhem.

Mary led the walk to her car, feeling a heaviness she had never known, her heart a weight. It was a grown-up perspective, new to her, but she was coming to the understanding that not every ending could be a happy one.

'I'm gonna catch a cab,' Bennie said abruptly, waving a hand, and Mary looked over, surprised. In the lights from the building, she could almost see the boss's expression, impassive. They hadn't exchanged a word in private, like a couple keeping their fight before a dinner party a secret.

'I can drop you at home,' Mary said, anyway. They had all come together, and she felt funny just letting Bennie go, an attack of separation anxiety. She wondered if they'd ever work together again or if she'd ever even see her another time.

'Understood, but I'll get a cab.' Bennie's blond

393

hair curled in the humidity, a fuzzy topknot, and her trenchcoat hung open. She turned to Trish and extended a hand. 'It was good meeting you. Don't worry about your mom.'

'Thanks, Bennie.' Trish smiled wanly. 'I guess I shoulda told you, I don't know how soon I can pay you. If we could do installments — '

'Don't worry about it,' Bennie answered easily, turning toward the street. 'This one's a favor to DiNunzio.'

'For real?' Trish sounded as incredulous as Mary felt.

Huh? 'You don't have to do that, Bennie.'

'Don't worry about it. Trish, take care now. I'll keep you posted.'

'Thanks,' Trish called after her.

But Mary didn't know what to say. 'Bennie, can we talk?' she blurted out. 'Maybe tomorrow?'

'Tuesday's better, nine o'clock,' Bennie answered, then she walked to the street, her trenchcoat billowing.

'That was nice of her, not to charge me,' Trish said quietly.

'It sure was.' Mary nodded, watching her go. She was thinking about what Judy had said about Bennie's clients not paying. Maybe it was because she'd been doing nice things, like that.

They got into the car and slammed the doors, and Mary turned on the ignition, rewinding the events of the night like a video. Mrs. Gambone had confessed, and Bennie had proposed a plea bargain that would reduce the charge to voluntary manslaughter, with a two-to-four-year term. She had argued that the murder was the misguided act of a loving mother, the inevitably tragic response to domestic abuse, and that Mrs. Gambone deserved credit for coming in voluntarily and preventing an all-out Mob war. The young A.D.A. had said he'd take the offer to his boss and even he appreciated the sympathy factor. The whole time, Mrs. Gambone had remained stoic, if shaky, but Trish had cried hard.

Mary cruised through the drizzle, and her thoughts clicked ahead. She was already thinking of ways to help the cause, maybe with a well-placed leak to the press, to help spin the story in Mrs. Gambone's favor. She could even notify women's groups and domestic abuse organizations and tell them what had happened. They might file briefs on Mrs. Gambone's behalf or support her in the media. Certainly the neighborhood groups would get involved, and Mary made a mental note to contact local magazines like *South Philly Rowhome* and the newspapers, too.

Mary stopped at a light and glanced over, with concern. Trish's face was turned away to the window, her shoulders slumped. 'How you doin'?' she asked.

'Okay.' Trish's voice was hoarse.

'It was a really good deal.'

'I know.'

'Four years, if they go for it, isn't forever. She might not even serve the whole time.'

'I know.'

'Your mom did the right thing. The smart thing.'

'We'll see.'

'Brinkley and Kovich will take good care of her. Believe me, they take no satisfaction in locking up someone who could've been their own mother.'

'I saw.'

Mary stopped trying to make conversation. She couldn't begin to imagine how Trish must be feeling, knowing that somehow she was responsible for her mother's ruin, and even Bobby's murder. It would change her life. It would change everything. In time, they hit South Philly, and Mary steered the car through the neighborhood. Most of the houses stood dark at this hour, and Mary flashed forward to how difficult it would be for Trish in the morning, when everybody in the neighborhood knew.

'One more thing,' Mary said, and Trish turned, shadows flashing on her face as they drove under the streetlight haloes.

'What?'

'I was thinking we should call Giulia and the girls. Have 'em come over. Agree?'

'Nah.'

'Why not?' Mary asked, and Trish looked away again, out the rainy window.

'What're they gonna do?'

'They can help.'

'How?'

'Be your BFFs. Do girlfriendly stuff. Hold your hand. Listen to you cry.'

'Gimme a break.' Trish reached for her purse, anticipating Mary's turning onto her street.

'I don't think you should be alone tonight.'

'I'm fine.'

'It would be nice to have some company. Who wants to go home to an empty house?'

'I better get used to it, huh?'

Mary didn't reply, but pulled up in front of the Gambones' and set the emergency brake. 'Hope you're not mad at me, but the girls are inside waiting for you.'

Trish turned in surprise. 'What girls? Who is?'

'G, Missy, and Yo-Yo Yolanda. I called Giulia when you were with your mom, at the Roundhouse.'

Just then the front door opened, sending a sliver of warm yellow light slicing through the darkness, and there appeared in the threshold three curvy silhouettes, topped by curls. In the next second, the girls hurried down the steps in the rain to meet the car.

'It wasn't your *worst* idea,' Trish said, her voice suddenly thick. She looked back, her eyes glistening. 'By the way, that thing with Joe is over.'

'Good,' Mary said, relieved. Before she could say goodbye, Trish got out of the car and closed the door, and the girls surrounded her, then swept her up the stoop and inside the house. They closed the door behind them, plunging the street back into darkness.

Mary sat alone with her thoughts, in the idling car. She'd worn a brave face the entire night, the professional mask that came with her law degree. Now that she didn't have to pretend for anybody else, the reality was hitting home. She stayed in the car for a minute, watching the raindrops creep down the windshield, then pressed the gas and cruised down the deserted street. She steered the car toward Center City on autopilot, then fast-forwarded to a picture of herself at home, in bed, under her comforter in her Eagles jersey.

Who wants to go home to an empty house?

On impulse, she turned left two times and headed back. She knew the address; she remembered it. She didn't know if she was ready, but she was going anyway. She figured she'd know for sure when she got there, or maybe six months from now.

In no time, she found herself parked in front of the rowhouse Anthony was renting, looking up at the second floor, where a light was on. In the window she could see his head and shoulders as he sat in front of a laptop. The monitor lit his handsome profile with white shadows, and he typed quickly, working away. Mary turned off the engine, dug in her purse for her BlackBerry, and texted him:

Come to the window

She hit Send and waited, her heart starting to pound. She wasn't a forward girl. She'd never even asked anybody out. She didn't know if it was crazy or not, or if she was getting ahead of herself, or him, but she didn't care. She wasn't thinking of the end point, or the destination, or even the purpose. The future or the past. She was thinking only of the present, and her heart was telling her she couldn't do anything but

398

what she was about to do, right this minute.

And upstairs, Anthony jumped from his seat, came to the bedroom window, then left just as quickly, and Mary climbed out of the car, hurried to his front stoop, and reached it just as he threw open his door. She didn't say anything because she was crying, and Anthony scooped her up in his arms and took her inside.

Finally, out of the rain.

45

The morning sun shone through the window, making a lemony parallelogram on the comforter over Mary's feet, warming them like a curled-up tabby cat. The house was quieter than in Center City, and the bedroom was larger. The walls were a darker blue than hers, the bedroom had a neater dresser, and the air smelled of better coffee.

The other side of the bed was empty, with only a messy white comforter, a thin pillow, and an excellent instant replay to remind her that she had slept with Anthony. She squirmed, happily nude under the covers, and checked the clock on the night table. It said 9:20, in numbers big enough to read without her contacts, which must have gotten lost in the melee.

'You're up, huh?' Anthony appeared in the doorway, holding a mug in one hand and with a newspaper tucked under his arm. He was barefoot but dressed, wearing a pair of jeans, his white shirt partway open. His dark hair glistened wetly from a shower, and he came into the room, smiling. 'I let you sleep. You needed it.'

'Thanks.' Mary pulled up the covers, self-conscious. She didn't know if her body was ready for daylight, though she'd shown the good sense last night not to worry about it. Anthony came over, set the coffee on the night table and the paper on the bed, then propped himself on one hand while he leaned over to give her a soft kiss. Mary clamped her lips shut. 'No, stop. Save yourself. You'll die on contact with my breath.'

'Aw, come on.'

'Let me have the coffee, then let's try again.'

'You're being ridiculous.' Anthony handed her the mug, and Mary accepted the coffee and took a quick swig, which tasted hot, sweet, and delicious.

'Okay, now.'

'Done.' Anthony leaned over again and gave her a softer, slower kiss that tasted of Colgate, and Mary felt himself respond as naturally as she had last night. He smiled and stroked her hair from her eyes. 'Nice.'

'My thoughts exactly.'

'I like the way you kiss.'

'Kissing is fun.'

Anthony kissed her again. 'I'm so glad you came over last night.'

'Me, too.'

'I have a craving for peppers and eggs. How about you?'

Mary smiled. 'Is this a dream?'

Anthony smiled back. 'You have time before work?'

'Work is Tuesday, so yes. Is that a newspaper?'

'Yes, and it's good news.' Anthony opened the paper and handed it to her, headline first: **A MOTHER'S JUSTICE**, it read, and Mary held her breath until she turned the page and skimmed the article, which reported that Mrs. Gambone had allegedly confessed to killing the mobster who had abused her daughter for years.

'They're with her.' Mary gathered that Bennie had leaked the story already, before she'd had a chance. 'If public opinion goes with Mrs. Gambone, the D.A. will be more likely to give her the deal.'

'I'm sure, and who's gonna object? Ritchie and his father? Is the Mob gonna stand up for law and order?'

'Good point, but he does have a family.' Mary skimmed the article again, but there were no quotes from Rosaria. 'On the other hand, Mrs. Gambone will do time.'

'The punishment will fit the crime. It's fair.'

'I guess that's right.' Mary's eye caught the sidebar. 'The neighborhood will be behind her.'

'They already are. My mother called this morning.'

'What'd she say?'

'You can imagine, they're with Mrs. Gambone. Hell hath no fury like an Italian mother, and she took down a Mob guy.' Anthony hesitated, and Mary saw doubt flicker across his features.

'What?'

'Nothing.'

'Tell me.'

Anthony paused, eyeing her frankly. 'There's talk about you.'

'Oh no,' Mary said, her heart sinking. She set down the paper. 'What now?'

'It's gossip.'

'Tell me.'

Anthony shifted over on the bed, touching her arm with a warm hand. 'Rumor is that you turned Mrs. Gambone in.'

'I would have, but so what? What's the point?'

'That it wasn't fair, it wasn't right. You know, you snitched on somebody from the neighborhood.'

'All over again?' Mary gulped her coffee. 'I can't take these people. They're impossible to please. They hate me when I lose Trish, they love me when I find her, they hate me again when I take her mother in.' Mary felt the caffeine kick in, making her angrier. 'They're unprincipled.'

'Right.'

'Emotional.'

'Exactly.'

'They don't have all the facts.'

'Not in the least.'

'And they're laymen, on top of it. They're not lawyers. They don't know.'

'Of course they don't.' Anthony cocked his head, his smile sympathetic. 'So why let them bother you?'

'Who said I'm letting them bother me?' Mary almost wailed, then heard herself. 'Okay, I am, but I can't help it.'

'Of course you can. Why can't you just consider the source?'

'Because the source is my client base.'

Anthony scoffed. 'That's not what's bothering you. You'll always get business from the neighborhood and you know it. You're our girl.'

'I'm not too sure about that.'

'The problem, if I may say, is that you want them to love you. You want them to approve.'

It struck a chord. 'Okay, I do. Guilty.'

Anthony eyed her, his brown eyes soft. 'You need to stop being guilty, and you need to understand that it's your opinion that matters and not theirs. Not anybody else's. Not even mine.'

Mary listened, and Anthony's tone was tender enough that she didn't hit him.

'Are you proud of what you did, babe?'

Babe? Mary couldn't let herself be distracted by any instant replays. 'Yes.'

'You think you're in the right?'

'Yes.'

'Then let it go, let it all go. Some people will agree, some will disagree, and the ones who stay with you are the ones who count.'

Mary considered it, and Anthony leaned over and gave her a quick kiss on the cheek.

'For what it's worth, I agree with you and I'm staying. If you'll let me. Will you?'

Mary looked at him, touched. He was staying. And she was happy about it, she could feel it inside. She didn't hesitate before she kissed him back. Slower.

And after another kiss, Anthony slid the coffee from her hand and set it on the night table.

46

Mary and Anthony dropped by her parents' for a quiet dinner, but the first clue that something was different was the music playing when they opened the front door. They got inside and stood mystified by the sight: octogenarians packed the living room, their gray heads and bald pates bobbing as they fox-trotted or stood in groups, talking, laughing, and drinking beer. Mary was astounded. It was getting crazier and crazier at her parents, and she suspected AARP was behind it.

'What's going on here?' Mary asked, but no one even noticed they were inside. The dining room was full, too, even though it was usually reserved for Christmas, Easter, or another occasion when something really good had happened to Jesus Christ.

'Ma?' Anthony asked, and from the middle of the crowd, Elvira Rotunno turned around, brightening behind her glasses. She had on a pretty blue dress, worn without an apron, and held a green bottle of Rolling Rock beer.

'Ant! What're you doin' here?'

'Maria!' Mary's mother emerged with open arms. 'Maria, I was so worry.'

'Honey!' Mary's father materialized at her mother's side, dressed in his Sunday best. 'I'm so happy to see you.'

Both parents threw their arms around her, and

405

when they broke up their clinch, everyone had turned to watch, their smiles a sea of dentures. Mary spotted the Elmo-red comb-over of Tony-From-Down-The-Block, the Mr. Potato-head glasses of Tony Two Feet Pensiera, and the tiny, tanned head of Pigeon Tony. But she was surprised to see Bernice Foglia, hoisting a bottle of beer. In the background, Frank Sinatra launched into 'Just in Time.'

'How do you like our mixer?' Her father beamed, gesturing at the crowd with his heavy hand. 'It's the Sinatra Society and the Dean Martin Club. We did it together.'

'You're kidding.' Mary laughed, delighted. 'How did *that* happen?'

'I knew you were busy with Trish Gambone and all, so I figured I'd pick up the phone and call Mrs. Foglia myself.' Her father grinned, and behind him, Mrs. Foglia came forward with Tony-From-Down-The-Block. You didn't have to be an amateur sleuth to see the new warmth between them.

'It's like this,' Mrs. Foglia said, wagging a finger. 'Tony said he was sorry to me and Frank, and that's good enough for me.'

Tony-From-Down-The-Block nodded. 'Then she apologized for what she said about Dean. Now everything is copasetic.'

Mrs. Foglia looked over sharply. 'You apologized first. Then I apologized.'

Mary interrupted before the truce collapsed. 'I think that's terrific. No more litigation, no more fighting. Peace is better than war, and love came just in time.'

'I did good, huh, Mare?' her father asked, grinning, and in response she gave him another big hug.

'I love you, Pop.' Mary hugged him one more time, then her mother, and just when she thought the hugfest was over, Anthony threw his arms around her and gave her a big kiss.

'You're amazing,' he said, looking down at her, his dark eyes warm, and suddenly from the crowd, came a gasp. Elvira Rotunno stood aghast, her forehead creased with bewilderment and her eyes focused on her son.

'Ant'n'y, honey? What are you doing, kissing Mary like that?'

For a minute, Mary didn't understand, then she remembered.

Anthony smiled. 'Ma, I have something to tell you.'

The room fell silent except for Frank Sinatra, and everybody held his breath.

'Ma, I'm not gay. I never was gay and I'm never going to be gay.'

'Ant, it's okay. I know you're gay and I love you anyway.' Elvira gestured at the crowd. 'We all know. I told everybody, it's like Rock Hudson. We're all fine with it, aren't we?'

The room murmured in approval, though Mary spotted two members of the Dean Martin Fan Club exchanging looks in the back of the crowd. Everybody Loves Somebody Sometime, but only if the somebodies were a boy and a girl.

'Mom, no.' Anthony laughed. 'I'm really not gay. I just like books and wine and opera.'

'That's not true, son. You don't have to lie. I

like it that you're gay. It makes me feel special.'

'Listen, I'm straight. I can't help it. I was born this way.'

'It's possible, Elvira.' Mary's father looked over with a half smile, but her lined mouth was set with skepticism.

'No, it's not. What about Celine Dion? That's proof!'

Mary saw a chance to broker a settlement. 'Elvira, he was gay, but I converted him, and if I keep at it, he'll stay on the straight and narrow.'

'Right, Ma. All it took was the love of a good woman.' Anthony threw his arm around Mary and gave her a squeeze. 'This woman.'

Mary's parents beamed, and Elvira looked from Anthony to Mary and back again, then broke into a smile.

'That, I can understand,' she said, finally.

47

A pale yellow sun climbed a cloudless sky, and Rittenhouse Square was just beginning to flower, the coldest of March gone for good. The hedges lining the park popped bright green leaves, and the grass, recently seeded, sprouted behind cordons of cotton string. People strode through the park, bearing briefcases and gym bags, full of purpose and caffeine, on their way to work. Mary sat next to Judy on a wooden bench, dressed in a khaki suit, white shirt, brown pumps, and her starter trenchcoat. She was betting it would help get her job back, if she dressed like a mini Bennie Rosato.

'She'll take you back, I know it,' Judy was saying. 'All you have to do is go into her office, sit in a chair, and tell her that you're sorry.'

'What am I sorry for, again?' Mary kept forgetting.

'You're sorry for walking out that day.'

'I'm not sorry for that. I'm sorry I lost my job. Does that count?'

'No. You need to say you're sorry if you want your job back.' Judy looked concerned, which was a neat trick in a jeans jacket and a cherry red minidress, worn with black-and-white-striped leggings and yellow Dr. Martens boots.

'She might not take me back. At the Roundhouse, she barely spoke to me.'

'Don't worry about it. She'll come around.

409

She was really upset last week, after she'd come back from court. She won her trial and she still wasn't happy.' Judy flared her eyes. 'Unprecedented.'

'Really.'

'Weird.' Judy nodded.

'She left me no choice but to go,' Mary said, thinking back. 'The truth is, I wouldn't do it any differently.'

'You're *not* going to say that.' Judy brushed a spray of bangs out of her eyes. 'It sucks working there without you. Anne feels the same way. We want you back.'

'I want to go back. It's where I belong.'

'Good. Then do it for me. Say the magic words, and Bennie will accept your apology. Even if she's still mad at you, it makes business sense to take you back.'

'I've lost some clients.'

'You'll get them back and plenty more. In fact, I forgot to tell you, Nunez called this morning and he's rehiring you.'

'That's great.' Mary felt her heart lift.

'It's just the beginning. Of course Bennie will take you back. She just needs to save face, which is why you have to apologize.' Judy pointed her finger. 'Say it first. 'I'm Mary and I'm sorry.''

'I'm Sorry Mary.'

'Stop joking around.'

'I'll crawl in on my knees.'

'That works, too.'

'I hear you.' Mary was thinking about Mrs. Foglia and Tony-From-Down-The-Block. 'You know, Bennie should apologize to me.'

'Don't be a baby.'

'I'm just saying. I didn't do anything wrong and in the end, I caught the bad guy. Even if it wasn't my job and she was somebody's mother.' Suddenly Mary wasn't feeling so strong. She was destroying her own self-confidence. She needed to shut up. 'At least I have a boyfriend.'

'True, and he sounds great.'

'He is.' Mary had told Judy every delicious detail. Twice. Of course, she'd never admit as much to Anthony. Not all conspiracies of silence were wrong.

'But now you need a job.'

'Can you believe this? For a long time, I had a job and no boyfriend. Now I have a boyfriend and no job. How do you get both at once?'

'Stand up. We're going.' Judy rose to her full six feet and checked her ridiculous Swatch watch with the tumbling baby heads. 'You meet with her in fifteen minutes.'

'Okay, I'm ready.' Mary rose with a self-assurance she didn't feel, and Judy raised a hand to slap her five.

'Come on, give it up.'

'No. You always do it too hard.'

'Now. For luck.'

Mary obeyed, and Judy slapped her palm too hard, as she knew she would. 'Jude, ouch!'

'Sorry.' Judy threw an arm around her and they joined the flow of the people with jobs, walking to the office down the main diagonal of the park. 'It's nothing compared to what

411

Bennie's going to do to you.'

'Thanks.'

'I'm kidding. You'll be fine.'

'You'll come in if I scream?'

'Goes without saying,' Judy said anyway.

48

Mary lingered at the open door to Bennie's office while the boss skimmed the newspaper, standing up behind her desk the way she always did, her hands braced on either side of the front page. Even upside down, Mary recognized her own photo below the newspaper fold, and it reminded her of what she'd been through in the past week. For some reason, she felt suddenly impatient.

'Bennie, you ready to see me?' Mary asked, and her voice sounded authoritative, even to her, who knew better.

'DiNunzio.' Bennie looked up pleasantly and motioned her in. She had on a navy suit and white oxford shirt, with her curly hair pulled back into a simple, albeit tangled, low ponytail. 'Take a seat.'

'By the way, congratulations on your trial. I forgot to tell you the other night.'

'Thanks,' Bennie said with a smile. She sat down in her desk chair while Mary took a seat opposite her desk, thinking about what Judy had told her.

She just needs to save face, which is why you have to apologize. It has to be the first thing you say.

'I'm pleased with the newspaper coverage, aren't you?' Bennie asked. 'The media attention bodes very well for Trish's mother. The pressure

413

will build up, especially if the Mob murders stop. So far, so good.'

Apologize. 'I thought the same thing.'

'Against my nature to have her confess, but it really did serve the client and the greater good.'

'It did. Thanks for coming to the rescue.' Mary smiled, softening. As angry as Bennie must have been, she dropped everything, no questions asked. 'I was so blindsided by her confession. I don't know what I would have done without you.'

'You're welcome.' Bennie waved it off. 'How was Trish later? She was so upset.'

'She'll be fine, I think. Her friends will help.' *Now. Say it.* 'I'm sorry about the other day, when I left the office.'

Bennie looked at her for a minute, puckering her mouth slightly, and Mary sensed she was waiting for a second helping of crow.

'I would like to have my job back, if that's possible.'

'First things first.' Bennie rested her elbows on her armrests. 'I appreciate your apology. I suppose I owe you an apology, too.'

'You do?' *I mean, you do.*

'Now that I'm involved with the case, I see what you were dealing with and I can understand why you went to such lengths to find Trish. I'm sorry I gave you an ultimatum.'

Wow! 'Thanks,' Mary said, shocked.

'You know, I was remembering when you came in, that morning not long ago, asking me to hire you help.'

'I remember.'

414

'You said you were bringing in a significant amount of new business, and that would justify hiring an extra person.'

'Yes.'

'You were right, in a way. The fees you brought in for the past year have been very significant to the firm. The past two years, in fact.'

So Judy had been right.

'It's not that my cases don't bring in money, but they are a slow pay. They're bigger, as you know, and so many of my fees are recoverable only by application to the court, under the civil-rights statutes and such. It creates a chronic cash-flow problem.'

It was just what Judy had said.

'Big picture, the firm has enormous resources. We have several million dollars from the class-action representations, and for a long time now, I've been planning to move our offices.'

'You mentioned that.'

'Yes, but what I didn't tell you is that my long-term plan is to buy my own building, not keep leasing.' Bennie's blue-eyed gaze didn't waver, and her tone of voice changed, newly serious. 'It requires a lot more capital, organization, and coordination than merely reupping.'

'I bet.' Mary had had no idea, and Bennie grinned for the first time, excited.

'It's a good time, and I feel ready for the move, but that's why I didn't want to hire anybody right now. I'm in negotiations to buy a building uptown and I expect the deal will be final by the end of next month.'

'That sounds great.' *But will I be working there?*

'You should also know that the other relevant part of my business plan was that after the move, I planned to offer you a partnership in the firm. I thought you had matured in the past few years, and your numbers justified it.'

Gulp. Mary couldn't believe her ears.

'Bottom line, I'd like very much for you to come back to work. I think you deserve your job back, and you're a terrific lawyer and associate.'

'Thank you,' Mary said, but the sudden darkness in Bennie's facial expression made her hold her breath.

'That said, it's only fair to tell you that I don't see making you a partner anytime soon, not after what you did. I'm no longer sure that you'd make a terrific partner.' Bennie's blue eyes hardened, like ice. 'You walked out on me when I needed you, and I can't have that in a partner, my sole partner. I hope you understand.'

Surprisingly, Mary did. But it didn't mean she liked it. She shifted in her chair. A sunbeam from the window caught the prism of a cut-crystal award and sent shards of light shooting around the office.

'I run a very successful law firm, DiNunzio. That takes planning, professionalism, and mental toughness. To a certain extent, you're still ruled by your emotions. You haven't fully matured as a lawyer or a businesswoman. You're too impulsive.'

Mary felt an ember of resentment flare in her chest.

'You identify with your clients, and that's the reason they love you. South Philadelphia's throwing itself at your feet because of your loyalty. But that strength can also be a weakness, in a partner. I need your first loyalty to be to our firm as an entity, and to me.' Bennie's features relaxed a little. 'You can't throw a temper tantrum, even for the sake of a client like Trish. For you to ever make partner, for you to be *my* partner, you would have to show me you understand that.'

For a second or two, neither woman said anything. Bennie's mouth remained taut, and Mary sensed she was her mirror image, just in a tinier suit.

It was Bennie who spoke first. 'I'm sorry if this hurts your feelings.'

'No, it doesn't,' Mary said, though it did. She'd always liked being an employee, but she didn't like being told she couldn't be a partner. She thought that even though a firm was composed of many clients, it made sense that some matters would be more urgent than others.

'So, DiNunzio.' Bennie clapped her hands together. 'You ready to get back to work?'

'No,' Mary heard herself answer. She felt like walking out on her job, right now, but that would be impulsive, proving the wrong point. And she needed the job, to finally get her house.

'Pardon me?' Bennie blinked.

417

'I don't want to come back on the terms that I may never make partner.'

Bennie blinked. 'Okay,' she said slowly.

'I'd like to come back, do my job, and talk about partnership in six months.'

'Really.'

'I think I deserve it, and the business I bring in justifies it.' Mary was making it up as she went along, but she was convincing herself. 'We have our different spheres of influence, but that's good. The fact that you don't agree with the way I handled one situation doesn't mean I'm not mature.'

Bennie said nothing, but eyed her with annoyance, or new respect, Mary couldn't tell which.

'What do you say?' she asked.

'No,' Bennie answered flatly.

'No?'

'Six months isn't enough. One year.'

'Let's split the difference,' Mary said, relieved. She'd thought she was getting fired again. 'Nine months, then.'

Bennie nodded, mulling it over. 'And what if, after nine months, I say you don't make the grade? Do you leave or stay?'

'We'll see, then. I can't decide now, on impulse.'

'You don't make impulsive decisions.'

'Never.' Mary smiled, and so did Bennie.

'Fair enough. Done.'

Yay! 'Good.' Mary rose and extended her hand across the desk, and Bennie stood up, took it, and squeezed it hard.

418

'Now get back to work, DiNunzio.'

'You're not the boss of me.' Mary turned to go, with a smile.

'For nine months I am.'

'There's gonna be some changes made — Rosato.'

'Out of my office,' Bennie said, chuckling.

And Mary ran.

Acknowledgments

I wanted to thank you readers for picking up this book, and especially those of you who remember the women of the Rosato firm from my earlier books. They've been gone for five years now, and I know some of you have wanted them to return, so permit me to explain why they took such a long vacation. As you may recall, *Killer Smile* was my last Mary DiNunzio novel, and it was written before my father, Frank Scottoline, passed away from cancer. When I started to write about the DiNunzio family again, I began to realize how much Mr. DiNunzio was like my father. It was simply too hard to write about the DiNunzios, and oddly, it wasn't until I wrote a novel entitled *Daddy's Girl* that I got my mojo back. So, bottom line, the Rosato girls will return from time to time, because I've missed them. Thank you for your loyalty as I stretched myself to create other characters. I'm a fan of making new friends, but I'll always keep the old.

Of course, in that regard, thanks very much to the great gang at HarperCollins, for publishing my books so well for fifteen years — CEO Jane Friedman, Brian Murray, Michael Morrison, Jonathan Burnham, Kathy Schneider, Christine Boyd, Liate Stehlik, Tina Andreadis, Heather Drucker, Adrienne DiPietro, Ana Maria Allessi, Wendy Lee, and my wonderful editor, Carolyn Marino. Thanks to all of the supertalented people like Virginia Stanley, in addition to some of the best sales reps in the business, including (but hardly limited to) Gabe Barillas, Jeff Rogart, Ian Doherty, Brian Grogan, Brian McSharry, Stefanie Lindner, Nina Olmsted, Carla Parker, and the world-famous John Zeck.

Thanks to my amazing agent and dear friend Molly Friedrich, as well as Paul Cirone and now Jacobia Dahm, at the Friedrich Agency. I love you guys and I appreciate you more than you know. Thanks to Lou Pitt out on the West Coast. Thanks and a big hug to my assistant and resident genius Laura Leonard, for everything.

As is usual with research, I consult a number of experts, though any and all mistakes are mine. First thanks to Carolyn Romano, my friend of twenty years now, who provided all sorts of expertise and reviewed the manuscript for accuracy as well as fun. Thanks to Franca Palumbo, my BFF of thirty years (yikes), who helped me understand the details of special education law and who works so hard every day to champion children with special needs. Thanks so much to my cousin Elaine Corrado for the tip about Carlo Tresca, who I sense will get his own book some day. A special thanks to my favorite legal ethicist Lawrence J. Fox, Esq., with admiration. Many thanks, as always, to Glenn Gilman, Esq., and Detective Art Mee, my legal and law enforcement experts, who always keep me in line. This time around, I got a special assist from Special Agent Jerri Williams of the Philadelphia Division of the FBI, who helped me put a human face on an agency that works so hard for all of us. And a huge hug of deepest thanks to Neuman-Goretti High School of South Philadelphia, including Principal Patricia Sticco and Dorothy Longo in Development, and all of the wonderful teachers, alums, and nuns who helped me so much with this novel and who do so much for the community.

As you may know, I permit worthy causes to auction off names in my novels, so my books are always populated by generous and good people. Thanks to Joe, Dawn, and Bethann Coradino (special thanks to Dawn, who contributed to the YMCA of Philadelphia), Mary Alice Raudenbush (Walnut Street Theater), Jimmy Kiesling (Downingtown East Hockey), Elka Tobman (Key to the Cure, purchased by her son, Alan Tobman), Rhonda Pollero (Sleuthfest), Theodora Landgren (Center for Literacy), Jo-Ann Heilferty (University of Pennsylvania Law School's Equal Justice Foundation, bought for her mother by my galpal Dean Jo-Ann Verrier), Marc Robert Steinberg, Esq. (Child Advocacy Center), Carolyn Edgar (St. Dominic School, Brick, NJ), Sharon Satterfield, M.D. (Howard Center, Burlington, VT), Sue Ciorletti, Julia O'Connell, an eight-year-old who loves dogs, bought by grandfather and lawyer extraordinaire Tom Morris, to benefit Women's Way.

And last hugs and much love to my family, because they're the beginning and the end.